CRITICAL ACCLAIM FOR
*Eve's Apple*

"A quietly powerful exploration of a theme as old as
the story of Adam and Eve . . . a subtle
psychological examination."
—*New York Times*

"*Eve's Apple* is the work of a natural master: Jonathan
Rosen's headlong narrative is propelled by psychological
acuity, balance, penetration, and a racing metaphysical
beat. *Eve's Apple* introduces a strikingly achieved young
chronicler of a ripened and roiling inner world."
—Cynthia Ozick

"Intention and desire. love's chaos, sadness that cannot
be extinguished—the emotional nuances that Rosen
brings to *Eve's Apple* are haunting."
—*New York Review of Books*

"A harrowing, close-up look, through a male gaze, at
what an anorexic consciousness does to love."
—Naomi Wolf

"An impressive debut. A highly original addition
to the distinguished line of Jewish-American
family romances."
—*The New Yorker*

A graduate of Yale, JONATHAN ROSEN is the cultural edi-
tor of *The Forward* and a creator of the newspaper's Arts
and Letters section. His essays have appeared in the *New
York Times Magazine*, the *New York Times Book
Review*, and *Vanity Fair*, among other publications.

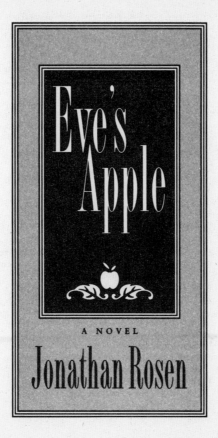

# Eve's Apple

A NOVEL

## Jonathan Rosen

A PLUME BOOK

PLUME
Published by the Penguin Group
Penguin Putnam Inc., 375 Hudson Street, New York, New York 10014, U.S.A.
Penguin Books Ltd, 27 Wrights Lane, London W8 5TZ, England
Penguin Books Australia Ltd, Ringwood, Victoria, Australia
Penguin Books Canada Ltd, 10 Alcorn Avenue,
Toronto, Ontario, Canada M4V 3B2
Penguin Books (N.Z.) Ltd, 182–190 Wairau Road, Auckland 10, New Zealand

Penguin Books Ltd, Registered Offices: Harmondsworth, Middlesex, England

Published by Plume, an imprint of Dutton NAL, a member of Penguin Putnam Inc.
This is an authorized reprint of a hardcover edition published by
Random House, Inc. For information address Random House Inc.,
201 East 50th Street, New York, NY 10022.

First Plume Printing, May, 1998
10 9 8 7 6 5 4 3 2 1

Grateful acknowledgment is made to the following for permission to reprint
previously published material:

*American Psychiatric Association:* Diagnostic criteria for Anorexia Nervosa,
Bulimia Nervosa and 307.5 (Eating Disorders Not Otherwise Specified) from
the *Diagnostic and Statistical Manual of Mental Disorder, Fourth Edition.*
Copyright © 1994 by American Psychiatric Association. Reprinted by
permission of American Psychiatric Association.

*Harold Ober Associates Incorporated:* "The Story of Laura" from *The Fifty-
Minute Hour* by Robert M. Lindner. Copyright © 1954 by Robert M.
Lindner. Copyright renewed 1992. Reprinted by permission of Harold Ober
Associates Incorporated.

PUBLISHER'S NOTE
This is a work of fiction. Names, characters, places, and incidents either are
the products of the author's imagination or are used fictitiously, and any
resemblance to actual persons, living or dead, events, or locales is entirely
coincidental.

*For Mychal, body and soul.*

Of Man's First Disobedience, and the Fruit
Of that Forbidden Tree . . .

John Milton, *Paradise Lost*


"I always wanted you to admire my fasting,"
said the hunger artist. "We do admire it,"
said the overseer, affably. "But you shouldn't
admire it," said the hunger artist.

Franz Kafka, "A Hunger Artist"

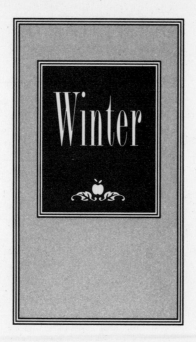

Winter

The first thing Carol Simon does when she enters a room is water the plants. It doesn't matter whose house it is, she runs around sticking her fingers in flowerpots, and, if things are dry, she finds the kitchen and emerges carrying a glass of water. She's like an animal staking out territory. And because I was living with her daughter, she may have felt a special urge to lay a claim to our place. Her daughter, Ruth, sat glowering beside me with a shawl over her shoulders—huddled, shy, enraged.

"Mother, sit down," she said between her teeth. "You're being rude."

"Not at all," her mother said. "I'm doing you a favor. I've never seen plants in such terrible shape—it may be too late for them."

The plants were indeed starved. The coleus had lost its purple, the leaves of the ferns were edged with brown, and the spider plant, in its crisp dying, looked alert, as if it had been watered with coffee.

"I hope you don't treat *him* like the plants," she said, stretching out her arms and dragging the cat toward her. The plants were Ruth's. The cat, Max, was mine.

"No," said Ruth, "Max eats like a horse. I don't think he's really a cat. I think he's some other animal in disguise."

Max could eat the cream cheese off a bagel in the time it took to answer the telephone. He would jump over the serrated tops of shopping bags and land face-first in the groceries as soon as the bags were set on the floor. And Ruth hated him for it. He was like her hunger gone out of her— prowling in the kitchen, nosing in the cabinets, leaping on the table at dinnertime. He gave away the secret of her appetite. And if I had learned anything about Ruth in the time we were together, it was this appalling mystery that at first I refused to believe—that she was always hungry.

Max's gray bulk lay purring on Mrs. Simon's lap, and as she stroked him she talked about movies. Mrs. Simon had recently finished a PhD in film theory, and much of her time was spent in screening rooms.

She was an attractive, energetic woman with abundant, unruly red hair. It was, Ruth had assured me, her natural color, and though I preferred the muted fire of Ruth's own auburn wavelets, there was something mesmerizing about her mother's high-voltage hair. She had a strong, faintly freckled face and her gaze was keen and attentive—the kind of absorbed, giving gaze professors focus on in class and direct their lectures to. Apparently more than one professor had focused on it in the last twelve years, and the list of her affairs had grown longer than the course catalog.

Movies and sex. To hear Ruth tell it, ever since her mother gave up being a housewife to go back to graduate school when Ruth was a little girl, her mother seldom came out of the dark. Her degree coincided almost perfectly with her divorce, so that by the time her dissertation was approved the final papers were ready for her signature at the lawyer's, and she was ready for a new life.

Despite lost time, she obviously had a good career ahead of her. She was in her mid-forties, having married right out of college, and though Ruth remembered days from childhood when her mother could not get out of bed, she was clearly full of energy now. Carol Simon had played field hockey at Wellesley and there was a restless athleticism about her, a vitality that recalled for me a photo Ruth had of her mother, taken in the early sixties, that showed her at a team practice. Wielding her hockey stick like a scythe, hair aflame, she looked, in her high socks and pleated skirt, more like a Highland warrior than a college sophomore. The picture stirred in Ruth the same ambivalent admiration that most of her mother's achievements evoked.

It was hard not to admire Carol Simon. The glow of success was on her. Her dissertation, "Here's Looking at You, Kid: Images of Women in the Cinema," had been published by Harvard University Press. Her position at a small college in Boston was untenured but secure. As she immodestly told us, "I virtually *am* the film department." She attended conferences all over the country and received invitations to film festivals in France, Austria, Venice, from which she returned looking younger, more exotically intellectual, and, despite hours of consecutive viewing in dark theaters, as tan as her fair complexion allowed. She even wrote a column, "Talking Pictures," which appeared in a small journal once a month.

And how did Ruth feel about her mother's academic adventure?

"She wanted to have her kids and eat them, too," she told me once, bitterly. "She wanted to escape, which is fine, except that I had already been born. How could I compete with Katharine Hepburn when I was only five?"

Ruth could not forgive her mother for abandoning her to frozen dinners, to public transportation, to an empty house when school was over. And she could not forgive herself for not forgiving her mother. She wanted a mother who was educated. She wanted a mother who worked. She wanted a mother who was independent—after all, she wanted these things for herself: was it fair to deprive her mother? But try as she might, she could not root out an implacable longing for a storybook mother, someone who would love her above all, who would fill the kitchen with warm food smells, who would tuck her in, who would convert her own suffering into love energy. And that was why she wanted me.

I had mastered the ability to banish the ghost of sadness from my own life, and Ruth no doubt sensed this power in me. People have always valued me for my calm exterior, for my carefully cultivated optimism. In my self-persuading cheerfulness I brushed aside all Ruth's fears and warnings. Little did she realize that darker desires lurked in me as well. I did not know it myself. Ruth's illness seemed the sole obstacle to our happiness, not the source of my fascination. It was only much later that I came to see that Ruth, hoping for health, unleashed the opposite in me. At the time I would not have believed it. I told myself I was an ordinary young man and in large measure that was true. The tormented, the obsessed, the needy filled me with fear. But Ruth filled me with desire.

Even as she sat at the table fighting the demons riding on her fork, weighing down her food and giving her face a damned and distant look, even then I could not take my eyes off her. She suffered during every meal, I knew it deep in my gut, and I monitored her with unnatural attention. I felt her moods the way a blind man feels a face—some part of me was pressed up close against her, always, reading her, feeling the contours of her emotions, her thoughts, her moods, her hunger. She shrank at times from the grope of my intuition, but at other times she posed for it, holding herself up for my inspection, baring her misery like nudity that has put aside shame.

Not tonight, though. Ruth barely spoke during the meal with her mother. She sat hunched over her food, focused on her plate, staring at the troubled surface of her own reflected beauty. Her face wore a look of complete and painful absorption, unappeasable and unappeasing. When she looked at *me* that way my blood froze. But she had no eyes for me at all during dinner.

She looked down as if she were enchanted, working her food slowly across her plate, slowly onto the fork, slowly into her mouth, observing a thousand invisible rituals I could only guess at. Her face had grown very white, as if hunger made it incandescent. Ruth stared at her plate, and I stared at Ruth— Narcissus and Echo, frozen on the brink of a transformation. I felt that at any moment we might both become flowers and that Mrs. Simon would water us on her way out.

Mrs. Simon seemed oblivious of her daughter as she ate. She talked on unperturbed—a lively talker, a wonderful eater. She was teaching a class on women in cinema, which she called "All About Eve."

"Of course the kids call it "Chicks in Flicks," but what can you expect?" She laughed. "I know the guys take it so they can see Marilyn Monroe movies, but I like to think I'll get to them in the end. If they could only understand how horrible it is to be stuck in a movie, a whole generation of women imprisoned in a permanent image—of femininity, expectation, desire. These films are there forever, and what scares me most is that we love them, we return to them, we fall back into them so easily. The lights go down and we start with the old roles all over again."

We had moved into the living room, full of furniture plundered from Ruth's parents' home—the spoils of divorce supplemented with chairs rescued from the sidewalks of fancy neighborhoods. It looked comfortable enough, I thought, with Mrs. Simon seated expansively in an armchair, Ruth on the couch beside me and Max cruising below our feet. He nosed Ruth's foot and jumped into her lap. She had no patience for him, and after stroking him absently a few times, dumped him back onto the floor. She was, I knew, still thinking about dinner, reviewing each bite in her mind, like a chess master replaying a finished game.

"I'm tired," said Ruth. She lay back on the long couch, her head on the armrest, and shut her eyes. I wondered if she looked like this in analysis, lying on her back, peopling the room with her troubles—with her mother and Max, with me.

Looking down, I was struck by how much she resembled her mother. Seen from above, Ruth's face, white and very still, appeared infinitely older. With gravity sinking the shut eyes, darkening them, and pulling at the corners of her mouth, she looked like her mother's death mask. But then she stirred and stretched and the dreadful vision passed. Really, she was beautiful.

For a woman who was always hungry, Ruth kept herself in excellent shape. She was slender-waisted and, despite full hips and strong legs, delicately proportioned. She was five foot six, appeared even taller beside me (for I am barely five foot nine) and bore herself with elegant grace. But though not as tall or broad-shouldered as her mother, Ruth had a sturdiness about her that she resented. It resided in her bones, beyond the reach of diet or exercise. Nevertheless, the needle of the scale was always at 112 pounds. She lived by the scale, regulating herself not by appetite but by sheer will. It amazed me that she could remain true to this ideal, adding to or subtracting from herself like someone weighing meat in a delicatessen, throwing on or taking away slices as necessary. I often wondered how she managed it.

She had no inner sense of her body at all—she felt either cavernously starved or else stuffed and obese. When I insisted that no one saw her as she saw herself, it enraged her. I felt sometimes that her body was real only to me. Her own view of herself had nothing to do with the soft, solid reality I laid my head against at night. I felt sometimes that her body and I had an agreement that excluded Ruth. Thinking this way was unsettling, as if I were cheating on her.

—

Mrs. Simon was still talking, her long legs stretched out before her, her feet up on an ottoman. She had removed her shoes, and I looked at her over the webbed toes of her stockinged feet. I knew that it was Ruth's father who paid the gigantic bill from Dr. Hallo, her analyst, but I could not believe that Mrs. Simon had managed to put her daughter's sad history completely out of her mind.

So when Ruth left to go to the bathroom, I was not surprised when Mrs. Simon leaned toward me and said, dropping her voice to a whisper, "How is she? Still so gloomy? Still troubled?"

Her feet were on the floor now, and her hand was on my leg. She kept it there as if she were afraid I would follow Ruth out of the room. The distance she leaned across pitched her toward me in an almost desperate way; her face was upturned and the smell of her perfume misted around me.

"She *is* doing all right, isn't she? Ruth and I don't communicate very well just now, so *you* tell me." She laid her freckled hand on my thigh.

"Don't let her seduce you," Ruth had told me that afternoon before her mother arrived, and I'd laughed. But here was Carol Simon, squaring her padded shoulders like one of Hollywood's powerful women of the 1940s, looking at me hard under extended lashes. If she had pulled a cigarette holder out of her little gold bag, loaded it and lit up with an embossed lighter I wouldn't have been a bit surprised.

"What's wrong, Joseph? If you know something, give it to me straight."

"I think a lot of her gloominess has to do with you," I said at last. "Why don't *you* ask her how she is? I think all she really wants is for you to treat her like . . . for you to act like a . . ."

I faltered, and Mrs. Simon said, still whispering, "A mother?"

The word had a bitter sound.

"Listen, Joseph, I know Ruth blames me for most of her problems. I know she's in analysis. But is she going to spend the rest of her life chewing over something she bit off in childhood? The answers, believe me, are not in the past. She has to look to the future. Look at me—I had a miserable childhood and a narrow, dull marriage and now I've changed. Changed!

"She's a grown woman," she continued. "You should see that. What does she need me for? Besides, she's got you. You're wonderful for her. I can see that in one meal. You're a nourisher. Marry her. You're better for her than I could ever be."

And then she looked at her watch.

"Oh my, I've really got to get out of here. Honey!" she called in a loud voice. "Ruthie, I'm leaving." And, turning to me, she said, "Be a dear and find her, please." She began to gather herself up, looking about for her shoes. "I've got to go this instant."

I rose and went into the long hall that led to the bathroom, and there, at the end of it, stood Ruth, balanced as if listening in on a conversation inside the bathroom. All I heard as I approached was the hiss of plumbing.

She looked up, startled, when I was almost before her. She seemed hunched, contracted, like a frightened child. There was something consumptive about her, something pitiful, and for some reason this made me want to kiss her. I put my hands on her shoulders, silently, and pressed my lips against hers. My kiss was passionate and selfish, my eyes were shut, and I did not realize until she pulled her head away that she did not want to kiss me. I released her, but a taste, like poison, had crept into my mouth.

"Ruth!"

"Leave me alone," she said.

I swallowed it, this fleck of vomit, and it fell like a seed, spreading roots deep inside me, blooming with the odor of decay.

"Honey!" called Mrs. Simon. "Ruthie! I'm going. Will someone call me a cab?"

Ruth had squeezed past me and was heading toward the room where her mother stood.

Mrs. Simon embraced her and Ruth melted briefly in her mother's arms.

"I love you, baby."

"I love you, too, Mommy."

"Take care of yourself."

"You take care of *yourself.*"

"Oh, don't worry about me," said Mrs. Simon, detaching herself. "You've got a good thing here," she added, nodding in my direction.

"I know I do," said Ruth. "Joseph, since you *are* such a good thing, will you go downstairs and get my mother into a cab? I'm exhausted. I'm getting right into bed."

"Are you eating?" asked Mrs. Simon, reproachfully.

"Mother!" said Ruth. "You just saw me eat. Do you want me to have my stomach pumped so you can examine the contents?"

"Ruthie, the way you talk," said Mrs. Simon, embracing her daughter again hastily, kissing her on the forehead and looking her over pityingly, a little fearfully.

"Joseph, stay here with her—she needs you more than me. I've been hailing cabs all by myself for years—besides," she said, laughing, "these days it's my only exercise."

But I already had my sneakers on and I felt the need for a little air myself. Ruth's kiss was sinking through me, spreading concentric circles of fear. Ruth hugged her mother once more, avoiding my eyes as she shut the door behind us.

Sunday nights are dead even in Manhattan and as we stood on bleak, deserted West End Avenue I was glad I had not let Mrs. Simon go down alone. The cabs were dammed up at a red light two blocks above us and Mrs. Simon stood staring at the empty street. Suddenly, she turned and faced me.

"Ruth told me about your sister," she said.

I winced. I had not wanted Ruth to tell anyone, least of all her mother. It changed how people looked at you. It gave you an unearned aura—it inched you a little out of this world. People pitied you and at the same time suspected you of something. I always felt a suspicious shadow fall on me when people asked me about Evelyn.

Mrs. Simon, however, was all sympathy. "Your poor parents," she said, putting her hand on my head with surprising gentleness, as if to soothe a bruise. "Parents never recover from something like that. How long ago was it?"

"Ten years."

"How old was she?"

"Sixteen."

Mrs. Simon shook her head sadly. "That's a very vulnerable age. Ruth's past that stage now, thank God. I used to worry. She was always such a morbid child. Drawn to suffering. She used to play 'Underground Railroad' and hide her friends in the basement. Then it was 'Anne Frank' and they all moved up to the attic." She gave a low, husky laugh. "Oh, Joseph. Daughters are difficult."

She turned to me with naked curiosity. "And your poor sister. How did she . . . ?"

"Pills," I said bluntly, in the hope of laying the subject to rest. But Mrs. Simon was not to be put off. She stared at me with her dark, bold eyes—she had, I noticed, the same extra fold of lid that Ruth fretted over as a sign of early aging, though on her mother the delicate, furled skin, brushed with blue and traced in black pencil, seemed, like her red hair, merely a royal excess. There was no malice in her face and I felt strangely drawn to her, as if we shared something. She looked at me with her Cleopatra eyes—Ruth's eyes—and I could see a further question behind her questions.

"You don't think," she said softly, "that Ruthie would ever do something . . . like that?"

The thought had crossed my mind. Ruth was fascinated with my sister, almost to the point of jealousy. Like her mother, she'd wanted all the details, and I felt her curiosity straining, like her hunger, toward an invisible point beyond satisfaction. I wanted to say something to Mrs. Simon about this, and tell her that sometimes I was genuinely scared. That there were times when I felt it was my sister Ruth reached for when she held me at night. I wanted to tell Mrs. Simon about the evening's appalling kiss, though Ruth's warning not to trust her mother was ringing in my ears.

Suddenly a pride of yellow cabs came roaring by and Mrs. Simon, waking from a dream, shook herself and, raising a heavily fur-draped arm, yelled, "Taxi!"

Turning to me she said, "I'm going to miss my train."

A yellow cab slid to a halt. I opened the door for her and she kissed me on the cheek before ducking to get in.

When she was seated in the back, she rolled down the window and leaned her luminous head out.

"Take care of her," she said. And the cab veered off into traffic.

Ruth was already in bed when I returned, and if she was not asleep, then she was pretending.

———

Later that night, Ruth woke up and padded silently into the kitchen. She opened the door of the refrigerator and stood there for a long time. It was something she did when she couldn't sleep and was tormented with thoughts of food. Perhaps it gave her troubles a focus.

I stole out of bed to see where she was. The kitchen was dark, but her body was lit by the light from the refrigerator. She wore nothing but the underpants she slept in. A cold smoke was rising from under the freezer and filling the air around her. She was too absorbed to see me, and I quickly went back to bed.

I dozed but woke as she crept under the covers. Instinctively, I put out my arms for her. She clung to me like a rescued animal. Her breasts and belly were cold, as if they weren't a part of her body.

"I love you," she whispered, nestling into me. I kissed the top of her head and smoothed back her hair. Slowly she warmed up and fell asleep. I stayed awake a long time watching her. She lay at my breast like an infant, but it was a man's breast, empty and unprepared.

The bed was empty when I woke up. I heard Ruth moving softly in the kitchen, a temple priestess shifting among the sacred mysteries of her cult. I half thought about getting up, striding naked into the kitchen and challenging her about last night. But I knew better than to confront Ruth during breakfast.

It was at breakfast that the tone of her day was set—the whistle of the kettle, the pop of toast, the crunch and swallow were the first bars in a fugue that would play itself out during her long day of eating and not eating. Nutritionists are right about breakfast being the most important meal; if Ruth missed it, no quantity of food later in the day could fill the loss, and if she ate too much, then for the rest of the day there was fasting, weeping, wailing and gnashing of teeth.

I strained to hear the sounds of her preparation, picturing that look of childlike intensity that filled me with the pitying ache of love parents must feel when they see their child alone in the playground, off in a corner, absorbed in some solitary game of the imagination.

Max drifted through the open bedroom door and leaped onto the bed, walking over my stomach and face before settling on Ruth's pillow. The animal presence soothed me, though he carried a faint odor of the litter box with him, a few grains clotted in his fur behind. I made a mental note to do laundry.

The refrigerator opened and shut, the kettle lifted its shrill voice, and the shattering sound of coffee beans in the electric grinder made Max raise his head, ears twitching, before sinking again into cat sleep. Ruth kept the beans in the freezer—an unusually fragrant assortment of Swiss chocolate almond, mocha Java, blackest French roast—and often slipped an un-ground bean onto her tongue and sucked it like a lozenge. Sometimes she examined the glossy beans in her palm, cloven like tiny hooves or sex organs, potent with caffeine. They enchanted her—look, boy, magic beans!—but no bean stalk, no fairy-tale world grew out of them. Those sterile seeds were not for planting.

Coffee occupied a sacred place in Ruth's life, and she spent much time at the great barrels in Zabar's, choosing her mixture carefully. It was easy to picture her plucking the old filter out of the coffeemaker, where it had spent the night, as if she were reverently extracting a Dead Sea scroll from its burial jar.

It was a pleasure for me to watch Ruth handle food. She made salads with the skill of a surgeon, snapping beans with quick fingers, plucking with care the rolled leaves of romaine, fingering small mushrooms the size of champagne corks, skinning a cucumber so that it retained a jade-green luster. Oh, those salad days! My kosher childhood, with its separate drawers of silverware and dishes for milk and meat, was nothing to Ruth's prandial preparations. She scrubbed spinach leaves as if she wanted to bleed out the chlorophyll and then spun them dry in a lettuce spinner. She peeled an onion as if unwrapping a gift. She would steam an entire brain of cauliflower and eat it sprinkled with Parmesan. She was queen of the vegetable kingdom, introducing me to greens I had never known—hearts of palm, endive, radicchio *ad absurdum*. She even brought home flowers with bright petals, orange, yellow, burgundy, to adorn our salads.

But a serpent crept among the flowers and foliage of the kitchen. I had tasted its poisoned kiss the night before.

Ruth came into the bedroom wearing her red kimono with white embroidered flowers. She held a coffee mug, not by the handle, but gripped in both hands as if she were cold. I shut my eyes fast. I heard the swish of her silk robe, the small thud of her naked feet. The tickling vibrations of Max's purr forced me to swallow a sneeze. I heard every sound with blind clarity. A floorboard creaked under her delicate weight. She set her mug down on the dresser and slid open a drawer on easy runners. I heard the silk fall from her body. The scent of coffee, acrid, sweet, warm, reached me, smelling as it would taste on my lips if she bent and kissed me.

Ruth began to dress. Through slitted eyes I watched her, unnoticed, a sly angel sensing the sadness of even a beautiful body, seeing it there, alone in space. The full-length mirror held her like a magnet. The naked points of her beauty shone in its cold surface. I had seen her when she seemed to relish the sight of herself and I had seen her, as now, profoundly displeased, as if, in the concave chamber of her self-esteem, the reflected image grew monstrously distorted.

Ruth never dressed plainly. Even undressed she did not seem naked. Always a veil, a haze of concealment, lay over her. No matter how long I stared I would merely glimpse her. She kept stepping into shadows and shadows kept stepping into her—darkening her from within.

Through fluttering lids I admired her narrow shoulders and slender waist, her broad hips, unslimmable and therefore hateful to her. I wanted to reach out my hand and touch her, but instead I watched as she stepped grimly into sky-blue underpants.

She favored lacy underthings, stockings that rose to the upper thigh—but not beyond. The flesh above had been waxed smooth by the strong hands of Russian refugees—they were, she felt, the best—who tore off the hot waxed strips with savage speed and then slapped the skin to prevent pain. Her underpants arched up to the thigh's hollow, courting the hair beyond, which was tamed and tweezed as if for the beach. Her breasts were couched in lace or silky camisoles. She mistrusted the natural packaging of the flesh, lovely though hers was. The first time I undressed her—we were still in college—the vision of her body, not merely given but gift-wrapped, nearly knocked me out. That her physical unease should express itself so erotically, should prove so gratifying, gave me a vague pinch of guilt, but a greater pinch of desire.

—

I'd known about Ruth and food from the beginning. And, I must confess, the air of tragedy she brought to meals, to bed, had drawn me to her from the first, as if she expressed something I'd secretly harbored all along. I remember vividly the hidden elation I felt when she told me, in a coffee shop on our very first date, that she had once—for a brief period of her life—been very sick.

"I've had—problems," she told me darkly. "I can't believe I'm telling you this, but I had to spend time in a hospital once."

"Really," I said, greatly concerned. "Was it something serious?"

"Guess," she said, surprisingly playful.

It made me uncomfortable to flirt with her about illness, but I hazarded a few diseases, all off the mark, and Ruth seemed hurt that I was unable to divine what it was that had sent her to the hospital.

I was certainly glad she hadn't had cancer, lupus or meningitis, but I was running out of diseases and the pleasure of imagining her nude, which had been the immediate result of Ruth's insistence on playing this verbal game of doctor, had taken on an unpleasant medical aspect. I was now trying to imagine her at the molecular level, wondering what could possibly have been wrong with her.

"Nothing so clinical," she finally said, though she would not let me surrender.

"Can you give me a hint? A symptom or two?"

"I was wasting away," said Ruth, melodramatically.

"Consumption?"

"You're getting warmer. Actually it was the opposite of consumption," she said, coyly. "I stopped eating."

"Were you on a hunger strike?"

"You might say that."

Telling me was, perhaps, a kind of test, or a warning, or maybe she really sensed there was something different about me.

"Just to do this," she said, raising her cup of black, fragrant coffee and gesturing with it—at the slice of cake before her, at me, at the little round table, at the whole room, "is a victory, an achievement."

Later, she would not always be so talkative about her unhappiness, but she communicated, at all times, the same current of occult sadness mingled with tough humor that I had noticed on that first date. To my college mind, the mystery of women seemed bound up in her. Her intense secrecy spoke half of sex and half of hidden sorrow. We sat, that first date, late into the night and did not leave the coffee shop until the restless waiters were vacuuming the floor and turning chairs upside down. I walked her back to her dorm, and though Ruth, to my surprise, invited me up, I declined, saying I had a paper due. I'd felt suddenly that the invitation was not intended to further the revelations of the evening but to terminate them—even, in some way, to terminate us.

I knew I'd have a better chance of being with Ruth, really being with her, if I allowed her slowly to unfold. And I felt, from the start, that I really did want to be with her.

She seemed astonished by my refusal, briefly stung but also stirred.

"I want to see you again as soon as possible," I said.

"Just not right now," Ruth said, tartly.

"That's right. Not now."

She laughed and so did I and at that moment I pushed forward, striving for a kiss. Our teeth struck and she started back, laughing. My spine tingled, as if we had clinked skeletons.

With Ruth, a kiss was not just a kiss, a smile just a smile. I had tasted truth and I craved more. Ruth offered knowledge that I could not resist. From that moment on, I knew I needed to be with her. More than that, I knew she needed me.

It had been months since graduation and still we were together, living now in the same apartment. But the mystery about her had not abated, it was as ripe as the night we first went out.

Is it any wonder, then, that I did not leave her after my lips had learned a new secret? If anything, that kiss by the bathroom door, like our first kiss, bound us together. The memory of it drew me on like a whispered, half-secret word. I wanted to know more.

And perhaps, though I shudder to think it, I wished her illness back as it had been when she was a teenager and had given up food altogether, wished it to show its face, not cloak itself in her fine body. Wished it back so I could heal her, make her whole and drive out hunger once and for all.

Wished it back so that I could be with her as she had once been, troubled and gaunt at seventeen, help her through that time and, by so doing, erase the past. And perhaps, too (though it shames me to confess it), I wished to learn something from Ruth, to study her, ill, for Ruth knew something or embodied something that I sensed, vaguely, was of vital importance to me.

—

"Good morning," said Ruth, as soon as I opened my eyes. She wore a gray blazer buttoned over a cotton camisole, a short skirt and black stockings.

She still held her coffee and took a quick sip. "Was it fun watching me dress?"

"Yes," I said, "it was."

"You'd make a terrible spy, Joseph."

She kissed me, tasting of toothpaste and coffee and the waxy almond flavor of lipstick.

"Did you sleep well?" I asked.

"Yes," said Ruth, looking at me suspiciously.

A conversation was taking shape in my brain and Ruth was studying me, recoiling faintly, as if, connected as we were, my words were forming in her mouth, and she tasted their meaning.

"Can we talk?"

She put a finger on my lips.

"No," she said. "There's no time. I don't want to be late for Dr. Hallo."

"When then?"

"Later."

"Wait," I said. "Come here."

I pulled her down to me.

She set her coffee cup on the dresser and descended, all scented, crisply clothed, made up and lovely. Forget last night, I thought. This is a new morning.

Max rose as Ruth entered the bed.

"Beat it, fuzzball," I told him.

"Two's company," said Ruth, helping him off the bottom of the bed with a gentle stockinged foot.

Ruth put her head on my lap and curled up, puppyishly, with burrowing affection. She was trying to smother desire, not stoke it, but desire popped up like a bad bedspring. Ruth looked startled.

She did not want to have a conversation, she did not want to have sex. She rose, smoothed her skirt and looked at her watch.

"I'm late," she said, stepping into her shoes, gathering things, sliding quarters and dimes and tokens off the top of her dresser and into her cupped palm. Her back was to me.

"Something happened last night that I wanted to ask you about," I said, before I realized what I was doing.

Ruth did not respond, and for a moment I thought that perhaps I hadn't spoken after all but only practiced the sentence in my mind, something I occasionally did when talking to Ruth, since the wrong word, the wrong phrase, could trigger her considerable anger.

But she turned and faced me, and I could see by her white cheeks and pursed lips that an emotional change had taken place in her.

"Please," she said, imploringly. "Not today. Not now. I didn't sleep well. I'm not feeling one hundred percent. I think I've got some kind of bug."

"Is that why, when we kissed . . ." I could not finish my sentence.

"Can't I even be sick in private?" Ruth said, her voice breaking. "Do you have to know every secret?"

She was crying now and I felt ashamed.

"I had an upset stomach, is that a crime?"

I leaped to my feet, penitent, mortified, but she turned away from me.

"I'm sorry," I cried. "Forgive me, please."

"Just because I told you about my problem in high school," she said, "you suspect me of the sickest things. I shouldn't have shared so much with you. I knew it was a mistake. I knew you'd use it against me."

"No, Ruth. It wasn't a mistake," I said, amazed to discover how great my need to know was, how terrifying the prospect of her future silence, the loss of her secrets. "I'll never ask you again. Always tell me things."

"I'm late," said Ruth.

"I'm sorry," I said, going over to her.

"It's okay," she murmured, snuffling, blotting her tears gingerly with a tissue to avoid smearing her makeup.

"I'll lock up after you."

"Don't bother."

She went into the hall, looked at her face critically in the mirror by the door, blew her nose and struggled into her coat. I sat on the edge of the bed and heard the locks tumble in the door—the final word, it seemed, in our conversation.

I counted to ten, rose and went over to Ruth's dresser. The radiator steamed and above it a parched spider plant, which Mrs. Simon's roving finger had missed, dangled its blackened babies over the rising heat. I touched the soil with my finger and felt how dry, nearly dead the plant was. I started to the bathroom for water but interrupted myself and returned to the dresser.

The crime I was about to commit required my complete concentration. I took a deep breath and studied the room around me the way a thief might look at a house he is about to rob. So powerful was Ruth's presence that I felt secretly observed, and I stood for a moment collecting myself, fearing that at any second I would hear the door unlock and find Ruth rushing in to catch me red-handed. I hesitated and stood quietly, regarding the room.

If our apartment had a sex it would be female. Not only was Ruth beautiful but she had the ability, almost instinctive, to make things beautiful. Though I am a slob, the apartment ignored me and organized itself around her presence and, with the exception of the houseplants, bloomed.

Beside the ailing plant, the window was hung with pear-, teardrop- and heart-shaped crystals that cast brilliant rainbows on the wall. These were Ruth's flowers, grown with light alone, as if the whole room were a window box. Our window faced the river and had no shade or curtain, so that most mornings, though the western light was not yet strong, it was like waking up in a cathedral, with muted pink rainbows hanging in the air. Ruth insisted on letting the sun wake her—she feared oversleeping, as if, missing the morning, she would never wake up again. As a result I had trained myself to sleep in sunlight and had even come to appreciate the rainbow dazzle of our walls.

Whatever it was her hands touched—a simple piece of woven cloth she decided to frame, an antique toy, a Japanese screen she had found thrown out on the sidewalk and repainted in glowing black enamel—created a sense of order and beauty.

There was one closet in the bedroom, which was mine. Ruth kept her clothes on a bar mounted on wheels, the kind you see pushed through the garment district. Her dresses and skirts and shirts hung in plain view, creating the feel of an actress's dressing room. Underneath, her shoes and boots were neatly ranged. She was a hard walker and the heels were melting away even on newer shoes.

Not only the soles of her shoes but also the soles of her feet became strangely worn. She inserted pads in all her shoes but still developed white, lichenous callouses on the bottoms of her feet, as if she had been snapped off a pedestal. But her shoes, like her feet, were small and shapely. Just by looking at one of those shoes I could, as if rubbing a magic lantern, summon up the foot and even the whole body.

It was not only the bedroom that was filled with Ruth's presence. In a little cherry-wood revolving bookshelf in the living room were the books Ruth prized most, Freud and Melanie Klein and Karen Horney, a host of writings by French feminists, as well as books with titles like *Fat Is a Feminist Issue* and *Overcoming Overeating*, with the spines facing in. But mostly the shelves contained her collection of fairy tales, Mother Goose rhymes and children's tales from many countries. It never ceased to amaze Ruth—we talked about it often—how in every culture ogres devour children, stepmothers are cruel, fathers lock their daughters up in towers and parents abandon their children in the woods. Chief among Ruth's many artistic desires was her wish to illustrate children's books, and she was drawn to fairy tales most of all.

Indeed, everything in the house that was hers seemed, however attractive and tasteful in itself, to serve a double, symbolic function. Innocent objects—masks, screens, fabric, books—

became tame symbols of her deeper nature, aesthetic tropes for inner torments.

—

There were no rainbows on the wall. The morning was fading and the winter sky was overcast. I stood before Ruth's dresser, my heart beating.

Slowly I slid the top drawer open. There, tied with a purple ribbon, amid postcards and spools of thread, loose change and unmatched earrings, a subway map, Italian telephone tokens, a diaphragm and spermicidal jelly that saw little action, lay Ruth's diary. I pulled at one end of the ribbon, slowly, and it whispered open. I did not dare lift the book out of its place in the drawer, I merely opened its cover and then, page by page, having already read most of them, shamelessly, sneakily (for Ruth was wrong, I made a very good spy indeed), turned to see if she had added anything that morning while I slept.

There was a fresh entry, written as always in the third person, a disconcerting habit Ruth had, as if she saw herself only in a mirror.

Dec. 2nd.
Mother was here last night. She really got along with Joseph.

Chicken with ginger and garlic, potatoes and broccoli. Ruth had two helpings of salad, no bread at all but ate a thigh and a wing. No potatoes. Mother brought cookies from Just Desserts—chocolate chip with pecans. Ruth was a pig and ate two with her coffee. The second one was gone before she knew it. Mother saw and smiled, a smile of triumph. Sworn she wouldn't eat a single one of the cookies. But that is not the terrible part. Threw it all up afterward. But that is not the terrible part. That happened like something in a dream. Feeling every ounce inside her, bloating her like her period. Her pants were suddenly too small and like a dream she was in the bathroom and as soon as she lifted the lid it happened. Barely had to tickle. Didn't forget how, though she'd been so good. Like riding a bicycle. Amanda in Twin Oaks showing her. Her pink throat. Like sex, Amanda said, better than sex. She was crazy but here Ruth was, no better. It felt good, afterward, to step on the scale. 109. One pound less than before dinner. Is that possible?

The terrible part is Joseph. He kissed her when she came out of the bathroom. He knows. If he knows she will die. She will kill herself. If he knows he will loathe her and leave her. He will be right to. It's gross and disgusting, the worst part of her. The part she must keep hidden. Must be careful. Terrified. The terrible part is Joseph.

That was all. I noticed, with horror, that I had smeared a little soil on the page, a telltale fingerprint of dust. But it was dry, and quickly blown away.

Ruth's diary was on my mind as I headed downtown for work. I had a folder of assignments to correct but gave up marking the scraggly foreign letters with my own jumpy subway script. I was a teacher of English as a Second Language to Russian refugees. I worked from one to five.

This was not exactly what I had planned for myself on graduating, but since I hadn't actually planned *anything,* my current employment didn't really surprise or distress me. I had majored in English but started out wishing to become a doctor and occasionally thought of returning to Columbia to finish the year's worth of pre-med courses I'd never taken. The application was in a drawer, along with an application to Cornell's Graduate School of Veterinary Science: I'd dreamed briefly of some kind of pastoral life, slapping cows on the rump, ramming giant pills into the mouths of horses, earning the admiration of farmers. Though in truth I'd probably have wound up giving distemper shots to overbred dogs and chasing gerbils around an office in the suburbs, work with animals seemed preferable in some ways to work with people: simple, soothing, with little room for tragedy. I'd been deeply affected by *All Creatures Great and Small* in high school, and occasionally played doctor with Max, cupping his head in my hands and examining his teeth, trimming his claws from time to time, and casting a cold, curious eye at his stool to check for worms.

My other options, though numerous, had, like veterinary work, temporarily gone the way of the buffalo. Law school was a word I kept lodged at the back of my mouth, like a cyanide tablet, *just in case.* Then there was a vague thought of becoming a foreign correspondent, but since I'd never worked for a newspaper, or lived abroad, it seemed like a long shot. And after all, the foreigners had come to me.

My Russians weren't a glamorous group, but they did hold a certain interest. I felt oddly at home in their dislocated company.

I had drifted into the work some six months before, quite by accident. It was summertime, I had just graduated and, having decided to move in with Ruth, put off the travel plans I'd vaguely entertained. I began substituting from time to time for my friend Kenneth. When fall rolled around and I discovered that I had nothing to do, I slid into a part-time routine that left me free in the mornings to look around for something better and contemplate my options.

This morning, however, it was Ruth who was on my mind as I sat in the rattling subway, whose posters all seemed to preach the perils of the flesh. There were condom ads in two languages, diagrams of feet with bunions and corns, a poster that asked, shamelessly, "Hemorrhoids? Fissures? Fistulas?" Homeless beggars drifted through the car, looking as if they'd risen rotten from the grave. Absently, I fished out a coin or two from my pocket, but my thoughts were full of Ruth and the revelations of the morning. Mentally, I reviewed the story of her earlier illness, what Freud might have labeled "The Case of Ruth S." and Alfred Hitchcock, or perhaps Mrs. Simon, would have called *The Lady Vanishes*.

Ruth had fallen ill in her junior year of high school, though sickness had been brewing for a long time. She was attending an expensive prep school where she'd been sent during the cold war of her parents' separation. There she learned French and Latin, lost her virginity and fell to a weight of seventy-eight pounds. In response to an alarmed phone call from Ruth's guidance counselor, Mrs. Simon had driven up to the stately Spalding School in New England, where she found her daughter looking like a ginseng root in blue jeans, and burst into tears. She screamed at the school authorities for half an hour and, though she had promised never to speak to him again, called her ex-husband.

Carol Simon stayed in a motel near campus with her morose daughter, who refused to touch food and spoke in whispers. Will Simon drove up the next day and the three had an awkward conference in the offices of the school therapist. Ruth sat, wasted but triumphant, in a large black chair as the therapist told them it would be best for the time being if they withdrew their daughter—temporarily, of course—while she regained her strength and received the proper treatment. She recommended a specialist, a man who ran a clinic in upstate New York called Twin Oaks, where a number of Spalding girls had received excellent care. Several had even made it back for graduation. His name was Sandip Ranji, a psychiatrist, Indian-born, very skilled in these areas.

"What areas?" Mr. Simon, a management consultant with a booming voice, demanded.

"Anorexia," said the psychologist. "I'm afraid it's really very common."

"It was the first time," Ruth told me, "the word was spoken, and it went through my parents like a nail."

Ruth had kept a careful record of herself, first of her illness, later of her treatment, tape-recording sessions with her therapists, keeping track of what she ate and when she ate it, documenting herself with photographs and records of her weight. Despite her shame and shyness, Ruth was a meticulous recorder, the Pepys of eating disorders.

Such was my privileged place in her life that she opened the archives of her suffering to me. I was privy to her secrets and, indeed, her sharing them had formed a part of our courtship—though it would have mortified her to know that I had continued the practice by reading her journal. It was in an old journal of Ruth's, which she handed to me with the page open, that I had read the transcript of the encounter with the school therapist. I had even heard a tape recording of her first meeting with Dr. Ranji.

Ruth had played the tape the night we first slept together. We sat on her double bed—a rare item for a college dorm—with the tape recorder between us. It was almost as if the sex had been incidental: here was the real revelation.

Ruth explained, before pushing "Play," how Ranji had refused to see her unless the whole family came, divorced or not. Ruth drove up with her mother. Her father arrived soon after.

Dr. Ranji gave Ruth a thorough examination in his office, weighing her, listening to her heart and even pinching her skin with what she called Nazi instruments. Then they joined her parents in the large, furnished outer office where they had been squirming in an agony of proximity and unspoken accusation. They all sat at a round table, silently, expectantly, until the doctor cleared his throat and said, in slightly accented English, "You understand, I hope, that for your daughter to get well again, you must confront your own relationship."

"We confronted it," said Mrs. Simon quickly. "We got divorced."

"But you did not divorce your daughter?"

"Ruth and I have a very loving relationship."

"And I suppose you, too, have a loving relationship with Ruth?"

"Why don't you ask her?" Mr. Simon said testily.

"Because I do not have to," the doctor responded. "I only have to look at her. Let me explain something to you two," said Dr. Ranji levelly. "Your daughter is a reflection of the lives you built, of the choices you made, the love you gave— and the selfishness, too. She is the mirror of your innermost selves.

"Look at your daughter, Mr. Simon. Look at her and tell me what you see."

"I can see that Ruth has lost a good deal of weight," said Mr. Simon.

"The therapist at Spalding told us it was anorexia," Mrs. Simon said, trying to be hard-boiled.

"That is just a word," said the doctor impatiently, "and not a very accurate one, for it means lack of hunger, and I suspect that that is hardly the case. There is a great deal of hunger hidden in that little body. Starvation is another story, and, certainly, she has the symptoms of starvation. I know them as a doctor and from experience in India, where one sees bodies like your daughter's in many gutters."

"If you're so interested in starvation, why didn't you stay in India?" Mr. Simon burst out rudely.

"Will, shut up!" said Mrs. Simon.

"Please," said Dr. Ranji. "Here everyone may speak for himself. There are many kinds of starvation, Mr. Simon," the doctor said placidly, almost as if to a child. "In the country where I was born, starvation is the province of the poor. In America it is a luxury for rich people. You give it to your children when you run out of gifts. Or perhaps it is the biggest gift you give, this hunger that eats up little girls."

"What are you telling us, Doctor?" asked Mrs. Simon, like a student straining to understand a lesson. "Come to the point."

"Let me explain something to you," said Dr. Ranji, in his fluty voice. "I have examined your daughter thoroughly, though my medical findings should be apparent to the un-trained eye—even the cloudy eyes of parents. Can't you see what has happened?"

"Tell us!" Mrs. Simon practically shouted.

"This is a good part," Ruth had said to me, stopping the tape. I was always impressed with the dispassion she could summon in the face of her own past illness, as if it were someone else's entirely, and yet there was a note of pride, too, in her appreciation for the whole production.

"Your daughter," said Dr. Ranji, "is dying. Fortunately, she's doing it in slow motion, which gives us time to investigate. What will the charge be?" he asked cunningly. "Suicide or murder?"

This nearly broke up the meeting. Mr. Simon smacked the table ("I thought he was going to hit the doctor," Ruth told me) and declared that he would not be bullied by anyone, and Mrs. Simon announced that she would not subject her daughter or herself to psychological warfare. But the doctor calmed them.

"Please sit down," he said, soothingly. "Forgive my dramatic tone. I find, in the long run, it is best that way. I know I am provocative. To make an omelette, one must break eggs, eh?"

The doctor then said, as he had at the beginning, that he wanted to tell the Simons again that it was brave of them to come, family therapy is crucial in a case like this but with divorced parents there were certain obstacles. Not everyone would have done it.

"We're doing it for Ruth," said Mrs. Simon. "Because we love you, darling."

"But you seemed to know," said the doctor. "You seemed to feel, instinctively, when you called on your husband for help, that you were both implicated."

"Ex-husband," said Mr. Simon.

"We're here for Ruth," said Mrs. Simon again. "He and I have been at each other's throats too long."

"Ah, that's just it," said Dr. Ranji. "You were at each other's throats, but it was your daughter you were choking."

"Before this there was never anything the matter with Ruth," Mrs. Simon said. "It was almost scary. She was a perfect child, she cooked herself dinners when I was out late at classes, she shopped for the family, she baked wonderful cookies after school. And she *wanted* to go to Spalding. She asked to be sent away, there was that wonderful language program you said you wanted, Ruth. Remember? I just don't understand it."

"She was never a normal eater," said Mr. Simon. "First came cottage cheese and fruit. Then just cottage cheese. Then just fruit—bananas all day, nothing else, or blueberries by the bowlful, fanatically. Then just vegetables: broccoli all the time. Or carrots—I swear, doctor, her fingers went orange. I called her my little carrot."

"And what did you do about it, besides calling her your little carrot?" asked the doctor.

"That was a difficult time for me, I was just starting my own consulting firm, the pressures were huge and you know how teenage girls are."

"Only too well," said the doctor.

"I always made time for Ruth, though. We watched TV in the evenings while this woman was out at movies and God knows where. I helped her with math homework when she was younger, not that she needed much help, she was a natural. She's very smart."

"You worked until ten o'clock at night," Mrs. Simon broke in sharply. "Why do you think I decided to go back to school in the first place?"

"Don't pin this on me," said Mr. Simon, "when it's probably your diets that started this in the first place. I remember you from that time, changing yourself, willful, slimming down, dressing up."

"I was trying to please you, God help me."

"Not to mention your diet of men."

"Will!"

"Is that thing on?" Mr. Simon suddenly roared. "My God, Ruth, are you crazy? Can she have that on?"

"Believe me, Doctor, I know this fight by heart, I don't need a tape recorder." It was the first time Ruth had spoken and she sounded near tears.

"That's just like you, Will," said Mrs. Simon, more afraid of embarrassment than anything. "Do you think she wants to blackmail you?"

"She's blackmailing me already."

After this there was a pause of several minutes that, like the blanks on the Nixon tapes, was rich with imagined possibility. Ruth had turned off the machine to please her father, switching it on again without his noticing. The voices came back abruptly and something—Ruth insisted she couldn't remember what—must have happened, for suddenly everything on the tape sounded hurried and compressed, and no one waited for anyone to finish speaking.

I could hear Mrs. Simon, angry, alarmed, cutting off the doctor and saying, "I don't approve of these tactics," and Mr. Simon saying, "Stop attacking the doctor," and Ruth saying, "Both of you stop it!" and the doctor saying, in a surprisingly matter-of-fact fashion, "Shut up, little girl, you're not acting like an adult and don't deserve to speak," and Mrs. Simon saying sharply, "You're out of line, Mister," and Mr. Simon, bellowing suddenly at his wife, "You've killed my daughter! You've killed my daughter!" and then, in a coddling, cajoling voice, saying, "Come on, Ruthie, why don't we go out and get a bite now?" and Ruth, in a smaller, thinner, harder voice than I had ever known, saying, "I'm not hungry," and Mr. Simon suddenly erupting, "Who the hell do you think you are, Gandhi? Haven't I bought you everything you ever wanted? Where are you going? Get back here, you ungrateful bitch!" and Mrs. Simon yelling, "You'll hurt her," and the doctor saying quietly, "I think that will do, Mr. Simon," and then the sound of struggling, of a chair toppling and Mr. Simon shouting "Ruth!" and the next moment weeping like a child, saying, "Don't die, honey, don't die, don't die," and Mrs. Simon saying, "You see what I've had to put up with, Doctor?"

I strained to pick out each note of this atonal quartet, to hear each disembodied word. Mrs. Simon, as if she knew I'd be listening someday, exclaimed, shortly before the tape ran out, "Oh, this is a soap opera, I can't believe I'm here." This was family drama all right, such as my own family had never engaged in. If only they had, my sister, who had so silently made her exit, might have stayed a little longer. Because Ruth was sitting beside me, playing her tape for me, there was something triumphant about the performance, almost magical. Like an opera star who falls to her death as the curtain comes down, she was standing again, waiting to take her bow, when the curtain rose.

Ruth's pain was real enough, however, and though she had played me the tape to teach me what she had been through, it was clear she was giving me a larger message, a warning about the consequences of loving her. It was a warning I had ignored. The tape made me love her more. It did not unlock the riddle of adolescent sadness or female misery or the burdensome body that Ruth had been so keen to throw off. But it brought me closer.

Now, as I rattled downtown, I thought again about what I had heard on the tape and I couldn't help feeling that a note of that distant music had escaped from the past. I wondered whether the adolescent illness that she had told me about so blithely on our first date had reemerged, broken through the surface of our present life.

Despite her hunger, I had always considered Ruth cured in the fundamentals of her illness. After the meeting whose recorded minutes I had heard, she was checked into Twin Oaks. Her parents managed to come for several more sessions that grew increasingly chaotic, but it did not seem to matter. For, strangely, as Ruth confessed to me, after that first meeting she began to eat a little each day.

"Something died in that room with my parents," she told me. The hospital was a kind of afterlife, unearthly and not altogether unpleasant. It had the romance of a nineteenth-century tuberculosis sanatorium, stocked with pale, wasting girls who pressed themselves like flowers between the pages of enormous novels, pouring out their troubles in late-night journal entries, whispering together in huddled circles while brisk nurses made the rounds, taking the pulses in their tiny arms.

Of course there was terror and madness at the clinic, too. Screaming refusals to eat, IVs ripped out, food stolen from the kitchen, gorged in the bathroom and vomited up. Girls in white robes at midnight, defying the order to rest, frantically trying to exercise, wheeling their glucose units beside them as they flew by on stick legs until a nurse caught them and led them kicking back to bed.

There were bars on the windows.

Snapshots of Ruth from this period broke my heart: large-eyed, waiflike, numb and startled, her hair close-cropped and brittle, like the hair of a cancer victim. But with a look of hard determination, too.

Ruth was a good patient, not like many of these terminal girls who competed with each other to lose weight, who took pride in outwitting the nurses and Dr. Ranji. Ruth wanted the doctor to like her, and he rewarded her weight gain by treating her as an adult, by sitting in the garden and discussing her parents with her, and sometimes telling her about France, where he had lived for several years after leaving India and where Ruth dreamed of going some day. Dr. Ranji helped her eat, coaxing and calming her. He had a hold over her. She trusted him.

"He took my pulse the way gentlemen used to kiss a lady's hand," Ruth told me, and I could picture the dark doctor suavely approaching her bed and taking her hand with elegance and detached ardor, lifting her wrist so that the fingers hung down, smiling into her eyes before looking at his watch. "As if he wanted to press my hand to his heart. I suppose I had a kind of crush on him that helped heal me," Ruth told me, adding, "In some ways, you remind me of him."

My heart leaped.

Brooding over Ruth, trying to recall those days when she had courted me with tales of her illness, I nearly missed my stop, forcing myself through the closing door at the last second. It was cold when I emerged from the subway, the sky was white, the air scented with snow. The city seemed quieter in the heavy atmosphere, muffled, and the jangle of my fears about Ruth grew less intense.

Many of my students were already crowded into the lobby of the twenty-eighth floor, and I walked into a roar of Russian. There was a camped caravan quality to the assemblage. I expected to find chickens and ducks underfoot, though my students were for the most part an urban lot, and it would be more accurate to say they resembled people in an airport where all the flights have been grounded. They played chess and gossiped and filled out forms and nursed babies and ate out of their pockets and pocketbooks and smoked cigarette after cigarette.

A man was passing around his newly acquired driver's license with immense pride, as if it were the photograph of a newborn child.

He had been a student of mine before moving on to a more advanced class and he rose to show me his prize.

"Mr. Joseph—see, I make my examin."

"Boris, that's great."

"Now I must to get car," he said, laughing heartily. He was a large, bearlike man, but there was a tremulous, rabbity nervousness around his eyes and he fell suddenly silent.

"You let them call you Mr. Joseph?" barked a voice behind me. "You'll turn them out into the world like idiots."

All my students called me Mr. Joseph; I enjoyed the title, incongruously formal, like Mr. Ed, the talking horse.

"Oh, good morning, Mr. Blitstein."

He ignored my greeting.

"Do you think someone will hire a man who puts 'Mister' in front of his first name? To be a janitor, maybe. To be a garbageman."

Fortunately, my boss was too impatient to stay put long enough to reprimand me further. Out of the corner of his eye he had caught sight of a Russian newspaper and he ran to confiscate it from the hapless immigrant hidden behind it, for only English newspapers were permitted in the ETNA offices.

"*Abizyana!*" muttered Boris, and the others smiled sheepishly, embarrassed to have witnessed their teacher's humiliation. Some were still so formal as to stand up when I entered the room, though they were the new ones and would learn soon enough how things were in America. Off in the corner Blitstein was brandishing the Russian daily over his head as if he planned to beat the man who'd been reading it like a bad dog.

Arthur Blitstein single-handedly ran ETNA—English Training for New Americans—where I taught basic English to Russian immigrants five days a week.

On his office door he had a poster of the three monkeys covering their eyes, ears and mouth. Under the poster, in block letters, Blitstein had printed in his furious hand: "See No English + Hear No English = Speak No English." Beneath this equation were the words "Don't Be a Monkey."

For this the Russians referred to him as *Abizyana*—the Monkey—and I suppose Blitstein, despite his height, did bear a certain resemblance to one. His dark-haired head was unusually round, he had large ears and his mouth worked with unconscious perplexity, as if he were waiting for speech to evolve on his tongue. But he could speak, superbly, seven languages, and each language, he once told me, had saved his life: Polish in the forest, Yiddish and German in the camps, Russian during the Liberation, and a host of others as he made his way, a teenage boy alone, across Europe toward his final escape into English.

What bent Blitstein most cruelly into animal shape was a small bulge on his back, unnoticeable from most angles, but, once discovered, impossible to ignore. Whether he had always been a hunchback or whether some calamity had bowed him into one I did not know, but the lump rose beneath the fabric of his brown sports jacket as if, having once drunk deeply of disaster, he kept it like a camel, stored—he could cross a thousand deserts nourished on bitter knowledge.

Straightened out, he'd have stood over six feet tall, and as it was he cut an imposing figure. He fled through each day with crazy energy, shouting, pushing, poking his head into classes and herding stupefied immigrants through the halls. The Russians respected his fierce temper and loud voice. The teachers—soft, friendly, sloppy young Americans like me—were more fun, perhaps, but deep down you could see he answered to some Soviet expectation of the brutality of education.

And though he cursed and derided them, Blitstein needed his students as much as they needed him. As they stood munching apples in the hall, ruminative, immobile, he bounded against them like a pinball and they absorbed his ferocity, buffered his impact. They saved his life daily. Without them he would have dashed out his brains.

Blitstein worked fourteen-hour days and it was rumored that he scrambled files at night so that he could sort them out the next morning. He interviewed students and reinterviewed them and then assigned them to impossible classes, calling numerous meetings to sort out these self-created problems. He drafted tests he did not give, collected tests he would never correct, hired assistants he fired the following day. He took no vacations. His life was perpetual motion concealing what I am sure was absolute stillness. He cared about the students at ETNA, and certainly, in his mad way, he helped them. But that was a by-product. In truth they were merely a dream, a distraction for him.

As I headed for my class I passed him in the hall (in his manic fashion, he seemed to have ricocheted off the length of the building, coming at me now from the opposite direction, though he had been behind me a moment before). He said nothing as he passed, but he stared at me strangely with his penetrating black eyes.

The bell rang.

—

Heavy and slow, the Russians entered my class like children back from playing in the snow. Even in summer there was something encumbered, bundled up, about them. Although many were in their forties or fifties, you could imagine them with mittens clipped to their coat sleeves. There were a few young and slender beauties among the women, but mostly there were matrons, heavy legs, heavy breasts, heavy hair. They sat in the back row, wearing too much makeup, round and silent like painted Russian eggs. The men were thick, sullen, tired but inexhaustible in their oxlike determination. In some, eyes sparkled with quick understanding. Others would never learn: English was for them a wilderness in which they would die. Only their children would achieve the promised land.

The class fell silent when the bell rang for a second time, but began murmuring as I took attendance.

Kurasik, Igor.

"I am."

Yevdosin, Boris.

"Yes."

Zhdanov, Marina.

"Here."

In the wrong place.

Mrs. Zhdanov had crept beside her husband, but that was forbidden and I exiled her to the back row. It was ETNA policy to separate husbands and wives when they turned up in the same class. Every morning I moved them and every afternoon they worked their way back to each other. Most of the wives learned faster than their husbands, who sat gruff and resentful beside them. The women whispered answers and the husbands, looking down, repeated the words with despair.

Mrs. Zhdanov pleaded comically, "Oh, Mister Joseph, I must please to sit, I very need please my man, okay?"

Despite Blitstein's reprimand I did not correct her, for I knew they could never bring themselves to call me by my first name alone, and I did not wish to be Mr. Zimmerman.

Mrs. Zhdanov was panting with anxiety, but I knew if I did not move them now by persuasion that Mr. Blitstein, who often burst into class unannounced, would drag them apart by force. Her husband, unmoved, sat eating crackers out of his briefcase.

Gennady Zhdanov was a man of impressive silence with a complete set of gold teeth. That he had been a "worker" was all I could get out of him and he looked like one—he always wore a white T-shirt that exposed his compact, muscular torso. He had close-cropped red hair and an extra bulge of forehead, the head of a whale. He refused to answer questions, bribing me with a gold smile when I called on him and returning his face to the window. His wife whispered furiously from behind but he ignored her, ignored everything as far as I could tell.

I had a new student, a young woman named Yelena. She sat in the front row, brown hair framing an angelic face. She was hunched in her chair, her thighs were thick, her hands awkwardly roving over her books, but her face was beautiful, with small full lips, fine eyebrows and blue-gray eyes. She had studied to be a midwife in Russia and an aura of light and babies surrounded her. She refused to answer my questions.

"Tomorrow I speak," she said, blushing. "Tomorrow."

I finished attendance and began my dull litany of questions. It always took me a while to get warmed up at the beginning of a class. Teaching exhausted me like travel, and my own slowed speech—essential for making myself understood—was as tiring to me as a foreign tongue.

"Where are you from, Igor?"

"I am Odessa."

"I am FROM Odessa," I corrected.

"I am from Odessa," came the dutiful echo.

"Mr. Zhdanov, do you like sports?"

Mr. Zhdanov showed me his teeth, shifted in his seat, groaned. According to Mr. Blitstein, who had a foreigner's love of puns, there were two kinds of students: immi*grants* and immi*grunts*. Mr. Zhdanov was an immigrunt. He cleared his throat, looked away, coughed.

"He very like sports!" his wife exploded.

"Thank you, Mrs. Zhdanov, wait your turn, please. 'Likes a lot.' But not now."

"*I* very like sports," came suddenly from Mr. Montau. "I like sex my wife."

"Thank you, Mr. Montau." Fill in the preposition? Ignore him? "Is that an Olympic sport?"

But Mr. Montau had been absent when I taught "Olympic" and though the Russian word is *Olympiada* he could not make the leap.

"*Shto?*"

"*Olympiada.*"

"*Olympiada!* Yes. Gold medal. Ha ha."

"Mrs. Chodorofskaya, what is your profession?"

"I am dentical technician."

"Do you work as a dental technician in New York?"

"No, I am unemployment."

"You are unemployed."

"No bees no honey, no job no money."

Somehow, they all knew this rhyme and recited it at every opportunity. All that remained of *Das Kapital*.

"Is milk a dairy product, Mrs. Kurasik?"

"I am a dairy product."

Poor Mrs. Kurasik had no handle on the world of things and so she became whatever she talked about. I could see it was going to be a difficult day. A roomful of open mouths and I had to drop English into every one. The sheer weight of their wanting—to know, to be—exhausted me in a moment, shrank me. They seemed lined up against me, cars at a red light waiting for green so they could run me down.

"Mr. Kurasik, what time is it?"

But Mr. Kurasik seemed uncharacteristically distracted and did not hear me. I soon understood why.

"*Snay!*" one of my students exclaimed, pointing, and I did not have the heart to correct him. The whole class was transfixed and I entered into their trance. Gazing out the window I noticed, for the first time, that the building opposite had a row of bronze lion heads on its cornice. They stood out, green in the whirling white, oddly mobile in the falling snow, as if they were moving toward me. I felt the spin of the earth in the fall of snow; the view, twenty-eight stories up, seemed alive. The Metropolitan Life building and the Chrysler building, shrouded in mist, might have been steeples in Eastern Europe, the city might have been any city, all of us packaged for traveling in clumps of soft white. I felt carried away by my students to the places of their birth: Tashkent and Kiev and Moscow and Leningrad, back through time and the gates of Ellis Island into an immigrant past I had never known.

Galina Kurasik, the dairy product, brought me back.

"My son," she said, pointing to the door. "My son, Oleg."

Her son's face was pressed against the glass. A surly teenager who had been in my class for two days and refused to remove his Walkman, he had dropped out to go to public school and then dropped out of that.

"Go," I said. "Go."

The bell came like a blessing.

———

No one at ETNA was what he wanted to be. The students wanted to be Americans, but they were refugees. They wanted to be rich, but they were poor. Those who had been doctors wanted to be doctors again. Those who had never been doctors also wanted to be doctors. Instead they were all students, sitting in small wooden chairs designed for children, learning the alphabet.

The teachers also wanted to be something else. Felicia, David and Margot all wanted to be actors. Kenneth wanted to be a poet. Carlotta painted.

And what did I want? So far, I was merely outside, waiting as if for a visa, though there was no other land I wanted to go to and no one was keeping me from doing anything. I envied the Russians their clean distinctions, lives defined by powerful negatives. "Dissident" and "refusenik" were terms one heard less in those days, as the iron hold of communism was loosened, but still they had built their lives against a powerful "no." They carried this energy and defiance with them and the teachers, in one way or another, were all under their spell. A number of ETNA teachers actually fell in love with their students, including Kenneth, who during the break showed me a poem he had published in a small academic journal. I read his poem respectfully, with great curiosity:

### LOST IN TRANSLATION

Once you recited Mandelstam
To lovers and friends on winter nights.
Recite the alphabet to me
And, my love, it will suffice.

Amerika's building a tower—the curse is
We all speak English.
My mother's father spoke German
And *his* father spoke Polish.

Although my lips are poor,
Kiss me with your Russian smile.
Language is a door which only leads
From right to left. Or left to right . . .
Where will you sleep tonight?
Is all I want to know.

Politics—you have no use for.
"I live my life from day to day"
Is a phrase you learned in school.
"I hate Brooklyn" you taught yourself.

Why not live from day to day?
The N train will take you out of Brooklyn.
And the F, R, B, Q, D.
The alphabet is waiting.
These letters will carry you away.

"What about Chinese?" asked Margot, reading over my right shoulder. "Chinese goes up and down. So does Japanese."

"Who's the girl?" asked Carlotta, reading over my left shoulder. "Anyone in my class? Nina Naroditskaya? She's hot."

Carlotta was the funkiest of the teachers, an artist who had almost had a painting in a trendy SoHo gallery. She was dressed in shades of chaos, long underwear, leather miniskirt, boots and raveling black top, but she had chalk on her ass, which diminished the effect of nihilism and branded her on her leather bottom the same as the rest of us: schoolteacher.

I wondered what her students could possibly have made of such clothing. She, I know, admired what she called their "gorgeous immigrant ugliness." It is true that their clothing, like their English, had an unmistakable accent. The stilted fashions of an arrested culture gave them an antique look, like cars with tailfins. The women began to remake themselves from the bottom up, and I looked down at Fourteenth Street footwear: white plastic boots, leopard-spot boots, fake-alligator boots, boots with pink feather fringes, slick black boots with what looked like fins and gills.

And of course everyone ran out and bought blue jeans. "The great prewashed masses," Kenneth called them. But at present he was in no mood for joking.

"Why is it," he asked, "that because I want to be a poet I have to surround myself with illiterates?"

"Do you mean us or the Russians?" asked Margot, pouting.

"Take it as you wish," said Kenneth, lighting a cigarette.

I was the only teacher who did not smoke. The ETNA teachers' room was the last stronghold of chain-smoking in America. They could not talk during a break without cigarettes, and when I observed other classes I often noticed that the teacher held the chalk between two fingers, flicking imaginary ash onto the floor.

I left them arguing, gesturing, inscribing the air with smoke, and stepped into the hall.

The corridor smelled like a deli. As soon as the break bell rang, the students removed their snacks from pocketbooks and plastic bags, briefcases and coat pockets. They filled the hallway, munching and talking quickly, feasting on Russian and Russian food between classes. Sausage sandwiches, pickles, apples, puddings eaten out of reused yogurt containers, blintzes wrapped in plastic.

I turned away from the great feast. I was sick of the hungry and tired and poor. And on the Upper West Side of Manhattan somewhere was Ruth, hungry and tired and poor in her own way, yearning for a far more elusive freedom. I wanted to go to her and comfort her, tell her things would be all right. I turned and saw Arthur Blitstein shout at a student at the far end of the hall. As he yelled he noticed me and fixed his dark eyes briefly on mine and I felt, as I had on many occasions, that despite his having humiliated me that morning, he took a special interest in me.

He had intuited something about me—loss, perhaps, hidden grief. Sorrow was a language he had mastered like all the others.

———

Back in class, the women reapplied their lipstick and blotted their lips in preparation for the more refined pursuit of English. They settled in for the final hour. Fortunately (for me) I had nothing to do but observe them over the top of my newspaper as they guessed their way through another of Arthur Blitstein's famous placement exams.

I felt a surge of powerful sympathy for all of them. They cheated shamelessly, twisting their large bodies out of their little chairs, whispering and poking and pointing. It was a naked display of their worst qualities: greed, competitiveness, utter disregard for the rules, but this only endeared them to me more. For one brief second, I felt I loved them.

Suddenly, Blitstein burst into the room, leaning on the doorknob as the door swung open.

"Let them cheat and you're no better than they are," he said in a low tone. Then he gave a great sniff.

"It stinks in here. Pfeh! Open a window."

He spoke in Russian and a woman in the back turned bright red and seemed on the verge of tears. Blitstein swung himself out with a slam.

Murmuring, with sheepish, insulted faces, they fell to work again until the spell wore off and they grew bolder and began to cheat with renewed and almost spiteful vigor.

I opened the window a wide crack to let "Moscow Nights," the perfume of choice among women in ETNA, escape the room. Having smuggled it out of the USSR these women must have watched with sadness as their supply diminished daily until there was nothing but the smell of their own cooking to remind them of home. The powerful fragrance, mingled with the odor of their overheated bodies, passed into the chill New York afternoon. It was no longer snowing and the lions across the way, now maned in white, had grown small and tame.

I remembered my high school demonstration of osmosis, a beaker of perfume that evaporated to fill the whole room evenly, and I thought of Moscow Nights vanishing into Manhattan, and of how my students would soon follow.

I used to wonder, lying in bed, if my sister's spirit still lived in our house and if she was able to filter through my shut door at night. Could she see me in the dark, under the covers where I lay? Was she near or far? I felt, looking out at the white lions, that old stirring ache, the light, invisible presence pressed against the glass.

When the bell rang, I collected the papers hastily, suddenly tired and eager to leave. My small outburst of affection for my students had vanished. Their clattering, childlike commotion oppressed me. I wanted to go home.

I can almost do something extraordinary," said Ruth, taking a sip of tea.

"So do something ordinary," I told her. "There's no shame attached."

"I hate to," she sighed, "but I suppose I have no choice."

Still, she hesitated, forming words silently with her lips, as if in prayer.

It was Ruth's dream, playing Scrabble, to use up all her letters in one spectacular word. Mine was to have every word on the board reveal a secret about the players.

I considered what was on the table: BONE—FLIRT—NAG—MANGE—MUD—GRAVE—TRELLIS—RELISH. Hardly a useful map of our lives, and yet, in the manner of Scrabble boards, almost meaningful. Ruth's nimble fingers added FLOAT—using the F of FLIRT. The T was a triple-letter score and she wound up with fifteen points.

"Not bad, after all," I said.

"Not amazing," said Ruth, plucking out her new letters from the bag with shut eyes, dropping them into her lap and then transporting them one by one to the surface.

We were seated at the dining-room table. The crumbs of dinner were all around us, but the Scrabble board had flattened the meal's discomfort, and the cool letters drew us playfully together as food never did.

It was only nine o'clock, but Ruth was in a pink flannel nightgown with a frilled collar. Her contact lenses were out for the night and the round, tortoise-framed glasses that she now wore gave her an owlish look, but her face had a warm, sensual glow from the abundant heat that came ringing up into the apartment. Her full hair fell around her shoulders, her legs were tucked up under her on the chair and she was studying her letters intently, glancing occasionally at the board, already preparing for her next move.

She was creaming me, as always. Having spent the day tangled up in other people's alphabets, I was not eager for the game. But I felt that Scrabble might ease us indirectly into a conversation touching on the night before, and I was already wondering if I might not make an observation about the difference a single letter can make—between fast and feast, for example, or diet and die. My own letters could do nothing so dramatic and, biding my time, I held my tongue.

That evening I was having particularly bad luck. I had two consonants, a c and an n—the rest were vowels. Already losing interest in the game, I considered my meager options: GUN if I borrowed from NAG, CANE if I built on GRAVE, NARC if I made use of TRELLIS—but was NARC a word? Then I saw, with wicked satisfaction, that I could use the T in FLOAT. I placed three letters in quick descending order on the board.

"Joseph!" said Ruth. "How can you?"

"It's a word," I said.

"Substandard. And gross."

"A perfectly good Anglo-Saxon noun. See Chaucer."

"Perfectly disgusting," said Ruth. "See *Penthouse*."

"Do you challenge me?"

"I should."

"Shall I get the *OED*?" I asked, pointing toward the bookshelf.

"Fuck off."

"Hey! I go where the letters take me."

"And is that where they take you?" Ruth demanded.

"Occasionally."

Ruth glowered. "It's only worth seven points."

She sank back into contemplation of her letters. Max, who had been sleeping under the table, woke, yawned and glanced upward, shaking his head, as if he had dreamed of eating the alphabet. Ruth stirred uneasily. My word was a wedge driven into the midst of soft innocuous syllables, disrupting our game. Ruth eyed it, disgusted, aroused, on guard as if it threatened to expose her, or me. She eyed me along with the word, suspicious.

The flannel of her nightgown gave only a muffled echo of her body's shape, for though she favored erotic fashions in the morning, when she was halfway out the door, at night, close quartered, she preferred the plain and the protective.

She could not, however, keep me from feeling her body stirring under the table when she shifted her legs, crossed them or tucked them back up under her. She seldom sat still. I stretched my own legs under her chair and sometimes she rested her feet on the slope of my shins. Occasionally I removed my slippers, leaned back and laid my feet in her lap. She stroked them as she would a cat as she plotted her move, but when they grew too alive against her thighs she flung them off.

Now she was stiff, alert. My word broke the surface of the table as if it had leaped from the depths below.

"Did anything happen today at work?" Ruth asked, for at dinner we had not exchanged much information. "How are all those Borises and Natashas?"

"I think Kenneth's having an affair with one of the Russians."

"Anyone you know?"

"No names have been mentioned—it's only a rumor."

"It's probably true," said Ruth, without looking up. "Don't they all want green cards?"

"I don't know. Probably."

She lifted her head. "Does it give you ideas?"

"I don't need a green card," I said.

Ruth was silent, placing four letters on the board with great deliberateness, pressing each square down with her thumb.

"IRATE."

"Six," I said.

"Twelve," said Ruth. "It's a double word score. That's 103 for me. You have sixty-four. If you stayed away from words that belong on bathroom walls you'd be doing better. Sex doesn't score well in this game."

"Are you kidding?" I said. "The x alone is worth eight points."

Ruth shut her eyes tightly and thrust her hand into the letter bag I held out to her. She withdrew a delicate fist and opened it under the table, dumping the letters in her lap.

"Lucky letters," I said.

"Are you looking, Joseph?"

"Of course not."

Nevertheless, she lifted the bottom of her nightgown with one hand, making a tent over the letters, baring her smooth thighs while she transferred the letters to their little wooden ledge on the table.

"Is this strip Scrabble we're playing?"

"Joseph!" said Ruth. "Go!"

I put a P down in front of Ruth's last word.

"PIRATE."

"Seven," Ruth counted, jotting down the number.

She stared down at her letters with absorption. I waited for her to say something but she was silent, ordering and re-ordering the little wooden squares, composing an epic poem in seven letters.

Suddenly she began to smile.

"What have you got there?" I asked.

"Oh, nothing," Ruth said, smirking behind her letters.

"Come on, poker face, bring it out."

She smiled airily, the canary who had eaten the cat. "I'm not sure I want to. It may not be worth enough points. Maybe I can do something better."

"Ruth," I said coaxingly, "let's see what you've got."

"Don't put it that way," she said, blushing. But the letters were already in her hand, and she spelled them out neatly.

"Substandard," I cried. "Gross. Disgusting."

We both burst out laughing.

"It's a bird," said Ruth. "A male chicken."

"We're going to wind up like that couple in Dante's *Inferno,* Paolo and Fresca."

"Francesca," said Ruth. "Fresca's a diet soda. And they weren't playing Scrabble, they were reading."

"But not for long," I said, laying my hand on her thigh.

She slapped it playfully, but with a look of creeping discomfort.

"Can we go back to the game, please?"

"The game. The game. I speak of pressing matters and she speaks of the game."

"You just don't want to lose," said Ruth.

"There's more than one way to lose."

"It's your turn."

"Your words know more than you do, Ruth."

"Don't say that," she warned.

"Well, it's true," I said. "Just look."

"It is not!"

"My God, Ruth," I said, unable to contain myself, "there's more sex on the board than in our bed."

"That's not funny!"

"Maybe it's not a joke."

"Go to hell!" Ruth suddenly shouted, banging on the table so that the letters jumped and Max, cleaning himself, lowered his leg in a hurry.

"Since we moved in together, Ruth—do I have to spell it out?"

"You already have," she said, grimly.

We both fell silent. I sat, contemplating the table set with words, the frozen remains of our conversation. We had both studiously avoided discussing what had happened the night before. Sex somehow was the substitute subject, the embodied secret that, though perilous to talk about, was safer than discussing food.

Ruth seemed on the verge of tears and I was sorry to have raised the issue, just when we were getting along so well. I would have liked to spell out some kind of apology, it was my turn, but all I could do was make MANGE into MANGER, a vague allusion to the approaching holiday (which neither of us celebrated) but it didn't do much for Ruth's expression. Her glasses were mysteriously crooked, as if I had actually slapped her.

"I'm sorry," I said.

"Twelve points," said Ruth, writing it down. She held out the bag to me and I drew another useless vowel.

"Would you boil some more water?" Ruth asked.

She held out her empty mug like a peace offering and I took it from her.

"Witches' brew?"

"What else," said Ruth, smiling faintly.

In the kitchen I filled the kettle and cracked an egg into a bowl for Max, who had trotted in after me. I began beating it with a fork.

"What are you making?" Ruth shouted from the living room.

"Nothing," I called back.

"You'll give him diarrhea," she shouted.

"It's good for his coat."

"It's bad for the carpet."

"You'll behave, won't you, Max?" I asked, squatting before him, but he was already whisker-deep in the egg, lapping it industriously and chomping occasionally on the gooey strands of white.

I sat at the kitchen table waiting for the kettle to boil, puzzling over the sexual knot at the heart of my life with Ruth.

When Ruth and I began going out, she had evinced a peculiar blend of passion and reserve, a sexual style that had evolved out of her illness but had also been a means of combating it.

Her first year of college had been misery. The clinic had let her go, her parents had let her go, but she'd fooled them all, she'd smuggled out a sad starving girl cloaked in the body of a healthy woman.

There was no help for her from home. Her mother called dutifully and breathlessly from all over the world, asking if she was eating and if she'd met any boys yet and what classes she was taking; her father wrote brief loving notes printed in his bold hand on office stationery attached to salamis from Zabar's, which disgusted and embarrassed her, though they touched her, too, even as she wrapped them at once in newspaper and buried them in the garbage.

She had to turn her back on home, she'd learned at least that much from Dr. Ranji. To do this, boys were indispensable. They seemed not to care what mood she was in, whether she was sad or happy inside, hungry or full. They carried her in their arms a little further through the night, a little further from her parents and the self she did not like.

Over the bare patches, the warped and buckled surfaces of her soul, she unrolled the carpet of sex. Boys wanted to sleep with her and she let them, aroused but always alert, wary, holding herself still inside, even if she moved outwardly to accommodate the action.

In college we had many passionate encounters, but I quickly realized that this was a habit with her. Sex spared her a certain amount of conversation, of revelation, of sharing that would, she felt sure, drive everyone away. And maybe it would have. But I could not rest until I had gotten at the hard core of her. Gradually I began to seek a deeper understanding and a fuller physical rapport. I was so keenly bent on making her happy, on satisfying her, on plumbing her depths, that I could not rest till I knew how she really felt, what she really wanted. And that unsettled her terribly. Whenever I polled her, in the midst of passion, about how she was feeling and what I might do to let her enjoy herself more, she grew vaguer and vaguer.

"Why don't you just enjoy yourself?" she would say, anxiously, in answer to my questions. But I wanted her to enjoy *herself*. I was hell-bent on making her feel good, but how could I, sensing her there, so *abstract*?

All this would lead to the two of us lying side by side, engrossed in long, naked conversations. She would offer up, not sex, but information about herself. And the more I coaxed out of her, the more she played me her tapes, read me her transcripts and shared the extraordinary knowledge of her illness in an effort to explain herself, the closer we grew. Yet the closer we grew, the less we made love. Invariably I wanted more. Her revelations answered some deep and inexplicable need of my own to hear them. But at the same time, a painful balloon of desire was building inside me, rising beyond the conversation—like my penis, which seemed to peer, curious, above the sheets, reproaching me as it stood up on the smooth highway of my reclining body, rubbernecking to see, past all our pointless words, the sad wreckage of our sexual life.

Secretly I had believed that when we moved in together, physical intimacy would follow, but in the six months we had been living together we had made love less and less and, a disturbing development, I was not permitted to enter her. It suddenly occurred to me, with horror, that Ruth thought it would make her fat, as if I too were some kind of taboo food. Ruth no longer said, "Why don't you just enjoy yourself?" I had talked my way into her secrets but out of her body. I had joined her on the far side of the physical realm and the price I paid for standing there beside her was that I shared the mood of privation she lived with.

I wished at times to return to an earlier simplicity, but it was no longer possible.

"Not yet," Ruth would say. "Not yet."

But when? If not now that we lived together, when?

"Aren't you coming back?" Ruth shouted.

"Have you gone yet?"

"No, but I miss you. You must have filled the kettle too full. Wait in here."

But just then the kettle began to sputter and sing. I made Ruth a mug of her special health-food mixture—her "witches' brew" of senna leaf and camomile—whose odor I could scarcely endure, and drowned a buoyant Constant Comment tea bag in a mug for myself.

—

"Ruth," I said, "is it possible you still haven't gone?"

"Yes," she said, "the board's gotten very full."

"You don't have to get a double or triple word score every time."

"I know," she said, "it's not that. There just isn't anything I can do."

"If you'd use your blanks you could go."

"I can't believe you looked at my letters!" Ruth cried.

"Well, the way you hold them I can't help it."

"Joseph!"

"Look," I said, "you're winning, so it's hardly made a difference. But if you'd like, I concede. I resign, in disgrace, for my behavior. If I had a king I'd topple it. Instead, I'll have to topple the whole board." I leaped to my feet.

It was a deluxe Scrabble set, with a raised border around each letter, so I virtually had to turn the board upside down in order to scatter them. Max pounced on a letter, batted it and then bounded out of the room.

"You're a lunatic!" Ruth shouted.

"Oh, am I?"

"Yes!" said Ruth, retreating to the couch.

"Is it crazy to want to sleep with you?"

"Is that what this is all about? Is that all you want out of me?"

"I don't want it out of you, like plunder," I said. "I want it with you. Once it wasn't such a problem."

"You weren't satisfied," said Ruth.

"I wasn't satisfied because you weren't satisfied."

"What makes you think I wasn't?" she demanded.

"Were you? You told me, and I could tell, that all those men . . ."

"It wasn't so many," said Ruth, coloring. "Why are you always harping on the numbers?"

"You made me feel that, with them, sex closed a door. We were going to open one. But maybe you'd rather have it that way. Maybe you want to be left alone."

"No, Joseph, you saved me. I was dead inside and you saved me. You know that."

"Well, you don't show it."

"I don't know what you want from me."

"I want you to enjoy yourself!" I shouted, foolishly. "I don't want to feel like something you want but don't want at the same time."

"What does that mean?" asked Ruth.

"I don't want to be treated like a piece of food."

"Food!" gasped Ruth.

"Yes, food!" I shouted. "That's what I feel like. The dinner you can't enjoy. I'm your dinner," I cried, losing control. "A kosher meal. A male chicken."

The saltshaker was still on the edge of the dining-room table and I grabbed it and began shaking salt maniacally onto my head. It sifted down my face like freeze-dried tears and made my eyes sting.

Ruth was crying, sobbing. Real tears, of course.

I stopped, suddenly, my heart pounding, my eyes stinging, my anger spent. Breathing hard, I sat down beside her on the couch.

"What do you want from me?" she asked, in a small voice.

What I wanted was to have sex with her, to be a cock and not a chicken, but I couldn't say it. I felt cruel, terrible.

"Do you want to be like the others?" she asked, seeming to read my mind. "Do you want me to go back to that?"

"No! No!" I cried. "Teach me not to be like the others," I said, though of course, at that moment, I did want to be like them. "Teach me how to make you happy," I added. Her face wore a pained look, but she was no longer crying. She was holding her mug of tea in both hands, cowering behind it, allowing it to fog her glasses.

I placed it on the coffee table. I touched her hair. Carefully I slid the thick glasses off her tear-streaked face and set them down next to the mug. I eased her back on the couch and ran my hands down her sides, skirting her breasts, stroking her belly, her hips, trying to soothe her. She lay stiffly, like a volunteer at a magic show about to be sawed in half.

The magician himself was nervous.

The air between us grew thick, charged. Max, as if sensing animal activity, trotted back into the room and curled up on the floor.

"All I want is to learn what makes you happy," I whispered.

Ruth took my hands and moved them off her body.

"I'm much better at . . . doing things . . . for myself," she said finally.

"Show me," I breathed.

She hesitated, and then, without a word, drew her nightgown slowly above her thighs. My whole soul rose with the hem of her gown.

"Go ahead," I whispered. "Don't be shy. I don't mind."

She was bare to her belly. A faint female odor, tangy and pure, rose from her body. My heart was beating furiously.

Then, without looking at me, she touched herself gingerly, sinking two fingers into her black hair as if she were feeling soil for water.

"Oh, I'm embarrassed, I can't," she said, pulling away almost at once.

"Yes, you can. Imagine you're alone. I'm just a dream you're having."

Soon, to my surprise, she relaxed. Her two fingers returned and took on a natural rhythm, a slow trill played on herself, and then, the tempo picking up, she played a faster trill and then a chord for the whole hand, striking down and down and losing time all together. But a deeper rhythm took hold of her. Her mouth was open, she gave a surprised groan and shut her eyes, but mine opened wider and wider.

My pulse was racing, my hands were dying to help, but I was irrelevant, and she was a closed circuit, lighting herself up, her face pink, her teeth flashing white. On the sidelines it looked astonishing—her passion, without me as an object, seemed like pain, as if she were giving birth. I found myself strangely moved. And despite my desire, I kept my own body in check. Withholding myself seemed to intoxicate and purify me. I behaved like a pervert, but I felt like an angel, hovering above her, her body unfolded, its mystery laid bare.

For this divine pleasure I would give up all physical claims. I became a fine diffused presence, filling the room like love itself.

And then it was over. The hand that had been in her was out and in my hand; she drew her legs together and gasped, up from the deep.

"Oh, that was remarkable!"

"I wish I could take the credit for it."

"You can," she said. "I could never do that in front of someone before."

I did feel a strange, powerful pride. I cannot deny this sense of triumph. Something her Dr. Hallo had never seen, some deep form of knowledge had been presented to me. And I would help her, free her. I was better for her than Hallo. He had her on his couch and I had her on mine. We would see. . . .

Ruth gazed up inquisitively at me. I sat beside her, appreciative, apprehensive, looking down, taking her in. The lower belly, domed like a forehead, the widow's peak of pubic hair.

My body was thrumming with desire but I was afraid to touch her, to alarm her. At last I lifted my hand, gently touching the hollow place formed by her neck and collarbone. I dipped my fingers into the shadows of that shallow pool, filmed with delicate moisture. Her chest rose and fell with her breathing, and through the twisted opening of her nightgown I saw the gleam of one sloping breast.

The phone rang.

"The machine will get it," I whispered. The phone rang four times and soon my father's voice broke over the answering machine and we both froze. Ruth's hand cupped herself protectively, like Giorgione's *Venus*.

"Joseph?" said my father. "Joseph, are you there? Are you well?"

His voice passed over us like the voice of God walking in the Garden, seeking me out.

"Joseph? Joseph? Call me when you have time." It was a voice darkened by an indelible stain of sadness. There was a permanent catch in it, like the last traces of an accent that cannot be wiped out. "We love you. Are you all right?" The tape clicked and whirred briefly, and then, silence.

Was it because of that voice, and the loss behind it, I asked myself suddenly, that I was in this strange situation? I could not avoid the thought as the metal ear of the recorder coiled up my father's words.

Ruth was already standing, her nightgown pushed down once more, her glasses back on. She stooped to pick up the Scrabble tiles that had scattered on the floor. I admired the strong curve of her body from behind.

"Would you like to take a bath?" I asked.

"I've already showered once today," said Ruth, without turning around.

"I really feel like taking a nice hot bath," I said.

"Good idea," said Ruth, dropping a handful of tiles into the bag. "Why don't you do that?"

The kitchen was spotless—and bare—when I got home the following evening. A note had been stuck with a tiny magnetic ice-cream cone to the door of the fridge.

Dear Joseph,
    Went on a cleaning spree. Chucked the leftovers. Sorry. There's pasta in the cupboard. I'm going downtown to meet Nadia and will be eating on the fly. I promised her I'd go to a meeting. Home late.

Love,
R

It was clear enough from the sparkling refrigerator and gleaming linoleum how Ruth had spent her afternoon. I wondered what "eating on the fly" might mean for her. It made me nervous when Ruth didn't eat dinner with me.

Nadia, who took art classes with Ruth at the New School, was not my idea of a helpful friend. She was a large-boned midwestern girl with sandy hair and a face so pale it looked like an overexposed photograph of itself. I understood from Ruth that Nadia's childhood had been dark and violent—there were hints of incest, of drunken paternal disorder, of siblings serving time at the local penitentiary. Nadia might have been a guest on *Oprah* for any number of shows, but she had pulled herself together, made it to New York and set out to become an artist. The only example of her work I'd ever seen was a sculpture called *Wrapped Fruit*, an orange and a banana covered in thousands of sheets of plastic wrap until the orange became a gray basketball and the banana looked like a foot in a cast.

"The fruit is the seed of a plastic creation," Nadia explained to me. "The world is natural at the core but on the surface it's, like, fake."

It seemed sad to me that she had escaped hell for this, but Ruth thought Nadia had a future and found her work fascinating. I suspect it appealed to her alimentary anxieties more than her aesthetic sense, for Ruth herself had a fine artistic eye.

The meeting Nadia was going to was at Alcoholics Anonymous. Ruth, who was obsessed with her newfound friend, often went with her as a show of solidarity. Ruth had confessed to me that she drew strength from the meetings herself—all those substance abusers publicly acknowledging weakness and failure. It pained me to picture her in that seedy setting—the abandoned Quaker meetinghouse or moldering church common room—surrounded by the smug misery of all those yuppie junkies and ruined lawyers, actors, suicidal housewives, the secretary and the CEO linked in a sordid hour of self-abasement.

No, I did not like her going. Too many bloodshot eyes looking for love and scoping her out. At the end of the meeting, Ruth had told me, everyone held hands.

Max's yellow food-and-water dish had fallen prey to Ruth's cleaning fit and stood empty on the floor. I filled its two compartments and Max, who had been sitting in the sink, reduced to nibbling water from the barely dripping faucet like a giant gerbil, leaped gratefully onto the floor.

I scrubbed a potato, pierced it and popped it into the microwave. Ruth hated the appliance, mine from before the move, mistrusting its methods. Hearing its hum I was, myself, made slightly queasy by the notion of invisible, radioactive fingers stroking the molecules of my potato one way, then another, back and forth. I felt I should be wearing a lead blanket over my genitals as during a dental X ray. I headed for the bedroom, thinking about Ruth.

"Trying, trying," were the first words she had written in her diary that day. "Things are getting difficult." Alarmed, I read on.

—

Cleaned out the fridge. Literally. Everything into a box and then the garbage. All but the eggs and the milk. Scrubbed the crisper with Fantastik. Removed the racks and used steel wool on the bars. Like cleaning a big thermal cage. Her cage.

Afterward she made a big pot of popcorn. Her reward. Too much. Buttered. Flung it all out the window into the courtyard. The birds discovered it in seconds, diving off the windowsills where she hadn't even noticed them before. Filthy creatures. First one goes for it, then they all do. Like they've been thinking about food all day. Watched them gobble it up, fighting over it. Mostly pigeons. A few sparrows, skipping in between. Ruíz was hauling out the trash. He was singing and looked up. He stopped singing, smiled, and said something in Spanish. It sounded like *sweeno porkita*. You little swine? Ducked out fast.

She felt weird but free. Every day she should cook food and throw it out the window. Ballast for her balloon. Must rise higher.

Yesterday, Joseph noticed her belly and chubby thighs. Can't believe she wasn't ashamed to show them. Must exercise more. Can't stop thinking about the case of Laura. Turning into Laura.

"Cleaned out the fridge" could be given an ominous interpretation, but I didn't think Ruth would lie to her journal. If she'd eaten all that food, surely she would have said so. The observation about the belly and thighs pained me, for I had thought nothing of the sort—indeed, I considered our session on the couch a breakthrough. Most perplexing was the reference to "the case of Laura." I had never heard the name before. Who or what did it refer to? I must, I decided, find a way to draw it out of her.

Having carefully stowed the diary back in its place, I noticed the answering machine blinking on its stand beside the bookshelf. I half expected it to contain more of Ruth's diary. I pushed a button and the machine rewound, slurping backward.

There were two messages. First came Nadia's intemperate voice, strong but somehow diffuse, unstrung, inviting Ruth downtown. "I could use you, babe," she said, in a tone of intimate collusion I loathed but that I knew had flattered Ruth and drawn her out on a cold night. Then my father's voice entered the room: melancholy, loving, reproachful. He spoke against the backdrop of WINS news. Shot between his sentences were phrases like *A Bronx woman was fatally stabbed* and *in an unrelated incident.* . . . "Joseph dear," my father began, as if he were dictating a letter, "I thought we'd hear from you. We want you to come out and see us. Your mother doesn't understand why you don't come." (That explained why my father, who seldom did the calling, was on the phone for the second time in two days.) "Call us. Bring Ruth. We love you. Are you there?" Something in me quivered as he paused, waiting for me to step forward, while the announcer's voice said *Anyone with information relating to this crime should contact the New York City Police Department.* "We love you," said my father. "Bye-bye."

—

Something had gone wrong with my potato. Either I had not pierced it enough, or ten minutes was too long, for it had reorganized itself into a kind of dinosaur egg. I sawed it open with a bread knife, but it was impossible for me to mash it with a fork and I was reduced to treating the wrinkled halves like pieces of bread, making an unsatisfying, slimy margarine sandwich, margarine being the only item left in the fridge besides eggs and milk.

Eating, I found myself worried about Ruth. I hoped she would take a taxi home. The image of the Bronx woman murdered on a subway platform haunted. As always, the subliminal undertow of my father's words were more powerful than anything he actually said. I imagined him sitting in the kitchen with the radio on, the endless information about disorder an ironic source of comfort.

My father goes to bed with a portable radio. He falls asleep to the news and wakes up to the news and during the night the radio lies grumbling beside him like a restless sleeper. On the pillow the sound quality is poor, the words muffled and disturbed, as if the radio had an accent. I don't know how my mother ever sleeps. In the morning, my father adjusts the station and raises the volume. He leaves behind his private dreams and wakes into the nightmare of history. At breakfast, he sits with the radio on and the newspaper folded in his lap. He reads with frantic intensity, a lost man consulting a bad map. From time to time he lifts his head and listens to the radio with a dissatisfied expression, as if it were not what he was expecting to hear—the wrong news after all.

In his dental office my father plays opera, and the open mouths of his patients seem to be holding long ecstatic notes. But as he bends over them, he looks as if he is staring a great way down, and that at the very bottom the news is still audible, a ceaseless transmission of the misery of the world.

My mother works in the office as his secretary. She wanted to be a singer when she was young and her voice, though haunted by its own secret note of grief, sings out musically when she answers the phone: "Dr. Zimmerman's office." She is my father's public voice and handles all the calls.

Attended as he is by voices and music, my father is nevertheless a silent man. To avoid direct speech he surrounded us with the events of the world—like fragile glass wrapped in newspaper—or with the high voices of singers that made me tremble.

—

I frittered the rest of the evening away doing laundry, watching television and waiting for Ruth.

Down in the basement with the laundry machines, amid the subterranean roar of the furnace and the occult rumble of pipes, clutching my bulging sack of clothes, I experienced a sensation of sudden terror. The super's dog, from somewhere in the basement, began yapping and scratching against an unseen door. As I threaded through the dimly lit concrete passageway that led, at sharp angles, to the laundry room, I felt certain that at each corner someone was lurking. The laundry room was empty, however, and freezing cold—a window had been left open. I poured in my quarters, my soap and my clothes and fled with the empty sack. As I passed the boiler room, the super's dog began to bark again, louder and closer, and from behind me a voice said, "She keep you busy."

I whirled and saw the super himself, grinning.

"Your wife," he said, "she keep you busy."

I laughed in huge relief and agreed, not bothering to point out I wasn't married. Instinctively, I fell into my slow, English-as-a-second-language voice.

"I see her today," said Ruíz, "feeding the birds. She love the birds. She has a good heart."

"Yes," I replied, stupidly, eyeing the ratlike Chihuahua that had come trotting out of the darkness and deciding that Max could have eaten it in two bites. "She loves the birds."

"You see this," he said, tapping a button pinned to the pocket of his brown shirt, above the heart. It was a white dove against a purple background. "This is the spirit. The spirit save me. In Puerto Rico I found the spirit. Before that I was no good: hangin' out, dreenkin', swearin'. I was no good and the spirit save me."

"That's great," I said, inching toward the elevator.

"Maybe your wife find the spirit," he said.

"Maybe so," I said. "Good night."

"Good night," he called, as I stepped into the elevator.

When I went down to transfer the clothes to the dryer forty minutes later I heard only his dog and when I went down a final time, they both seemed to have gone to sleep. I sneaked by in petrified silence, like a thief. In my impatience to get out of there, I took our clothes out of the dryer too early, discovering only upstairs that they were hot but not dry.

Overdone potato, raw laundry.

Spreading everything out on the bed to locate the few dry items, I found myself suddenly moved by Ruth's clothing—the fragile, puckered undergarments, the "Peds," socks that dipped below the ankle that she wore with her sneakers, tiny and white and touching as baby shoes. All the lineaments of her body seemed scattered on the bed. Most of her delicate articles were dry, and I gathered them up with almost trembling tenderness, matching underpants to underpants, tights to tights, bras to bras, occasionally lifting whatever it was I held—a T-shirt or camisole or clean but discolored pair of panties—to my lips and kissing it in a sudden transport of sad love, as if I knew that she would never come back.

Communism was collapsing on the eleven o'clock news. For some reason I felt inclined to click off the sound and watch in silence. I always decline the earphones on an airplane and whenever I see a silent screen I get the unconscious impression that I am 30,000 feet up in the air, the sterile chill of alien space pressing against the window, the hum of artificial atmosphere in my ears. Gorbachev appeared, Napoleon in gray flannel, pressing the flesh in some republic or other. My students hated him, distrusted him utterly. The crowds now on the screen combined the frenzy of Times Square on New Year's Eve, the earnestness of a sixties war protest and the proportions of a Nuremberg rally. It was thrilling. The Ice Age was ending and enrollment at ETNA would be up.

My father, watching the same broadcast across the river, would take no pleasure in these historic events. He had a dim view of the past and, since my sister's death, a dim view of the future as well. America, which, while I was growing up, he had always spoken of with the enthusiasm and patriotism befitting a child of immigrants, now seemed to him a lethal environment. Though every fire, every car crash, seemed to make the evening news, the war that had claimed my sister was never reported on television. Suicides, and the mysterious forces that made them, went unreported. Still—or perhaps for that reason—my father watched, letting the news wash over him, sitting in the living room like a man in a rainstorm, trying to drum out inner voices with a torrent of outside information.

I used to join him for these evening rituals. We said little, but I felt an unspoken closeness to him that I felt now, knowing that this was his channel and his hour. I, however, was watching in inverted fashion. He muted the commercials and I muted the news. A commercial came on, for which, perversely, I snapped on the sound, wishing to hear the voice that went with the beautiful body now whispering into the camera.

—

Ruth had not returned by midnight, when I crawled under fresh, damp sheets and shut my eyes. A dream, of wind and snakes and torture, awakened me. It was 2:00 A.M. and Ruth's side of the bed was flat, cool, sealed like an envelope. The hooped *whoosh* of air, the crack of a whip that had woven itself into a troubling dream and yanked me upright was audible. Though my dream had vanished, I felt I might still be within it as I sat in darkness, listening to the creaking, thumping, whirring slap—ominous, complicated, sounds inside sounds. Frightening, hinting at flagellation, the sound was also innocently familiar. Suddenly, wide awake, I knew what it was. I heard the telltale *swish* of a rope and knew that out in the high hallway of the apartment Ruth was exercising. I pictured her now, vividly, skipping intently into the smiling mouth of a jump rope. I lay back in bed without saying a word, listening to the soft, rhythmic thump of her bare feet on the floor, like the beating of a giant heart.

There were bands of haze over New Jersey the color of Saturn's rings when I woke up the next morning. Somewhere under that lurid orange light my father was in his office bending over the open mouth of a patient. Ruth, on the Upper East Side, was lying under the silent eye of Dr. Hallo. I was alone.

The day was unnaturally warm. It had snowed on Sunday, but whatever snow remained was turning to applesauce underfoot as I walked to the subway. All along Broadway, Korean markets offered asparagus at ninety-nine cents a bunch. The abundance of this spring vegetable in New York City in late December, the unnatural warmth of the day and the stirred emotions of my growing alarm over Ruth disoriented me in my own neighborhood, so that it was a relief to enter the permanently displaced ambiance of ETNA.

At ETNA, many students had mistakenly dressed for more snow. They roamed the halls topped with astrakhan hats the size of television sets. Some had huge mittens of the sort worn by Peary to the North Pole, and a few women even sported muffs of rabbit or sable. Blitstein was scolding a man wearing a particularly fluffy hat, for he had warned ETNA students repeatedly to leave their furs at home and to buy wool watch caps.

"They—will—shoot—you—on—the—subway—for—your —hat," Blitstein explained, with staccato ferocity, separating his words as the Blitstein method dictated, while the man, furry earflaps down, nodded aggressively in deaf bliss.

In the teachers' lounge a small commotion was under way in a corner.

"Close the door," Margot hissed at me fiercely when I walked in.

"What's going on?" I asked, prying the lid off my coffee and noticing suddenly that the table was strewn with contraceptives. "Some kind of experiment?"

"Margot wants to be the Dr. Ruth of Russia," said Felicia, adding in the accent of the popular sexologist, "Use a condom, foam, and haff fun!"

"She's going to teach the poor deprived proletariat about the indiscreet charms of the bourgeoisie," said Kenneth.

David looked up from *Rosencrantz and Guildenstern Are Dead,* which he was memorizing for an off-off-Broadway tryout, and sang, in a surprisingly fine tenor, "Ukraine girls really knock me out, they leave the west behind. . . ."

"You think it's a joke," Margot said hotly, slapping the lid down on a diaphragm case, gathering up colorful condoms, a banana, an applicator for foam and a tube of spermicidal jelly and dropping them all into her pocketbook. "But it's not. You know Ina Karpinskaya, that sweet young bookkeeper from Baku?"

"Does she wear a leopard-skin bodysuit, purple eye shadow and go-go boots?" asked Kenneth.

"Sometimes. She's not a very good dresser," said Margot, smiling, but then, regaining her earnest intensity, added, "Do you know how many abortions she's had?"

"How many?" we all said.

"Five!" Margot shouted. "She's twenty-one years old!"

"That's disgusting," said Felicia.

"I asked her how she prevents pregnancy," Margot continued, "and she just shrugged. Sometimes she gets them to pull out."

"Vatican roulette," said Felicia.

"Russian roulette," said Kenneth.

"Not to mention the risk of disease," Margot said. Of all the teachers she was on the most intimate terms with her students, often going to the Russian baths on lower Broadway with the women, or drinking with them in Brighton Beach bars. She had been to their homes and played with their babies. She prided herself on knowing the personal details of their lives.

"So you're going to give the whole class Sex Ed?" I asked. "Why not tell the social worker?"

"The social worker couldn't find her ass with both hands," Margot burst out, lighting a cigarette nervously.

"What if Blitstein comes in? If he finds you waving a diaphragm around he'll fire you in a second."

"Fuck Blitstein," said Margot, taking an angry drag. "I'm sick of this job anyway."

Just then Blitstein did come in. "No bell today," he announced, avoiding eye contact, for he was a little afraid of the teachers despite his bullying manner. "Get to your classes. What are you all doing in the corner, plotting revolution?"

"Yes," said Kenneth.

David looked up from *Rosencrantz and Guildenstern,* singing: "You say you want a revolution, weh-eh-el, you know-wo-wo," but Blitstein was already out in the hall, directing human traffic.

"Are you okay?" Felicia asked me. The other teachers had filed out and I was leaning against a table, suddenly aware of a faint glow in my brain.

"Fine," I told her, but I had a feeling that after a reprieve of several months, I was about to get a horrible headache.

She put her hand on my shoulder and if I hadn't been preoccupied I'd have asked myself what that hand meant.

"I think you need a vacation," she said, and then hustled down the hall.

A few moments later I found myself standing before my class, framed against the dark night of the blackboard, moving the hands of a cardboard clock back and forth and quizzing my students on the time.

"It is noun," a man was saying.

"Noon," I told him, but even as I spoke I felt, to my horror, the insidious stirrings of pain. I stopped what I was doing as if that could indeed freeze time, but there was no question about it. I felt, with grim certainty, the slow dawning of a migraine. It was, as yet, a gentle heat, a mere halo of pain, but I knew that soon enough the heat behind my left eye would sharpen into fire. Already my eye was beginning to tear.

"Excuse me," I said to the class.

And without another word I walked out, avoiding the perplexed moon faces, the exclamations of surprise and concern. I left them suspended in their seats, though I could hear, as I closed the door, an explosion of Russian.

The teachers' lounge was empty, the lingering smell of smoke still haunting the air. I switched off the light (light is deadly at such times), shut the door and stumbled through the room in the dark. There was a row of folding tables pushed against the wall and I climbed onto one of them, though my impulse was to climb under it. Something about the pain drives me down, drives me under, but the darkness was complete and buried me enough.

Already the velocity of the headache was increasing, the cloud of pain had contracted into molten rock, hardening and searing, my eye was streaming water and a cold nausea made its way down my limbs. I glanced at my watch, glowing green in the dark. In fifteen minutes, I knew, the pain would peak. Fifteen minutes more and it would begin to fade away. I hoped I could beat the break, for I did not wish to be found writhing in the dark.

I lay on a table, my head in both hands. I pressed my skull, pulled my hair, worked my jaw, my fingers seeking out some secret trigger to end the pain.

My body rolled over the slick surfaces of the Formica top where, half an hour before, Margot had displayed her contraceptives. I kicked away pencils and textbooks, a coat. Something dug into my back. I groped and flung it away and heard the crash of heavy glass on the far wall. An ashtray. When my hand returned to my face it was dark with the smell of ashes. The bitter taste streaked across my lips.

Pain unleashed fury. I felt if I could hurl the desk, tear down the walls, throw the very room through space, my pain would be appeased.

—

I experienced my first headache when I was a sophomore in high school. It came in the early hours of the morning, did not last long, and I attributed it to a hangover, for I had gotten drunk the night before for the first time in my life. But the next day I got one again, at 4:00 A.M., and the next day I got another. Just when I decided I'd see a doctor, they disappeared. Perhaps it was a hangover after all, I decided, and thought no more about it.

My next batch appeared three months later. It was Sunday and I had been shooting baskets at the playground near my house. It was early morning and I'd been at it about an hour when I felt the strange ghost of pain pass through my skull and enter my brain. I was at first more curious than alarmed, though I decided to knock off for the day and walk home. By the time I got there, three minutes later, I could barely walk upright. I flung the basketball into the driveway as if the ball and not my head were in pain. I watched with envy as it rolled into the garage. No one stirred in the street. The steps to my house seemed endless and unmountable.

I dived behind my parents' car, which was parked in front of the hedges surrounding the yard. I squatted down between the car and the hedges. It was spring, but there were leftover fall leaves mashed into the ground, and the smell of earth and decay sickened me. I shut my eyes.

It seemed to me then, though perhaps I dreamed it, that the door opened and my father came out. He walked down a few steps and looked around, having heard, no doubt, the ball dribbling itself down the driveway. Did he see me, too, crouching and shaking the bushes? To this day I do not know. The pain passed, I brushed myself off and, weak and white, entered the house, where my father stood waiting.

Immediately, he asked me what was wrong, cupping my head in large, protective, inquisitive hands when I told him. He suspected some misalignment with the jaw and sat me in a dining-room chair, my coat still on, gazing into my mouth, which I opened and shut at his command. When that failed to turn up results, he called a host of specialists who, because they knew my father, agreed to see me immediately. Every day that week I suffered the same headache, shutting myself in my room so my parents would not see me. My father drove me to different doctors, while my mother, panicked and pale, awaited the results with a look that, more than the pain itself, convinced me I was going to die. I was sixteen, the same age my sister had been when she died, and I could see, in my mother's eyes, a look of tragic expectation.

But I was not going to die, as the specialists quickly confirmed. I suffered from a peculiar sort of migraine that came in clusters, cycling through my life at irregular intervals, no one knew why. Usually men were older when they got it, though it had been known to exist in boys as young as twelve. I was given medicine that lowered my heartbeat and chilled me to the tips of my fingers. My head was stored, like ancient pottery, under special conditions—the pressure lowered, the temperature reduced. And, as the doctor predicted, in a few weeks the headaches disappeared. But as the doctor also warned, they returned, sometimes after months, sometimes only after years. And so it was, an odd mysterious pattern of pain cutting across my life.

The causes were unknown, the doctor assured me, but I could not help associating the invisible pain with my sister. Once, during that first week, hiding my headache from my parents, I had gone into her room, which had been left much as it had been at the time of her death, and lain on the floor. I had not been there since just after she had died, two years before. I had disgraced myself at the time by failing to cry at the funeral or show much emotion at all in the days that followed. And I'd disgraced myself further by something strange that had happened soon after her death. About a week after Evelyn's funeral, after people had stopped coming to our house, I woke up in a sweat, heart pounding, in the middle of the night. Impulsively I got out of bed and went into my sister's room. Her nightgown, long white flannel with a frill of pink at the neck, was still at the foot of her bed. She must have worn it not long before her death because it had the sweet, spiced, powdery odor of everything she wore. Evelyn wasn't fat, but was built on a larger scale than me. I could eat anything, whereas my sister was always dieting, exercising, and fretting over clothes. It horrifies me to confess it, but I teased her often and mercilessly. It was the great trump card I played whenever we fought.

Evelyn's nightgown fit me except for the sleeves, which were too short. I put it on, climbed into her bed, curled up under the covers and almost immediately fell into a deep, dreamless and mysteriously peaceful sleep. In the morning, so early that light was barely glowing through the curtained window, a hand on my shoulder shook me gently awake. There was my mother, standing over me with a look of unspeakable tenderness and pain on her face.

Perhaps she had mistaken me, briefly, for the corporeal ghost of my sister. Or perhaps she had known it was me all along and had watched me sleep. She didn't scold me or seem outraged. She merely said, quietly, "Joseph, it's time to get up now." She left me to change back into my T-shirt and underpants and when I saw her downstairs at breakfast she did not allude to where I had spent the night. In fact, she never mentioned it again and, if she ever told my father, he did not let on. That was the last time I had been in my sister's room until I went in to lie on the floor two years later, as if in penance for her death.

Was pain my sister's way of inhabiting me from time to time, putting on my body as I had once put on her nightgown? I lay on the desk in the dark of the ETNA lounge, my head fragile as glass, the pain hot as live tungsten, worming through the dark. I was lit up by my suffering until the door opened and a shaft of real light struck me like a club and then—a horrible flash. Then more lights, like an exploded sun.

I raised myself up, my back against the wall, my head in my hand as if pain were an idea I was turning over in my mind, a persistent thought I could not rid myself of.

"What's going on?"

It was Blitstein, his dark eyes blazing close. The light was excruciating. I felt like the Cyclops blinded by the burning brand, all eye and all pain.

"What's wrong with you?"

Again the high, frantic, familiar voice. There was more than a note of hysteria.

"What are you, crying?"

"No," I breathed, and the breath cost me. "I have a headache."

"A headache?" cried Blitstein. "This is a headache?" He was bending over me, stooping beyond his naturally bowed state.

He fixed on me a look of caught and contagious misery. "You shouldn't come in if you're sick. You should call. What are you, a martyr?"

I said nothing. The pain spoke louder than he did.

He waited, poised above me, humped up with anger and sympathy.

"Ach! I'll teach your class."

I imagined then that he reached out to pat my arm, but I shrank away, fearing contact. He turned without a word, switching off the light before closing the door.

When the bell, fixed, clattered fifteen minutes later I was already sitting upright, like Lon Chaney, Jr., waking after a spell as the Wolf Man, the hair and teeth and claws having receded, leaving only a vague memory of murder, guilt, exhaustion.

I could pass, in the sallow light of my smoking fellow teachers, who straggled into the room, for tired, wasted, hungover. No one inquired. Only a speck of vanishing pain remained, like the dot of light on an old TV set.

Distantly their conversation came to me.

"It was a disaster. The men started inflating the condoms. They're gorillas. The women blushed under their blush and wouldn't say a word."

Kenneth was roaring with laughter. "I saw them in the hall, tossing the diaphragm like a Frisbee. I hope you don't still use that one."

"Shut up!"

I staggered out to the hall to drink at the water fountain and ran into Blitstein.

"Go home!" he said. "You look like hell."

But I refused.

I finished the last hour—pale, hollow, slow—pain still sparkling in my head. I felt I had died and this was my heavenly, or perhaps my infernal, task: to teach immigrants English. My students stared, goggle-eyed, murmuring, as if they had seen a ghost.

A middle-aged woman from Tashkent, with iron-gray hair and dark, Asiatic eyes, raised her hand.

"Mr. Joseph, please, I am doctor. May I help?"

At once the other students began to holler, razzing her.

"She kill you. She kill you. KGB." (They pronounced it Ka Gah Beh.) Several raised their hands, squeezing imaginary syringes in the air. The woman had worked in a psychiatric clinic in the Soviet Union.

"Thank you, Lyudmila," I said. "I'm fine."

The class quieted down and I returned to writing vocabulary on the board. I felt like a spirit in their presence—the healthy, eager bulk of immigrants, weighted in their chairs, and I, light as chalk dust, drifting before them.

It was already growing dark when I left ETNA. Rather than go home, where I was longing to nurse my head, still dented with pain, and to shower away sentence fragments and stray, meaningless syllables, I headed south for a rendezvous with Ruth, her mother and her mother's friend, Ernest Flek.

I didn't know much about Flek, but what I had heard intrigued me. He had grown up in Hollywood, where his father, Victor Flek, a German refugee, had been a director whose films enjoyed enormous popularity in the thirties and forties. "Flek magic" suggested a bittersweet world where humor, love and irony kept poverty and misery at bay and where a miraculous ending typically swept sadness aside. Carol Simon, who was a big fan of Victor Flek's films, had met the director's son while researching a chapter on a book about Hollywood's refugee directors. Ruth wasn't sure if her mother and Flek were lovers, though on the whole she assumed her mother slept with every man she befriended.

Ruth spoke about Flek uneasily, and not simply because of his suspected relationship with her mother. Flek, who had built a successful career in California as a psychoanalyst, had gradually lost his faith in the talking cure. He had backed away from Freud, but remained involved in the recovered-memory movement, coaching numerous young women through traumatic memories of childhood abuse, until, finally growing disenchanted with that form of therapy, too, he had abruptly given it up when one of his former patients suddenly "remembered" that not only her father and her uncle but Flek himself had molested her. Though her lawsuit was dismissed, Flek had quit California some years ago for Manhattan and had become a crusader against the entire psychoanalytic movement, which he now saw as the pernicious underpinning of much that was wrong with American culture. He lectured at the New School and had published two scathing and much-debated articles: "Freud's Superego" in *Harper's Magazine,* and "The Shrink-wrapped Society" in *The Atlantic Monthly.* Within the therapeutic community, Flek was famous.

All this made Ruth—who still believed in the buried treasure of forgotten trauma, and trusted Freud's map of the unconscious to lead her to the mother lode—extremely anxious.

I was buzzed into Flek's apartment, the top floor of a converted factory on Mercer Street. The elevator button didn't light up when I pushed it, and I experienced a brief pang of claustrophobia in the battered, immobile box, but moments later the elevator rose of its own accord, summoned from above. I soon found myself in a small vestibule facing a single door. It was an imposing entrance of rich, dark wood that contrasted strangely with the graffiti-scrawled, forbidding exterior of the elevator.

Through the door I made out the unmistakable strains of *La Bohème.* It was early in the opera, the scene in which Rodolfo, to the applause of his friends, burns his play to keep the fire going. There was an elegant brass knocker in the center of the door. I knocked lightly. Then loudly.

"Come in," a voice from beyond the door called at last.

The door was unlocked and I pushed it open, revealing a huge loft, the ceiling high enough to accommodate clouds. There was a man seated in the middle of the giant room and not far from him a little girl crouched under a table. I waited for the man to stand up, but he only smiled and raised his eyebrows expectantly.

"I'm looking for Ernest Flek," I said.

"You've found him," the man said genially, though still he did not stir. The operatic mirth of Puccini's bohemians rang through the loft. Flek sat as if onstage. He wore a ribbed cashmere turtleneck of forest green and held his thick upper body powerfully erect. There was a drink in his hand, a dark blanket over his lap. He had the arranged look of a king on his throne and I resented his assumption that I would come to him. Leave it to a shrink, I thought, even an ex-shrink, to make every encounter a test of wills.

"Should I come back later?" I asked, annoyed.

"Forgive me for not standing up, Joseph," he said after a scrutinizing pause. "Believe me, I wish I could."

No one had bothered to tell me that Ernest Flek couldn't walk. Only after approaching and bending low to shake his hand did I see the crutches lying next to him. They were not the temporary wooden crutches you get when you break your leg, but the permanent sort, made of metal, that grip each forearm with a gray padded plastic cuff. Against the wall, beyond the plush furniture, a wheelchair was folded against itself, big wheels and little wheels, like a ten-speed bicycle mated with a shopping cart.

"I'm sorry," I said, burning with embarrassment. "I didn't expect you to be—"

"A cripple?" he suggested cheerfully, cutting me off.

"Seated," I offered lamely.

"I like that," he chuckled. "Seated. God knows it's better than 'challenged' or 'handicapped,' though I prefer 'cripple' myself."

He had a crushing handshake, and as we shook hands he pulled me down to him so that he could get a better look at me. I got a better look at him, too. He had a large, handsome head, very tan and almost bald, but with two tufts of white hair pressed back like wings on a Viking helmet. His face had a Roman nobility, strong, but with a great capacity for weeping in the eyes. His nose was thick, powerful, nostrils flared, but his lips were lifted in a smile.

There was a small gap between his two front teeth, and strangely, it was this tiny imperfection more than his paralysis that unsettled me. If only he had fixed his teeth, I thought. My father's dental view of the world had clearly rubbed off on me. Fix the smile and everything will follow.

"Please sit down," he said, when he released me.

I sat on a nearby love seat, from which I took in the true size of the apartment that soared above us like an airplane hangar. Because of the great height of the ceiling, the apartment had at first seemed larger than it actually was, but it was still impressively vast and beautifully decorated, with antique carpets set down like gorgeous beach towels on the pale floor. Paths of wood ran between the carpets that I imagined allowed him to navigate the large space.

I apologized again for having expected him to get up when I'd arrived.

"Forget it," he said gently. "Why on earth should you be sorry?" And then, as if in answer to my unasked question, he said, "I had polio. In 1954—the year my father made his last film, which was a flop. I was thirteen and I got sick at camp—it was the last epidemic before Salk wiped the damn thing out. I'm sure someone your age doesn't even think about that illness. We're veterans of a forgotten war."

There *was* something of the soldier about him. Even the blanket of red-and-black plaid that hung over his lap and legs gave him, like a kilt worn with conviction, a surprisingly rakish appearance rather than the look of an invalid. He radiated a robust virility and it did not seem at all impossible that he and Mrs. Simon were indeed lovers. I'd felt, shaking his strong hand, a kind of electric charge, a macho condensation of his lost motility in his swelling chest and arms. On either side of his chair two squat black dumbbells weighted down the elegant carpet. And I guessed from the presence of the little girl, who bore a certain resemblance to Flek in her wide eyes, that not all under the blanket was paralyzed.

"This is my daughter, Miranda," he said, following my gaze and pointing to the little girl under the mahogany dining table. She had curly blond hair and was playing with a naked Barbie doll who also had curly blond hair.

"Miranda, why don't you come out and say hello to Joseph?"

I smiled at the child, who did not smile back but only shrugged shyly. She showed no inclination to emerge from under her table, and I could see why so small a girl, in the dwarfing height of the apartment, would crave a lower ceiling. I felt half inclined to crawl under a piece of furniture myself, and it occurred to me that the height of the ceiling made me feel the way Flek himself must have felt in his chair—farther from the sky than he ought to be, closer to the ground.

"My daughter," Flek said again, proudly. "Her mother," he added in a lower voice, turning back to me, "lives in France. Miranda's just here for a few weeks."

A wave of sadness passed over his strong face and I felt drawn to him still more. It was clearly painful to him to be separated from his child, and I wondered if his marriage had been a casualty of the scandal in California. I wanted to ask him something more about his daughter, but the music in the background shifted and grew stronger, the violins rose, and Flek touched my arm to call my attention to it.

"Listen to that," he said, shaking his head in marveling appreciation, something my father himself used to do during Saturday afternoon broadcasts from the Met, on the rare occasions when he wasn't at the office, but sat listening in the living room. I recognized the "Mimi" theme and knew the tubercular heroine was going to make her entrance. She was climbing the stairs, her candle about to blow out. "It's hard to make a cough musical, but she does it," said Flek. "Do you like opera?"

"I grew up listening to it," I told him. "My father plays opera in his office. He's a dentist."

"It must help distract the patients while he works."

"Mostly it distracts my father," I said. "It keeps him sane looking into all those bloody mouths."

"I understand that," said Flek. "It's nice to have a reminder that out of the encumbered body so much ethereal beauty can come. At least that's how I feel listening to opera."

There was something enormously appealing about the way Flek spoke, an odd mixture of blunt directness and refined reflection that made everything he said familiar and yet somehow surprising. Some of this must have been the compensatory verbal energy of a chair-bound man, but despite the occasional florid excess of his speech, there was something unabashedly open, bracingly honest and truthful about not only his words but his whole bearing. I found his voice, enriched by the merest hint of an accent, unusually captivating, almost hypnotic. No doubt it was the music in the background, but I had the impression that he was somehow singing himself.

"Joseph, are you feeling all right?" He was staring at me with his pale, penetrating eyes. "Forgive me for saying so, especially since I've only just met you, but you're looking a little green around the gills."

He was right, of course. I was still feeling the aftereffects of my migraine. My head felt like a pumpkin the day after Halloween.

"Just a long day," I told him.

"Would you like a drink? I'm sorry, I'm not being a very good host. I haven't offered you anything."

"Please don't trouble yourself."

"It's no trouble," he said, pushing the button of an intercom that rested on a small table that also held a portable phone and a book whose title I could not make out.

"Magda!" he roared. "Come here, please." His voice, which had been soft and refined, became effortlessly loud. I attributed this to the thick construction of his upper body. His belly seemed an extension of his chest, as if the rib cage traveled all the way down to his hips, and powerful lungs inflated his whole length.

A plump, kerchiefed middle-aged woman, who might have been one of my students, scurried into the room from a shadowy passageway in the rear that concealed some hidden depth of the apartment. She spoke English with difficulty and stood trembling like a woman awaiting punishment. Flek was very patient with her, repeating several times my request for a seltzer and his own for scotch, while she nooded her head in the obliging manner my students used when they had no idea what was being said.

While Flek arranged for our drinks, the girl under the table and I engaged in a brief staring contest. The girl stuck out her little pink tongue with sweet defiance and scowled at me. I smiled back.

"No ice, only water," Flek was saying to Magda, "very important." She left the room repeating, "nice vater, nice vater."

"You teach English to immigrants, don't you?" Flek said when she had left the room. "I admire that. It's such an important job. I don't think I'd have the patience for it, I'm worn out just giving orders to Magda."

He seemed, unlike most people I encountered, to be entirely sincere in his praise of my occupation.

"I don't always have the patience for it myself," I admitted. "It's really just a temporary job."

To my relief, Flek did not ask what it was I truly wished to do, but only nodded. The music had risen in intensity again and we sat together without speaking, listening. In a moment, I knew, Mimi would collapse into Rodolfo's arms.

"What do you suppose it is about a sick woman that nineteenth-century men found so desirable?" Flek asked suddenly.

I told him, truthfully, that I had no idea.

"It's interesting, though, isn't it, this fantasy of a woman in distress? In medieval tales the damsel was held captive in a castle. But in Puccini's day she was held prisoner by her body, wasting away like Mimi. Finally, she was a prisoner of her own mind. Freud certainly believed he was a modern knight, galloping to the rescue, storming the fortress of the unconscious. I once believed that myself."

"What do you believe now?"

Flek sighed and looked down thoughtfully. "Now I believe that you cannot always help people. You cannot always keep people from the mistakes they have to make. You can, of course, give comfort, support, love. But you can't travel back in time and fix the past. The past no longer exists, it's not a place we can ever visit, much as we wish we could."

Listening to Flek, I had a sudden inspiration.

"Have you ever heard of the case of Laura?" I asked. "Is that one of Freud's?"

Flek thought for a minute. "No, I can't say it rings a bell. Any reason in particular?"

"Not really," I told him. "Someone mentioned it recently, that's all." Could I admit to reading my girlfriend's diary?

"It wasn't Ruth, was it?" he said. "I know how much she loves reading case histories."

"No," I said quickly. "It wasn't Ruth. But please don't tell her I asked you."

Flek gave me a curious, sympathetic look.

"Of course not," he said. "By the way, how is she?"

"Oh, she's doing all right," I said.

"You don't sound very convinced."

I hesitated a moment. I was not accustomed to confiding in other people, especially the professional class of listeners Ruth had so much faith in. But for that very reason, Flek appealed to me. He was and was not a part of that world—an anti-analyst who nevertheless knew the intricacies of illness firsthand. I found his face so open and intelligent that it seemed capable of receiving the most extreme revelations with perfect equanimity.

"You're right," I said. "I'm worried about her. She's one of those people you were talking about. She thinks she can visit the past and fix what's wrong."

Flek nodded as if he'd known what I was going to say before I said it. I could see how good a therapist he must have been. He created an atmosphere in which confession seemed a natural extension of conversation. I was on the verge of telling him everything, beginning with the astonishing detail of our kiss—though Ruth would have felt it a terrible betrayal—but Flek spared me by saying suddenly, "Joseph, do you mind if I tell you a story?"

"Go right ahead," I said.

He did not, however, begin speaking immediately. This gave me a chance to study him. I realized I'd avoided looking directly at him, though he had the kind of concentrated appearance that imposes itself on your vision whether you stare or not. Flek held himself very straight, with the slightly uncomfortable look of a man in a barber's chair halfway through a haircut. From time to time he shifted uneasily, pushing down on the armrests to resettle his body, adjusting the blanket and reaching underneath, surreptitiously, to adjust his legs. For all his robust presence, I sensed the complex difficulty of his incapacity, a lifetime of adjustment and physical compromise.

I found myself mysteriously drawn to him, and waited eagerly to hear what he'd tell me. I felt that his story would touch on Ruth, and though Ruth disliked him for having abandoned his faith in Freud, I felt certain that he could help me—and help me help her.

"I was thirteen," he said at last, "when I got sick. I know something about the wounds the body can suffer and the ways it can heal. And the ways it can't heal." He was silent again, shifting in his chair.

"It's not easy growing up in Hollywood," he continued, "when you've lost the use of your legs. Especially in a house where movie stars sit by your pool. I ought to have been grateful just to be alive. Two of my bunkmates, who also got sick that summer, died. But I didn't feel lucky. One night, after everyone was asleep—and we had a big house, with servants—I rolled myself right into the pool. I wasn't wearing my leg braces and though the chair sank right away—they were incredibly heavy in those days—I rose to the top. Did I swim up? Float up? I wasn't sure. It was a beautiful night, the moon was out and the air was fragrant and warm. I was gasping for air and struggling desperately, but I still saw how beautiful everything was, the mimosa, the moonlight on the Spanish tile. I began to swim. Just from hauling myself around on crutches all day my arms had grown strong. When I reached the shallow end of the pool safely I didn't crawl out, I turned around and swam back the other way. Then I swam back again. I swam laps all night. And when the sun came up and our groundskeeper came out to clean the pool, there I was, still swimming."

Flek's face glowed with triumph as he recalled for me this story of rebirth. I did not begrudge him the boastfulness in his voice, it was undoubtedly such defiance that had saved his life. If only my sister, I thought, had possessed that kind of defiance. If only someone had told her a story like that. I wanted to ask Flek about those who don't swim but sink—whose fault is that? But he was speaking again.

"After that, I spent most of my time in the pool. Hydrotherapy was big in those days anyway, and I swam for hours. Besides, from the waist up, treading water, I looked like a normal teenager. Better than a normal teenager. I was strong and dark from all those hours in the pool. I had hair then, too, and I wasn't bad-looking. And of course, there were all those beautiful women who came and sat and swam and sunned. I was there so often they just accepted my presence. They took their tops off and sunned themselves and talked as if I wasn't there. Maybe because I was a cripple they felt sorry for me, or decided I was safe. And eventually they talked because I *was* there. These women, aloof and elegant, began to talk to me. They began to talk to me in a way they did not, I believe, talk to anybody else. And what I found out was how miserable they were. Starlets were always turning up dead in people's pools. They fished them out like goldfish. Nobody seemed to find it that unusual that so many young, beautiful women wanted to die.

"This made a very big impression on me. These women, who looked so lovely, so divine, so whole, felt worse about themselves than I did. *And they could walk.* This, I must confess, was enormously helpful to me. Eventually it gave me the courage to begin asking women out. If some gorgeous Goldwyn girl thought, deep down, that she was ugly, what could be said for the women I went to school with? This is not something I'm proud of, but I pulled myself back into life partly on the knowledge that many women hate themselves."

I found what he said deeply disturbing. Had I bound Ruth to me with knowledge of her unhappiness? Did I too use an intimate acquaintance with female misery to my own advantage?

"I had to make a stark choice forty years ago," Flek was saying. "Swim or drown. Walk or crawl. Fight or surrender. Live or die. I chose life, but I understand the other impulse too. What I saw once in Hollywood," he said, looking hard at me, "I now see everywhere. Polio has been wiped out in this country, but the number of attractive women who hate themselves—well, that's something of an epidemic. Hollywood culture is universal culture now. Everyone wants to step out of life and into the flat perfections of a movie screen. My own wish to drown was not so different from the desire those girls had to leave their real lives behind, to receive new names and wardrobes and perfectly scripted lines. Most people don't want to die, but they don't want to live either. I am speaking about men now as much as women. They look for a third way, but there is no third way."

"Why are you telling me this?"

"I saw Ruth when she was sixteen," he said. "I didn't treat her, but I saw what she looked like. I know." he said.

I felt a shiver pass over me, as if the mercury had sunk in my spine.

"But she isn't like that anymore," I said, as much to convince myself as to convince him.

"I'm not saying she is. But you said yourself you were worried about her."

"Yes," I admitted.

At that moment the buzzer rang and Magda went running through the living room and out the front door to send the elevator down.

"Joseph, we'll have to talk some other time," he said. "I hope you don't mind my speaking so directly—Ruth's a wonderful young woman and you seem like a fine young man. I only want to give you a word of caution."

I nodded without speaking.

"By the way," he said, "it occurs to me that there is a case of Laura. It isn't one of Freud's, it's in Robert Lindner's *The Fifty-Minute Hour.* I don't know if anybody reads that book anymore but the chapter on Laura was one of the first case histories to apply psychoanalytic principles to eating disorders. Of course the theory's all horseshit—I urge you not to look for answers in books like that. But whoever told you about that book," he said meaningfully, "may be looking for help."

"What kind of help?"

He did not have time to tell me, if in fact he knew, for at that moment Carol Simon burst into the apartment.

Mrs. Simon was wearing a fox-trimmed leather coat and large pink-lensed glasses. She looked like one of the movie stars from Flek's childhood.

"Oh, Ernest, have Doris make me a drink," she said, peeling off the heavy coat and dropping it over the back of a chair, which swooned under its weight and fell back like an animal, legs sticking up. "I'm dead."

"Doris is sick. I got someone new from the agency. Magda!" Flek shouted, not bothering to use the intercom.

Carol leaned languorously down over Flek and kissed him, not on the lips but on the tanned top of his head. In this way he was greeted directly by her breasts. How could Ruth not be sure? I thought. There's no question. None at all. But this confirmation didn't bother me as it would have Ruth; I felt oddly comforted by it.

"Carol Simon," said Flek, reading the name tag she still had stuck to her blouse.

"Ugh!" She tore the tag off like a Band-Aid in one savage rip. "Oh, those awful parties."

I righted the chair Mrs. Simon had capsized and stood waiting for her to acknowledge me. She shifted her glasses to the top of her head and looked around. Her bright hair was pulled back in a bun pierced by lacquered chopsticks.

"Joseph, you're here," she said, bypassing my outstretched hand and kissing me. "So good to see you," but she had spotted the child under the table and moved on.

"Miranda!" she cried, and swooped down to kiss her, murmuring in cooing off-kilter French. Ruth's mother had grown up in Montreal, and Miranda laughed at her accent—which Mrs. Simon exaggerated for comic effect—coming alive under her caressing attention.

"Scotch?" Flek asked, as Magda came into the room bearing our own drinks on a tray.

"I've been drinking wine," Mrs. Simon called back, abandoning Miranda, flinging herself into an easy chair and removing her shoes. Flek gave the order and then took his own drink from the breathless Magda, who had combined the two previous orders and made us both scotch and sodas.

"Where's Ruth?" I asked, setting down my drink as soon as I scented the alcohol, fatal to my tender head.

"Don't you know?" she said. "I thought she'd be here."

"She had an art class at the New School, but I thought it would be over by now."

"Oh yes," said Mrs. Simon. "Still life. If she wanted still life she should have been at my conference. What a bunch of stiffs. Someone should colorize those people. My God! Where's my drink?"

"It's coming, my dear. Patience." Flek was smiling, though he kept his teeth concealed. He had taken on an extra glow in Carol's presence.

They fell into a brief conversation about someone I did not know, while in the background Act Three of *La Bohème* was ending. The warmth of the apartment and the length of the day caught up with me and I shut my eyes. For a moment I felt the way I did in childhood, sitting with my sister on the cracked leather couch in my father's waiting room, waiting for my parents to close the office so we could all go out for dinner.

The buzzer rang and I jumped up, startled.

"Magda will get it," Flek said.

A moment later Ruth appeared, dwarfed by the giant doorway.

She stood, bundled beyond the demands of the weather, unwinding a long turquoise scarf from around her neck. Her large black thrift-shop coat, slightly padded at the shoulders, was roomy enough to conceal a child under its folds without detection.

Seeing her filled me with excitement. A moment before I'd felt lost, adrift. Suddenly I was found. I felt a great urge to rush over and embrace her but Flek, to my surprise, got to his feet at her arrival, and I stood watching him instead. He'd risen with awkward ease, reaching down and grabbing the crutches, then poling himself up on them and fitting his arms into the metal bands. His trousers were of thick, charcoal-gray flannel; a few threads of red from the blanket clung to them. He took a single, stiff step forward, like a statue coming to life. Misshaping his trouser legs were the iron outlines of leg braces. He advanced toward Ruth with a muffled clank.

Flek's blanket had fallen to the floor and I scurried over to pick it up, holding it draped over one arm and feeling oddly protective, ready to lunge should he fall. But Flek himself did not seem embarrassed or reluctant or in any danger. And Ruth did not seem to notice the trouble he was taking for her. She did not spare him the walk, but stood her ground, slowly taking off her winter things while he advanced.

"Hello, Ernest," she said, reluctantly unbuttoning her coat. It was a smuggler's coat—potatoes might have fallen from the sleeves, loaves from the pockets. Ruth liked to dress up, and not long before had bought a beautiful and expensive cashmere coat at Bloomingdale's, but she had a more careless mode, and she indulged it most often when seeing her mother.

"Ruthie, that coat," said Mrs. Simon, coming up and kissing her daughter. "Where did you get it?"

"Alice Underground," said Ruth. "What's wrong with it?"

"Nothing at all," said Mrs. Simon. "I'm sure the homeless man who owned it got a lot of use out of it."

"I think it has character," said Flek, who had come to a halt in front of Ruth and stooped to kiss her. Even leaning on his crutches he was tall.

He insisted on taking the coat from her and managed, with great dexterity, to free one arm, tossing the coat over his shoulder and catching his crutch before it fell. Ruth seemed to shrink away from him, but Flek, unperturbed, chatted amiably with her. I admired his fortitude.

Ruth's eyes brightened when she saw me. She left Flek holding her coat and came over to where I stood. She had a red spot on each cheek that could as easily have been from the heat as the cold. But when we kissed, I felt the chill on her.

"Get me out of here," she whispered, and I kissed her again.

What was going on inside her? I must, I thought, get my hands on "The Case of Laura." I repeated the title, *The Fifty-Minute Hour,* over and over to myself like a mantra, afraid I would forget it.

Magda came back with Mrs. Simon's drink, took an order for mineral water from Ruth, and left carrying Ruth's coat.

"You can keep it," Mrs. Simon called after her.

"Mother!" said Ruth.

"Relax," said Carol. "She doesn't speak English. I don't think this is wine I'm drinking. Really, Ernest, you can do better."

Flek, who had reestablished himself in his old chair, laughed good-naturedly. He seemed to take enormous pleasure in the presence of Mrs. Simon and her daughter.

He lit a cigar taken from a drawer of the little table beside him. Miranda, who till then had remained glued to her spot, crawled out to receive the paper cigar ring, which she slipped immediately over one of her little fingers.

Ruth waited until Flek had taken his second puff before she erupted. "If you don't put that out," she said, "I'm really going to throw up."

Mrs. Simon supported her daughter. "Ernest, you're positively killing that child," she said, a reference not to Ruth but to Miranda. "There's no air in here, no natural light."

Suddenly, as in the elevator on the way up, I felt a shudder of claustrophobic dread and noticed, as if for the first time, that the huge place indeed had no windows. We were in the old meatpacking district and the apartment, full of ghostly noises, seemed still to whir with the spirit of its old machinery, the shouts of workers, the lowing souls of cattle. The only natural light came from above, two great skylights thick with city soot, woven with chicken wire, glowing with the night-blue hue of a winter sky. The cooing shadows of nesting pigeons darkened the corners of the glass.

"She's not a houseplant," said Flek. "But you're probably right, I should give this place up and get some bright house in the suburbs." He extinguished his cigar, which had scarcely had time to form an ash, and sighed.

"I like it here," said Miranda suddenly, from under the table where she had once again crawled, speaking for the first time.

Flek brightened and looked lovingly at his daughter.

"Thank you, darling. You like visiting Daddy, don't you?" But she had gone back to combing the blond curls of her doll and did not look up.

"You see, she's doing fine," said Flek, looking triumphantly at Mrs. Simon. "She's playing with Barbie and she has Zazu."

"Zazu isn't here now," said Miranda, without looking up.

"Who's Zazu?" asked Ruth.

"Zazu is her imaginary friend," said Carol Simon.

"How sweet," said Ruth, smiling at Miranda. Although somewhat fearful of them, Ruth loved children, and often pointed out the cutest babies on the street, establishing meaningful eye contact as they rolled past in their strollers.

"He's not imaginary," said Miranda. "But I'm the only one who can see him."

"Well, that takes imagination," said Flek. "That's not a bad thing."

Miranda seemed to sulk.

"Oh, I see him," cried Mrs. Simon, sliding out of her chair and onto all fours so that she and Miranda were at eye level, a lioness and a cub.

"No you don't," said Miranda. "Zazu lost his passport and didn't come."

"That's not him over there?" asked Mrs. Simon, pointing.

"That's just an old Indian mask."

"No, under the mask," said Mrs. Simon, coaxingly.

Miranda squinted and looked, shaking her head vigorously back and forth so that her blond curls flew.

It was touching to see Mrs. Simon maternally engaged. Ruth seemed to resent it, staring at me as if to say, "Don't be fooled."

"Are you sure?" urged Mrs. Simon.

"No no no no no no," the child sang.

"But I see him," Mrs. Simon said.

"What does he look like?" Miranda demanded.

"Well," said Mrs. Simon, "he's green and friendly and he has a beret and he's smoking a pipe."

"That's not Zazu," said Miranda condescendingly. "That's Zazu's cousin, Peepee."

"Ah," said Mrs. Simon.

"Ruth had an imaginary friend," said Flek. "I can see it in her face."

"I had an imaginary enemy," said Ruth dryly.

Flek laughed.

"She means me," said Mrs. Simon from the floor, where she was discussing with Miranda what Peepee ate for breakfast.

"No, Mother, you were real."

"Ouch," said Mrs. Simon, without looking at all hurt. Flek chuckled good-naturedly and I felt myself smiling, but Ruth wasn't happy. She was staring at the blanket, which I had absentmindedly laid over my own lap.

"Cold?" she asked.

I stood up and offered the blanket to Flek, who flung it casually over one shoulder like a bullfighter.

"I'm still not used to winter in New York," he said.

"Are you thinking of going back to California?" Ruth asked, rather cruelly, I thought.

"Actually, I *am* thinking of going back," said Flek. "At least for a visit."

"Ernest, I had no idea," said Mrs. Simon. "How terrible you are for not telling me. Are you serious?"

"I am serious," said Flek. "But I decided only this morning. There are some papers of my father's I've been meaning to sell to the UCLA library—you know about that. And I've discovered an unfinished screenplay I actually think I might sell to a studio."

"Oh, Ernest, how wonderful!" cried Carol Simon. "You must tell it to us immediately."

"Do you think," Ruth asked, "that you could turn off that music first?"

"It *is* giving me a dreadful headache," Carol Simon agreed. "And I had one to begin with."

"Well, Joseph," Flek said, turning to me, "it looks as if you and I are alone in our passion." With a wave of the remote control he terminated Mimi before the TB could finish her off. We all sat for a moment in the silence of the huge apartment.

"Oh, that's better," sighed Carol, taking a sip of her wine. "Now tell us about that movie. Is it a bedroom comedy?"

"I suppose you could call it that," said Flek. "That was my father's specialty."

For some reason we all glanced at the child under the table, but she seemed happily lost in her own world. She had neatly removed the head of her Barbie doll and was carefully combing through its curls with a tiny pink comb.

"It's called *The Affair*," said Flek. "My father had set it in Vienna, but I'd move it to New York. It's a very simple idea, really. It's about a man who has an affair."

"What's unusual about that?" said Mrs. Simon.

"Well, he has it with his own wife."

"Are they divorced?" she asked.

"Not at all, although things are a little rocky. That's when he gets his great idea. Rather than cheat on his wife, he'll cheat with her. They live in a suburb of New York. Every Thursday night they meet in Manhattan at a different hotel. They come in separate cars. They sign in under false names. They pretend to be lovers.

"At first, they're awkward, embarrassed. The wife thinks the idea is crazy. But then, though it was the man who forced the idea on his poor wife, she takes things in hand. At first it is to shame him, but soon she too gets drawn in. She buys clothes he has never seen before. She says things she has never said. She does things that are new to her and she finds that she feels more alive when she is out on Thursday night than when she is home the next morning. The affair takes off. They murmur to each other: 'My wife must never know.' 'My husband can't ever find out.'

"They never speak of their Thursday nights when they are together during the rest of the week. Their children are off at college. They both have successful careers. But they live for their Thursday trysts, which grow more and more passionate. Feelings they did not know they had, passions they had not felt in years, overtake them. She comes to him, naked under her coat. Or in exotic lingerie. They murmur wild words. But then a strange thing happens.

"The husband, after his initial delight, begins to grow jealous. His wife, he cannot help feeling, is cheating on him. Even if he is both the lover and the husband, it's beginning to drive him mad."

"Oh, how exciting!" said Mrs. Simon, breathlessly.

Ruth shifted uncomfortably in her chair.

"And then, one Thursday night," Flek continued, "in a moment of passion, the wife cries out, 'I wish I could leave my husband. It's you I want. I wish he was dead!'

"The husband is horrified. A terrible fight follows. He wants a divorce. No, that won't do. He wants to kill her. His hands are around her throat. She has betrayed him and now she must die!"

Here Flek paused.

"What happens?" whispered Ruth, her eyes big with interest and horror.

"I don't know," said Flek. "My father never finished it. That's where it ends."

"Oh, you're terrible, Ernest!" cried Carol Simon. "How can you do that to us?"

"Well, what do you think should happen?" Flek asked, looking around. "You can probably help me."

"I think the man goes ahead and kills her," said Mrs. Simon. "No, wait, he tries to kill her and she stabs him with a knife in self-defense. Yes! *She* kills *him*."

"That's lovely, Mom," said Ruth, sarcastically.

"Hey, it happens a lot," said Mrs. Simon. "Read the papers."

"Joseph," said Flek, "what do you think should happen?"

"I think they should stay together. They've learned too much, they've shared something too extreme to let them break apart. The man should come to his senses, realize his hands are around her throat, realize what he's about to do. Instead of killing her, he begs for forgiveness."

"I disagree," said Ruth with surprising vehemence, cutting me off. "If he can't accept her the way she is, she should leave him."

"Then you agree with your mother that it can't last," said Flek. "You just disagree about the method of resolution."

"No, I don't agree," said Ruth. "I think they should get married again."

"But you just said they can't stay together."

"Not at first. She has to leave him. They get divorced. But then, let's say a year or even five years later, he sees her in Paris, on a bench. In the Luxembourg Gardens. The leaves are just starting to turn. It's getting cold and she's bundled up, but it's her, looking older. Maybe there's a little gray in her hair, but she's still lovely. And he comes over to her and says, 'Excuse me, Madame, is this seat taken?'

"And she says, 'It's not Madame, it's Mademoiselle. And yes, this seat is free.'

"So he sits down and they start talking. And you know that this time it will be for real."

Ruth's eyes had filled with tears, and I myself was moved by her romantic vision. It delighted me that Ruth should want a happy ending after all. Flek too seemed pleased.

"I love it," he said. "And I think the studio will love it. You should get a credit."

Ruth's moist eyes shone. I wanted to go over and take her in my arms. I felt that she had just made me a promise of eternal love.

"Too derivative," said Mrs. Simon. "Preston Sturges, *The Lady Eve*. Henry Fonda courts Barbara Stanwyck and then courts her again, not realizing it's the same woman."

"That's completely different," said Ruth.

"Who cares, Carol?" said Flek. "You of all people know a good love story doesn't have to be original."

Ruth did not look mollified by this defense. She'd been stung by her mother's words and was about to say something when she was interrupted by a small, determined voice that came from under the table.

"Tell *me* a story," said Miranda. Everyone looked over at the child. "Not one of yours," she said, in a sweet voice. "Tell me a real story from Japan."

"If you'll all excuse me," said Flek, stirring in his chair and reaching behind him for his crutches, "I'm going to go read my daughter a story."

"Tell it here," said Miranda emphatically.

Flek looked apologetically around the room, but Carol Simon said, "Oh, absolutely. We'd all like to hear another story. I love being read to."

Even Ruth, who had, after all, her own collection of fairy tales, nodded in agreement.

"Well," said Flek, smiling down on his daughter, "go and get the book."

Miranda scrambled out from her hiding place and disappeared down the passageway. A few moments later her tiny rapid footsteps returned and she appeared, carrying a tall book. Flek placed her on his lap, over which he had again spread the blanket. I felt I could hear the faint muffled clank of iron as his daughter settled herself. From somewhere he had produced a pair of gold Benjamin Franklin half-glasses. He held the book out in front of Miranda—so she could see the pictures—and looked at the open pages over her shoulder, holding the book with outstretched arms, the way you hold the handlebars of a bicycle when giving a girl a ride on the bar. But the glasses gave him a grandfatherly aspect.

"Sorrowful Sorrowful or Congratulation Congratulation?" he asked the little girl.

"Sorrowful Sorrowful," she said without hesitation.

"But we had Sorrowful last night," said Flek, smiling.

"Sorrowful again," said the girl.

"At six she knows the world." Flek sighed, flipping through several pages. How about 'The Rice Demon'? " he asked her.

She nodded approval. Flek cleared his throat and looked around the room briefly. Ruth had moved beside me on the couch. Mrs. Simon had stretched her legs out before her, shoes off.

" 'The Rice Demon,' " said Flek, "or 'The Wife Who Ate No Rice.' "

Once upon a time there lived, in the province of Echigo, a man who was very rich and very stingy. He had no wife, and though his friends constantly reminded him of possible sickness and the discomforts of a lonely old age, he refused to listen to their advice and remained unmarried. In reality, he wanted a wife very much; but whenever he remembered that marrying meant doubling the number of bowls of rice at each meal, he counted the bales of rice in his storehouse and sadly shook his head from side to side.

He did not enjoy being alone, and sometimes thought of getting a dog or a cat for company, but when he considered that he would have to share with them the fishbones from which his soup was made, he sighed and again sadly shook his head from side to side.

Years passed. He grew richer and richer, but his health began to fail and he found it was not pleasant to look forward to old age; so at last, after a great deal of hesitation and many sighs, he decided to marry.

In arranging with the go-between he demanded a maiden of many virtues. She must be young, he said, and as beautiful as the cherry blossoms in the dawn of spring. She must be as industrious as the busy ant of summer, as obedient and submissive as the autumn grass bending in the wind, and lastly, so considerate of her husband's welfare that she would never lessen the treasures of his storehouse by eating even a single grain of rice.

The gods who plan marriages were good to him, for a wife was found who was beautiful, industrious, obedient, and who never ate a single grain of rice. The bridegroom was so pleased that he gave a grand wedding; but after this one generosity he was as stingy as before.

The bride brought a fine dowry of many clothes and she was not only pretty and gentle, but cheerful also, and, best of all, possessed the virtue of a quiet tongue.

And she was always busy. The *tap, tap, tap* of her paper dusting stick was heard at sunrise, and until the last lantern in the village was dark, her hands were never idle. She brushed the mats, she wiped the porch, she polished the lacquer, she spun, and wove, and sewed; and she never failed to have ready for her husband's return a meal of rice and browned fish, delicious soup and juicy pickles with eggs and vegetables. Yet his garden remained as full as before and the rice bales in his storehouse did not seem to lessen. Of course he was the happiest and proudest husband in the province of Echigo.

Just on the other side of the bamboo fence lived a neighbor whose wife was a good woman, but she possessed an overwhelming curiosity. Naturally she took a great interest in the pretty bride next door, and it was not long before she noticed that every day, after the husband had gone, there was a long, continual, regular *swish-swash, swish-swash*— the familiar sound of someone washing rice before cooking it. Also, she noticed that immediately after the sound ceased, a large quantity of smoke came pouring from the lattice windows beneath the ends of the roof ridge. Curious to know the meaning of this, she one day peeped through the bamboo fence and saw an astonishing sight. In the midst of her neighbor's kitchen, the bride was kneeling beside an enormous kettle of steaming rice. Plunging both hands into the steaming rice, she ate hungrily. No longer was she a pretty, gentle maiden, but one of the wild imps of the mountain who are sent to teach the wicked.

The horrified neighbor could scarcely wait until her husband's return to tell him the story. He did not believe it, but he remained at home the following day and watched with his wife through the bamboo fence. He saw the same terrible sight and, convinced and frightened, he went that very evening to the rich man and told him what he had seen, excitedly declaring the bride was not a woman but some wicked fairy in disguise.

The husband, startled but only half believing, hurried to his storehouse and counted the bales of rice. Not one was missing. In a great rage he berated his informer as a malicious talebearer, and his confidence in his wife remained untouched.

The curious neighbors kept watch at the bamboo fence. The husband spent so much time at the opening that his work was neglected and the contents of his storehouse grew smaller as the hole in the bamboo fence grew larger.

One day he formed a plan. He invited the rich man to dine with him. Although still angry, the stingy man would not lose so good an opportunity to save a meal at home, so he accepted, counting in his mind that in this way several bowls of rice would be saved. The day came. The neighbor's wife was a clever woman, and she placed the two little tables so they would face the garden, beyond which was the bamboo fence. As the weather was warm, the sliding doors dividing the room from the porch had been removed, and the rich man, while eating, could plainly see his own house-roof and the top of the big pine tree that grew beside his rice storehouse. The host was very entertaining, and his guest was kept so busy talking and eating that he did not hear the *swish-swash, swish-swash* of the rice washing, nor did he notice the smoke pouring from beneath the roof ridge, but the host carefully noted everything, and at the proper moment he cried out suddenly,

"A rat! A rat! Oh, Honorable Neighbor, it has gone through the bamboo fence and is running toward your rice storehouse."

Flek paused and looked around the room. The dark faces on the wall held their breaths and the living faces all stared, masklike, enchanted. A pigeon shifted on the roof. Flek savored the dramatic silence and inhaled deeply.

"Go on, Daddy," Miranda said, softly. Flek continued:

Up sprang the stingy man and, hurrying to the fence, he anxiously peered through the opening. He saw not a frightened, scurrying rat, but his own wide-open kitchen. The fireplace was red with hot embers, over which was hanging a huge kettle full to the brim with steaming rice.

His wife—his young, beautiful, industrious, frugal wife, who was always cheerful and busy and who never ate a grain of rice—was leaning over the kettle, her ever-busy hands tossing handfuls of rice up to her face as fast as wind blows the autumn leaves. Her entire face from brow to chin seemed a great chasm, and as she ate her eyes became shining coals, horns sprang from her forehead, and the horrified husband saw before him, clothed in his wife's dainty garments, one of the dreaded imps of the mountain who are sent to teach the wicked.

Here Flek paused once more. His eyes fell on Ruth and she shuddered. His glance then turned to me. At last he returned his gaze to the book. He stroked his daughter's head absently and resumed reading in a hushed voice.

Faint with terror, he dragged himself back to the neighbor's porch and for a long time waited, fearing to return home. The time came, however, when he must go. Stealing quietly into his house, he went to his room and, hurriedly spreading his sleeping cushions, he crept into them and covered up his head.

Soon his wife came in, pretty and merry as usual, and greatly surprised to find her husband hidden in the bed clothes.

"What ails you, my lord?" she asked anxiously.

"Pray let me be alone," came in a terrified voice from under the covers. "I am not well. Pray let me be alone!"

The obedient wife bowed and retired, but soon she came again.

"Allow me to rub away your ailing," she pleaded. "My hands may give you ease."

"Oh, no, no! Pray let me be alone!" he cried faintly, his face still hidden.

Again she submissively bowed and went away, but soon she returned with a cup of boiling water on a little tray.

"Here is hot water, my lord. It may wash your ailing away."

"Pray let me be alone," he whispered, almost fainting with terror.

Again she bowed and obeyed, but once more she returned.

"Let me bring you medicine, my lord, to cure your ailing."

The poor man was so faint with terror he could make no reply. As he did not command, the need of obedience was gone, so the wife sat quietly for a moment by the bed. Then she took hold of the edge of the cover and began slowly drawing it away. The terrified husband looked up and saw his pretty, gentle wife smiling shyly into his face—but only for an instant. As he gazed, her eyes began to blaze, horns pushed through the smooth forehead, her mouth opened from side to side, and as she spoke flames burst forth with every word.

"You did spy!" a hissing voice mocked. "And now you see the truth."

The husband was almost dead with terror. He could only gasp over and over, "Pray let me be alone! Pray let me be alone!"

"You expect fire without fuel," she went on. "You demand untiring labor and not one grain of rice for food."

"Oh," he gasped, "I pray you let me be alone. Take every single bale in my storehouse. Sweep clean from the floor every grain of rice, but I pray you let me be alone."

With a mocking bow of thanks, she turned away, and left the terrified man cowering within the bed cushions.

All night long a storm raged furiously. The sky seemed split asunder with flashes of fire and crashes of thunder. The winds roared a hoarse *"gow-gow!"* The bending branches of the big pine tree snapped and crashed: *"Ach-za-ra! Ach-za-ra!"* The torrents of rain poured: *"Bara-bara!"* and in the midst of the noise and confusion the awestruck neighbors saw a great wheel of fire dart down the pine tree by the storehouse, then, with a thunderous roaring and vivid flashes of light, spring upward and go whirling through the air toward the distant mountains.

The next morning the sun was shining brightly on the dripping thatch of the house, and finally the frightened husband found courage to creep to the porch. A blackened path reached from tip to root of the big pine tree and the wind was blowing cheerily through the wide-open doors of the empty storehouse. Not a single bale was there and even the floor was swept clean of every grain of rice.

Flek closed the book slowly. "Sorrowful! Sorrowful!" he said, Miranda joining in, echoing sweetly, in her small voice, "Sorrowful! Sorrowful!"

For a moment, no one spoke. I looked over at Ruth, who was sitting entranced, a look of horror on her face.

"That's me!" Mrs. Simon cried, breaking the silence, sitting very straight, as if she had seen a ghost.

"Carol?" said Ernest Flek.

"That's me and William! He wanted me to do everything and ask for nothing. Desire that wasn't trained on him was demonic. He made me feel like a witch just for being a woman."

"Sorrowful sorrowful," said Ruth, mockingly.

She had risen and was asking Flek for her coat.

"But we haven't eaten yet!" Mrs. Simon cried.

"It's nine o'clock," said Ruth. "Dinnertime is over."

"What are you talking about," said Flek. "There's a great bistro two blocks away. In Europe, no one eats till ten."

"This isn't Europe," said Ruth.

Flek looked truly concerned, even, I thought, a little hurt.

"I was just going to put Miranda to bed and we'll go," he said.

"I don't want to go to bed," Miranda piped up. "I'm not tired."

"What if we eat right now?" I suggested, rising. "Wouldn't that be okay?"

Ruth shot me a deadly look. She could throw her emotions the way some people can throw their voices, and I would find her feelings somehow passing through me—a chill wind of anger or a sudden bolt of mirth. Now her anxiety literally shook my heart.

"We'll eat at home," I said. "I've got some work to do."

"Really?" Mrs. Simon asked.

"Mother!" shouted Ruth.

Ruth had found her coat and began winding her long scarf around her neck as if she was going to hang herself.

I confess I was disappointed. Flek intrigued me and I would have liked to eat with him. While Ruth was bundling up, Magda touched me on the arm and handed me a business card. It had Flek's name and office address and phone number on it. I saw him looking at me warmly; his kind, intelligent eyes seemed to say, "It's up to you." On the back of the card he had written, "Come."

"Joseph, I hope we'll meet again," he said when I went over to him to shake his hand.

The good-byes were hasty. Ruth, in the elevator, was crying before we hit bottom.

I stroked her face, trying to soothe her, but she sniffed distastefully.

"You smell like him," she said.

The next day I went to the library to find the case of Laura. Having surreptitiously written down the name "Robert Lindner" and the title, *The Fifty-Minute Hour,* on the business card Flek had given me, I slipped it into my pocket that morning as I dressed. It is difficult to say why I was so desperate to get my hands on that book, but I experienced, waking up, an exhilarated sense of purpose. I had no guarantee that Flek had correctly identified the reference in Ruth's diary, and he certainly seemed to think very little of its value. Nevertheless, I was sure that if I could only find Laura, then Laura would lead me to Ruth.

Ruth had left the house early, as she generally did, to begin her morning on Dr. Hallo's couch. My classes didn't start until one o'clock, so I would have several undisturbed hours to pursue my research.

I felt Flek's card tingling with almost talismanic power in my pocket as I walked to the library. As I got closer, I kept taking it out and reading it.

I had decided against Butler Library at Columbia, where I'd been an undergraduate, because I still knew teachers and students there and did not feel like exposing my research to the curious eyes of acquaintances. At the Main Branch of the New York Public Library, that grand, impersonal vault, I felt I could conduct my investigation privately.

My heart was racing, my palms sweating as I approached the big white building. The stone lions on either side of the long granite steps looked unusually alert and forbidding, the guardians of secrets. I was both excited and ashamed. Never had I felt so fully a library's illicit appeal. All knowledge has about it a pornographic lure. Hadn't I felt my Russians, for all their exhausted gaze, focused on me as on some mysterious instrument of desire? Hadn't I seen the dullest face suddenly lit by the possibility of understanding, panting after knowledge?

But my intentions, like those of my students, were pure. I was desperate to understand Ruth so I could help her. If I needed a new vocabulary, I would learn one. If I could have stepped inside her slender body, slid her head on like a magic helmet, felt her feelings, thought her thoughts, suffered her appetites, I'd have done it. But all I had were books. I had raided her diary with a daily desire for understanding. Now I was expanding my investigations.

In my haste, I hadn't bothered to check the library hours. Though the great brass outer doors had already been swung open, the revolving door flung me back when I hurled myself against it. I looked up, startled, to see, through the glass, a sullen guard holding up both hands—ten minutes.

It was a chilly morning but I was too eager to begin my search to look for a place where I could get some coffee. I stood at the top of the stairs and watched the early holiday shoppers scurry across Fifth Avenue, the Christmas decorations snaking around streetlamps, a pretzel vendor's smoky cart. But everything I wanted that morning was inside the library. I turned away from Fifth Avenue and peered impatiently through the glass door. This time the guard pretended not to notice me.

As I scanned the facade of the library, I noticed the statue of a woman off to the left and went to take a closer look. She was set into a large scalloped niche, part of a fountain on the left side of the building's grand portico. She was slender and smooth, sitting on a winged horse, naked, but with one marble thigh draped chastely so that the folds fell between her legs. Above her, carved in stone, were the words:

BEAUTY OLD YET EVER NEW
ETERNAL VOICE AND INWARD WORD

On the right side of the portico, balancing Beauty, was a beefy marble man, designed on a grander scale than Beauty but meant to match her. Above his statue were the words:

For a few moments I shuttled back and forth between the two figures. The inscriptions intrigued me. You would have thought the designers of the library knew just what I was there for, as if my research, far from being eccentric and illicit, lay at the heart of the library's function. Beauty and Truth. And Truth beareth away the victory.

Ruth would have found the assignment of Truth to the man and Beauty to the woman sexist and archaic. Perhaps it was. But to me, that morning, the nude stone man, seated on a sphinx, was Doctor Flek. He had the same defiant nobility, the same imperious but benevolent presence. He also had bird shit on his head and a pigeon perched on his shoulder. But for all that there was something impressive, knowing, about his expression that seemed to say, "Sure there's bird shit on me. That's part of the truth. *You* stand out here naked to the elements and see what you get on your head."

Of course, I thought of the goddess on the left as Ruth. Ruth was prettier, but the statue's mix of vulnerability and stubborn strength made her uncannily familiar. The sculptor had not produced a mere ideal. If you looked at the statue long enough, even at the implacable face alone, you could feel the out-of-work turn-of-the-century art student sitting naked in the chilly studio, waiting to be turned to stone. It occurred to me that the artist had been in love with this woman.

Ruth would have found the statue too plump, of course, though Beauty's hairless arms and legs would have impressed her. No trips to Columbus Avenue Hair and Nail for her.

By the time the guard opened the door and let the early arrivals in I was in a highly allegorical mood. A sign standing just inside the entrance, NO FOOD OR DRINK BEYOND THIS POINT (I was reading everything in sight), seemed as portentous as if ABANDON HOPE ALL YE WHO ENTER HERE had been engraved above the door. But I bounded past the sign and the guard and took the marble steps two at a time, straight to the third floor. I arrived, a little out of breath, in the catalogue room that served as antechamber to the vast main reading room. At last I could begin.

I took out Flek's card for the hundredth time and read "Robert Lindner—*The Fifty-Minute Hour*," though by now I knew those words as well as my own name. I found the call number, filled out a request form and handed it to a clerk, who, without comment, sent it, enclosed in a plastic tube, down a pneumatic chute.

I went to await my book's arrival in the main reading room, where a dumbwaiter carries the books up from the bowels of the building. As each book arrived, a number flashed on a large electronic board like the departures and arrivals bulletin at Grand Central. The whole reading room, in fact, looked like a giant train station, the high ceiling, the vast space suddenly filled with people, a rush hour of readers.

I was waiting, I felt, for much more than a book, and half expected Dr. Lindner himself to appear from out of the shadows to unfold the deepest mysteries of the human heart. But though the board was now filled with lit numbers, my number was not among them.

The longer I sat there, the more the mute activity of the library unsettled me. The air seemed to vibrate with a static charge that both exhausted and agitated me. The yellow glow from the high, globed lights hanging from iron chains seemed antique, light from stars that had already died. Unlike the catalogue room, which had recently added computers—a plaque told me they had been paid for by Bill Blass, the fashion designer, more fodder for my allegorical mind—the reading room was frozen in time. Even the antique clock above the pickup desk looked as if it told old time. I had a sudden premonition of disaster. Why was I here instead of with Ruth? What could I possibly learn in this place that I couldn't learn in her arms? Everyone was paired with a book, as if this were a giant ballroom where people came to dance with the dead.

Out! I thought suddenly. Out! But at that moment the number on my receipt flashed on the board and I went to claim my book.

It must have been a first edition, for it was sheathed in plain gray cardboard folded around the book and held in place with two rubber bands. Pandora's book. The slender, clean-shaven librarian who handed it to me stood very straight and looked at me shrewdly through gold-framed glasses. He had a smooth, self-cleaning, catlike look. I wouldn't have been surprised to see him lick the back of his hand and drag it across his face. "Be careful," he said as he handed me the package, "it's falling apart." I took it back to my seat, set it on the table, removed the rubber bands and opened it.

The book was indeed a first edition, printed in 1954 but already crumbling. I flipped through it gingerly. Robert Lindner had also, I saw, written *Rebel Without a Cause*. Had the case of Laura been turned into a film? Glancing through the book, I found snippets of dialogue that read like an overheated movie script from the fifties.

There were often asides, too. For example, "I lit a cigarette and settled back in my chair to listen," as if Lindner had been imitating Hammett or Chandler—a hard-boiled shrink. Lindner, I read, had worked at a number of federal penitentiaries. Was he afraid of being taken for a sissy? I imagined Dr. Lindner in a dark smoky office, a notepad in one hand, a Lucky Strike in the other, a fedora perched on the back of his head.

"The story of Laura" opened like this:

Laura had two faces. The one I saw that morning was hideous, swollen like a balloon at the point of bursting, it was a caricature of a face, the eyes lost in pockets of sallow flesh and shining feverishly with a sick glow, the nose buried between bulging cheeks splattered with blemishes, the chin an oily shadow mimicking human contour, and somewhere in this mass of fat a crazy-angle carmined hole was her mouth.

Her appearance astonished and disgusted me. The revulsion I felt could not be hidden. Observing it she screamed her agonized self-loathing.

"Look at me, you son-of-a-bitch!" she cried. "Look at me and vomit!"

Was this a case history or a fifties psy-fi thriller? The crumbling pages gave off a mulchy, mellow odor, a whiff of rot, as if the girl's wide mouth were indeed close to mine.

I looked up. Through the high arched windows I could see the overlapping ugliness of midtown Manhattan, obliterating what must have been uninterrupted sky when the library was first built. It occurred to me that the city itself was overweight, with tons of concrete and iron and granite piling up greedily around me. Time to go, I thought, but I knew, even as I thought it, that I wouldn't. I had peered through the keyhole and I knew I'd keep looking until I'd seen all there was to see. I turned back to the book.

"Yes—it's me—Laura. Don't you recognize me? Now you see, don't you? Now you see what I've been talking about all these weeks—while you've been sitting back there doing nothing, saying nothing. Not even listening when I've begged and begged you for help. Look at me!"

The face was Laura's, but I heard Ruth's voice. Was I betraying Ruth, picturing her in the form she most feared? My damp fingers left dark spots on the dry, nicked pages. I felt half inclined to shut the book and get out, but I read on.

"Lie down, please," I said, "and tell me about it."

A cracked laugh, short and rasping, came from her hidden mouth. The piglike eyes raised to some unseen auditor above, while clenched fists went up in a gesture of wrath.

"Tell him about it! Tell him about it! What the hell do you think I've been telling you about all this time!"

"Laura," I said more firmly, "stop yelling and lie down"— and I turned away from her toward the chair behind the couch. But before I could move she grabbed my arms and swung me around to face her. I felt her nails bite through my coat and dig into the skin beneath. Her grip was like a vise.

She thrust her face toward mine. Close up, it was a huge, rotting wart. Her breath was foul as she expelled it in a hoarse, passionate whisper.

"No," she said. "I'm not going to lie down. I'm going to stand here in front of you and make you look at me—make you look at me as I have to look at myself. You want me to lie down so you won't have to see me. Well, I won't do it. I'm going to stand here forever!" She shook me. "Well," she said. "Say something! Go on, tell me what you're thinking. I'm loathsome, aren't I? Disgusting. Say it! Say it!" Then suddenly her grasp loosened. Collapsing, she fell to the floor. "O, God," she whimpered, "please help me. Please . . . Please . . ."

From that opening description I formed a hideous image of Laura, big as a grand piano and making a terrible racket, until I read on and saw that she was actually an attractive young woman, not fat at all. "The ascetic regime she imposed on herself between bouts of abnormal eating kept her fashionably thin," Lindner wrote. This only made the portrait scarier, for she wasn't, outwardly, a freak at all. It was just that from time to time, in sudden fits of depression or despair, a terrible hunger opened up in her.

"It's like a hole in my vitals appears," she explained. "Then the emptiness starts to throb. . . ." Even though it wasn't really hunger, Laura would begin to eat, trying, in her own words, "to fill the hole." If she paused in her feeding frenzy for even a moment, the hole got wider, deeper, more terrifying and unappeasable until, twenty-four or sometimes forty-eight hours of nonstop eating later, she fell into a swoon, exhausted. Sometimes in this state she slept for two whole days and nights.

The case history was long, more than sixty pages, but I plowed through it without looking up. Reading about Laura's hunger was like reading about black holes in a physics text—there was something so profoundly strange about it that it seemed almost physically impossible. Could Lindner have made the whole thing up? Black holes had always seemed to me a dream in the mind of some frail, earthbound astronomer fantasizing a dark force gulping down stars and moons and entire galaxies, sucking light and even time out of the universe. But the scariest things are usually true and I had a dread feeling that for all his melodrama, Dr. Lindner was telling the truth about Laura. Is that what Ruth really was?

The case offered very little practical information. Laura's relationship to food was presented more as a bizarre aberration than as a sickness other women might share. When Lindner talked about it, he adopted the tone of *Ripley's Believe It or Not*. I did not find this helpful:

"In the literature of morbidity," he wrote, "occasional reference was made to a disorder called bulimia, or pathological craving for food, and I had of course met with numerous instances of related disorders." Here the doctor made a long digression recalling "one of the most amusing incidents of my career" involving a prisoner at the Atlanta Federal Penitentiary who ate razor blades and whose stomach was found, after emergency surgery, to contain, along with the aforementioned blades, "two spoons, a coil of wire, some bottle caps, a small screwdriver, a few bolts, about five screws, some nails, many bits of colored glass and a couple of twisted metallic objects no one can identify."

I was not at all amused, but I read on, waiting for him to get back to bulimia, but he never mentioned the word again. In fact, he scarcely discussed food at all. Lindner's tale of horror, I now saw, was going to be useless. I would have to go looking myself through "the literature of morbidity" to find what I needed. But still I read on, page after page, in the hope of finding some crumb of useful information.

Laura's story was touching. She had been a poor girl. Her father was an alcoholic. Her mother, crippled by an unnamed illness, was in a wheelchair. One day, after her father came home drunk, her mother screamed at him once too often and he left the house for good. Laura blamed her mother for driving him away. She lived on her own now and worked in an art gallery and I felt that she and Ruth had other things in common besides an interest in art, despite their different backgrounds. Laura, for example, had dark hair and high cheekbones that gave her "an almost Oriental flavor." I suspect—indeed I know for sure—that the doctor, who described in detail how Laura tugged her skirt nervously before a session, found his patient not merely intriguing but attractive.

Then there was the matter of sex. Laura was afraid of it. She seemed to have had a fair amount of it but she'd only had what she called "the real thing" a few times and only "as a last resort."

"I'd do anything to keep them from getting inside me—poking into me," she told the doctor. Ruth again! But Lindner's solution—he solved this in one session by analyzing a dream in which Laura finds herself in a complex contraption, her legs spread for some sort of gynecological exam—wasn't as useful as I'd hoped. Lindner helped Laura realize an unconscious fear that sex would turn her into an invalid like her wheelchair-bound mother. I would like to have learned more about this, but Lindner moved on to other things. He seemed to have forgotten about food too, and I was beginning to lose patience with him.

I looked around for a moment, absorbing the dull anxious atmosphere of the library, the hermetic bustle of scholars, the weary look of extension students—men and women bending over their books as if they were performing manual labor. For all that, there was still the erotic energy that libraries always engender, the darting eyes of bored men and women, the accidental touch of a foot under the table. The throat cleared with no words following.

Sitting at the long wooden table, I was filled again with the old undergraduate sensations, a powerful mix of boredom, longing, excitement and despair. The sounds of the library were disconcerting: the shuffling interim noises of a concert hall during the break between movements. But the orchestra never starts playing. It's all coughing and turning pages, a perpetual pause that never ends. At any moment someone might scream. It might be you. But you don't. No one does.

I turned back to my book. The next thing I knew, Laura had slit her wrists. The information struck me not as if it had happened to a woman I had never met and who, if still alive, would have to be in her seventies. (Lindner himself, I'd learned from the card catalogue, had been dead for thirty-five years.) I read about this as if it had happened to some young person I knew well. Did death lurk behind every illness? Did Laura really wish to die? Did Ruth?

I stood up for a moment, noisily pushing my chair back. Several readers looked at me in irritation. Where was I going to go? I didn't even know precisely where Ruth was at that moment, though I knew she had a class somewhere in the New School. And even if I knew, what then? I sat down again slowly and it was only after I looked down at the blurred book that I realized there were tears in my eyes.

But Laura didn't die. She started to scream as soon as she'd finished cutting herself and a doctor who lived in her building came at once.

Laura had tried to kill herself when Lindner had canceled one of their appointments so that he could attend a conference. He raced back to town and saw her in the hospital, sedated, wrists bandaged. She not only recovered quickly—the cuts were not deep—but the episode seemed to help with her psychic healing. The suicide attempt "furnished us with vast quantities of material for analysis in subsequent months," Lindner wrote, though he didn't say what that material was.

Those months were telescoped into a handful of pages and there were only a few pages left in the whole account when at last he returned to the subject that had interested me about Laura in the first place. "No progress at all had been made against the strange complaint which brought her into treatment: the seizures of uncontrollable hunger, the furious eating, and their dreadful effects."

Until one day when Laura failed to show up for a session. In the course of that day, the doctor received a call in which he heard a groggy, mumbling voice on the line. This happened several times throughout the day and again that night when he was hosting a dinner party. This time he knew it was Laura.

He asked her what she was doing and the single, horrifying word came back: "Eat-ing."

Those were the days of house calls. Lindner rushes over to the apartment, where he finds Laura bloated, dazed, surrounded by empty plates and cartons and boxes of food spread out all over the floor, on every surface, even in the bed. Laura is wearing a sheer nightgown and under the gown, shockingly, the doctor sees a pillow strapped to her belly. It makes her look pregnant.

Lindner calls a nurse, who puts Laura to bed and airs out the apartment. A few days later the riddle is solved. Lindner makes the triumphant discovery that Laura has always wanted to bear her absent father's child. Laura is overjoyed by the discovery. "It was," Lindner concludes, "for this impossible fulfillment that Laura hungered—and now was starved no more. . . ."

Congratulation! Congratulation!

Teaching English seemed more unreal than ever that afternoon. Fragments of the case of Laura kept floating up in my mind, frightening me about Ruth. What had she meant when she wrote in her diary that she was turning into Laura? Where was she at that moment? What was she thinking? What was she doing? What was she eating? Or was she—God forbid—lying in the bedroom, her wrists cut, unable to move? Is *that* what she meant about Laura? I couldn't wait for the day to end—I was desperate to see for myself that she was all right.

Fortunately it was "Job Day," and for the last hour of class there was an assembly devoted to the quest for employment. Blitstein gave a gloomy lecture in Russian and English, a social worker talked about green cards and H-1 visas and a few of the actors who taught at ETNA put on a skit in which they played job-hunting immigrants. They borrowed the great floppy hats and spoke in funny accents, which enraged Blitstein, though the students found it hilarious, especially when David, conducting the interviews, shouted, in Blitstein's voice, "If you don't learn English you'll never get a job. If you never get a job you won't learn English." Halfway through the skit, I slipped out the back door.

Ruth was cooking when I got home. I smelled garlic and ginger out in the hall and was reassured. If she was cooking, she was all right.

Or was she? After all, I was home early. Would I peer in and see her, like the rice demon, devouring dinner by the handful? Would the apartment bear the naked remains of an unspeakable feast? Would Ruth come to the door looking like Laura, her face swollen, her belly puffed out by a pillow?

But Ruth was lovely. She opened the door while I was still fumbling with the key and kissed me warmly.

"You're home early," she said, smiling, until a look of concern suddenly crossed her face. "You didn't have another headache?"

"No," I told her, touched by the way she reached up and stroked my head. "Today was Job Day, when we teach them that America has no economic future. I left early."

"I'm glad you're here," Ruth said, kissing me again before turning away. "There's a surprise for you in the kitchen."

"A surprise?"

"Follow me," she said mysteriously.

Max ambushed us in the hall. It was a measure of Ruth's good mood that she laughed when he flung himself at my untied shoelace. But when I bent to pry him loose and spend a moment scratching his narrow neck and shoulders, Ruth called out impatiently, "Hurry up."

She had covered the kitchen table with a clean white cloth and laid a long-stemmed rose across each of our plates. There were two blue candles, still unlit, standing in slender silver holders—wedding presents to her parents that neither had wanted after the divorce. There were linen napkins rolled and threaded through round wooden holders that Ruth herself had painted with bold orange and blue flowers. There was Billie Holiday singing "God Bless the Child" from the tape player on top of the refrigerator, and there was the warm smell of soup bubbling on the stove.

"Wow!" I said. "Everything looks terrific."

Ruth stirred her soup and looked over at me shyly.

"You like it?"

"It's beautiful."

"You really think so?" she asked, beaming with pleasure.

"Absolutely. Is it . . . a special occasion?"

Ruth was always keeping time, announcing our one-and-a-half-year anniversary, the six-month anniversary of our living together, the three-month anniversary of my employment at

ETNA. Although birthdays made her anxious, they were important to her, and even Max was given a little party on the anniversary of his acquisition. It was hard for me to keep up with Ruth's calendric calculations. I lived in fear of missing some key milestone that called for presents and flowers.

But I hadn't forgotten anything.

"I was just feeling how lucky I am to be with you," she said, going to the sink to rinse vegetables for salad. There were tears in her eyes and though there was a diced onion on the sideboard, I knew the tears were for me.

I was flooded with warm feelings and went over to her, embracing her from behind. She did not turn around to face me but when I started to let go of her she said, "No, keep holding me, please."

So I stood behind her while the water ran and her clean white fingers explored spinach leaves for hidden grit.

"I realize how much I rely on you. Especially after seeing my mother last night . . ."

She grew silent, focusing her energies on the salad. We hadn't talked about the previous evening. Ruth had been too distraught and I'd been drained by the day's headache and the medicine I'd taken when I got home.

I was still behind her at the sink, waiting for her to speak again. Her hair was tied back with a length of the same purple ribbon she used to secure her diary. If only I could untie that velvet cord, I thought, and glimpse the mysteries concealed beneath the beautiful binding of her auburn hair. I kissed her on the head and held her closer, my arms wrapped around her. I felt my heart beating against her back.

"I can't breathe," Ruth whispered.

"Sorry."

I released her, kissing her again, and sat down on a stepladder just behind her.

"It was nice," Ruth said. "I just couldn't breathe."

She didn't say any more and I waited for her to take up the thread of conversation again. Lindner had finally cured Laura when she made a Freudian slip. She'd said "Mike a baby" instead of "make a baby." Her father's name was Mike and it had turned out she'd wanted to bear her father's child—that was the reason for the pillow, the frenzied feeding. Should Ruth make a similar slip I wanted to be there to catch it.

But Ruth said nothing. Lined up along the counter were canisters with HELLO MY NAME IS . . . labels stuck to them. Ruth had printed in neat letters each can's contents, introducing a cheerful anthropomorphic element into our kitchen. HELLO MY NAME IS: Flour. HELLO MY NAME IS: Sugar. HELLO MY NAME IS: Rice. HELLO MY NAME IS: Oatmeal. A conference of comestibles.

"Was there more you wanted to say about last night?" I asked finally.

She stirred her soup again and went back to the sink. "You seemed to hit it off with Ernest," she said, looking not at me but deep into the sink, watching her own hands at work.

"Dr. Flek?" I said cautiously. "Yes, I liked him."

"You shouldn't call him 'doctor.' He's given that up. And it was just a PhD to begin with."

I didn't say anything.

"Of course he doesn't act like he's given it up. He's always watching. He's always observing. He's always passing judgment."

"What do you mean, 'passing judgment'?"

"That story he told, for one thing."

"About the man who has an affair with his wife?"

"No," said Ruth. "The other one. The one he read to Miranda."

"The Japanese story. What was it called?"

" 'The Rice Demon,' " Ruth said.

"Right. Miranda seemed to really enjoy it."

"It wasn't meant for Miranda."

"No?" I said. "She asked him to read it."

"She only chose the book. *He* chose the story. And he chose it for me."

I didn't say anything. Billie Holiday was now singing "All of Me"—"Take my lips, I'll never use them. . . ." What would Dr. Lindner have made of that?

"Your mother thought it was about her," I said.

"My mother thinks everything is about her," said Ruth acidly. " 'That's me and Will! That's me and Will.' " She mimicked her mother's hoarse, melodic voice. "Please! He meant it for me."

"You really think so?"

Ruth turned and looked at me sharply. "Of course he did. I'm sure my mother told him all about me. Didn't you see the way he looked at me when he was finished? That judging look!"

Her voice rose, drowning out Billie Holiday.

"Ruth, calm down. I really think you're overreacting."

I stood up and went over to her but she shrank under my touch.

"Are you afraid I'll turn into a demon?"

"Don't talk nonsense," I said, secretly abashed. "I'm sure he meant it for Miranda. It's a bedtime story."

"That's a bedtime story? A woman who never eats anything and then all of a sudden eats everything? That's what you read to a little girl?"

"That's what fairy tales are. You know that. It's a cautionary tale—about misers," I said. "It's not a parable about . . ."

"About what?" said Ruth.

I was walking on eggs and I knew it.

"About food."

"It's called 'The *Rice* Demon,' Joseph. And don't you think anorexics are misers?"

"But you're not anorexic."

"No," said Ruth, hastily. "I'm not."

"What are you?" I asked.

"What does that mean?"

"Is there anything you want to tell me about, Ruth?"

"No," she said, without looking up. She was now shredding the spinach into a bowl. When she was done she mixed in the chopped red onion and began peeling an orange to add to the onion and spinach, a combination I did not care for but that Ruth liked.

I had hoped, in a casual way, to bring up the story of Laura, or at least refer in some way to its contents. I wasn't sure if our conversation was the way in to the subject or a signal to hold off. I rubbed Ruth's back and she allowed me to, relaxing. I could feel her heart beating through the thin wool of her turtleneck. She grew calmer under my touch.

"I'm sorry, Joseph," she said, "I know it's not your fault. I wanted this to be a special dinner."

"Ruth," I asked, "do you ever think of having children?"

I felt her stiffen under my hand. The question had blurted itself out and surprised me as much, I assumed, as it surprised Ruth. At least I hadn't said, "Ruth, do you strap a pillow to your belly when I'm not home, and eat everything in the house?" At least I hadn't said, "Ruth, do you want to have your father's baby?" I began to stammer an apology, but it was Ruth who apologized. She turned around and faced me with tender eyes.

"Oh, Joseph," she said. "I'm sorry, I'm just not ready to think about children now."

I felt myself blushing.

"I'd want to have them with you, though. I think you'd make a wonderful father."

This wasn't quite the conversation I'd intended. But it seemed to cheer her up so perhaps, in some way, I was on the right track. Maybe Lindner wasn't a crank after all. Ruth had taken my question as a kind of offer. Perhaps I should propose. What better way to hold on to Ruth than in marriage?

"Do you really think I'd make a good father?" I asked.

"Wonderful," she said. She looked at me with great affection. She wiped her hands on her apron and put her cool fingers against my cheeks.

"Well, you'd be a wonderful mother."

"Me?" She asked doubtfully. "I don't think so."

"I do."

Ruth smiled. And then, pulling away, she said, "The soup's ready. It's that butternut-squash soup I made that time and you liked it so much. The one from the *Times*."

I couldn't recall precisely what soup this was—Ruth was always clipping recipes out of the newspaper and sticking them to the refrigerator like children's drawings—but I told her I remembered it well and she seemed pleased.

The soup was delicious, full of warm spongy chunks of squash, tiny fragments of garlic and a few unexpected fibers of ginger. Ruth didn't talk much during dinner, but she seemed happier than she had in a long time. She ate an entire bowlful of soup, a small plate of salad and even had a slice of bread. I couldn't help but feel a little surge of protective power. Perhaps my words could heal her after all.

After dinner, though, she grew distant. She remained at her place, playing with the rose that had lain on the table beside her while she ate. She snapped off the thorns absentmindedly and lined them up on the rim of her plate, like tiny sharks' teeth. I offered to wash the dishes, but Ruth insisted, spending a long time at the sink in a sort of sudsy trance.

I graded my students' homework at the kitchen table, and the homey atmosphere made me more tolerant of their childish errors. I even found the odd stains, which often streaked the pages and blotted out whole words, touching. They had probably done their homework in the kitchen, the warm center of an immigrant home, while dinner was cooking or tea was being served. It gave me pleasure to know that I was grading their papers in the same spirit.

When Ruth finished the dishes we moved into the living room. Ruth, to my delight, asked if she could work on her sketch of me for a portrait she'd been planning to paint for months. It was always a sign of affection when she took out her large, stiff-backed pad and resumed work on it.

Ruth was very protective of the sketches she made. She wouldn't open her pad until I had taken up my position across the room and she refused to show me how the sketch was progressing.

"When it's done," she would say, when I begged her for a peek. "Not before."

Strangely, I respected this request. Though I knew where she kept the big pad—in her bottom drawer, under her sweaters—I never violated that trust. As often as I broke into her diary, I prided myself on respecting the privacy of the bottom drawer.

Although I knew the pose, I was pleased that before we started Ruth had come over and positioned my head, like a tender barber, pointing my gaze down and to the left. I think she also wanted to get a fix on my face with her hands.

She was very authoritative while she worked. With the big pad resting on her lap, she allowed herself to look at me with open, penetrating eyes. There was none of the shielded shyness of her usual glance. It was I who became furtive, stealing peeks at her as she worked. She seemed to erase more than she drew, but I was happy to think of myself taking shape under her hands. Her face wore an expression of beautiful absorption and it pleased me to know that I was the focus of her attention.

Max had settled down peacefully in the corner, his head on his paws, as if he too felt himself under loving, watchful eyes. My earlier fears floated away as I sat before her. I felt, posing for Ruth, as if no harm could come to either of us. We were bound together in a firm, if distant, embrace.

We went to bed early. When I woke up in the middle of the night, Ruth wasn't beside me. The light was on in the kitchen, where I found her drinking a cup of tea.

"I couldn't sleep," was all she said when I asked her what was wrong. She sipped the dark brew without saying more.

"I didn't hear the kettle," I said.

"I made it in the microwave. I didn't want to wake you."

"Why not, Ruth? I can help."

"There's nothing to help with," she said. "Go to sleep."

I bent and kissed her, tasting the night on her soft, tea-warmed lips.

"Were you serious about having children?" she asked, before I turned away.

"Someday," I said.

"We should name the girl Evelyn." Ruth spoke so softly I wasn't sure she'd actually said it.

"What did you say?"

I waited for her to repeat it but she only whispered, "Go to sleep, Joseph," as if I was already falling asleep. And indeed I was. Exhaustion from the previous day's headache, the medicine I was still taking, the morning in the library, the fear and stress about the meaning of Laura's story had all worn me down. I looked at Ruth. She was neither smiling nor frowning, but her lips did not seem neutral. I kissed them again, as if that would tell me the meaning of her expression, but I learned nothing more.

"Go to sleep," she whispered, and I obeyed.

Lying in bed, I trained my ears for telltale sounds, vowing to stay up until Ruth returned. Before I knew it, though, I was asleep. I dreamed that I was wandering through the main reading room of the Public Library, following a trail of rose petals, looking for Laura who was also Ruth who was also someone whose name I did not know. I didn't wake up until Max stepped on my stomach at eight the next morning.

Ruth was already gone.

Once again I found myself consulting Flek's business card, not for the information I'd scrawled on the back but for Flek's phone number, printed on the front. I fed Max, drank a quick cup of coffee and dialed.

Flek answered on the first ring. As soon as I heard his blunt, friendly voice I felt mysteriously reassured.

"Joseph!" he said, not sounding at all surprised. "I thought you might call."

"What made you think so?" I asked.

"You seemed, the other night, like a man with a lot on his mind. If we hadn't been interrupted, I felt we might have had a longer conversation."

"I read the case of Laura," I said abruptly.

He was silent a moment and I could hear Humperdinck's *Hänsel und Gretel* in the background. I'd always liked the opera, but suddenly wondered how Ruth would have reacted to Flek's selection. Would the heartless stepmother, the edible house, the lost children and the cannibal witch appear as painfully symbolic to her as "The Rice Demon" had? More and more I found myself trying to think as Ruth might.

"And was it helpful?" Flek asked finally.

"I'm more confused than ever."

"Hardly your fault," said Flek. "Plenty of people would find the idea of a young woman trying to have her father's baby by eating herself into a stupor confusing."

"It does sound absurd when you put it that way."

"I don't mean to make light of your concerns, Joseph," Flek said. "Anytime you'd like to come by I'd be happy to talk. I can probably suggest a few things more . . . relevant."

"Are you free this morning?"

Flek laughed in his gruff, genial way. "Sure," he said. "Come over now."

—

Flek had a small office at the New School. He worked on his books there, and held office hours for the few classes he taught. It was a spartan room. Except for a large, simple desk, a few chairs, a single crammed bookcase and a CD player—which was still playing *Hänsel und Gretel* when I got there—the room was bare.

Flek was seated behind the desk in a padded, high-backed swivel chair. He was wearing a bulky gray fisherman's sweater, the sleeves pulled halfway up his bare, powerful forearms. They were the kind of forearms thick enough to sport tattoos of mermaids and anchors without embarrassment, though the tan expanse of his skin was bare except for a fine tangle of graying hair. His legs were hidden behind the wood-backed desk.

"I'm sorry to bother you," I said, after I'd shaken his hand and seated myself in the chair across from him.

"Stop apologizing, Joseph. I gave you my card, after all. I wanted you to come. How is Ruth?"

"Oh, I don't know. That's the problem. I don't know. I thought Laura might give me some kind of clue . . ."

"You seem to have put an awful lot of faith in an out-of-date case history. How did you say you heard about it in the first place?"

"I didn't say."

"It was Ruth who told you about the case of Laura, wasn't it?"

"She didn't exactly *tell* me."

Flek shifted in his chair, pushing down on the desk as he settled himself more comfortably. He did not take his eyes off me as he did this and I felt as if I was the one squirming in my seat. He seemed, for all his movement, steady, level, at ease. Why not tell him everything? But he saved me the trouble.

"Do you read her diary every day?" he asked.

I felt myself blush.

"No, I don't," I told him. This was not strictly a lie, for I had been so eager to get myself to Flek's office that I had, for the first time in a long while, forgotten to see if she'd written anything new that day.

"But you do read it?"

"Sometimes, yes. Because she doesn't tell me everything and there are some secrets it's important to know. For her sake."

Flek sighed. "I see."

"She wrote that she's turning into Laura!"

"Are you even sure which Laura she meant? Maybe she has a friend or an acquaintance by that name. I wish you'd told me more before I opened my mouth. That's my own fault. Oral impregnation was a big theory in the fifties, when it came to women and food. I can't see how Lindner's story could be helpful to you now. It hardly represents the latest thinking."

"What does?" I asked.

"So you can run back to the library and look it up?"

"I'm worried about her. Even the story you read Miranda upset her. She thought it was about her."

"It *was* about her," said Flek. "It was also about you. And about Carol. And about me. It was even about my daughter, Miranda. She asks for that story all the time."

"But Ruth felt the part about . . . food . . . was particularly about her. You've seen her. You saw her when she was sixteen. And she thinks she's overweight!"

"We are all overweight," Flek said with a sigh, tapping his broad forehead with a thick finger. "Right here. We are all three pounds overweight."

"What does that mean?"

"It means that the things that makes us human often make us ill. Call it a Darwinian contradiction. We come down from the trees and walk upright and what do we get for it? Foot pain! Bad backs! We cease living sexual lives regulated by mating seasons, by hormonal tides or the rotation of the earth, and what happens? Marital misery. Divorce. Rape. As a species, we're not very well evolved. Our brains, the crown jewel of our collection, may be the most flawed thing about us. But tell me more about Ruth. I know these generalities aren't what you came here for. Tell me more."

Flek was a good talker but he was an even better listener. The occasional adjustments he made to keep himself positioned comfortably in his chair seemed like efforts to incline his body more fully to my words. He seemed to listen with his whole self. His hands were spread before him on the desk, his broad face open, accepting, genial, unjudging.

And so I told him.

I told him about the bathroom scale she lived by. I told him about Ruth's rituals in the kitchen. I told him about the restaurants we walked out of before even ordering, not because we'd quarreled but because Ruth had panicked or the mood had set her off, or she'd overheard a voice, or imagined one, whispering that she was fat. Or the menu was too long or too short. The portions too big or too small. And I told him about the restaurants we seemed unable to leave, as if some spell had been cast on our table. How we sat for hours in silence while Ruth sipped her bottomless cup of coffee and while the waiters vacuumed the floor and turned the chairs upside-down around us. I told him there were days when I saw Ruth eat nothing and there were days when I suspected she ate a great deal, in secret—days when Ruth might indeed have a good deal in common with Laura.

I finished talking and Flek was silent for a long time. He seemed to be considering something carefully, looking me over with his large, knowing eyes. I wondered if his monumental head held a brain heavier than the three pounds he'd alluded to. His broad forehead was richly tanned and slightly speckled, like a scrubbed potato—especially one scrubbed by Ruth, who always complained that when I washed vegetables I left some dirt on them. Ruth washed potatoes as if she were trying to erase them.

"Joseph," Flek said slowly, "I'm beginning to wonder if there isn't something you haven't mentioned."

"About Ruth?"

"About yourself."

"Like what?"

"I don't know. Perhaps, if we get to know each other better, it will emerge."

"Why can't you believe that I just want to help her?"

"I can believe that. I do. It's not that I doubt the sincerity of your feelings for Ruth. It's just that the wish to know someone, to really know all about someone, to master as much information as you have, to know her symptoms and thoughts and dreams, to know all that and to still want to know more can be dangerous. And knowing it in the name of love doesn't change that."

"Are you saying I don't love Ruth?"

"I'm sure you love Ruth," Flek said. "But I want you to understand how seductive illness can be. Our own as well as other people's. We tell ourselves it isn't. That we want health. We crave life. But put a thermometer in the mouths of most people and they will wish, secretly, for the mercury to rise. We live in a society that spends endless energy and money on health clubs, but it is illness that steals our hearts. Everyone wants to be rescued from the world of the ordinary. Everyone craves the care and comfort a sick child receives, the loving touch, the warm embrace. And if they can't get it, they settle for giving it."

"I don't understand," I said. "We're talking about something very specific. We're talking about Ruth and food."

"Are we?" said Flek.

"You mean Ruth's obsession with food isn't really about food, don't you? Isn't there supposed to be something behind it—a need for love or control or something like that?"

"Maybe," said Flek. "Maybe not. Nobody really knows. Not everything is a substitute for something else, despite what my former colleagues might believe. Why discount the material aspects of our lives? More wars have been fought over food than over love. Our civilization exists because we found a way to make our food reliable. All we are, all we make, all we do, arose because we found a way to make food our servant instead of the other way around. Ten thousand years ago we stopped being hunter-gatherers and learned to domesticate plants and animals. We tamed the earth and made it grow food for us instead of foraging for what we needed. These early cities grew, and with them art, culture, literature, history. We fought over land and the resources the land possessed."

He seemed to sit up straighter in his chair as he warmed to his subject. He began talking with the muscular, mesmerizing energy I'd experienced in his apartment. He may have been bound to a chair, but while he was talking he seemed to fly.

"The danger," Flek was saying, "is in our belief that we are perfected beings. That everything that plagues us is psychological and that once we resolve it we will be free. That we have conquered nature and can now sit back, resting on a bed of lettuce. But our bodies won't let us forget where we come from. The old foragers in us, those ancestors who never had enough, haunt us. We have their genes, the urges that made it possible for us to survive but that have now become inconvenient in a civilized world. We are a flawed species, and all our technologies, all our ingenuity, can't defend us against the old biological imperatives."

I thought what Flek was telling me was interesting, but in an abstract way that didn't seem to take the urgency of the situation into account.

"You said you could give me more relevant reading," I said impatiently.

Flek shook his head sadly.

"I'm trying to give you a larger lesson, Joseph. One it took me a long time to learn."

I looked at him, waiting for more. "Tell me where to start. If *The Fifty-Minute Hour* is the wrong place, tell me where to begin."

"Why not at the beginning," said Flek. "In the Garden of Eden. 'The day that thou eatest the fruit thereof thou shalt surely die.' Food has been causing trouble ever since."

"Isn't there anything more contemporary?" I asked.

Flek gave a short, gruff laugh. "If I don't tell you what to read, you're just going to start grabbing books off the shelf, aren't you?"

"Probably," I said, though it was hard to do that at the Forty-second Street library.

I was pleased when Flek, however reluctantly, took a piece of paper from his desk and a pen from his top drawer and began writing.

The opera was just ending. The witch was about to be baked into her giant cookie and the little boys and girls who had been cookies were about to turn back into children. How had my life become so symbolic? Flek had careful, deliberate handwriting, and I watched him write, feeling a certain pathos in the way his big hand gripped the slender pen.

"I don't recommend it, but here," he said, looking up at last and sliding the paper across the desk. "These are a few books, past and present, that might help you. Not all of them are books of science and none of them holds the key. You could spend the rest of your life reading and never come to the end. You have to remember that."

I took the paper and stuffed it into my knapsack.

"Thank you," I said.

"Don't go thinking there's something magical about these books. They're just books."

"I understand," I said, but already I was wondering if I'd have time to get to the library before class.

"You teach immigrants," Flek said. "Perhaps you should think of Ruth as another immigrant. The world expects her to speak the artificial language of modern life, but the language of the body is her secret tongue. The language of food. The primitive language that truly shapes us and that we can never escape. That is the language you will have to learn if you are going to understand her. We're all immigrants from the tree-tops, after all. Learn the language of the body. The language of blood and bone and appetite. The body is our one great book. Unfortunately it is written in a language we no longer understand. All other books, even our most cherished, are merely efforts to understand our one great book, which holds the secret of ourselves. Our most brilliant writers haven't come any closer to the body than those chalk outlines policemen make on the ground after a murder. The body is our true Bible. All other books are commentary. You've been studying Ruth, it's clear, but you have a lot to learn and you can't do it by tracing her life endlessly in the air. You can't do it by going to the library."

"I should let you get back to work," I said.

"Do you want to read something really helpful?" Flek asked suddenly. "Before you go?"

"Absolutely," I told him.

"Go to my bookshelf."

I got up and stood in front of his bookshelf, which I looked at closely for the first time. The books did not appear to be in any particular order. The complete works of Freud, in German, filled the bottom shelves but the rest was a hodgepodge. The uniform Yale Shakespeare, bound in blue, was bracketed by books of natural history and anthropology and the collected letters of Charles Darwin. The CD speakers and various CDs—opera and jazz, mostly—were wedged in beside three silver volumes of *Remembrance of Things Past*. A book about drug addiction stood beside De Quincy's *Confessions of an English Opium Eater*. A battered copy of *Moby-Dick* leaned against *Gray's Anatomy*. There were medical textbooks interrupted by volumes of the uniform Oxford Dickens. There was more than one edition of the Bible.

"There's a book on the third shelf up from the bottom, a few in from the right-hand side. A brown book."

"I can't find it," I said, scanning the packed shelf.

"Next to *Paradise Lost*. A little book."

I found a small brown volume with the gilt letters half rubbed off the spine. I pried it out of the shelf to check the title page.

"Sorry," I told him. "I must be on the wrong shelf."

"Why?"

"It's the letters of Keats."

"That's it," said Flek. "Give it to me."

It was a small, neat hardcover and Flek handled it reverentially. In his large hands the open book looked tiny.

"I forgot my glasses," he muttered, flipping pages. "Hard to read a damn thing. Hold on. Here!"

He looked out over the little book like a man with a full house whose bluff has just been called. He cleared his throat and began to read.

"Several things dovetailed in my mind," he read, "and at once it struck me, what quality went to form a man of achievement, especially in literature and which Shakespeare possessed so enormously—I mean negative capability, that is when man is capable of being in uncertainties, mysteries, doubts, without any irritable reaching after fact and reason . . ."

There was a knock on the door and Flek bellowed, in his suddenly giant voice, "One minute." Then to me, more softly, he said, laying the book facedown before him, "Do you hear that, Joseph? Negative capability. The ability to do nothing. To make peace with uncertainties, mysteries, doubts. Yours about Ruth, for example. That is something to strive for. That was written by a sick man who knew, despite his sickness, that life is not about finding a cure. And this is true for any man of achievement. I'd say simply for any man. Something to think about when you're in the library." He picked up his watch, which lay in front of him on the desk, and said, "I've got office hours. My students are starting to arrive. But please, let's keep in touch. Stop by again. Come and talk to me about what you read."

"I will," I said.

"And call me whenever you feel like it."

I shook his hand warmly and thanked him again.

"People are who they are, Joseph," he said as my hand was on the doorknob. "Not what we wish them to become. Remember that. And at some level we are all unknowable—even to ourselves."

There was a young woman leaning against the wall outside Flek's office. She was about Ruth's age and build but thinner. She didn't look like Ruth, but there was something strangely familiar about her. I felt, as I looked at her for the few seconds it took her to gather up her books, that I knew her. I smiled as I passed but she avoided my gaze, or perhaps she didn't notice me at all.

Her brown hair was in braids that began high on her head, a fashion Ruth also had considered, though I had dissuaded her from it since it made her look twelve. I turned around and saw her disappear inside Flek's office. The door shut behind her. Had I known her in college? Was she a friend of Ruth's? For a fleeting moment I had the urge to double back, to press my ear against Flek's door.

I stood still and listened. I felt I could hear the low notes of Flek's voice and then a higher, softer sound. It had a kind of strangled, indistinct quality. The woman might have been crying—or laughing, for that matter. More likely she was merely talking. But who was she?

Eager though I was to get to the library, I remained frozen. The muffled, indistinct music filtered through the door and reached me across the still air of the quiet hall. I was desperate to hear even a single sentence, though I told myself there was nothing to learn from the conversation, even if I had been able to hear it. Still, I strained, unsuccessfully, to catch a few words—but the words were simply sounds, lapping unintelligibly at the door.

For Ruth, cleaning was an aerobic activity. She dressed for it as for a sport, slipping into gleaming black workout pants and a sweatshirt, tying back her hair and putting on music with a strong beat.

I knew even out in the hall, where I heard James Brown singing, "Get up off of that thing, and shake it, you'll feel better," that Ruth was either cleaning or exercising. I found her in the living room, sweeping. She did not hear me come in and I stood for a moment, watching her as she worked in time to the music. She pushed a chair out of the way with her foot, twirled to bat Max away from the dust pile as if he were a croquet ball, and then squatted to shoot the long wooden arm of the broom under the couch.

I touched her on the shoulder and she jumped up, screaming inaudibly, the music pounding. When she realized it was me she smiled sheepishly, panting. She kissed me, took a sip of water from the Evian bottle she'd placed on the bookshelf, blotted her chin neatly with her sleeve and went back to work.

It had been a week since I'd visited Flek. I had been to the library four times, and as I watched Ruth from my place on the couch, under a reproduction of Klimt's *The Kiss* that Ruth had owned since college but had recently reframed, I fished out from my knapsack the notebook I'd begun keeping of my findings. It was a speckled black-and-white notebook like those I'd used in elementary school, with wide lines to allow for horrible handwriting (mine had hardly evolved since I was ten). It was the same kind of notebook in which I kept track of my

ETNA students, and I'd chosen it so that Ruth wouldn't grow suspicious when she saw it. Ruth wasn't the sort of person who would go through my things as I went through hers, though to be safe I kept it in my knapsack.

I placed a bundle of homework on my lap alongside the open notebook but Ruth seemed entirely absorbed in her cleaning. She had momentarily laid aside her broom to clean a streak on the window she'd missed earlier. It was dark enough outside for me to see her reflected features, focused intently as she shot the glass with Windex. Then she was sweeping again. I lifted my feet obligingly as she stooped to clean under the couch before migrating to the far side of the room. There, where the absence of furniture allowed her to work with uninterrupted strokes, she seemed to fall into a kind of rhythmic trance, offering herself unself-consciously to my sight, almost as if she were posing. I glanced up discreetly, eager to match my library findings against her physical form. From time to time she looked over at me and smiled. I smiled back. The clean, dark windows mirrored the room's glow.

On the first page of my notebook I had copied the section Flek had read to me from Keats's letters about "negative capability"—the ability to be in mysteries, doubts and uncertainties without reaching after fact and reason. I wasn't sure how much faith I had in those words, but I valued them because Flek did, and for the more practical reason that anyone peeking into my notebook and finding that quote probably wouldn't look much farther. I'd added Keats's letters to my pile at the library for much the same reason, placing it over the more nakedly physiological texts.

I quickly turned the page, where I'd copied the "Eating Disorders" entry from the *Diagnostic and Statistical Manual* of the American Psychiatric Association. It was dry and technical but it had been on Flek's list and I'd written out whole chunks of the entry word for word. I reread it as Ruth swept, glancing up only to watch her crawl, dustpan in hand, under the dining-room table. Her Lycra workout pants shone as she stretched, catlike, under the table. Her legs and neat behind were sleek beneath the synthetic material. I admired the compact curves, the taut lines of her strong, slender thighs. Too slender? I didn't think so but I had begun to wonder. I very much wanted to know how much she weighed.

### DIAGNOSTIC CRITERIA FOR 307.1 ANOREXIA NERVOSA

A. Refusal to maintain body weight at or above a minimally normal weight for age and height (e.g., weight loss leading to maintenance of body weight less than 85 percent of that expected; or failure to make expected weight gain during period of growth, leading to body weight less than 85 percent of that expected).

B. Intense fear of gaining weight or becoming fat, even though underweight.

C. Disturbance in the way in which one's body weight or shape is experienced, undue influence of body weight or shape on self-evaluation, or denial of the seriousness of the current low body weight.

D. In postmenarcheal females, amenorrhea, i.e., the absence of at least three consecutive menstrual cycles. (A woman is considered to have amenorrhea if her periods occur only following hormone, e.g., estrogen, administration.)

Except for B, "intense fear of gaining weight," and C, "undue influence of body weight or shape on self-evaluation," I found these elements too harsh for Ruth's present condition, however much they might have described her in high school. She had regular periods and was not, I thought, underweight, though hovering perhaps on the border. According to the DSM there were two main types of anorexics, those who simply reduced their intake of food to almost nothing—these were called "restricting types"—and the "binge-eating/purging types" who not only cut back on food but used laxatives and vomiting to lower body weight.

I was interested in "binge-eating/purging types" but I had doubts, particularly since Ruth did not seem unnaturally thin. The second entry in my notebook, also from the *DSM*, seemed a better description of her.

A. Recurrent episodes of binge eating. An episode of binge eating is characterized by both of the following:

1) eating, in a discrete period of time (e.g. within any 2-hour period), an amount of food that is definitely larger than most people would eat during a similar period of time and under similar circumstances

2) a sense of lack of control over eating during the episode (e.g., a feeling that one cannot stop eating or control what or how much one is eating)

B. Recurrent inappropriate compensatory behavior in order to prevent weight gain, such as self-induced vomiting; misuse of laxatives, diuretics, enemas, or other medications; fasting; or excessive exercise.

C. The binge eating and inappropriate compensatory behaviors both occur, on average, at least twice a week for 3 months.

D. Self-evaluation is unduly influenced by body shape and weight.

E. The disturbance does not occur exclusively during episodes of Anorexia Nervosa.

Then two specific types were listed, further complicating things.

Purging Type: during the current episode of Bulimia Nervosa, the person has regularly engaged in self-induced vomiting or the misuse of laxatives, diuretics, or enemas.

Nonpurging Type: during the current episode of Bulimia Nervosa, the person has used other inappropriate compensatory behaviors, such as fasting or excessive exercise, but has not regularly engaged in self-induced vomiting or the misuse of laxatives, diuretics, or enemas.

Whether or not I really had tasted the truth on Ruth's lips the night I kissed her when her mother was in the apartment, I still had reason to suspect Ruth of much of this behavior. Certainly excessive exercise seemed possible. She jumped rope late at night when she couldn't sleep and even the present cleaning fit—Ruth had now sheathed the bristles of the broom in an old T-shirt of mine and was standing on a stepladder tilting at cobwebs—seemed excessively energetic.

As Ruth pursued the cobwebs from one wall to the next, I read on in my notes. Most confusing of all was the third entry from the *Diagnostic and Statistical Manual*, category 307.50: Eating Disorder Not Otherwise Specified.

> The Eating Disorder Not Otherwise Specified category is for disorders of eating that do not meet the criteria for any specific Eating Disorder. Examples include:
>
> 1. For females, all of the criteria for Anorexia Nervosa are met except that the individual has regular menses.
> 2. All of the criteria for Anorexia Nervosa are met except that, despite significant weight loss, the individual's current weight is in the normal range.
> 3. All of the criteria for Bulimia Nervosa are met except that the binge eating and inappropriate compensatory mechanisms occur at a frequency of less than twice a week or for a duration of less than 3 months.
> 4. The regular use of inappropriate compensatory behavior by an individual of normal body weight after eating small amounts of food (e.g., self-induced vomiting after the consumption of two cookies).
> 5. Repeatedly chewing and spitting out, but not swallowing, large amounts of food.
> 6. Binge-eating disorder: recurrent episodes of binge eating in the absence of the regular use of inappropriate compensatory behaviors characteristic of Bulimia Nervosa . . .

Thus my attempts to exempt Ruth from the previous lists now had become irrelevant. One could, according to section 307.50, be sick almost without visible symptoms. According to paragraph 2, one could even be anorexic without being thin. I had already learned, from the "nonpurging type" exception to section 307.51, that one could have bulimia without throwing up. According to number 3 of 307.50, one might have only rare outbreaks of unnatural behavior and still be ill. According to number 4, a woman could consider two cookies a binge and behave as if she'd eaten as much as Laura on a bad day. You could binge without purging and purge without binging. How on earth could I possibly track Ruth's behavior, given the infinite varieties indicated by the *DSM*?

By examining her teeth, for one thing. I had copied out a few telling sentences:

> Recurrent vomiting eventually leads to a significant and permanent loss of dental enamel, especially from lingual surfaces of the front teeth. These teeth may become chipped and appear ragged and "moth-eaten." There may also be an increased frequency of dental cavities. In some individuals, the salivary glands, particularly the parotid glands, may become notably enlarged.

I had no idea what the parotid glands looked like, but I knew as much about teeth as most people. I used to look inside my sister's mouth with the dentist's mirror my father brought home for us to play with when we were young. It had always been mysterious and thrilling to peek inside Evelyn's mouth at her pink gums and small white teeth. Evelyn had always endured this patiently, sitting with her mouth open while I counted her teeth and pretended to fill her cavities. If only I could get Ruth to do the same.

The room was suddenly very quiet. The CD had ended and I looked up to see Ruth, framed in the kitchen door, leaning on her broom, watching me.

"Mr. Blitstein doesn't pay you enough," she said. "I'll bet you're the only teacher who prepares so much."

"How long have you been spying on me?"

"I haven't been spying," said Ruth, offended. "I've been admiring you."

I closed my notebook.

"I've been admiring you, too."

"You have?"

"Yes," I said. "With your hair pulled back and those metallic pants, you look like the statue of Joan of Arc on Ninety-third Street."

"Really?"

Ruth, I knew, loved that statue. When we took walks together down Riverside Drive she often made us pause at the equestrian statue—one of the few in the entire city, as Ruth often told me, designed by a woman.

"Yes," I said. "If you hold that broom up you'd have it exactly."

"Like this?"

To my surprise, Ruth gripped the broom halfway up from the bristles and raised it high, skimming the surface of our twelve-foot ceiling. She put one hand on her waist and spread her legs as if she were sitting on a horse. Her face assumed a remote, inspired expression, her body the fearless pose of Joan as she brandished her sword over the Hudson toward Jersey.

Ruth's playful display stirred me. She really was a soldier, tougher, probably, than I knew. I stood up, put my arms around her slender waist and kissed her. She let the broom fall with a crack.

"Oh, Joseph," she said, giggling strangely, "I'm not really a saint."

"Good."

She smiled up into my eyes but I was looking down at her mouth. The warning from the *DSM* flashed into my head. There was nothing "moth-eaten" about Ruth's teeth, that much I could see. But would I be able to detect decay if I looked inside?

"Have you been to the dentist recently?" I asked.

Her smile vanished at once.

"Why? Is there something wrong with my teeth?"

"I thought I saw something."

A look of anxiety and discomfort came over her.

"What does that mean? What did you see?"

"I don't know. A chipped tooth, maybe."

"Really?"

"Let me see."

"Which tooth?"

"I need to see again. Say *cheese*."

Ruth didn't say *cheese* but she forced an unhappy smile.

"It must have been a back tooth," I said. "Can you open?"

Reluctantly, Ruth opened her mouth. Her gums looked pink and healthy. She had good, even teeth, though faintly stained from coffee. I gazed deep into the moist back of her mouth, where her tongue widened beneath the pink teardrop of the uvula and blended into the dark channel of the throat.

"Wait a minute," I said. "I think I see something." Quickly I placed a finger into her mouth, pressing my nail into her molar to see if it was soft.

Ruth pulled her head back and snapped her mouth shut. I barely withdrew my finger in time.

"What the hell are you doing?"

"I was feeling your molar. Sorry."

"*Feeling* my molar? Joseph, what's wrong with you?"

"Well, my father's a dentist. I know about these things. Wisdom teeth can irritate the gums and I thought I saw some inflammation. Did it hurt?"

"My teeth are fine, Joseph."

I was inclined to agree with her, though I wouldn't have minded going back in there to press on the other side. But it was too late for that. She took up her broom and went back to work, sweeping with concentrated energy, covering ground she had already covered. She seemed angry, snapping the bristles toward her as if striking a giant match against the floor.

I sat back down and flipped forward in my notebook to some notes I'd made on a book, *Starving in a Sea of Objects* by a John A. Sours, M.D. I liked the name of his book and, even more, I liked his own name, which captured the bitter taste of an eating illness and made me feel a sort of confidence in his abilities. A Dr. Sweets would have been hard to take seriously, but Sours inspired trust.

According to Dr. Sours, rich girls suffered from eating disorders more than poor girls, smart girls more than dumb ones. I couldn't help feeling a flush of pride as I read that "high intelligence has always been linked with anorexia nervosa." I wondered if Ruth knew the statistic. Sours cited a 1979 study that for anorexic girls aged 11 to 14, 90 percent had IQs above 120. The older you were when you got it, the more this percentage decreased. Ruth had first gotten sick at fourteen and was, in that sense, at the top of her class—something that had always mattered to her.

She would not have cared for the next entry I made, in which Sours noted that the anorexic's "goal is power, expressed by a grand gesture which gets its energy from the fact that it is difficult to stop anyone from starving herself. She wants to avoid any kind of accommodation to the demands of others, contrary to the compliant, sweet posture she maintained in her earlier childhood."

But Ruth wasn't starving herself. At least I didn't think so. That was part of the difficulty I had making sense of my notes. Sours, like the *DSM,* also noted that there are so many varieties of the disorder, including those in which weight remains normal most of the time, that diagnosis, not to mention a cure, was unbelievably difficult.

Sours claimed the illness dated from the nineteenth century but Flek had included a book called *Holy Anorexia,* about women in the Middle Ages, which I had also taken notes on. Written by Rudolph M. Bell, a contemporary scholar who documented the ways the cloistered women of medieval Italy starved themselves to gain authority and independence, the book argued that fasting was a way for powerless women to rebel against the patriarchal world they lived in. They could exercise dominion over their own bodies and the control they gained over food somehow translated into a sort of mystical authority that helped them in their quest for sainthood, one of the few roads to power for medieval women.

Catherine of Siena would put a stick down her throat to make herself throw up if she ate more than a pinch of herbs a day.

Eustochia of Messina prayed to God to take away her appetite, rejoicing when her prayers were answered and the very smell of food made her vomit. She wept so copiously when at table that her fellow nuns had to carry her sobbing from the room.

Veronica Giuliani, a nun who, like Eustochia, later became a saint, refused food from the kitchen until once she found her plate covered with cat vomit, and only then ate with relish. Given Ruth's feelings about Max, I doubted the story would appeal to her, and yet there was something in the stern will of these Italian women, their mastery over what they took into their bodies, that made me understand why Flek had put *Holy Anorexia* on my list.

These women won such renown for their acts of self-mortification that word of their deeds spread far and wide and they achieved the power to command kings and stand up to popes. They were taken as instruments of God, able to go without food for months or years or to eat only occasionally and then the vilest meals—the scabs of lepers, washed down with pus.

The images were startling. They frightened me. Hadn't Ruth cheerfully mimicked a saint only moments before? Joan of Arc, to the best of my knowledge, had not been included in the study. But the enthusiasm with which Ruth had struck the pose of a woman burned at the stake seemed suddenly ominous. That I had suggested she do it seemed beside the point.

"Ruth," I said, "haven't you swept enough? Come sit down."

"Why? So you can feel my teeth?"

"I got carried away. Come sit down."

"No, I still haven't used the sponge mop."

"Shouldn't we eat dinner first?"

"I'm not hungry," said Ruth. "And the apartment's gotten filthy. Where does all the dust come from?"

"Skin," I said, closing my notebook and slipping it back into my knapsack.

"What do you mean?" asked Ruth, looking at me. "What kind of skin?"

"Human skin. Our skin. We slough it off all the time."

"Like snakes?"

"Sort of—except it doesn't shed in one piece. Little by little, dead cells flake off our body. We just don't notice."

I wondered how Ruth would respond to this. In the book about holy anorexia I'd read how Saint Veronica had cleaned her cell by licking it with her tongue, not only licking the floor and walls, but lapping up the spiderwebs that lay in her path, gobbling the spiders along with their webs.

Could Ruth exhibit similar tendencies? Would Ruth, four hundred years ago (leaving aside the fact that she was Jewish) have joined a monastery and tortured her flesh, fasting and then dieting on disgusting foods as a test of will? I'd always assumed cleaning was no more than her way of burning calories, but perhaps there was some link between dirt and a sinful sense of the body that I needed to explore.

Ruth looked down at the dust pile. She seemed intrigued.

"You mean this is both of us mingled? Like Cathy and Heathcliff?"

"With a little Max thrown in."

"How much comes off a day?" she asked.

"I don't know."

Ruth stared at the gritty pile gathered at her feet, and I couldn't help imagining that she was weighing it in her mind, trying to establish how much she lost in dead cells each day. She'd resumed sweeping absently as we talked, moving not with her earlier energy but languidly, in small circles, as if she and the broom were the last contestants left in a dance marathon.

"Is it really skin?"

"Haven't you ever heard that the human body is mostly water and about ninety-eight cents' worth of chemicals? Dust to dust. We're basically reducible to a package of Kool-Aid."

"And what about the soul?" She said this diffidently, not making eye contact.

"What about it?"

"Is it part of our body, or separate? Where does it go—afterward? Does it weigh anything?"

Again I saw in her flashes of the medieval women I'd read about. Perhaps there *was* a religious side to all of this that I had to take more seriously. I should definitely ask Flek. It had never occurred to me that Ruth, with all her fretting over her body, thought about her soul.

"What makes you so sure we even have souls?" I asked.

"Oh, we do," she said with conviction, though still looking away shyly. "We definitely do. Don't you ever wonder where your sister is?"

"I know exactly where my sister is."

"How can you be so sure? Maybe the best part of us is the invisible part."

That very day I had copied into my notebook an observation by Sours: "She treats her body as though it were a threatening entity which, like a demon, needs to be controlled at all times. As her flesh falls away, her soul is revealed, made free again. . . ." This passage struck me now as ominously prophetic.

"Ruth," I asked casually, "how much do you weigh?"

Her eyes went big with fear.

"You think I'm fat!"

"No. Ruth, you're not fat at all. Not at all!"

"It's these pants."

She put her hand on her belly and looked down, panicky, studying her lower body, smooth as a seal in the Lycra pants, though much more slender.

"It's not the pants. It's not anything. I was just curious."

"You must have had a reason for asking."

She had taken up the broom again, and her inability to disappear behind it seemed to confirm her worst fears.

"Ruth, I didn't. You look great."

"You have a reason. You think I'm fat."

"Not true. I don't."

"Then why'd you ask? Why are you looking at me like that?"

"I'm afraid you're too thin, not too fat."

She looked at me doubtfully.

She'd begun resweeping the already clean floor. I listened to the *swish swish swish* of the broom, waiting for her to speak, but for several moments she was quiet.

"When I die," she said suddenly, "I'd like to be cremated."

"What are you talking about?"

"I'd like to be cremated. And scattered somewhere beautiful."

I had just begun to respond to this when Max, who had become hypnotized by the absentminded arc of the broom, made a run at the dust pile, pouncing, sneezing and bounding away, leaving a trail of dust behind him as if in fulfillment of Ruth's final wishes.

"I hate you!" Ruth shouted, shaking her broom and suddenly bursting into tears, her body convulsing with sobs.

"Come here, Ruth," I said.

She looked at me through her tears but did not move.

"Ruth," I said again, holding out my arms, as if for a child who has just learned to walk, "come here."

She laid down the broom, and came over to me. She sat on my lap, allowing me to enfold her. Her damp face pressed against my chest, she continued to cry.

"No more talk of dying, all right?"

I held her, and stroked her arms and face, soothing her ruffled soul, kissing the fragrant top of her head. At that moment I was flooded with a kind of holy, inexplicable joy.

"Am I too heavy for you?"

"How can you say that? You're light as a feather. *Have* you been eating as much as usual?"

"Yes!" She squirmed on my lap but I held on to her and she settled back down. She sat there quietly, her feet touching the ground, supporting her weight. She was indeed very light.

She had gone slack in my arms. Resting against my body, her eyes closed, she seemed exhausted. I felt guilty that I may have tortured her into crying, and yet, even as I sat there, I wondered if I could check her pulse without her noticing. A low pulse might mean electrolyte disturbance, the result of an improper balance of fluids. My fingers were itching to feel the blood beating through her slender wrists. I resisted, though she seemed so fragile that I longed for the confirmation of her heartbeat. I felt suddenly helpless, unable to protect or help her.

I called her name softly and she stirred.

"Ruth," I whispered, "it's getting late. Let's eat something."

She nodded into my breast and stood up slowly, leaving the damp imprint of her face on my shirt. She took my hand and allowed me to lead her into the kitchen.

It took as long for Ruth to eat a small salad and a bran muffin as it took me to cook and eat a salami omelette. She was keenly conscious of the smell of my food. I could see it on her face, and in the way she would turn to watch me at the stove, so that I was embarrassed and wanted to apologize for cooking meat.

She hunched over her plate protectively. The smell of my omelette, like secondary cigarette smoke, seemed to threaten her, as if it might impart dangerous calories to her muffin. But I knew too that she liked it. She often joined me in the kitchen while I cooked, even if she ate nothing herself. It soothed her to sit silently amid the aromas.

Ruth ate her muffin as if there were bones in it, crumbling it onto the plate, mashing it with her fork and worrying it with her tongue once it was in her mouth. This was her most agitated eating style. She placed a small piece of muffin on her tongue with eucharistic care. The pressure of the evening, the lateness of the hour, had no doubt intensified her misery. I could not forget the kiss of a few nights before, still unresolved in my mind, but I dared not disturb her now, much as I was itching to urge more food on her, beyond the few greens and spartan muffin that lay in molecules before her.

Ruth did not dress her salad, but dipped each leaf into the little jar of dressing she had made. She mixed very potent dressings, using powerful granular mustard, as if she wanted to distill an entire meal into a single drop. She seemed to have a rule about how deeply she could dip—I noticed that the endive, when she lifted a piece from the jar, was merely tipped with dressing, like a poisoned arrow.

With her salad she allowed herself a single bread stick, which she ate like an ear of corn, nibbling the sesame seeds off and leaving the clean crust behind.

"Would you please not watch me eat?"

I could ruin a meal for Ruth just by staring, the spider who frightened Miss Muffet away. I filled the kettle and put it on the stove. A blue claw of flame gripped the steel bottom.

"Where are you going?" Ruth asked, alarmed.

She did not want to be looked at, but neither did she want to be left alone.

"Just the bathroom," I said. "I'll be right back."

On my way, Max heard me and scrabbled at the door of the bedroom, where he'd been shut up during dinner. He sounded like a dog. A faint fecal scent was in the air.

In the bathroom I cleaned his litter box. A dark starfish of cat shit lay on the sandy bottom. I removed it with an old slotted serving spoon I had once taken from home. I dumped it into the toilet and watched it sink with a few slow-motion grains of sand before flushing it down. Already the white throat of the porcelain bowl and its hard, concealing lip had grown fascinating and become a place of serious consideration. I had snooped and even sniffed into it, checking for traces of the behavior so clinically outlined in the *Diagnostic and Statistical Manual*. So far I'd come up with nothing.

I poked in the medicine cabinet briefly, looking for the laxatives, the enemas, the diet pills and other implements of unnatural weight loss I had read about in the *DSM*, though here too I came up with nothing except a dusty thermometer, a dented can of Band-Aids, cotton balls, moldering antibiotics, several boxes of single-use toothpaste samples I'd gotten from my father, and an old tube of spermicidal jelly hidden away, the half-extruded gel hardening into amber.

Before leaving I stepped onto the bathroom scale and watched the roulette roll of numbers settling at my weight. 170 was a bit much for five feet, nine inches. I had been a skinny kid and was surprised to discover that I'd become a hefty adult. Did Ruth think I was too fat? She never asked about my weight, but suddenly, standing on the same scale she stood on so religiously each morning, I felt, for a moment, judged and guilty.

Strangely, I did not feel particularly fleshy but, on the contrary, rather disembodied standing there, feet together, on the edge of a diving board ready to spring. The underweight boy I once had been still looked out through my eyes. Was weight, like the year when one was born, arbitrary, a number on a calendar irrelevant to oneself?

I stepped off the scale and watched as the dial spun back to zero, but it failed to do so. It stopped at seven. Stuck? A terrible fear that I had broken Ruth's scale gripped me. I stepped on the scale with one foot, pressed it up to thirty, removed the pressure and let the dial spin back. Again, it stuck at seven. On my knees, I picked the scale up and turtled it onto its back. I shook it and tried it again—and again, like loaded dice, seven came up. Then after several minutes of panicky investigation I discovered what should have been obvious in the first place: the scale was set at seven pounds over zero.

How long had it been that way? I did not weigh myself regularly and I couldn't remember the last time I had done so. I toyed with the idea of setting it back down to zero, but what would Ruth do when her weight suddenly plunged seven pounds—even if the weight it revealed would be her true weight? Was she really deceiving herself, with a thumb on her own scale? Or perhaps the extra weight was the soul she believed in, the invisible part that goaded her to fear the body that she could see and touch.

Ruth was still at her place in the kitchen when I returned. The kettle was whistling like an unanswered phone. I got two mugs and tore open the foil packet of a Constant Comment tea bag for myself. For Ruth I brewed a cup of her special herbal tea.

With a moistened finger, she was picking up the last of the crumbs. This was the most difficult part of a meal for her, facing the empty plate. I served us both tea and sat down opposite her.

"Ruth," I said, when her plate was as clean as if it had been washed and dried, "do you really want to be cremated when you die?"

"Oh, let's not talk about that now, Joseph," she said.

"But do you think about dying a lot?"

"I think about what will happen after I'm dead," said Ruth.

"To your body?"

"No," she said, looking down, "to the rest of me."

"And what is that? What do you see?"

"Different things at different times. Dr. Hallo thinks they're just the result of my bad body image."

"Really?"

She squirmed under my probing but I pressed on.

"Tell me one of the things you see. Tell me what you imagine."

"I shouldn't."

"Why not? If you can tell Hallo you can certainly tell me. I love you—he just gets paid."

"Don't say that."

"Why. Unless—does he love you?"

"Of course not. It's not that."

"Then tell me. If you can tell a stranger you can tell me."

"Dr. Hallo's not a stranger. I've known him longer than I've known you."

"You know what I mean."

"Okay," she said tensely. "This is more like a dream, only I have it when I'm awake."

She spoke without looking up. She stared into the depths of her wine-dark tea.

"I imagine that my mother goes into a movie theater. The theater is packed and the lights go down. When it's completely dark I appear on the screen. It's not a movie, it's really me, only I'm pure light and shadow. And I say, 'Mom, it's me, Ruth. I've been transformed.' Sometimes I think I'll curse her as she sits in the dark, but mostly I think I'll forgive her. 'It's okay, I'm up here now.' Like a voice from heaven. And then I rise off the screen and float transparently by. She tries to touch me but her hand passes through me. She tries to hug me but she can't. I'm just air. She calls after me, crying, calling me back, but it's too late. I float away . . ."

"What an awful image."

"No, it's not," said Ruth defensively. "It's like entering a dream without sleep. It's like those lines from *A Midsummer Night's Dream:* 'And I will purge thy mortal grossness so/ That thou shalt like an airy spirit go.'"

"But I love your mortal grossness. It's my favorite part."

"Well, I don't love it."

"You should."

"Why? I didn't ask for this." Her gesture encompassed her bust and the whole middle portion of her body.

"No one asks for a body, Ruth, but it comes with being born. And you're so beautiful."

"You're just saying that."

"Of course I'm not. I love you. All of you. But I wouldn't want you if you were just something on the overhead projector."

Strong feeling, though I would never have told Ruth, made the flesh under her chin and around her throat plump with emotion. Her lips always seemed fuller just before she cried.

"Well, I don't like myself very much. I don't know why you stay with me. I really don't. I'm bad news."

A tear tipped off her eyelash and onto her cheek. She pressed a finger on it as if it were a crumb.

"You sound like a bad movie," I said. "And you should know that once Marlene Dietrich tells a man she's trouble, he's hooked for life."

"Are you hooked for life?" she asked, coming over and sitting on my lap.

"Absolutely."

She gave me a very sexy kiss I did not expect. Her eyes, still moist with tears, were brown flecked with green, like a penny beginning to oxidize. We kissed for a long time. Flek had told me to trust not books but the body, and here she was. Kissing me, she seemed not the sick, distracted woman I'd been hunting through the stacks but the sweet girl I'd met in college. Her body felt solid enough on my lap. Her lips were warm. I admired her fine freckled nose, her high cheekbones, the eyelids with their extra, sensuous fold.

Only the taut pull of her hair distracted me. It gave her face a slightly ascetic aspect and revealed the delicate, blue-hued hollows of her temples. A pale vein rose tentatively beneath the translucent skin. There was something heartbreaking about this exposed, naked vein that the few stray tendrils of escaped hair failed to cover. I cupped Ruth's head protectively in my hands and kissed her again. My fingers groped up, seeking to unbind her hair, but she pulled away.

"Careful," she said, putting her own hands to her head and unwinding the elastic with expert fingers. "I'll do it."

When she had removed the elastic band she stood up and shook her head. A fullness returned to her face, her features grew more relaxed. For good measure, she bent over and, with her knees locked, pressed her palms to the ground, shaking her head at the same time so that her hair touched the newly swept floor. Ruth was extremely limber. She often stretched for the mere pleasure of it, to punctuate an activity or even to signify that a conversation was over. The fluid movement of her body as she bent entranced me. When she stood up again the blood gave her face a healthy glow that seemed to have reached even to the tips of her hair, which tingled with dark fire at the ends. She smoothed her hair in one final gesture.

"Better?" she asked, inclining her face toward mine.

Ruth's eyes were shut but I continued watching as we kissed. I noticed that a few hairs, shaken loose by all the activity, were floating free of her head. A thread-thin fiber clung to her sleeve, too long to be Max's. I brushed it to the ground. Were these loose strands more than normal? I had read that very day that hair loss, above and below, was a symptom of improper nutrition and often accompanied eating disorders. What would I find if I went through the hamper and examined her cast-off underpants? In the meantime, I tried to feel the health of the hair on her head with my fingers. Certainly it looked good. But as I ran my hand through it, I felt a tindery dryness, an unmistakable crackling of stray, parched strands. With my thumb and forefinger I isolated a single hair and tugged gently to see if it would come out easily.

"Ouch!" cried Ruth, starting back. "You did that on purpose. You pulled my hair!"

"I'm sorry. I thought it wasn't attached to your head."

"No? What did you think it was attached to?"

"I thought it was one of the loose ones. Sometimes they fall out on the pillow."

"They do?"

"Sometimes."

She looked mortified, smoothing back her hair protectively.

"Not a lot," I added hastily. "You never noticed?"

"No." She looked at me narrowly. "Joseph, what's going on?"

"Why should anything be going on?"

"Poking my teeth. Pulling my hair. Asking me all these questions. You tell me."

"Nothing. Come back."

But Ruth stalked off to get ready for bed. I had, as always, gotten washed up long before she did. Lying in bed, I heard the rich distant soprano of the opera singer who lived in one of the nearby buildings. I had seen her, on other nights, standing in the wedge of park that separated our little street from Riverside Drive and the larger park beyond. I knew she was out there now. I had spied on her many times as she stood, facing the park, the river, New Jersey, the night, bundled in her winter coat and, beneath that, bundled in her large stately body. She often sang Puccini, but tonight I recognized Marguerite's spinning-wheel song from Gounod's *Faust*.

I believe she was a black woman, but I had caught only glimpses of her under the yellow light of the street lamps. She always had two dogs with her, lean, surprisingly muttlike animals (she should have had borzois or Great Danes for her bearing was regal), who ran noiselessly back and forth while she sang. Sometimes she would break off abruptly in the middle of her aria and clap her hands for her dogs.

I lay there serenaded by the high, haunting melody that floated above the distant murmur of traffic. It was not strictly a good omen that she sang tonight, for Ruth was often made uneasy by her presence in the park. If Ruth was sketching late she complained she could not concentrate. On nights when she went to bed early, she complained that the woman kept her awake. But for me, nothing was more stirring than to hear that voice suddenly begin to sing.

Ruth seemed to take even longer than usual. The voice outside blended with the sound of rushing water from the bathroom, disturbing my peace. I thought of Ruth's wish to be a mere phantom in the dark, of the rice demon and the medieval women and the rigged bathroom scale, and I wondered what she was doing.

When at last she came to bed she seemed relaxed, affectionate. She lay down close beside me. She was wearing a long flannel nightgown and I slid my hand up inside, traveling the smooth surface of her thigh. She wasn't wearing underpants, as she normally did, and I laid my hand over the teased puff of pubic hair. To my surprise, she placed her own hand over mine, gently shifting my hand out of the way.

I lay still, excited, watching her focused face as she rummaged below. It lasted only a moment. She gave a sudden tug and drew her hand swiftly back over the blanket. Between pinched fingers she held a single, wirelike hair. She offered it to me, a wildflower from a forbidden field.

"For you," she said.

I became a binge reader.

My ETNA classes didn't begin until one o'clock. Every morning, before teaching, I spent several hours in the Public Library, plowing through stacks of books and articles, gorging myself on the horrific history of women and food, steeping myself in the melancholy of anatomy.

All around me, men and women were reading and taking notes, writing dissertations, articles, scientific monographs, novels and who knew what else? I also had my research project, my pile of books, my notebook. I, too, was scribbling notes for an investigation I might have called "Little Women," or perhaps, simply, "The Book of Ruth."

Once, absentmindedly searching for titles in one of the Bill Blass computers, I actually entered Ruth's name—as if there might indeed be a book devoted exclusively to her, uncannily explaining who she really was. To my surprise a Ruth Simon actually appeared on the screen. This one was born in 1917 and had written *Earthquake Interpretations: A Manual for Reading.* Would Ruth have been amused to discover she had such a namesake?

Further up the column of names was Ruth's mother, Carol, whose second book, *Screwball Comedies of the 1940s,* had recently been published. I refrained from requesting it, though who knows what clues to Ruth's personality I might have found in a book that devoted a whole chapter to *Bringing Up Baby?* But there were plenty of other books I did request.

In college I had been a good student but had never quite found the subject that suited me. At last I had. I thrilled to the strange sensation of researching Ruth. I could not have formulated exactly what I hoped to find, but I was drawn by some dream of salvation, as if Ruth's voice murmured to me out of the muffled echoes of the marble hall, whispering up from the riffled pages of borrowed books. She was the sphinx and the riddle, the question and the answer, the illness and the cure.

"Much study is a weariness of the flesh," King Solomon laments in Ecclesiastes, but my study *was* the flesh and I found it oddly invigorating. Was it merely coincidence that, in the weeks since I'd begun going to the library, I had not had another headache? I couldn't help feeling, for all the grim statistics I encountered, that there was something salutary about my research. If my own pain could be kept at bay by reading, soon enough I would be able to heal Ruth. Like my immigrant students and like all true Americans, I suffered from the delusion that there is no condition you cannot educate your way out of. I had only to understand the nature of Ruth's illness.

But that was not as easy as it had at first appeared.

To be sure, I accumulated plenty of descriptions in my notebook, beginning with the 1683 account by Richard Morton, an English physician, who wrote of a twenty-two-year-old patient: "I do not remember that I did ever in all my Practice see one, that was conversant with the Living so much wasted with the greatest degree of a Consumption, (like a Skeleton only clad with Skin) yet there was no Fever, but on the contrary a Coldness of the whole Body." Three months later the woman died.

But why this poor woman should have stopped eating, and why food should be the weapon of choice for young women in their war against the world, was anything but obvious.

I went back to my old friend Dr. Sours, who spoke of the "trauma of menstruation" and the difference between the male and female body. Girls and boys in early adolescence both needed more food to keep up with their suddenly developing bodies, but girls tapered off at about fourteen, after which, if they continued to eat at the same rate as when they were twelve or thirteen, they became fat. Boys, on the other hand, kept growing, getting stronger, needing calories and carbohydrates for height and muscle all through adolescence.

To become a woman, I now understood, was a far more radical alteration than anything boys experienced. And the more I read, the more the ruthlessness with which some women resisted these changes astonished me. The battle they waged against their own bodies gave me a context in which to consider Ruth's own struggle.

The terms were harsh. Words like "purge" and "gorge" and "binge" sickened me with their soft "g" sounds that seemed almost literally to catch in my throat and make me gag. "Bulimia," I discovered to my horror, meant "oxen appetite."

I began to devise a dictionary of alternate terms, wishing to save Ruth the indignity of such words. I replaced "bulimia" with "unrequited appetite." "Binging" and "purging" I replaced with "feasting" and "fasting," with their festive, almost religious, connotations.

"Anorexia" was a witheringly ugly word. It meant "lack of appetite"—an error, since those who suffered from it were hungry all the time. One study I read mentioned the German word for anorexia, *"die Magersucht,"* which I adopted as my own private name for the disorder. I preferred it not only because it was more accurate—it meant "a longing to be thin"—but because it was tinged with poetry, a sonorous fusion of beauty and death. It also gave to the illness a vaguely sinister, Nazi intonation. I thought Ruth, who kept a diary like her childhood hero Anne Frank, would prefer hiding from the shadow of *"die Magersucht"* rather than the ugly encroachments of mere appetite.

No name changes, however, could alter the grim reality of the illness. If it was a poetic disorder, it was one with harsh physical consequences. Fifteen out of every hundred girls with anorexia died of it—the highest death rate for any psychological disorder. Since Morton in the seventeenth century had described his mysterious skinny patient, eating disorders had risen steadily. In the nineteenth century, anorexia was given its name by William Gull, former physician to Queen Victoria. The queen herself seems to have had no trouble keeping food down but that was not the case for a growing number of her female subjects. England was becoming rich and industrialized and increasingly uncomfortable with the body. The more a well-to-do woman was liberated from working or raising children, the less she needed a robust physique and the more her body became an incongruity, an impediment to be refined and refashioned.

But also a source of power. It was in the Victorian era, as I read in a book by Joan Jacobs Bromberg, that "fasting girls" became prevalent. The dinner table in the nineteenth century had become the altar at which the middle-class family gathered. By refusing food, a young girl could seize control not only over herself but over her entire family. A modern class of self-starvers was born that helped update the abstinence of the saints, transforming a primarily religious phenomenon into a modern disease.

Perhaps these young women, who grew more numerous throughout Victorian England and America, were merely acting out the discomfort of an entire age. Maybe there was something about prosperity itself that spawned its own rejection. Or perhaps industrialization was the villain. With so much denatured around us, our biological selves came to seem by contrast false, faulty. The mystery of the flesh was replaced by mechanical detachment.

But just as technology was lifting us away from the body, evolutionary science dashed us back down. After Darwin, our animal natures were undeniable, an affront to our notion of divine origination. What, after all, *were* we? From the physiological perspective, we were merely an alimentary system maintaining a reproductive system. Our only purpose, in purely biological terms, was to sustain the species. That was why we ate. But of course we had come up with other ideas for ourselves. We wanted to be not hungry animals but spirits dressed in flesh.

No wonder the actual body was squeezed between these dissonant images. Hadn't Freud risen to prominence on the backs of unhappy women, hysterical housewives and their neurotic daughters? But why were women the shock troops in this war against human nature? Were they more bound to reproductive nature and therefore in more conspicuous revolt against it? And why, if repressive Victorian society had forced submerged appetites into unhealthy irruptions, did the sexual revolution of the 1960s in America unleash even more cases of anorexia? And why had the illness only become more common, diversifying beyond mere starvation, so that it was now impossible to tell simply by looking what the mental state of a young woman was, how she thought of food and her body? She might, like Ruth, be beautiful yet filled with secret self-loathing, beauty disgusted with itself.

So much reading began to shake my own sense of reality. The more I read, the more it seemed that the body itself was a problem for which there was no solution. Flek had been right: ever since the serpent had hissed into Eve's ear, food had been at the center of our struggle with human nature. Ruth's mystic impulse, to unzip the flesh and step out, a pure spirit, was merely an extreme version of the desire that had haunted human beings for thousands of years. I almost wondered if Flek had intended for me to make the discovery that I would have to solve the riddle of our civilization before I could solve the riddle of Ruth.

By the end of the third week I had read every book but one on Flek's list without feeling at all closer to a solution, much less a course of action. I'd put off calling Flek, believing that I would find some key in one of the books I had not yet read. Now, with nothing left but Kenneth Clark's *The Nude: A Study in Ideal Form,* I decided to give Flek a call.

I dialed from a pay phone in the library.

"Joseph!" Flek said. "I've been thinking about you. How are you?"

"I'm down to my last book. And unless Kenneth Clark is some kind of medical genius, I'm going to need more titles."

"Kenneth Clark isn't a medical genius," said Flek. "But I think you've read enough. What you're doing isn't helping Ruth. Why don't you come by my office instead of burying yourself in the—what library are you in?"

"The Public Library. The Main Branch on Forty-second Street."

"Joseph, listen. You're beginning to alarm me."

"Well, you *should* be alarmed. *I* am. Do you know that fifty percent of all college-age women would rather be hit by a truck than get fat?"

"That's not what's worrying me. I am worried about you. What you're doing isn't healthy."

"If you want to help me, think of some more titles. Or something I can *do*. I haven't gotten anywhere."

"Joseph. I'd like you to come by and see me." He sounded concerned.

"When can I come?"

"How about today?"

"I can't," I said, thinking of *The Nude,* which I had already requested.

"Then tomorrow," said Flek.

"I'll try," I told him, feeling suspicious.

"Good, I'll see you tomorrow, say, eleven?"

"I'll try," I said again. "I have to go now. I have a feeling my number is lighting up."

———

"It is widely supposed," I read, a few moments later, "that the naked human body is in itself an object upon which the eye dwells with pleasure and which we are glad to see depicted. But anyone who has frequented art schools and seen the shapeless, pitiful model that the students are industriously drawing will know this is an illusion."

Clark's "naked" and "nude" seemed uncannily relevant to my research, as no doubt Flek had intended. The naked body was the body as it actually appeared in nature—lumpy, bumpy, wrinkled, gross. The nude was what artists made of that body, an ideal representation. Clark was, I thought, rather hard on the naked body, describing it like a man who had learned about the human form from Holocaust documentaries. "A mass of naked figures," he wrote, "does not move us to empathy but to disillusion and dismay."

Ruth, I thought, would agree with Clark's judgment. Certainly she seemed to feel that way about her own nakedness. And yet disillusion and dismay were not what I felt when I saw Ruth dressing in the morning or stepping into the bath or sliding under the covers, or standing, half-dressed, in the dim light of the refrigerator.

The naked body had the virtue of being real, but this was not something Clark seemed to care about. And it was not, I suddenly understood, something Ruth cared about either. She wished never to be naked. She wished only to be nude. To be crafted, shaped, perfected. She wished, despite the hours she spent painting, not to make art but to be art, to sculpt herself into shape and rub out beneath her strong fingers all traces of mortality. She was her own Pygmalion.

I had only to look at the humpty-dumpty fragments of Greek sculpture reproduced in Clark's book, heads and hands and breasts broken off by time and cruel usage, to feel that nudes had their own sorrows, for all the perfection of form they approached. They seemed like models not of ideal beauty but of the fragmented self.

More than that, every age had its own idea of perfection. There was what Clark called "the Vulgar Venus," best represented by a chunky Neolithic fertility godling built like a matzoh ball. There was the "Celestial Venus," exemplified by a carved Minoan doll, slender as a Popsicle stick, which Ruth would have found more appealing, but, since its head was missing, it inevitably lacked a certain grace. And between these extremes was a world of mutable form, the smooth swells of Ingres nudes, the rumpled flanks of Rubens, the humbled flesh of Rembrandt, the delicate flowers of Botticelli.

What Clark called "the alternative convention" intrigued me most of all, particularly as embodied in the paintings of the Northern Renaissance. These northern artists had discovered the nude late. Unlike the classical perfections of the Greeks and the sumptuous renderings of the Italians, which seemed to obscure the body's complications as much as they revealed them, the nudes of the North retained a pale aura of Gothic shame. They also possessed the erotic charge of something long hidden and now brought out into the light. Sin still clung to their slender bodies—which is, perhaps, why so many northern artists favored portraits of Eve.

I was thinking about this, and poring over several sinuous examples of the "alternative convention," when I felt a tap on my shoulder and looked up into the gold grin of Gennady Zhdanov. He was wearing the same white T-shirt he wore to class and was carrying his ridiculous briefcase. He was looking past me at a painting of Eve from one of the side panels of Van Eyck's Ghent altarpiece. He turned to me and winked.

"You like naked womens?" he asked, not bothering to whisper.

"I like art," I whispered back.

He smiled conspiratorially and laid his forefinger against his lips. "I don't tell," he said. "I very like art too."

It was only then that I noticed Marina, his pudgy wife, sitting a few tables away. She waved shyly and then went back to her book. I couldn't see what she was reading but I recognized the Russian-English dictionary open on the table before her. Gennady had a copy of *The Wall Street Journal* tucked absurdly under his arm. He had circled a number of words in ink and annotated them in Russian. He winked at me again and went off to join his wife.

Who knows, perhaps someday he will strike it rich and leave a fortune to the library, like Martin Radtke, whose tribute to himself I had noticed carved into the marble floor of the lobby:

INSCRIBED HERE ARE THE WORDS OF AN
IMMIGRANT WHOSE LIFE WAS TRANSFORMED BY THE
LIBRARY AND WHOSE ESTATE NOW ENRICHES IT.

IN MEMORY
MARTIN RADTKE
1883–1973

Meanwhile, Gennady had opened his briefcase and taken out a sandwich, which he ate in rough, hasty bites. I returned my books and fled before the security guards could spot him and toss him out.

I ran down the stairs and into the main lobby. Only at the bottom of the stairs did I pause, stooping to tie one of my shoes.

"Hungry?" a voice said softly in my ear.

How did Flek get uptown so quickly? He seemed out of breath, and I wondered if he had rolled in his chair the whole way. He was dressed in an elegant cashmere coat open over a dark tweed jacket and thick corduroy pants. On his hands were black leather bicycling gloves with padded palms and cut off fingers. Around his neck hung a silver whistle on a string.

"You saved me a trip upstairs," he said, smiling.

"What are you doing here?"

"I came to meet you, Joseph. I thought I could tempt you to lunch. You look as if you're done for the morning."

"I am," I told him, remembering the munching Gennady Zhdanov upstairs. "I was reading Kenneth Clark. Did you suggest him because Ruth paints? Do you think she's absorbed bad ideas about the body from art?"

"What time do you have to teach?" asked Flek, ignoring my questions.

"One o'clock."

Flek looked at his watch. "That gives us an hour and a half," he said. "Let's go."

"Wait a minute," I said. "What was it about those northern artists—why didn't they accept the body the way Italian painters did? And where does America fit in? Clark doesn't mention America at all. Do we have no tradition of the nude?"

"We'll talk over lunch."

I would have liked to hash out such questions while they were fresh in my mind and we were still in the library, but Flek seemed eager to go, and his cheerfully commanding manner made resistance impossible. When he began wheeling through the lobby I followed him obediently.

We left by a way I had never been before—Flek needed the elevator and the ramp to get out. He kept up a pleasant banter, but when he had trouble negotiating the elevator and I grabbed the handles of his wheelchair, he suddenly abandoned his jovial manner.

"This is not a baby carriage," he said. "Thank you very much, I'll do it myself."

Out on the sidewalk he moved with such astonishing speed that I had to trot to keep up. Reaching back to grip the wheels of his chair, he hurled himself forward, pushing down athletically and letting the rubber tires hiss through his hands. The black fingerless gloves gave his hands a masked, menacing aspect. He powered along, swearing at the square curbs, muttering at careless pedestrians. He seemed a different person out on the street. He never blew the silver whistle, clenched between his teeth, but everyone in his path—bicycle messengers, dog-walkers, women with strollers—swerved to get out of his way. His eyes alone sounded the alarm.

I realized that alongside the good humor and the wonderful conversation and the broad intelligence was a bottomless fund of rage. He rode his wheelchair like a Roman charioteer, drawn by invisible horses.

"Where are we going?" I asked, a little breathless, as we zoomed up Sixth Avenue.

"Harvard Club," he said, letting the whistle drop from his mouth.

Trotting beside him, I imagined what an education it must be to move through the world waist-high. Hips and bellies, tight skirts, big behinds, drooling dogs, open flies, fuming tailpipes, bent-over beggars, laughing crying astonished children, dragged through life, looking endlessly up. No wonder Flek believed the body was our one great book.

The wheelchair elevator located to the right of the front entrance of the Harvard Club was broken and Flek refused to go around to the back, as the doorman suggested, where there was a ramp. "There should be a ramp here," he announced, winking at me. "I should be able to go in the main entrance. I'm not a dog. I pay my dues."

The manager came out and a brief commotion ensued which culminated not, as I'd imagined, in the police being called but in several obliging members, as well as the manager and me, hoisting Flek's chair up the outer flight of granite steps and then up the inner marble ones. Flek sat like a pasha carried in a litter, his great head royally impassive, his hands folded on his lap. He was unbelievably heavy.

It seemed like a lot of work for lunch. I had to borrow the blazer at the front desk. Flek had brought an extra tie rolled up in his pocket. The sleeves of the blazer were too short for me and I felt awkward, adolescent, as if I'd experienced a sudden growth spurt in the last five minutes. I was wearing a red-and-black flannel shirt, and the mustard-yellow tie Flek brought didn't match either the blazer or the shirt. Flek smiled at me, flashing the space between his teeth, as I emerged from the men's room.

"Perfect," he said, with the finality of a Brooks Brothers' salesman.

He had recovered his calm good humor. The maître d' led us through the long, crowded dining room, not unlike the main reading room of the Public Library in its heavy, muffled, antique style. The large room was humming with the low murmur of conversation, a kind of public whispering.

Flek ordered a bottle of claret with lunch, but when he tried to fill my glass I declined.

"Not even a little?"

"I don't drink wine."

"A young healthy man like you? It'll clear your mind after all that reading. And it's good for the digestion—that's not a myth."

"It's my head I'm worried about," I told him, "not my stomach."

"Migraines!" said Flek, as if confirming an earlier suspicion. He was still wearing the half-glasses he had put on to read the menu and he scrutinized me with interest.

"Sometimes," I admitted.

"Those can be terrible. Do they last long?"

"No more than an hour. Usually less."

"Have you had one lately?" he asked, with the professional curiosity of a doctor, though, as Ruth had reminded me, he wasn't an MD.

"Actually, I haven't had one since the day I met you. I'd gotten one that afternoon in class. That's why I didn't drink in your apartment. But I haven't had one since, for which I am very grateful."

"Well, don't thank me," Flek said, slipping off his glasses and laying them on the table, where they cast two burning shadows on the white cloth. "I am not a faith healer. I hope they never come back, but if they do it will be because there's a little faulty wiring in your head that triggers those things. Someday we may understand how it works, but until then it seems like magic."

Flek filled his own glass with the dark red claret and lifted it in a toast. The glass looked tiny in his large hand, which still bore, on its broad back, the circular imprint of the bicycle glove.

"To your head, Joseph. May it never cause you too much pain."

He drank, and, setting the half-emptied glass down, lifted the basket of popovers the waiter had just brought.

"Have one."

The popovers lay in the basket like dinosaur eggs. I took one—it weighed almost nothing—and tore it open, releasing a puff of steam.

"I'm hungry, too," Flek said, helping himself.

I felt, in his deliberate movements, that he was trying to teach me something. Was there a Zen-like lesson in the way he held his small knife and dipped it into the butter, spreading it generously over the yellow interior of the popover? Though he had rushed to intercept me at the library and then zoomed down Forty-second Street, up Sixth Avenue and along Forty-fourth to the Harvard Club, he had relaxed as soon as we arrived at our table, where he'd studied his menu with slow care. When, I wondered, would he answer my questions about Kenneth Clark? When would he ask me about my progress? But he sat chewing thoughtfully, making the occasional, surreptitious adjustments in his posture I was used to and looking around the large room with relaxed ease.

"Where does it come from?" I asked at last, unable to contain myself any longer.

Flek tore open another popover and dropped the two halves onto his plate. He began buttering the smaller half.

"Where does what come from?"

"Hunger."

Flek laid down his butter knife and gave me a long, sympathetic look.

"We're born hungry, Joseph. If we weren't, we wouldn't survive. Hunger isn't the problem. The denial of hunger is the problem."

Perhaps to emphasize this point, he picked up the concave crust he'd just buttered and bit into it.

"Not ordinary hunger," I said. "Unrequited hunger."

"Unrequited hunger." Flek, when he had done chewing, repeated the phrase. "You didn't find *that* in the *DSM,* did you?"

"No. I made it up. The scientific words are so ugly."

"Yes, they are," said Flek. "But so is the illness. Don't go making poetry out of it. That's part of the problem to begin with."

"Poetry is part of the problem? I thought it was part of the solution—you're the one who read me Keats's letters."

Flek sighed. "Yes, Joseph. I did. Perhaps it's both. I wanted you to be able to live with unanswerable questions."

"Do you mean there's no solution?" I asked in alarm. "Ruth's greatest fear is that she's locked in a hopeless puzzle. Are you saying she is?"

"No. I suspect that as she gets older, and more accepting of herself and of life, she'll get better and better. But it will take time. She's inching toward happiness, like a lot of people."

"I wish I could believe that. There's just so much I don't know about Ruth."

"And there always will be," said Flek. "We're all hidden, after all, like new moons. The sliver of a self you see is all you'll ever see. The rest is there, in shadow. If you strain you can see the outline, rounded by darkness. But that's only an indication of what you can never know. You're looking for the outline of the rest of Ruth. But she doesn't want to be discovered. And she can't be, fully. You can't expect to find answers. We are all mysterious—to ourselves and others—and the closer we get to someone else, the more the mystery deepens. Don't look for what's not there. That's all that Keats meant in his letter."

"But you told me to come talk to you."

Flek smiled. "I did, Joseph. And I want you to. Anytime. But not to look for answers. I don't have them."

"Who does, then?" I asked. My voice was louder than I intended. "Who else can I talk to?"

"What about Ruth? Do you talk to her about what you've read?"

"Not yet," I said. "Not directly. I don't want to scare her."

"I promise you," said Flek, "there's nothing you could tell her that she doesn't know. Are you sure you're not the one who doesn't want to be scared?"

I thought about this for a moment. I did not think so. Hadn't I sensed the dark glimmerings of Ruth's secret self and wished only to know more? To see more? It wasn't fear that drove me to her journal but something else. I felt equipped for any revelation, no matter how strange and secret.

"I'm not afraid," I said finally.

"Then let her know that," said Flek. "Let her know you want to help her. Let her know you understand and still accept. Ruth will be your best teacher if you earn her trust."

I nodded without answering.

"Don't think that you're alone in your quest," said Flek. "Or that Ruth is alone in her illness. Look around this room—at this well-dressed crowd. Look closely at the faces, not to mention the bodies. Read the eyes."

I did as Flek directed.

The room was full. There were more men than women, though most of the women were young and therefore noticeable. A surprising number were attractive, but with the trim, uniformed look of flight attendants. You couldn't tell much about them from their quasiofficial appearance. Some were eating, some talking, some listening. The older women did, I could see, possess a battered look about the eyes, but that was true for the older men too. Their suits, on the other hand, all had a kind of organic crispness that belied suffering. The younger faces might have belonged to former classmates of mine, but they seemed to be inhabiting another, more formal realm. Briefcases rested against the legs of their tables. They leaned forward, talking business with the look of elder associates while I sat, in my ill-fitting, borrowed blazer, waiting for a man in a wheelchair to share with me the secrets of the body. Of Ruth's body. My knapsack, with its disturbing hoard of information, lay slumped on the chair beside me.

"I don't see anything unusual," I said.

"You don't have to. What you're trying to understand isn't that unusual. Half the women in this room—more, probably—could tell you stories about 'unrequited hunger,' as you so delicately put it, that would spoil your appetite."

"But why is that?"

Flek shook his large head slowly.

"I don't know, Joseph. For everything that goes right with us there are a hundred things that can go wrong. Why do you get migraine headaches? Why did I get polio?"

"But this is different. You yourself said that we're born hungry. Eating is natural, like breathing. Isn't it?"

" 'Natural' is a funny word when applied to human beings," said Flek. "The barest savages living in the remotest tribe, cut off from western society and technology, isolated for thousands of years, are about as natural as a Styrofoam cup. Even if they run around naked, the men tie a tassel to their penises, or a string around their arms. They leave the mark of their own hands and minds on their skin, scratching a new man-made reality onto their faces and arms and backs. The mind that gave us cunning enough to survive in nature separated us from the 'natural' realm long ago."

"And where has it left us?"

"Confused," said Flek, smiling sadly. "The very things that advance us as a society make us sick, just as the things that make us sick may for a time advance us as individuals. Ruth's illness may offer her at least the illusion of control over a chaotic world, even though it ultimately makes her life chaotic. We are not rational creatures."

He fell silent, looking down at his plate. He had picked up his fork and, holding it upside-down like a pen, tines pointing up, wrote something invisible on the tablecloth. I wanted to ask him what he had written and even leaned closer to see if his words had left an imprint but he laid down his fork suddenly and began speaking again, still without looking up. His voice was calm, soft, measured, mesmerizing.

"We are an ill-adapted species, Joseph, but we disregard Darwin the same way people once disregarded Columbus. Deep inside, of course, we know the truth. That we are baffled animals. That our home is a round ball among billions of other round balls whose presence in the universe we barely understand. But we work hard to keep these secrets secret even from ourselves. *That* is the real work most people do. The truth of our isolation, of our frailty, shames us, mortifies us into silence—or into illness. We all have a skeleton in the closet—our own," said Flek. "We are all prisoners *here*." He thumped his thick chest with his fist, producing a muffled thud.

"If you want to help Ruth, you must first understand that. We are born naked, but, as Kenneth Clark told you, we wish to be nude, to be perfect. This ceases to be a philosophical abstraction and becomes a personal torment when we are continually told by society that this ideal can be attained, that we can style ourselves and educate ourselves out of our physical predicament. Women in particular suffer from the lie. Don't think men are free of it, but women are the primary victims, at least in this society. Fathers tell their daughters that they are angels, only to have them discover, at puberty, that they are something more—or, as some of them see it, less."

Flek was sitting up straight in his chair, looking right at me now.

"The womb, the belly, the nourishing body still pulls on the lives of women the way the moon pulls the tides. Inevitably the body breaks free and asserts itself and then—disaster."

"I read that educated women get sick more than uneducated women and that rich girls get sick more than poor ones," I said, trying to draw Flek back into a more practical dialogue. "Why should that be?"

"It's a good question," he said, adjusting himself subtly in his chair. "It may be that the poor lead healthier lives emotionally but I doubt that very much. I think they pay a different price. Interestingly, nobody really studies poor girls and food, since they don't seek treatment. But you see gigantic women on the street, barely out of their teens, silencing their babies with Hawaiian Punch, and you know that eating disorders afflict the poor as much as the rich. Poverty distorts one's sense of the body as much as wealth. Ghetto children have babies out of wedlock and believe that this way they'll strike a blow against powerlessness and poverty, only to find they've increased both. Using the body to rebel against the physical terms of our lives is never successful. Rich girls don't have children, they have eating disorders, but they are guided by the same principles. They use their bodies to try to negate the body, to exercise power over it. They think they will free themselves and gain control, only to find themselves prisoners. The body in this culture is the weapon *and* the wound."

"I thought that had changed—especially for women like Ruth. Didn't the sixties liberate women?"

Flek laughed.

"Eating disorders skyrocketed after the sixties," he said. "The sexual revolution only intensified the burden on women."

"But why?"

"When I had my practice," Flek said, "the secret shame of many of the women who came to see me was that they had failed. They could not live up to the new liberated ideals women had labored so hard to achieve. They couldn't do what they'd been told was now their birthright. They couldn't be educated, beautiful, fertile, strong, submissive, dominant, smart, sexy. They couldn't be ethereal animals, they couldn't be earthy angels. And who could blame them? It was too much. Secretly, they detected a true self lurking inside, a selfish self, a mysterious self, a self they hadn't been taught about and so couldn't accept or refuse to accept. They tried to abort, not the child in them, but the woman in them. And nothing is more dangerous than human beings in revolt against their own natures.

"America's bloodiest war was a civil one and we're in the midst of another one right now, only we're each fighting our own self. Einstein said the last war on earth would be fought with sticks and stones, but he was wrong, at least for America. Forks and knives, Joseph. Forks and knives. Speaking of which . . ."

Our food had arrived and Flek transferred his attention to the waiter serving it.

"Joseph, let's enjoy our lunch. I talked too much—wine on an empty stomach will do that. And your incessant questions." He chuckled. "Which, by the way, I hope you'll keep asking. But let's eat first."

He had ordered the red snapper. I had a hamburger. Flek took up the lemon half wrapped in cheesecloth and squeezed it with strong fingers over his fish.

"Why don't you start eating?" Flek demanded, his gaze fixed on me. "You haven't lost your appetite, have you? Be careful—we become our obsessions if we're not careful. Now eat. I want you to eat."

"Don't worry about me," I said, gripping the hamburger so that the juice ran down my wrists. I bit into it.

"Good," said Flek.

We ate without talking. I might have been back in the large empty murmuring space of the library, except that Flek's words reverberated in my mind. I had hoped for practical advice, but his sweeping pronouncements set my mind racing. Flek made Ruth's illness seem bound up with the whole of human history. I toyed with the thought that Stalin's Great Purge had been preceded by a Great Binge. Were the bodies in Hitler's ovens, like the children baked by the witch in *Hansel and Gretel,* part of an ancient grotesque war on physical existence conducted on a mass scale? Were all the great punctuating horrors of modern times linked to our war against our bodies, a war that technology had greatly intensified? And how did one make peace? How did one surrender?

I wanted to talk about these things, and about Ruth, but when I tried to take up the thread of our conversation, Flek stopped me, pointing at my plate with his knife.

"Eating is as important as talking," he said, draining his third glass of claret and sending the half-empty bottle away. "Let's finish our lunch and then pick up where we left off."

From time to time, as we ate in silence, I thought he was about to speak. He would place his silverware on the plate, absentmindedly fingering the silver whistle that hung around his neck. But then he'd take up his fork and knife and resume eating.

Vague questions formed and vanished in my head. I had skipped over the many paintings of the Crucifixion in Kenneth Clark's book, focusing instead on the women, but I felt suddenly that I should go back and see what those paintings were saying about the body. Had I ever seen a fat Jesus, the way one saw fat Buddhas? And what was Jesus doing on the cross if not fulfilling a western wish to destroy the body once and for all? Is this why the image was still so compelling after 2000 years? As for the Jewish God, he didn't have a body at all. And yet we were said to be made in God's image.

Was our conception of God part of the problem, a representation of the disembodiment we all longed for? Was the idea that God lay outside nature, separate from our bodies and the living world, destructive? Ruth, after all, had deep spiritual inclinations and these seemed inseparable from her illness.

What, I wondered, would Flek say about this? I ate faster, eager to finish my hamburger and start talking. Flek glanced at my clean plate with silent approval, much as I had formed the habit of surreptitiously reviewing the remains of Ruth's plate, a haruspex consulting the telltale guts of a sacrificial bird. But having my own eating habits scrutinized was disconcerting.

As soon as our plates were cleared, Flek put his half-glasses back on and studied the dessert menu. He insisted on dessert for both of us. I ordered apple pie and coffee. Flek ordered crème brûlée and espresso. The tiny cup looked absurd in his giant hand.

"Now," said Flek, clearing his throat, "I know I cut you off before. Whatever you'd like to ask, feel free."

"Do you believe," I asked, without having thought about it, "that we have divine natures?" I heard, in the strangeness of the question, an echo of Ruth's voice.

"Why do you ask me that?"

"Ruth does. She believes in the soul—an invisible piece of the sacred self she thinks remains after the body's gone away."

Flek took a sip of coffee and set the tiny cup back on the table.

"It's a comforting thought," he said.

"But you don't believe it."

He shook his head firmly.

"No."

"Is a belief like that just part of her illness?"

The question seemed to make Flek uncomfortable. He fidgeted with his silverware, studying his reflection in the convex bowl of a spoon. He clenched the silver whistle between his teeth and pursed his lips around it. I braced for the piercing blast that never came. The whistle dropped from his lips and he shrugged.

"I don't know," he said. "Religion is strange business. You shouldn't expect to figure these things out."

I waited for him to say more. Looking up, I noticed for the first time the giant heads of animals mounted high on the walls, deer and elk and moose, gazing glassily down on our conversation. It surprised me that I hadn't seen them before. Ruth would have noticed them right away. She would have felt humiliated on their behalf and seen cruelty in the hands that put them there. We had once left a fish restaurant because the walls were hung with nets and lobster traps. She wasn't a vegetarian, but she would, I knew, have pitied these animals and found it impossible to eat beneath them. And because I knew so well the mysterious pain that she would have felt, I began to feel it myself.

"What is it?" Flek asked.

He leaned forward, peering at me in concern. And in fact, something strange *was* happening. An enormous feeling of sadness had suddenly come over me and, to my astonishment, I felt my eyes fill with tears. I could not, of course, explain to Flek that, thinking so intently about Ruth, I had conjured her there in the Harvard Club. I couldn't tell him that Ruth, who cried so much, was crying now inside me, and that I, who never cried, was about to shed her tears.

"It's nothing," I said, and took a long sip of water.

"I know what Ruth's problem is," Flek said softly. "But what about you, Joseph? What's your wound? When are you going to speak about that?"

"What are you talking about?"

"I'm talking about your sister. Would you like to talk about your sister?"

I felt my face grow dark.

"Who told you about her!"

"What does it matter? *You* haven't. That's the interesting thing."

"Was it Ruth? Or Mrs. Simon?"

"It was Carol, if you must know. She mentioned it in passing. She thinks it's made you more sensitive to Ruth's needs. I'm sure that's true. But I think it's done more than that."

"What has it done?"

"Can't you see, Joseph? You're not just trying to save Ruth. You're trying to solve the riddle of female sadness itself. You're trying to solve the self-destructive urge of humanity. You're trying to crack the mystery of the body. Take it from someone who once tried to do these things for a living: it isn't possible. You've been hunting the white whale and it isn't going to end well if you don't take care of yourself."

I looked at my watch. It was 1:10. I had twenty minutes to get downtown.

"I've got to go," I told him.

"Joseph, why are you so afraid to talk about your sister?"

"I failed her," I said at last. "I'm not going to fail Ruth."

"You have to know you're not responsible for your sister's death."

"How can you be so sure?" I said. "You don't know anything." And with that I stood up.

Flek made no attempt to stop me.

"You'd better get to class," he said. He spoke casually, indifferently. "I'm going to stay and have another cup of coffee."

He seemed suddenly helpless in his low-slung chair, unable to rise and see me out. I looked down at him. It was a formal moment, and it felt final. He held out his large hand and I leaned down and took it.

"Thank you for lunch," I said.

Gripping my hand tightly in his, he drew me closer, so that I nearly fell onto the table. He looked up fiercely into my eyes, the same look of fixed purpose that I'd seen on the street, when he was barreling wrathfully down the sidewalk.

"Next time," he said in a taut undertone, "I won't talk to you about Ruth if you don't talk to me about Evelyn."

He knew her name!

He let go of my hand and I stumbled back awkwardly.

"Don't forget to return the jacket," he added, smiling with sudden warmth.

I nodded, hoisting my heavy knapsack onto my shoulder. Turning my back on Flek, I hurried out of the room.

Despite Flek's advice that I take Ruth into my confidence, and despite my own desire to do so, a week passed without my saying anything. In all that time Ruth and I scarcely had a meal together, let alone a conversation about food.

Ruth had suddenly become very busy. Almost every day I came home to find a message on the answering machine or a note stuck to the refrigerator, telling me that she had stayed downtown to attend a lecture at the New School, or that she and her friend Nadia had gone to an art opening. When she came home she'd insist that she'd had too much wine and cheese and crackers to eat another bite. I would have joined her at these events (though I hated art openings and disliked Nadia), but she didn't invite me and I felt that she was even more eager than usual to avoid letting me watch her eat.

When she came home, I confess, I was often quick to kiss her for the sole purpose of tasting her lips, absorbing the bouquet of her breath to see if she had in fact eaten and, if she had eaten, to tell, if I could, what had become of her meal. But I could deduce nothing.

Of course I continued to read her diary. Every morning, as soon as she left the house, I slid her top drawer open and peered in. I was more faithful to Ruth's diary than she was herself, for though Ruth sometimes skipped a day, I never did, and if the page was blank I wondered what might have driven her to silence.

After the lunch with Flek, I temporarily suspended my visits to the library. But all that week, with the regularity and anticipation with which some people lift *The New York Times* off the doorstep and unfold it on the kitchen table, I untied the lavender ribbon of Ruth's diary and carefully opened the clothbound book. Not war and famine and murder and fire but a daily dispatch from Ruth's inner life, her struggle with her body, with childhood, with sadness, with her mother, with food, with me, with herself. However narrowly focused, her entries issued from an inner world as vast and bottomless as the newsprint world of the *Times,* and beckoned to me with greater urgency. Her journal remained an infinite source of wonder and heartbreak, even when the entries were written with childlike simplicity.

"Oatmeal raisin cookies," for example, was all she wrote on Tuesday, followed by four words, printed over and over, like something a naughty student has to write on the blackboard: "I am a pig I am a pig I am a pig I am a pig." The entries could be maddeningly cryptic. On Wednesday she wrote simply: "Falling." The following day, "The naked dream again. Broadway. The lion." On Thursday she wrote nothing at all. On Friday I found an alphabet of obsessions.

Ruth would occasionally do this out loud when she was anxious, inspired by the little bear in *Bedtime for Frances,* one of her favorite children's books. When Frances can't sleep she makes up an alphabet song to calm herself: "A is for apple, B is for bear, C is for crocodile combing its hair . . ." But Ruth's alphabet was darker:

| | | | |
|---|---|---|---|
| A | is | for | appetite |
| B | is | for | bread |
| C | is | for | chocolate |
| D | is | for | dead |
| E | is | for | eating |
| F | is | for | fudge |
| G | is | for | gorging |
| H | is | for | head |
| I | is | for | illness |
| J | is | for | Joe |
| K | is | for | killing |
| L | is | for | love |
| M | is | for | mother |

| N | is | for | nuke |
|---|----|-----|------|
| O | is | for | orange |
| P | is | for | puke |

She didn't get past P. Had she run out of time? Out of rhymes? Or had she found the perfect word to end on, the word that canceled all others, so that there was no need to go further? I spent a few moments unsuccessfully trying to complete the alphabet for her. Q was a tricky letter, but Ruth was better with words than I was and I had a hard time believing that expert Scrabble player that she was, she couldn't come up with ten more letters. Clearly she'd ended on the word that for her served as a kind of final punctuation mark.

Equally disturbing was my own brief appearance on her list, flanked by "I" for illness and "K" for killing. This series intrigued me. She never called me "Joe" and the fact that she had shortened my name to fit me into her catalogue told me she must have been intent on listing me. But what was I doing there? Joe rhymed (sort of) with "love." But it was preceded by "illness." What in her mind was my relationship to her illness? The list was of things she liked: chocolate, bread, fudge. And of things she feared: illness, appetite. Which was I? Did she want to kill me? Love me? Or was love related to the word "mother," which followed it? That seemed unlikely. I took Ruth's list as a kind of code to be cracked, which is basically how I took everything about Ruth. Sensing this, perhaps, she had become more cryptic and self-protective than ever.

Several days after lunch with Flek I came home later than usual. I'd stayed downtown after class to celebrate another teacher's birthday and, though I'd called Ruth urging her to join us for dinner, she'd insisted she was tired and didn't feel up to the trip. I ate quickly and left early and when I got home I found the chain, which we used only at night, stretched across the door. Shades of the case of Laura! I hollered into the apartment, suddenly panicked. "Ruth! Ruth!" I shouted, and, when there was no response, was about to hurl myself against the door when Ruth ran dripping, a towel wrapped hastily around her, to let me in.

"I thought I'd have time to unlock it before you came home," she said. "You know I don't like showering when I'm alone in the apartment. I always use the chain."

It was true, of course, but I remained suspicious.

Ruth's showers lasted as long as most people's baths. She could stand, entranced, under the hot water for half an hour, oblivious of time. No wonder she felt vulnerable during such moments. But had she wanted the chain across the door only while she was in the bathroom? When Ruth went back to the bathroom, I headed straight for the kitchen.

Max, a silent witness, was sitting sphinxlike on top of the purring refrigerator, one of his favorite perches. If only cats could talk. Quickly I set to work examining the room.

The refrigerator, the countertops, the cabinets, the kitchen table, the garbage pail—a crime scene to be dusted for finger-prints, sifted for evidence. I had done this many times before without finding anything. Like the woman in the story who kills her husband with a frozen leg of mutton and then cooks it for dinner and offers it to the police, who are searching for the murder weapon, Ruth seemed constantly to commit the perfect crime, consuming the evidence—if indeed that's what she was doing—before I could figure out what had happened.

The average bulimic, I'd learned from my reading, could eat 5000 calories in an hour—twice what most people ate in two days. And that was just the average. Some consumed ten times that amount! Unless Ruth did her eating in odd places or at the oddest hours, unless she brought food home when I wasn't around and consumed it on the spot, I didn't see how she could possibly manage that kind of diet. But if my reading had taught me anything it was to doubt appearances. Q is for question . . .

What did I think I would find? I hunted with beating heart and mounting terror, as if I might pull from the crisper not a carrot or cucumber but the remains of an unholy feast, the white length of a shinbone. But this time, as I listened dis-tractedly to the distant rush of Ruth's shower, I discovered, buried under a suspiciously depressed layer of kitchen garbage, an empty container of ice cream (Ben and Jerry's New York Super Fudge Chunk). Inside it was another, and inside that, one more—like Russian dolls. And at the very bottom of the garbage—I went digging with both hands now—was one more.

My heart was racing. Should I run to the bathroom and confront Ruth with these excavations? She dreaded humiliation, but here was my chance to get things out into the open. And yet, did I need her confirmation? Could there be any question? The evidence was overwhelming. But how to explain my tunneling through the trash?

Ruth was still showering. The sound of rushing water reassured me, though usually I fretted about the length of her showers and poked my head in a couple of times to make sure she was all right. But today I left her alone while I considered what to do next. I had a powerful urge to talk to Flek and ask his advice. There was a wall phone in the kitchen. I could call if I hurried. But I decided against it. I hadn't liked the way our lunch had ended, the bargain he'd made as I said good-bye.

Suddenly, the water in the next room stopped. The whole apartment fell eerily silent. In a few moments, I knew, Ruth would appear. And still I stood, frozen, guiltily clutching the sticky evidence, wondering what to do.

Max roused me from my stupor. He leaped off the refrigerator and landed at my feet, lapping up a sweet, milky spill from one of the containers. He rubbed against my leg, begging for more. I thrust the containers back into the garbage, buried them as well as I could, and washed my hands quickly at the sink.

When Ruth at last appeared, warm and soothed by her long shower, her hair wrapped in a high, homemade turban, I had already put the kettle on. I decided to wait for a better moment.

And indeed, a few days later the subject came up by itself. It was Sunday, and Ruth and I were baking bread or, rather, Ruth was baking and I was assisting her. She often baked on Sundays. Though I generally helped her, and knew several of the recipes from *Beard on Bread,* the Bible of those Sundays, by heart, I was a mere factotum, sifting flour or measuring water as Ruth and James Beard directed.

There wasn't much talking. For one thing, Ruth usually had the stereo going. As with cleaning, she liked, while cooking, to move inside a strong beat. Our actions felt almost choreographed—we shared a sound track as if we were living in a movie, which lessened, for Ruth, the pull of her own physical reality and gave me an artificial feeling of vigor, the sensation of being inside the borrowed body of an athlete.

We talked as little as players on the same doubles team, but there was a physical bond of common purpose unbroken even by Ruth's irritability, inevitable where food was involved.

"Where did you put the wooden spoon? The big one, not that!" she would shout above the music. Or, "Don't squeeze the dough so much. Just use the heel of your hand." I knew her annoyance had nothing to do with me personally and I cultivated a controlled obliviousness that served me well. Her outbursts were the nails of a bed I lay on with the skill of a yogi: I made up in pride and discipline what I lacked in comfort.

At last the dough was ready. Ruth adjusted the knob of the oven to a perfect 350 degrees. She had a habit of kneeling before the stove as she turned the knob, like a safecracker listening for the tumble of locks. I greased two pans, and Ruth patted the dough into place, sliding the pans lovingly into the warm oven, putting her children to bed. We spoke in whispers and did not slam doors. The CD ended and there was silence.

I could almost hear the twin loaves rising, filling like lungs, taking a long slow final breath. The room was filled with the fertile odor of baking bread.

Ruth wiped her hands on her apron. A streak of white had gotten into her hair, as if she were going prematurely gray. She pried a little hardened dough off a nail and held her hands out before her, examining them. I had noticed her looking at her hands earlier, gloved elegantly in a fine dust of flour.

I would like to have taken a closer look at them, too. They were beautiful hands, full of slender strength, and I bent over and kissed the tips of her flour-dappled, tapered fingers. I wanted to examine the knuckles for the roughness I'd read was a sign of repeated induced vomiting. But Ruth turned from me to the sink and plunged her hands under a powerful stream of water.

I felt a dreamlike sense of dislocation as I stood a few steps behind her, watching her body bending over the sink. She was barefoot and dressed in an oversized football jersey that came down to the back of her thighs. Her hair was gathered up onto the back of her head, clamped in place with a large tortoiseshell clip that bit into her thick hair and held it. Her slender neck was exposed, bent so that two delicate vertebrae stood out. The wide opening of the football jersey disclosed a half circle of her smooth back—a freckle or two showing, stars in an early sky.

I was overcome, once more, with her vulnerability. How often had she told me that, growing up, she'd never expected to live past thirty. She'd never expected to find love or happiness or understanding. She'd never expected to feel worthy of love at all.

"Falling," her diary had said. She did look precarious, standing at the whispering sink, and I longed to spread a great net of love under her so that she never could fall.

I took a step closer to her with the intention of enfolding her in my arms, telling her that I loved her, putting my hands on her breasts and cradling her as I did sometimes in sleep. I wanted to tell her that I knew she had secrets and private sorrow, but what were these compared to love? I wanted to tell her that she was safe with me and that she always would be.

But I saw that she was crying, tears running quietly down her face as she washed the dishes.

"Ruth," I said, "what's wrong?"

"Nothing," she said, but even as she spoke the tears began falling faster and she choked back a sob.

I turned off the tap, as if that might stop her tears, though she only cried harder as I drew her away from the sink. I got a towel and, mechanically, she dried her hands.

"Ruth," I said, "talk to me. What's going on?"

Still she said nothing. She sniffled, trying without success to stop crying. I pulled her gently by the hand and she followed obediently, like a child. In the living room I sat on the couch.

"Come into my office," I said, lifting my arm and making room for her beside me.

She settled in next to me, resting her head on my lap. She lay curled up, eyes shut, as I stroked her hair and asked her again and again what was wrong.

"You're being so nice to me," she murmured.

"And why not?"

"I don't like myself very much right now," was all she said.

"I do, Ruth. I love you."

When I said "I love you" she sometimes gave me a searching, doubting look, but when she allowed herself to believe it her whole being glowed and her eyes grew big with wondering delight, like the eyes of a rescued child. She looked that way now. She had stopped crying. Something had been discharged that left her strangely peaceful. A kind of basking bliss lit her face, a gratitude that verged on tears. There was nothing I would not have done to keep that look on her face, to fill her heart and break the spell that so often trained her eyes away from mine. How could I ask about ice-cream containers when she looked at me like that?

"What do you love about me?" she asked.

"All of you."

"Be specific," she said, suddenly coquettish.

My eyes were drawn to her long smooth, waxed legs, charmingly knock-kneed, stretching out below me, but I thought it safer to start at the top.

"I love your hair."

"Too thick."

"I love your eyes."

"Too small."

"I love your nose."

"Too big."

"I love your cheeks."

"Too round."

I recited my litany, singing her praises, catechizing her in the love of her own body, trying to undo the dread alphabet I'd read not long before. She shook her head in disagreement after every compliment, but she seemed happy. The tears were gone and her face looked watered, clean, bright.

"I love your lips."

"Too dry."

"I love your chin."

"Too sharp."

"I love your neck."

"Too long."

"I love your arms."

"Too hairy." .

"I love your elbows."

"I never thought about my elbows," she said seriously.

"Well, you have beautiful elbows. And I love the insides of your elbows, which I don't know the name of."

"The underbow," said Ruth.

"I love your underbows." And I planted a kiss on the tender patch where doctors draw blood and junkies shoot up.

"My underbows are all right, I guess," she said.

"I love your hands."

"Yes," said Ruth, agreeing at last. "I do have nice hands." She held them up admiringly.

I admired them as well, and as I did I tried to see again if the backs of her hands were calloused.

"What are you doing?" Ruth asked, suspiciously.

I planted a kiss admiringly on her knuckles. It was impossible to tell, even brushing my lips against them. There was, perhaps, a certain chapped roughness, but washing dishes might as easily crack the skin there, and the weather had been raw the last several months. Did it have to be caused by the scrape of teeth?

"Joseph," she said again, somewhat uneasily, as I continued to study the back of her hand, "what are you doing?"

"I'm reading your future," I said.

"You're supposed to read my palm, not the back of my hand."

"Ah, that's where you're wrong," I said. "The back of the hand is even more expressive than the palm. Most people don't know that."

"Really?" she said, dubiously.

"Absolutely. Most people just don't know what to look for. But for those in the know, the back of the hand speaks volumes." I held her right hand up to my eyes for inspection.

"For one thing, you've been biting your nails again, haven't you? I thought you stopped."

Ruth withdrew her hand as if I'd bitten it.

"I'll stop again," she said.

I took her hand back. It fluttered in my own, an agitated bird. I wished I had a ring I could slide over the nibbled nail and rough knuckle, back to the web of her delicate hand. I wanted to band her like a bird so that I could never lose track of her.

"Long, slender fingers show an artistic nature," I said.

"Really?" she asked hopefully.

"Yes," I said. "And here, these fading lines on the middle knuckles, they show that the struggles of the past are going to disappear very soon."

Ruth said nothing. She had grown very serious and I noticed her eyes shining. If she hadn't been on her back, the tears would be flowing again.

Say something! I thought. Mention it now!

"What else?" said Ruth.

"You have a loving nature. A generous nature. But you can't always express everything you're feeling."

"That's true," said Ruth sadly. "But I'm trying. I want to."

"Yes, I can see that."

Coward! Ask her about the ice cream!

"Does it say I'll have children?"

"Oh yes," I said. "A lot of children. Beautiful and healthy."

She said nothing. I tried again to see if the skin was calloused around the knuckle.

"My hands are my favorite part of me," Ruth said suddenly. "They're the only part of my body I admire."

"Why is that?" I asked softly.

She ignored my question.

"I love working with my hands. Kneading. Beating eggs. Simple things," she said, apologetically. "I can't help it. I wish the rest of my body could be like my hands."

"Why is that?" I asked again.

"My hands obey me," she said darkly. "They do what I ask them to."

Her hands were still spread out in the air before her.

"Ruth," I said, "what do you ask them to do?"

She didn't answer me. She drew her hands into fists, the same little fists she had used to punch down the rising belly of the dough. I thought for a moment she was going to punch herself and almost reached out to stop her, but she unclenched her hands and covered her face with them. Was she about to start crying again? This was it!

"Ruth," I whispered, "I have a confession to make."

She uncovered her eyes. Surprisingly, she wasn't crying.

"You're in love with someone else."

"I'm in love only with you, Ruth—although frankly I do sometimes think the Ruth I love is different from the one you think you are."

"Don't be metaphysical," said Ruth. "Are you screwing a Russian or planning to leave me or something? Just tell me straight out."

"Of course not!" I was surprised by her bluntness. "But I've been . . . going to the library . . . without telling you."

"Oh God," said Ruth, with mock horror. "Not the library! How could you do that to me?"

At least I was cheering her up. She actually smiled.

"I know you're joking, Ruth," I said, "but the truth is, I went to the library to read about you."

"Me? Am I in the library?"

"I went to read about eating disorders."

Her eyes narrowed and she colored slightly.

"Really."

"Yes," I said.

"And why did you do that?"

"Because I want to help you. And you need help, Ruth."

She opened her mouth but no words came out. I braced for anger and insults, but none came.

"I know," Ruth said at last, in a small voice. "I've started binging." The very confession stuck in her throat. "Do you know what that means?"

"Well," I said, like a student being quizzed in class. "A binge is the rapid consumption of large amounts of food during a short period of time. It's defined as the consumption of two thousand calories or more during the span of one to two hours."

Somehow this sentence struck Ruth as funny. Or perhaps it was the general absurdity catching up with us. Whatever the case, Ruth, to my amazement and delight, began to laugh. "You really have been going to the library," she said at last.

"I told you," I said. "I'm a binge reader."

Ruth was laughing harder. I had begun to laugh too, more out of nervousness than because I found this funny, but Ruth was shaking with laughter. She laughed so hard that I became slightly alarmed. Tears had begun rolling down her cheeks.

"What made you go?" she said at last, blotting her eyes.

"I told you, Ruth. I want to help you. I want to understand you. Please let me help you. There's nothing to be ashamed of."

Ruth looked at me in a marveling, almost pitying way, stroking my arm.

"So?" she said. "Did you discover what's wrong with me?"

"As a matter of fact I did."

The smile faded from Ruth's lips. She said nothing.

"If you want," I said, "I can tell you what your problem is. Would you like me to?"

"No," Ruth said, bashful again and suddenly sitting up. I felt her getting ready to leave the couch altogether. She gave off the same gathering energy Max did when he was about to bound off your lap.

"You want to be a nude," I said.

"Excuse me?"

"You want to be a nude," I said again.

"Joseph, don't be offended, but it's been a strange day and I'm really not in the mood . . ."

"You don't understand," I said. "This is a philosophical observation."

"Of course it is," Ruth said, smiling again. She had grown more relaxed.

"No, really. I read about this in the library."

"And you learned that I want to be nude?"

"A nude. Or, more specifically, you don't want to be naked."

"What's the difference?"

"Naked," I explained, "is the natural form. The messy form we're born with and develop into. The bodily body. The one that sweats and thirsts and hungers. I think naked has a lot to recommend it, but art and advertising prefer the nude. The model posing is always naked. The portrait is of a nude. Do you get my meaning?"

"Sort of," said Ruth. She had grown distracted by Max, newly arrived, who, after a brief attempt to join us on the couch, lay down on the floor, raised a hind leg and began cleaning himself.

"Max is naked," said Ruth. "Right?"

"I disagree," I told her. "I think cats are nudes. They're not like people."

"Are you saying I want to be like Max?"

"Not exactly like Max. But Max always looks just right, doesn't he? He never goes out of style. He never looks too thin or too fat. He never has to look in the mirror. He never has dreams of being naked."

"How do you know I have dreams of being naked?" she demanded, startled.

"Everyone does," I told her quickly.

She looked at me skeptically.

"And is this information supposed to help me?"

"I haven't figured that part out yet," I confessed. "My research is in a kind of rudimentary state."

"You foolish boy," Ruth said, affectionately. "The answers aren't in the library."

Flek would have been proud of her.

I was feeling an enormous sense of release and possibility. For Ruth seemed not angry, as I had feared, but moved by my efforts to make sense of her life. She leaned over and kissed me softly on the lips. I had never felt so mysteriously close to her. I knew that I had crossed a threshold and stood on the brink of her body itself. Ruth lay back on my lap, stretched out like a small undiscovered country. She was going to take me in at last. I felt it. I would know her inner workings and unspoken secrets. My hours of reading had paid off. In my heart I thanked Flek, though had Ruth known he was responsible for sending me to the library she would have been furious and I would have lost her forever.

"What else did you learn in the library?" she asked. "It can't all have been about nudes. There must have something more practical."

And so I told her the stories of the new world I had been exploring. She lay listening, sometimes appalled—"Oh God, that's disgusting"—or nodding in agreement. She was amazingly knowledgeable about the subject and had actually read many of the same books. "I've heard some people try Prozac but I don't believe it's connected to depression, I just don't," she'd say, or "hormone therapy went out a long time ago."

But gradually I began to feel that our talk, even though it was taking place on a new level, wasn't necessarily going to accomplish anything.

"Ruth," I said at last. "What are we going to do?"

"There is something I'd like to try," she said. "Nadia told me about it."

"Nadia!" I said.

Ruth looked at me reproachfully and I bit my tongue. I did not wish to lose this new channel of openness so soon after finding it.

"I'm sorry," I said. "Tell me what she suggested."

Ruth told me that Nadia had persuaded her to attend a workshop for women who couldn't say no to food. Briefly, she sketched out the premise of the group. Though Ruth was a devout believer in analysis, she felt desperate enough to put her faith, this once, in behavior modification.

It was the philosophy of the workshop that people who binged or were obsessed with food lived in constant fear of its disappearance. They gorged like hunted animals who might not have a chance to stop and eat again. Love itself was at the root of this behavior, the therapist (I use the word loosely) told them. Fearing there would not be enough love, the patient turned to food and consumed it greedily. But the hunger was for love. Food was the compensation for affection never received, and since it was merely a substitute, it was never enough.

What was the answer? Go shopping. Buy everything you want, everything you secretly desire, everything you never had enough of. And not only that—buy twice as much, buy too much. Buy so that if you eat one box of Yodels you'll still have another in the cabinet. And when you eat one box, buy two more. And if you eat those two, buy four. Buy and replace geometrically so that it seems the very cookies in your cabinet have copulated and reproduced, the bread has bred and the fruit has multiplied.

And if you wish, buy dog food or a box of Little Friskies. No alimentary wish should remain secret, unanswered.

But whatever you buy, buy it in abundance.

The knowledge that there is more, always more, will sink in and curb the binging. No need to wolf down a carton of ice cream when you know there's another one there, waiting just for you.

Ruth was horrified by these instructions. She also found the idea intriguing.

I had not encountered anything in my reading to support what I took to be the crackpot notion that buying whatever you wanted was good for you. The treatment was based on the idea that if you had enough you'd stop wanting. How could I tell Ruth that I didn't believe this was true? That everything I'd read about hunger like hers indicated that its very nature was wanting too much? I couldn't. I merely listened and nodded, excited that we were embarking on an adventure together. She was sitting up beside me, reattaching the earring she'd removed so she could lie in my lap.

"Will you go with me, Joseph?" she asked shyly.

"Of course," I said at once.

"Tonight?"

"Absolutely."

"You're sure you don't mind."

"Not at all. I'll go anywhere with you."

She looked relieved and I felt flattered. But then her expression darkened.

"Dog food!" she cried, hiding her face in her hands in amusement, outrage and shame. "And believe me, there were people there who looked like they'd go for a can of Alpo. If Dr. Hallo knew I went there he'd skin me alive." A terrified look came into her eyes. "What if we meet him in the supermarket?"

"You can buy him a Ring-Ding," I said.

"It's not funny," said Ruth, but she was smiling and suddenly burst out laughing, a frenzied tear-filled excited fit, almost weeping. "Oh God, dog food! Dog food!"

I took her hand.

"You must really think I'm some kind of freak," she said.

"Not at all."

"I love you," she said.

"I love *you*."

"You're taking a big risk," said Ruth. "I might wind up looking like the ladies in the group."

"You won't," I assured her.

"But what if I do? Then what would you do?"

"I'll take my chances," I said. And I kissed her.

Mid-kiss she pulled away from me. I thought for a moment she'd lost it again, and braced for her tears, but then I smelled it too and tore after her into the kitchen.

Smoke poured out of the stove while Ruth, wearing two huge oven mitts, batted out the charred remains of the bread.

On the way to the supermarket Ruth lost all the ease and humor that confession had released. We stopped at a cash machine and both of us withdrew three hundred dollars. I had insisted on paying for half of whatever Ruth bought and this first extravagance at the cash machine made me feel the recklessness of the adventure. We each stuffed a fat green wad into our jeans pockets and held hands.

Broadway seemed unnaturally empty and threatening. It was close to midnight, and only the sidewalk vendors, their blankets spread with used books and old pornographic magazines, unmatched shoes and electric eggbeaters, were still there, encamped in doorways, sitting on cast-off beach chairs, wrapped in rags, sharing a bottle.

We headed for an all-night Food Emporium twenty blocks south. Ruth had wanted to reduce our chances of running into Dr. Hallo (unlikely, since he lived on the Upper East Side), and to eliminate unexpected encounters with friends or acquaintances. We moved, vulnerable, down Broadway, our pockets full of cash.

All my life I have loved supermarkets, from my earliest days, when I was small enough to ride the rumble seat of the shopping carts, pointing to every item my heart desired. When I was older I would race my sister down the sparkling aisles. Later, my mother would deputize us to shop with her, tearing her list in half and sending us off in opposite directions. My sister was a much more responsible shopper than I was—she compared prices on her own and always found the milk with the latest expiration date. I usually came back with the wrong kind of lettuce and an argument for the importance of Mallowmars.

When I was still in high school, I was a stockboy in Gristede's, my first job. On hot summer days I loved to step on the electric mat and enter the cool, ordered world of the supermarket. Like movie theaters, supermarkets have no windows, but you do not notice. They are their own environment. Aisle three—pet food, beer, crackers and soda—was my own. With my price gun and my razor for slicing the tops off boxes, I policed my aisle. I kept the puppy chow in line and the heavy bags of Kitty Litter neatly stacked. I called the women "Ma'am."

I taught a whole unit on supermarkets to my Russians, a subject that interested them keenly. They had not found the streets paved with gold but the walls of the A&P *were* paved with boxes of cereal and cans of soup and jars of jam. There were avalanches of apples, a rumbling abundance of cucumbers and peppers and melons of all sizes and shapes. "So many coffee," one of my students had told me, with tears in her eyes, recounting a trip to the supermarket. I had heard tell of another woman who had gone shopping her first day in America and actually passed out in a Brooklyn Red Apple, overcome by abundance the way tourists are occasionally overcome by art in the Uffizi and have to be removed by stretcher.

Once in the supermarket, Ruth put on sunglasses, which she'd brought as a joke but now wore, it seemed to me, with a genuine desire to hide. The Food Emporium, as big as Manhattan real estate prices allowed, was deserted.

"Let's leave, Joseph."

"Nonsense," I said. "We're already here. Don't be shy."

I did not want to lose the closeness we had shared in the apartment earlier that evening. I wanted to be inside her world, inside the secret domain of her dreams, her diary.

Though half of me was horrified, and though I had my doubts about the efficacy of the treatment, I did not want her to back out. I pried a shopping cart free and parked it in front of her. She gripped the round plastic bar mechanically.

"It's an assignment," I said. "Other people have done it. Relax. Feel free."

She took a few tentative steps. I had the sinister desire to push her along, to corral her through the aisles.

"Go on," I said, urging her on, eager to see what she would choose. But she did not want me walking beside her.

"Should I meet you back at the counter in an hour?" I offered.

"No," she said, suddenly unsure. "Just don't focus on me."

By the rules of the therapy, she should not have brought me along. She should have shopped in pure freedom. Whether it was an act of rebellion against the "appetite therapist" or merely fear of all that food—or whether it was because I had somehow been admitted into the inner chambers of her unhappiness—I do not know, but I was moved and flattered that she had let me join her.

She did not want me to watch her make her selections. In her shades, with me walking a few yards behind, she looked like a movie star trailed by a bodyguard. And isn't that what I was, more than anything? Her bodyguard?

Shy at first, Ruth chose tentatively. Her practiced restraint was too much to throw off all at once, to admit that cottage cheese and salad and rice cakes (only two-and-a-half calories each!) were a lie. She trembled in front of the superabundant avenues. She seemed paralyzed, glancing over her shoulder at where I browsed among the cereals a few paces away. She strolled empty-handed down the aisle, reconnoitering, touching nothing, while I remained, guarding the all but empty cart.

I wanted to appear as unobtrusive as possible, but there were no shadows to hide me. It was high noon under the fluorescent lights. I wished for wider aisles, with little chairs and tables set up so you could sit down from time to time as you could in the big bookstores. Why not a nibbling table? My mother often put a box of animal crackers in my hands as I rolled, enthroned, backward down the long aisles. Why shouldn't adults experience the same delicious ease?

Ruth had gotten nowhere. She stood only a few feet away from me, dazed, staring up at Froot Loops and Lucky Charms.

"Let me help you," I said, coming up to her. "After all, I'll see whatever you buy in the apartment, too."

"I know," she said. We were whispering as if in a library. A man with a bucket on wheels and a mop was washing the checkered floor at the far end, glancing at us from time to time.

So far she had two avocados and a box of Pepperidge Farm Orange Milano cookies. We'd be there till dawn if she continued at this rate.

"Why don't I get a cart," I said, "and whatever you take, I'll take a second. It's all your food, but I'll buy it. I'll be your double."

"Okay," Ruth said, compliant. She was still reluctant, embarrassed, and yet excited too.

I ran to the front of the store and returned with a cart. She had already added four tiny jars of Gerber's applesauce. Baby food. Was she going to eat her way up from childhood—or back into it? She saw me staring into the bright cage.

"Don't make me self-conscious!" she said, her voice trembling. "This is very hard for me."

"Why should you be self-conscious?" And I reached in and took two of the four jars and an avocado. "Should we get a second bag of cookies?"

"Don't suggest things," said Ruth. "You'll throw me off."

"Sorry."

"Do you think we should?"

"Up to you."

We did. Shyly, Ruth overcame her inhibitions as we wove up and down the aisles, and the walls of food began tumbling into our wagons. We wheeled together over the new-mopped floor, pushing our carts like twin baby carriages, though the contents suggested twin teenage monsters waiting at home. Our carts rose with Devil Dogs and Twinkies and ice cream in supermarket cinderblock-sized containers, bright maraschino cherries and corn chips and pretzels and Brie and Boursin.

We passed honeydew melons heaped like cannonballs, and I remembered Albert, who worked in fruit during my Gristede's days, lying to shoppers about the ripeness of his melons. Ruth wasn't interested in fruit.

Silently I wheeled my cart behind her like a shadow, filling it identically without asking or reacting, not wishing to throw her off or embarrass her. I dared not leave her for a moment. Her wagon wound a golden thread through the labyrinth of aisles. Was she the maiden or the Minotaur?

"Ruth, you don't drink milk," I said, in spite of my vow of silence.

"Yes, I do," she told me, in a quiet, faraway voice, and without another word I lifted a second huge container and placed it, cold and beaded with moisture, into my own cart. We also took a six-pack of Guinness stout each, which, I think because of the name, Ruth thought was more fattening than regular beer.

We shopped and shopped. While the Muzak played and the few lone customers came and went, Ruth and I stormed the high-stacked ramparts of food. We circumnavigated the supermarket with fixed purpose, voyaging through every food group and climate. We found frozen vegetables sleeping under permafrost and giant turkeys crusted with supermarket snow. There were hothouse vegetables, even fresh flowers.

Ruth behind her sunglasses seemed hypnotized. Her hands trembled slightly. She moved like someone in a dream, humorless, intense, deliberate. I, however, had never felt so awake. I passed behind her through the aisles of plenty, my blood singing. At last! I wasn't merely helping her shop, I was helping to heal her. The rising mound of food in my cart seemed like a testament to health. Mrs. Simon had said I was "a nourisher" and here I was providing. Joseph the provider. Or so I told myself.

The contents of my wagon were by now as heavy as a man. I thought uneasily of Flek, as if I was pushing his chair and not a shopping cart. I wondered what he would have made of this excursion. I did not think he would have approved, and yet surely these food-packed aisles were closer to real life than the dusty stacks of the library. And hadn't Ruth finally shared her thoughts with me?

But Ruth had stopped speaking, and I noticed that the more she bought, the more constricted she became. Was there a great release coming or an explosion?

"I shouldn't be here," she murmured suddenly, as we passed pet food. "I shouldn't be doing this."

But we kept on. Down down down we moved. Spaghetti-Os and Cap'n Crunch and Nutter Butter Peanut Butter Cookies (oh the added indignity of brand names!) and cheddar Goldfish and Nilla Wafers and little square cans of specialty coffees, scented and flavored: "Dutch Treat," "Vienna Special," "Mocha Delight"—down the stocked lanes, which, like the American highway, promised freedom but bred sadness, paved with abundance but bringing no escape, no satisfaction. There were no supermarket statistics but plenty of casualties—the starved, the bloated, the unhappy gorging before rented movies, children microwaving dinner alone, lovelorn teenagers gobbling chocolate and sometimes vomiting it up.

I began to feel afraid as we pushed our mountainous carts down the sterile lanes. I told myself that this is what she wanted—this overabundance, not abstention or starvation, is her inner desire. This is health. This will heal her. Still, I was afraid.

What was Ruth going to do with all this food? Again I shuddered inwardly. When would it stop? Would we be here till dawn? Would we ever go outside again?

But I had nothing to fear, for, in the back row of freezers, Ruth parked her wagon.

"Let's get out of here, Joseph."

"Okay," I said, turning my cart around.

"Leave it!" Ruth ordered frantically.

"What?"

"I'm not taking this shit home," she said. She was already walking swiftly down detergents and cleansers, the safest aisle in the store. I abandoned my cart with a little push and a feeling of release and caught up to her.

"Ruth, what about the workshop?"

"Fuck it," said Ruth. "Nadia's crazy if she thinks this works."

Like two criminals, we slid past the checkout counter. The sleepy woman at the counter ignored us. The door slid open and we were outside in the chill night air. I was dizzy and a little nauseated. God knows how Ruth felt. She was breathing heavily, practically panting.

"Ruth," I said. "Ruth."

She was crying, but she would not talk to me. I stopped a cab and we sped home up the giant aisle of Broadway.

All the way home she wept, while I held her hand, failing to calm her.

Only when we were home and Ruth was sitting on the bed did she speak.

"How could I do that?" she wailed. "I've ruined everything."

"What have you ruined?" I asked. "Nothing. We didn't even take it home."

"I'm such a pig! How could I do that?"

"But it was an assignment. You were supposed to do it. It wasn't your idea."

"I'd been so careful. I'm so ashamed."

"It was an assignment, Ruth."

"It wouldn't have worked."

"How do you know?"

"I know, Joseph, I know."

"But how?"

"Because I'm bottomless, Joseph. I'm bottomless!"

She did not look bottomless to me. She looked small and sad and finite. I wanted to take her in my arms, but when I touched her hand she pulled it away.

"How do you know?" I demanded again.

She was out of reach, staring off in transported misery, unwilling to be touched or consoled.

"Do you know why I bought two gallons of milk?" she said, finally.

I shook my head no, though I remembered reading that downing large quantities of liquid helped in the subsequent elimination of food.

She looked away and said nothing for a long time.

"Why?" I coaxed. I wanted to hear her say it.

"I would have eaten it all, Joseph. I would have eaten it and . . . gotten rid of it. The milk helps. I used to use it in high school."

She spoke in a hoarse whisper as if she had already consumed and vomited up the food we had almost bought.

"But Ruth," I said gently, "I thought that was okay in this program. It doesn't matter what you do with the food as long as you replace it. It takes time."

"I know *now*, Joseph," she said in a tiny, hard voice. "I don't need to see over time. I'm bottomless."

And suddenly, a thrill of fear went through me, despite the assurances I had given her. In that instant I felt in her something inhuman—a hard, alien particle in her otherwise soft, familiar presence. I realized that she was telling me the truth.

Spring

After the Food Emporium fiasco, Ruth seemed to intensify, if such a thing was possible, the spartan rigor of her meals. She spent hours working out to her exercise video or jumping rope. She brooded more, laughed less. She was punishing herself, I believe, for those two carts full of food, fasting off the contents as if she had actually consumed them.

The closeness we had enjoyed that Sunday baking bread had been replaced by a less communicative but even more compelling closeness. We were like accomplices in a terrible crime who both knew where the body was buried. There was an unspoken bond, an inner allegiance. I felt strangely twinned with her.

This is not to say that I didn't notice, at times, signs of mistrustfulness creeping into her glances. I don't believe Ruth blamed me for the supermarket excursion—how could she?—but I was, I believe, a constant reminder of her humiliation.

And I won't deny that I continued, the moment Ruth left the apartment, to consult her journal. The week following our trip to the supermarket, however, there was nothing to read. I took this to be another form of fasting. By midweek, I had gone back to the library.

What else could I do? Ruth's diary was the master text to which other writings were mere commentary, but the book was blank. And so I plunged into articles with titles like "Metabolic and endocrine investigations in women of normal weight with the bulimia syndrome"; "Psychoneuroendocrine investigations in 115 cases of female anorexia nervosa at the time of their maximum emaciation"; "A treatment of bulimia with monoamine oxidase inhibitors." Having exhausted Flek's list, I was now uncovering titles of my own.

The difference this time was that Ruth knew where I spent my mornings. In the evenings she would sometimes ask me what I had read, though she was far more pessimistic than I was about the possibility of uncovering useful information. More than that, a kind of exhaustion, a resignation had set in. Her old protective anger was gone. I was inside her secret and she no longer fought as hard to keep me out. Her illness, whatever it was, had become, more than ever, joint property.

Meanwhile, I felt myself growing more and more desperate. Like a gambler, I could not keep away from the library. The less I found the more I wanted. I'd go through one stack of books, cash them in at the return desk and get another. Chemical, cultural, historical, biological—each explanation offered a partial view but nothing I found in the library gave me the key. Was it gender? Genes? Genesis? The story in the Garden of Eden still expressed the paradox best: we reach for the apple because we want more. And we have wanted more since we reached for the apple.

When I didn't read, I looked at pictures. Sir Kenneth Clark's *The Nude* was almost always on the table before me. When I wearied of bleak statistics I refreshed myself with *La Baigneuse blonde,* the loving portrait Renoir painted of his plump wife sitting naked and unashamed on a beach in Sorrento. Or I turned to Titian's *Venus,* standing thigh-deep in water, wringing the brine out of her long, loose hair. Inevitably, though, I'd wind up in the chapter called "Alternative Traditions," examining grim, Gothic bodies tumbling naked into hell.

On such a morning, about ten days after my trip to the supermarket with Ruth, I was sitting in the library, my head buzzing with facts and names and statistics, my eyes blinking away images of nudes from Clark's book. It was still early, but I hadn't been able to do much real reading and had soon resorted to my familiar companions, sly Eves and seductive Aphrodites and melancholy Virgin Marys in every shape and style. I discovered that I had been absentmindedly making naked doodles in my notebook, trying to capture the lines of

Ruth's body. What I saw on the page alarmed me: faces without features floating above necks and arms and breasts of different size, scribbled obsessively and half-unconsciously over and over. I decided to call Flek.

I left my books and backpack on the table—I'd developed an odd trust for my fellow readers—and went downstairs. From one of the wooden booths in the basement, hot and close as a confessional in an old church, I dialed Flek's number.

He was not in his office, but I found him at home.

"Joseph, I was wondering if I was ever going to hear from you again. How are you?"

"I went shopping with Ruth," I said. "It was a disaster. We filled two carts with food and then left it all behind."

"Whose idea was that?"

"Nadia's. She's a friend of Ruth's who learned about this approach to eating where you don't deny yourself what you want, you simply buy everything you crave and keep the house stocked with food all the time. Gradually, you start eating like a normal person because you lose your fear that you won't have enough."

"What a stupid idea," said Flek.

"I know," I said. "I should have stopped her, but I was so happy that she wanted me to come along. We'd had a very nice talk earlier that evening. I told her about the library, as you suggested."

Flek was silent.

"I took your advice. And it seemed to be working, but then we went shopping and it all fell apart. It was the strangest trip to the supermarket I've ever had."

"Joseph, how about stopping by this morning? You've got a couple of hours before class."

"I can't," I said.

"Why not? Are you calling from the library?"

"No," I lied. "I'm home. I can't get away. I'm expecting the plumber."

"Did Evelyn starve herself to death?" he asked abruptly.

I knew when I called him that he would ask me about my sister, but hearing her name was still a shock. The phone booth was hot and I had closed the hinged door for privacy. It was getting hard to breathe.

"Joseph?" Flek repeated. "I asked you something."

"If I tell you, will you talk to me again about Ruth?"

But Flek only repeated his question.

"No," I said. "She didn't."

"Did she have a problem with food?"

"No. I don't think so. I mean, she was always dieting, but she wasn't like Ruth."

"What was she like?"

It struck me that I wasn't really sure.

"Was she depressed?"

"Sometimes. But she was also very cheerful. Very helpful. She worked in my parents' office. I never wanted to. I wanted my afternoons free. She'd go organize the files or straighten out the magazines in the waiting room. She even filled in for Gladys over Christmas vacation."

"Who's Gladys?"

"She assisted my father during extractions. She handed him the instruments and worked the suction. She put her hand on the patients' foreheads when they freaked out. My sister was able to do all those things. She was particularly good at comforting scared patients. My parents always talked about it over dinner. They were very proud of her."

"I'll bet they were," Flek said.

"My sister loved being part of their world. She was a really good student, but she loved being able to say, 'How's Mr. Fletcher's abscess—still infected?' My father actually talked to her when she talked about patients. And if she didn't go to the office, she'd start dinner while my parents were at work, and set the table so my mother wouldn't have to. Or make me set the table, which I hated."

"You didn't know how she felt inside."

"Actually I did know."

"How did you know?"

It had become unbearably hot in the phone booth, which seemed to be above some kind of heating duct.

"I don't want to talk about that now. I called because I'd like to talk about Ruth."

But at this point the operator came on and announced that five more cents were required.

"I thought you were home," said Flek. "Where are you—the library?"

I didn't answer.

"Let me call you back," said Flek. "What's the number?"

But the number on the phone was scratched out. And I didn't want him to call me back.

*Please deposit five cents . . .*

"Get out of the library," Flek shouted over the annoying atonal music that accompanied the operator's request. "Come see me."

The connection broke and I hung up the phone, which immediately began to ring. It was still ringing as I left the booth.

What was Evelyn like? Flek wanted to know. Why was that such a hard question? I had, after all, lived in the same house with her for fourteen years. But I lived with Ruth, too, and did I know—really know—what she was like? What, for example, was she doing right now? Where was she? What was she thinking?

But even as I wondered about her I knew, with eerie certitude, that she was in the library. She had asked me that morning if I was planning to go and I had admitted I was. Suddenly I knew why she'd asked. When I returned to room 315 I sensed, even before I saw her, that Ruth was in the reading room. She had found my knapsack and coat and was sitting in my chair, bent over the table with great intensity.

At the sight of her, a bolt of joy shot through me. The lonely hopelessness I had been feeling a moment before vanished. I wanted to shout her name—impossible in the dream-silence of the library. I walked quickly to where she sat, kneeled down beside her and touched her arm. She had been completing the weird sketches I'd made in my notebook, adding faces to the strange bodies, and she jumped when I touched her. As soon as she turned and saw me she smiled.

"What are you doing here?" I asked.

She put her finger to her lips and wrote, in my notebook, "I've come to rescue you."

*She* had come to rescue *me*. I was thrilled to see her handwriting, so familiar to me from her diary, appear in my own notebook. I kissed the hand that held the pen and then I kissed her lips. I felt half inclined to kiss the words on the page. The man across the table, staring at us over Plato's *Republic,* cleared his throat.

"Time to go," Ruth whispered.

Flek's questions to me about Evelyn, which had been reverberating in the back of my mind, vanished. Ruth had found me. As I pulled my coat on, I felt a new surge of hope. It was lunchtime and I felt certain that Ruth would join me—we never ate lunch together during the week, and I would sometimes wonder if she even ate lunch. Maybe the shopping experiment had indeed produced some unintended benefit. I began thinking of all the places nearby where we might eat. I had barely an hour before I had to teach.

But Ruth had not risen. She was staring across the reading room at what seemed to be a distant object.

"Ruth," I whispered, but she put her hand on my arm to silence me, indicating with a nod of her head that I should follow her gaze.

Sitting not two tables away was the focus of Ruth's attention. It was a woman, though it wasn't so much *her* that I saw as her outline, for a great band of late-morning light fell across her from one of the high windows, illuminating her from behind.

Her hair was pulled tight, but the sunlight set it ablaze around her darkened face, giving each stray strand a tungsten glow that formed a golden halo. She was looking down at a book that must have rested on her thighs, though the table obscured my view. She stared straight down into her own lap.

Her face was in shadow, but it wasn't her face that had captivated Ruth. The downward tilt of her head seemed to stretch and flatten her upper body. Her breasts made not the slightest dent in her tight-fitting shirtfront. Even with its turtleneck top doubled over, I could see, could almost feel, that her neck was unnaturally thin, giving her head, with its added burden of sunlight, an enlarged look.

My heart began to race with excitement. This woman might have been the risen ghost of Catherine of Siena starving herself in her medieval cloister; the emaciated Misses A, B and C, whose gaunt images had accompanied William Gull's 1853 lecture to the Royal Society at which he had first coined the term "anorexia nervosa"; the manipulative Mollie Fancher—"The Brooklyn Enigma"—whose lean figure had appeared in etchings that captivated American readers in the nineteenth century. This woman, conjured by all my reading, looked flat enough to have been pressed like a forgotten wildflower between the pages of a book. But what excited me most wasn't the presence of this woman, but Ruth's fascination with her. What did it mean?

Ruth was still staring, and as she stared the woman stirred in her seat and stretched, raising the book she had been reading in both hands and lifting it high above her head. It caught the light for a moment and I tried to see what it was.

"Don't stare," Ruth wrote impatiently in my notebook. She had lost the playful manner she'd had when I first met her. She was now grave and focused.

The woman set the book down on the table, and, looking neither right nor left, started to stand. She pressed down on the table as if she were raising herself up out of a swimming pool. When she had finally risen she stood very straight, pulling back her shoulders at an almost military angle.

There was something exhausted and invigorated about her at the same time. Taking up her book, she walked over to the returns desk. She wore, in addition to the dark-green turtleneck, a pair of navy running pants of some shiny material, not cut at all loose though somehow baggy on her thin legs. Their elastic gripped her above sharp ankles. She was wearing brown-and-blue argyle socks.

As she passed not far from our table, Ruth, who had not taken her eyes off the woman, suddenly let out a low gasp.

"What's wrong?" I whispered. "You look like you've seen a ghost."

"Shhh," Ruth hissed. Snatching up the pen, she scribbled hastily into the notebook: "I know her."

I was bursting with curiosity but Ruth would not talk to me in the library. She sank a little lower in her chair to avoid detection.

The woman, after returning her book, had gone back to her place; she stood there for a moment looking down at the table, as if she were saying grace.

I gathered my things, zipped up my knapsack and hurried to the returns desk. The book the woman had been reading was still there. *The Golden Cage: The Enigma of Anorexia Nervosa,* by Hilda Bruch. I recognized it at once. It had been in my hands only a week before.

*The Golden Cage* was published in the late seventies, when anorexia was just becoming widely known as an illness. I had copied the first paragraph into my notebook and knew it practically by heart. For me it was like the opening sentences of the Communist Manifesto—"There is a specter haunting Europe"—with its eerie, grim, prophetic tone:

> New diseases are rare, and a disease that selectively befalls the young, rich, and beautiful is practically unheard of. But such a disease is affecting the daughters of well-to-do, educated, and successful families, not only in the United States but in many other affluent countries. The chief symptom is severe starvation leading to a devastating weight loss; "she looks like the victim of a concentration camp" is a not uncommon description.

The woman in the library fit the description. But who was she? How did Ruth know her? And, though anorexics loved to read about themselves, why was she reading an old book on the subject? I did not like the change she had wrought in Ruth, who, clutching her coat, was surreptitiously watching this woman as she threw a cape over her shoulders that added to her awkward, angular elegance. She began walking toward the exit and as soon as she passed our place, Ruth sprang to her feet and followed her.

I followed Ruth following her, half convinced we would wind up at a secret door to an unknown passageway in the library where the riddle of appetite was answered. The woman merely nodded at the man checking bags at the security post on the way out of the reading room—he could have frisked her with a glance. Ruth, who had only her pocketbook, was quickly allowed through, whereas I had to stop, unzipping and displaying the contents of my messy knapsack. If Ruth decided to speak to this woman I didn't want to miss a word.

Ruth was waiting for me, alone, at the top of the stairs. She seemed shaken. I put my arm around her.

"Are you all right?" I asked.

She nodded, without speaking.

"Did you talk to her?"

"I wanted to," she said. "I just couldn't."

"Who is she?"

"Caroline Barnes. I knew her a little in high school, before she dropped out. She weighed seventy pounds then. She should be dead or better by now." Ruth spoke telegraphically, as if she were still jotting things in my notebook.

"Has she been like this all these years?"

Ruth shook her head. "I don't see how. Maybe."

"How about we get some lunch," I said. "You can tell me about Caroline Barnes."

But Ruth ignored my suggestion. With a disconcerting look of determination, she said, "You want to learn about Caroline? We're going to follow her."

"I don't think that's a very good idea."

But Ruth was already moving quickly down the stairs and I confess I had no desire to stop her. I remembered her telling me that when she herself had been anorexic many years before, she and all the other skinny girls had followed each other around, sitting together at meals and keeping mental score of who managed to eat the least.

We caught up with Caroline on the grand marble staircase leading down to the main lobby, slowing our pace so that we wouldn't overtake her. Ruth walked behind me in case Caroline turned around, but she showed not the slightest interest in her surroundings. She moved serenely down the marble steps as if she owned them and was descending to the door of her mansion to have a word with the butler. The fixed tilt of her head would have sat well in one of the gilded frames on the wall, and I had a feeling she could match iron will for iron will with the tough robber barons hanging there.

And yet there was something fragile about her. When she rested a bony hand on the broad marble banister I worried that her balance was delicately maintained and wondered if I was close enough to catch her if she fell. Her ankles wobbled in her Nike running shoes. Nevertheless she was moving fast, and Ruth, afraid of losing her, poked me gently from behind.

The security guard at the front exit let her go with a nod like the guard upstairs. Ruth, watching her through the glass door, gave the woman a head start and then passed through herself. I took longer and confess that this time it was intentional, dawdling as I zipped up my bag and coat. No good could come from this adventure. But what if Ruth simply vanished in pursuit of this phantom from her past? I began to run down the granite stairs that led to Fifth Avenue.

To my relief, Ruth was waiting for me beside one of the lions.

"Well," I said, taking her hand and kissing her, "that was exciting. Let's go get lunch."

"No," said Ruth. "You want to understand something about hungry women? I'll show you."

She started walking quickly, tugging me along. The day had grown suddenly overcast. The sky was white, the wet smell of snow muffling the mood of early spring. The woman was nowhere in sight.

"She turned up Fifth," Ruth said.

"I'm sure she's in a cab by now," I said. "Or the subway."

"First lesson," said Ruth. "Anorexics always walk. We'll find her."

And sure enough we soon caught sight of Caroline Barnes moving through the midday crowd. Her gait was high and light and awkward, like a wading bird in water, moving on high-stepping hollow legs.

"See?" said Ruth. She had put her sunglasses on, though they weren't needed. She was reacquiring her supermarket look, an Ahab intensity that both fascinated and frightened me. Instead of eating lunch together, as I had hoped, we were following this starving woman. Was I responsible for having drawn Ruth first to the library and then into this bizarre pursuit?

"I don't want to lose her," she said, hurrying down the sidewalk. Ruth, I realized—not for the first time—was in better shape than I was.

"Where do you think she's going?"

"She's not going anywhere," said Ruth. "She's just going. She has no destination. No goals except not to eat. The battle with hunger is a full-time job."

I was used to Ruth writing about herself in the third person in her diary and I felt she was describing herself as well as Caroline.

"Is your battle with hunger a full-time job?"

"Do I look like her?" Ruth snapped.

I assured Ruth she did not, but the exchange was unsatisfactory. I knew that Ruth had many of the residual characteristics of an anorexic without allowing herself to become emaciated. But for all I knew she worked just as hard, harder perhaps, for she managed to look normal. What, precisely, did she feel inside? Would she, describing Caroline, tell me how she felt, or only recall how she had been once?

"What's it like?" I asked, panting beside Ruth, "to be hungry all the time?"

"It's terrifying," Ruth said. "But it's also exhilarating. Everyone tells you that you need to eat but you don't. You don't need food. Of course, you're a prisoner, but you're also free. You can do things most people can't do. You feel almost omnipotent. Most people diet and cheat, they bend. Not you. You go all the way."

It was difficult to read Ruth's expression as she told me this, what with the dark glasses and her constant darting looks to keep Caroline in view.

It's harder to track someone on the streets of New York than you might think, especially in midtown, where the push and bustle of office workers flows into the stream of Fifth Avenue shoppers and eddies around sidewalk hawkers. I dodged and danced along the sidewalk after Ruth who seemed afraid that if she took her eyes off Caroline for a second she would be gone. But there was something so distinct about her carriage, so sharp about her image, that we never lost her for long, even when we lagged by half a block. Her skinny figure stood out and led us on, a compass needle pointing north.

She disappeared in front of the Plaza Hotel. Ruth looked panicked, wondering where she might have gone. She swept the milling crowds with desperate eyes, spinning in all directions. Horses and buggies lined the park. The horses were idle at this season and this hour, munching feed or merely standing, a foreleg balanced with surprising delicacy on the front edge of a hoof. One of the cabbies, a smooth-faced man, opened the door of his carriage and gestured inside with his frayed top hat.

"Let's," I said, suddenly eager to interrupt Ruth's chase. I'd miss work, but so what? A romantic ride in the park would be far better than this mad chase. And yet the chase too had a certain romance. Ruth gripped my arm tightly all of a sudden.

"There!" she said, pointing.

I saw our fugitive fording Fifth, diagonally, treading gingerly until she got to the other side. She headed east along Sixtieth Street. Holding hands, we dashed across after her. An angry cab honked and I hoped she would not look back—but she seemed dead to street noises.

On Madison it was smoother going. Caroline seemed not more relaxed but more distracted by the street life, glancing occasionally at the expensive art galleries and shops. Passersby seemed hardly to notice her, though her bearing was regal. She might have been invisible as she moved along with her oddly light, almost bouncing tread, her feet only pretending to touch the ground.

"Is she in pain?" I asked. "She looks kind of unstable."

"She's probably light-headed," said Ruth. "I doubt she's in pain."

"But what about electrolyte imbalance? And swelling of the joints? Edema?"

"*Edema,*" said Ruth. "See, you do that kind of reading, you don't learn shit. You're not thinking about your *joints* when you're like Caroline."

"What are you thinking?"

"You're *not* thinking. Your body's going *food food food* and your brain's going *no no no.*"

"Aren't there all kinds of secret thoughts? Beliefs that need to be reconditioned before you can get well?"

"Joseph, you really don't understand this. You know how in the movie *The Seventh Seal*—which my mother took me to when I was *nine*—Death comes to take the Knight and the Knight says, 'First tell me your secrets.' And Death smiles and says, 'I don't have any secrets.' That's what makes Death so horrible. He really doesn't have any secrets. Look at Caroline. She doesn't have any secrets either. You know everything you need to know about her at a glance. Before you're fully sick, maybe, and while you're getting sick, sure, you hide things. But when you're inside the illness you have nothing to tell. A shrink won't even talk to you till you gain ten pounds. That's why they force-feed you like a goose on a farm."

I remembered the growing blanks in Ruth's diary and considered what she had said about the illness having no secrets. But here she was, talking to me now. Talking more, in fact, than she had in a long time. Not about herself, of course—but could I be certain of that? Was she trying to communicate something through her skinny friend?

Caroline Barnes paused in front of an antique store where I thought she was looking at a grandfather clock, but realized, when we passed by a few moments later, that she had been looking at her own reflection in an oval mirror framed in gold.

"Note the mirror," said Ruth. "Narcissism. That's all you think about. How you look. It's a tyranny. And yet . . ."

And yet what? I glanced at my own face in the mirror and saw an unfamiliar, transfixed expression. I hurried on.

Caroline forged on and did not stop again until she passed a Mrs. Field's Cookies on Seventieth Street, where, to my surprise, she went inside.

"Don't worry," said Ruth, "she's just going in for the aroma."

"To torture herself," I said.

"It's not torture," said Ruth. "She's proving to herself she can withstand the temptation. And believe me, she can."

There was a note of admiration in her voice I didn't like.

"Like the devil sending Saint Anthony a naked woman," I said. "For her it's cookies, right? I read in *Holy Anorexia* . . ."

"Enough with the medieval saints," said Ruth. "It's really simple. Embarrassingly simple."

"She's hungry, but she won't eat?" I ventured.

"Alimentary, my dear Watson," said Ruth. "You're catching on. Here she comes . . ."

At Eightieth Street she looked in at E.A.T. Gourmet Foods, the breads stacked up in the window. There, too, she entered, spun around and left with a kind of orchestrated dance step.

The traffic light changed and we almost lost her again, but not before realizing that she was heading West on Eighty-fifth Street, back toward Fifth Avenue. We tracked her across Fifth, where I thought for a moment she was going to visit the Met, for she doubled back downtown and paused at the foot of the long flight of stone steps leading up to the museum. She began running up the steps, two at a time.

"She'll come back down," said Ruth with assurance. "She's just burning calories."

And sure enough, down she came, running with purposeful but stumbling steps, cape flapping behind her. Her mouth was moving strangely.

"Is she *singing*?" I asked.

"Yes," said Ruth. "An old trick. You burn more calories when you sing and exercise."

Caroline lurched past, dangerously close to where we stood, a strange murmuring music coming from her, though I couldn't make out any words. She slowed to a walk and, like Holmes and Watson, except that we were holding hands, Ruth and I took off after her. Caroline did not seem tired, and continued to hold herself very erect, as if she still enjoyed the perspective of a woman at the top of the steps of the Metropolitan.

From my reading (*Gray's Anatomy*) I had learned that the small intestine of the average person was twenty feet long, the large intestine was five feet long, both packed in economically. But what if we were unfurled to full size? Our insides are bigger than our outsides. Thought is larger than the brain.

Appetite is larger than the stomach. How big would this woman in front of me be if she were as large as her hunger? Taller, I imagined, than the trees flanking Central Park. She would have to get down on all fours to peer into the window of a bakery shop.

She kept on walking up Fifth, past the Guggenheim and the Cooper-Hewitt Museum, walking faster now on her strong, storky, herky-jerk legs until she came to the break in the park that led up to the track around the reservoir. She headed up the steps, her blue cape flapping in the chill air.

"She's going for a run!" said Ruth. Again I heard the note of admiration.

The track was uncrowded at this hour. Every now and then a die-hard runner flew past or, occasionally, a slower pair, talking haltingly as they went. A few people stood off to one side of the track, skipping rope or stretching, and Caroline began to limber up. She pressed her hands against the top of a bench, working the taut cable of her Achilles tendon and the overtaxed muscles that, in the absence of food or fat, nourished her body in what I knew to be the self-cannibalization of advanced anorexics.

The harsh lines of her figure spoke of the triumph of geometry over biology. She had succeeded in reducing herself to angles and planes. Did blood really flow beneath the skin stretched taut under those clothes? It was hard to imagine. She had squared the circle of the female form, corrected the chaos of the flesh with some invisible rule of her own. She stood up straight now, stretching high, her hands joined as if in prayer and pointing up above her head, triumphant, an arrow aimed at the eye of heaven.

"Let's go for a run, too," said Ruth. "Let's see how far she gets."

"A run? Ruth, I have to teach. In fact, I'm late. And if I wasn't, I thought we were going to eat lunch together."

"I thought so too," Ruth said, suddenly abashed. "I got carried away." She sounded apologetic.

I had to leave if I was going to get to work, but I was suddenly worried about Ruth. It was my turn to take her by the arm. She seemed to be waking from a sort of dream. She threw one last glance over her shoulder as I led her away from the reservoir, across Fifth and over to Madison.

"I'm going to catch a subway on Lexington," I said. "Do you want to come to ETNA with me? We can get sandwiches on the way and you can wait for me in the teachers' lounge."

She shook her head no, like a little girl.

"Then why don't you go back to E.A.T. and have a bowl of soup?"

"All right," she said softly.

"Do you promise?"

"Yes."

I kissed her and she returned my kiss halfheartedly. She seemed exhausted.

"This is my fault," I said.

"It's not your fault at all," Ruth said. "I'm the one who wanted to follow her."

"Maybe you wanted to help her," I suggested hopefully.

But Ruth shook her head vehemently.

"I didn't want to help her, Joseph. That's the final lesson you should learn."

"What is?" I asked.

"If someone wants to be sick," she said, "there's nothing you can do."

The dead can't come back to life," said Kenneth.

"How do you know?" Margot demanded. She was sitting cross-legged on a table, smoking.

"Trust me," said Kenneth.

"But people have near-death experiences all the time. They do come back from the dead. You haven't read the literature."

"The literature," said Kenneth, disgustedly. He took a sip of coffee.

We were in the teachers' lounge at ETNA.

Having spent the morning chasing a skinny woman halfway across Manhattan, I was eager to lose myself in the inane, intense office banter that usually preceded the class bell. But Ruth's parting words, that the sick cannot be healed, haunted me. How could I be sure Ruth hadn't gone back to the reservoir and was jogging after Caroline that very moment? I had grabbed a sandwich on the way to work and sat eating it and brooding about her.

"You just wait," Denise was saying. "The year two thousand is going to bring a lot of revelations."

"I don't believe in the year two thousand," said Kenneth.

"How can you not believe in it?" said Denise. "It's going to happen."

"It's just a number," Kenneth said. "A year like any other. We become obsessed with decades because we learned to count on ten fingers. If we had only eight we would have celebrated the octennium two centuries ago. There isn't anything special about the millennium."

"Time may be just an artificial construct, but we still get old and gray," said Denise.

"I hate to agree with her," added David, looking up from *Heartbreak House,* which he was now trying out for, having failed to win a part in *Rosencrantz and Guildenstern Are Dead,* "but weird things *are* going to start happening. Artificial constructs have a way of becoming real. If people believe in the Apocalypse, they'll make it happen. It's like the witches in *Macbeth.* They tell you you're going to be king and because you believe the prophecy, you make it happen."

"I hate the year two thousand," said Lisa, a morning teacher who often hung around the lounge in the afternoon. "All my life I've known I was going to be thirty-seven in the year two thousand. We figured it out in second grade. It's like being told how old you're going to be when you die. It's bad knowledge. Now I think something awful's going to happen to me."

"Like you'll wind up teaching English as a second language?" said Kenneth.

Lisa made a face and lit a cigarette.

"It would be a good class to teach, wouldn't it?" said Felicia, who had been grading papers. " 'Where will you be in the year two thousand?' It's the perfect future-tense exercise. You can talk about jobs, children, where they want to live. You can talk about their hopes and dreams. They love the future."

"If they only knew," said Kenneth.

"Only knew what?" asked Felicia.

"That the future isn't going to be what they expect."

"You do believe!" said Denise.

"Oh, please," said Kenneth. "I'm talking about the economy. I'm talking about America."

"What's wrong with America?" Felicia asked, looking up.

"The dream is over," Kenneth said, with surprising bitterness. "We make twelve dollars an hour!"

"But that's by choice," said Felicia. "I like teaching Russians."

"And we have other plans," said Carol.

"Other plans," said Kenneth. "My father was laid off by IBM last week. He'd been there twenty years. There isn't going to be anything left for us at all. Not to mention our children. Not to mention *them,*" he added, motioning toward the door, beyond which the Russians had assembled.

There was an awkward silence. People spoke intimately in the office but seldom personally.

"Maybe it would be just as well if time stopped with the year two thousand," Carol said finally.

"I don't want time to stop," said Carlotta, who had just walked in. "I haven't become famous yet."

"What about you, Joseph?" Felicia asked. "You don't want time to stop until you've finished that sandwich, do you?"

She said it playfully. Everyone turned and stared, laughing as I tried to swallow so that I could respond. I'd been caught with my mouth full and I knew that I was blushing.

Felicia put her hand on my shoulder before leaving for class.

"Chew slowly," she said. "There's plenty of time."

But the bell rang.

I wolfed the last of my sandwich, drained my ginger ale and took two quick bites of an apple I'd been saving for dessert.

My students were waiting in their seats with Eskimo patience, their fur hats—too warm for the weather—resting on chairs beside them. They, clearly, had eaten lunch. The smell of cured meats and pickled vegetables hung in the air, and I opened a window.

I'd been so intent on my bizarre adventure with Ruth that I hadn't managed to prepare a class. I immediately put Felicia's suggestion to the test.

"I will be big business in year two thousand," said Oleg Yevdosin.

"I will be Fifth Avenue," said Marina Chodorofskaya.

"I will be Cadillac," said Igor Kurasik. "Bleck Cadillac."

Their greedy optimism depressed me. Kenneth's words had made an uncomfortable impression on me.

"Forget it," I wanted to tell them. "You're too late." But I only corrected their grammar and pronunciation.

It was hard to concentrate. The skinny woman stuck in my mind like a fishbone that wouldn't go down. Why had Ruth followed her? What did she hope to learn?

"I will be baseball commissioner."

"I will be many money."

"I will be president United States."

The others turned on Boris Potimkin, who had ventured this sentence, with corrective indignation, showering him with "*nyet*s." They knew the law. Abashed, Boris shrugged sheepishly. They were practical even about their dreams.

I continued around the room, while their fantasies filled the air, weighing it down, oppressing me. Even if Kenneth was wrong and they did find their way to the pot of gold, what would they give up to get it? I thought of Ruth's self-absorbed parents, her broken home. My own grieving, driven family. No wonder Ruth had turned consumption into her private religion. And I had turned Ruth into mine.

"I will be will be," said Yelena, the midwife, in her mild, serene way. Was she being ungrammatical or philosophical? I didn't ask but I took vague comfort in her words.

After class I found myself standing on the subway platform at Union Square, waiting for the uptown train. It had begun to pour and seemed to be raining even inside the station. Across the tracks I could see my students. They were all headed in the opposite direction, downtown, to Brooklyn. They stood in huddled clumps, talking and smoking.

I watched a beggar thread through the crowd on crutches, a cup held low against the grip of one crutch. No one gave. Water dripped from the ceiling. The tracks crackled.

To my surprise, I heard my name shouted. In the cavernous space I thought at first the voice had come from behind me. I heard it again and this time saw Kenneth, on the opposite platform. With him stood David and Margot. They both waved. Kenneth called my name again. They wanted me to join them.

Standing near Kenneth was Ilena Tarkofsky. Even from across the tracks I could see her hot-pink lipstick and read the familiar longing in her eyes. She wasn't beautiful but her face held a volatile mix of elements, a kind of vampish innocence, stirring on a gray subway platform. Ilena had briefly been a student of mine before switching to Kenneth's more advanced class. She was, I realized suddenly, the inspiration of Kenneth's love poem.

Beside her was a young woman in a fake leopard jacket, a short skirt and low boots, whom I recognized vaguely from the ETNA lobby. Was she with David? And what about Margot, who must have put aside her millennial differences with Kenneth? I scanned the platform for a suitable Russian man for her. Had everyone gone native? Perhaps immigrant was a better word.

"We're going to Primorski," Kenneth shouted.

"Join us," yelled Margot.

Primorski was one of the nightclubs that had sprung up in the past ten years in Brighton Beach, aka "Little Odessa," where the first waves of Russian immigrants had settled. I'd been there once before, after my first day of work, and I pictured the red plush walls, the nonstop vodka and endless pickled hors d'oeuvres, the fat cubes of sizzling shashlik on swords. Ruth, who had been with me, had panicked and forced us to leave before dessert.

I had been thinking about Ruth all day. I was desperate to go home and see her and yet, for a split second, I wondered if I should go to Primorski. Seeing David and Kenneth and Margot, the made-up Ilena and her fur-clad friend, I felt a sudden pang of envy. The Russian women were beckoning me to join them.

A downtown train was coming. I'd have to run for it. I could call Ruth from Primorski, but I knew she would never join me. I stood rooted to my spot as the train screeched heavily to a halt. My mind was still with Ruth, still following her as she followed skinny Caroline endlessly up Fifth Avenue. It was a mysterious journey I needed to complete.

My own train arrived while the downtown train was still filling up. I got on quickly.

———

I let myself into a quiet apartment. A light was on in the living room. Ruth sat behind her desk—an oak door on trestles—sketching. Max lay on the couch, purring in his sleep. I didn't say anything. I wanted to catch her off guard, to see if anything about her had changed.

Ruth looked up at me slowly—she had heard me come in. She smiled nervously. There was a question clouding her lovely face. Would I make her talk about the morning? Would I reject her now that I had seen Caroline and discovered her platonic ideal, her obsession? But how could I reproach her for following her old friend? Hadn't I joined in the hunt, and found Ruth's pursuit strangely alluring?

Ruth's face relaxed as she looked at me. She seemed to intuit everything I was thinking. The silence was charged, intimate. Her thoughts whispered to me. Mine whispered back. Our minds touched.

But the moment passed and I felt outside her again, unsure. The doorknob of Ruth's desk, still in place, stuck up just below me. I twisted the knob absentmindedly and bent forward. Instead of kissing her, as I'd intended, I knocked, just above her lap.

"Can I come in?" I asked.

Ruth still said nothing. She covered my fist with her hand.

"Do you think I'm crazy?" she said at last, softly.

"Of course not."

I tried to move my hand but she wouldn't let go. I waited for her to speak.

She was wearing an old football jersey that had belonged to one of her high school boyfriends. The wide shoulders, intended to stretch over shoulder pads, dropped halfway down her upper arms, the three-quarter-length sleeves came down to her wrists. Ruth claimed not to remember the boy at all but his number, 12, taunted me with a suggestion of her sexual past.

She had slept with a lot of men, many of whom she had not liked and did not care to talk about. She described them merely as arms who had been there to carry her away from herself, through bad times when she had disliked herself and her body even more than she did now. These arms, despite her own feelings, had reached out for her and she let them have her, shutting her eyes and giving in before recoiling in guilt and running away. I knew that there had been desire on her part, too, not mere surrender, but it was something we seldom discussed. I was, she always assured me, the only man she'd loved or trusted. I believed that was true, but I envied the nameless arms nevertheless.

"Dance with me," I said, suddenly.

"What?"

"Dance with me beautiful lady." Ruth always found it amusing when I spoke in the bold but broken accent of my students. I felt somehow as if I had actually gone to Primorski and was drunk.

Ruth, to my surprise, got up from behind the desk and put her arms around me. Her legs, beneath the long tails of the football jersey, were bare.

I murmured nonsense words—invented, pseudo-Russian sounds. Ruth smiled faintly and rested her head against my chest.

We danced without music, swaying tightly. I turned off the lamp and we danced in the dark. I felt some of my drunken mood passing into Ruth. I danced her through the whole apartment. Into the kitchen, where the refrigerator loomed, through the narrow, pitch-dark hallway, huddling close. I danced her into the bedroom.

Ruth broke the silence, whispering.

"Sometimes I feel that God gave me this little body and there's just enough room in it for me. Not enough for love or anything else."

I slipped my hands under the faded fabric of her jersey which seemed indeed to shrink Ruth back into a high school student.

"What will happen to me, Joseph?"

"You'll stretch," I whispered, drawing her toward the bed.

She allowed me to undress her, holding her hands above her head in surrender as I worked the loose shirt gently off. I undressed myself.

Ruth kissed me, but she was leading me away from the bed. I pushed her back, but she resisted. A naked tango ensued.

"No, Joseph."

"Why not?"

She said nothing, only hugged me in resistance—Jacob and the angel on the brink of our bed. But I had lost my desire for angels and so, I felt, had Ruth. Though her fingers, as always, were cool, the rest of her felt warm and alive. She wanted what she did not want. She did not want what she wanted. I was inside the logic of her appetites and felt a strange assurance, a mastery of the facts.

I brought her down with me and she submitted. In my bones, I knew she was willing.

Ruth's emaciated friend had shot through us both like Cupid's arrow, drawing us together. There had been something sexual in Ruth's pursuit of her that I had understood, for all that Caroline's bodiless body seemed to signal the end of sex itself. Everything, I realized, contained its opposite.

Ruth was aroused, but she rolled away from me and I thought for a moment she was going to leave the bed. But she returned, moving sideways, crablike, on her hands. She shifted onto me so that she lay on her back, on me—her legs spread to straddle my legs, her bottom resting on my stomach. She was too tall to fit snugly and her head tilted off to one side, onto my collarbone. Her hair crunched in my mouth.

We were both facing upward, strangely fused. My organ grew between her legs. Her breasts rose where my own should have been. I cupped them with an eerie sensation and then let my hands play over her body, taut as it arced above my own. My fingers, finding the wedge of hair, slipped in as if it was myself I found. She shivered above me and my body felt the response. She rose and fell with the force of my lungs. Whose heart beat?

We lay in silence, superimposed, two bodies in a single space. I could see her ribs in the soft light of the bed lamp. Stretched as she was, she looked unnaturally thin. She was melting into me, dissolving back into my flesh. God opened Adam's body and plucked out Eve and now he was putting her back. But then Ruth toppled beside me, separate again, panting faintly.

There was a single condom in the night-table drawer. The blue foil packet, like a container for a fancy tea bag, had already been torn into one overoptimistic night. Could a condom go stale? I put the thought out of my mind.

Ruth put the condom on me with gentle and surprisingly practiced firmness. Her shadowed features wore a familiar look, a look I'd seen at the dinner table and in countless restaurants. She bit her lower lip and tried to hide the longing in her eyes.

In my enthusiasm I pulled the condom up tight, remembering the banana Margot had used to teach the Russians safe sex and laughing inwardly. Ruth, aroused, had also grown more shy. She insisted that we get under the covers and switch off the light.

She guided me to her and I tasted desire in her mouth when we kissed. The bedsprings cried like seagulls. We clutched in the electric darkness of tented blankets. Ruth's passion flared and then guttered, she held it in abeyance, mistrusting fulfillment, but I wanted more more more and listened, trancelike, dizzy, to the sound of our bodies and our breath, merging. Ruth, however, had a practical expression on her face: she was waiting for things to end. And when I was finished she became brisk, businesslike, flicking on the light, reaching for tissues. The covers fell away, but I still crouched above her, not wanting to let her go, eager to find in her face traces of the desire and satisfaction she had allowed me to glimpse.

But Ruth, when she turned back, let out a gasp. She was staring in terror at my middle. I looked down and saw, to my horror, that my penis now wore its condom like a turtleneck, the naked pink head bare above the latex sheath, as if the condom, too, had been circumcised.

"Oh, my God," said Ruth.

I stared blankly, watching my guilty organ, sheepish but irrepressible, not yet deflated but beginning to droop with shame. Oh, that this too too solid flesh would melt.

"How could it break?" she gasped.

But even as she stared at the tatters of our lovemaking I realized she was not so much surprised as grimly confirmed. For Ruth, the bubble of desire always burst with a bang. There was no safe sex.

And I could do no more than stare. I had mastered, too well, the miseries of women. In my zeal, I had deflowered myself.

I knew Will Simon from the crackling dispatches that issued from his car phone and appeared in abundance on our answering machine, most of them ending abruptly in midsentence, as if he'd driven off a cliff.

The message inviting us to Mother's Day brunch sounded as if it came from the Apollo spacecraft during a meteor shower.

"Dot and I want you here," his voice, hissing and popping, informed us, before it roared "Holland Tunnel!" and disappeared.

I gathered that inviting us to his house in Scarsdale was a strategic move on his part, securing diplomatic recognition for his second wife, Dot, as the real Mrs. Simon.

"My mother doesn't give a shit about Mother's Day," Ruth explained bluntly when she played the message, "but my father still thinks it's a big deal."

Even so, Ruth liked Dot and spent hours making a pair of earrings for her—tiny terra-cotta onions glazed gold and purple. Dot was from Vidalia, Georgia, home of the onion. Ruth had also bought a rattle made of smooth polished wood for her baby half brother, born just around the time Ruth and I had moved in together. I was pleased that she had done this, for she tended to view the child with suspicion as well as affection, a tiny pretender to the throne from which she had been displaced.

It had been six weeks since our ill-fated evening under the covers. Once again we had a secret that drew us closer, and another reason for silence. Ruth, at least, did not wish to speak about it. Her diary had swallowed the whole experience in four words: "Sex with Joseph. Disaster." There were many things I would like to have discussed—sex, for one thing, its relationship to disaster for another—but the less I probed, the more trusting and relaxed Ruth seemed. Ever since she had met me in the library and led me on the chase after Caroline, I had found myself more and more given over to her directives. Since that day, I had not been back to the library, waiting instead to see where Ruth would lead me next. And since that unlucky night with Ruth I had followed her lead into silence. I knew that in her own time she would reveal something of herself—though in what form I couldn't guess.

Ruth looked nervous as the train pulled out of Grand Central. She referred to Scarsdale as "the dale of scars," and as the scene outside the window changed from the crumbling decay of the 125th Street station to greener scenes of Harrison and Larchmont, she grew more and more agitated. I felt it was best to leave her alone when she was in this state, and contented myself with looking silently out the window, past the golden silhouette of her beautiful head. There is always something of winter about the city, even in May, and as we left behind the igloo brick of Manhattan, my spirits began to rise. When I took Ruth's cool, thin hand she did not protest and my heart, as always, beat faster, as if we were on a first date.

I had never been to her father's Scarsdale house, and Ruth had been there only once or twice while it was still being built to what I gathered were very elaborate specifications. Usually she met her father for lunch at the restaurant of her choice, and since this was generally a place I could not afford to take her, I often felt a pang when she came home, dressed up and glowing. Though she did not eat much, she loved good restaurants.

Ruth had given herself a different look. Her hair was pulled back behind her small ears, exposing simple pearl earrings, a gift from her father. She wore only a dusting of blush on the wide cheekbones that so vexed her (they suggested a plumpness she did not possess) and no eye makeup at all. She had on a jumper of soft cotton and delicate sandals with a thin single thong looping her big toe and running up her slender instep to the leather collar around her ankle.

I had, at Ruth's urging, worn a tie and jacket, but this proved to be unnecessary. We were greeted at the door by her father in an aquamarine sweatshirt with a Ralph Lauren logo, relaxed-fit jeans and gleaming white sneakers. I wondered if he had made a conscious effort to jazz himself up since the humiliation of his divorce.

"Muffin!" he cried, folding Ruth in a bear hug, while I stood peering into the vast expanse of lobby and tasting the refrigerated air of the house. The place still smelled of new paint and upholstery.

"How's my favorite daughter?"

"I'm okay," said Ruth, unwilling, as always, to admit to happiness but looking pleased.

At last he turned to me and a powerful handshake took my fingers hostage.

"I've heard a lot about you from Ruth. Don't worry, I don't believe everything I hear." He gave a deep, artificial business-man's chuckle. "Seriously, it's nice of your parents to give you up on Mother's Day."

"We don't celebrate it," I said, which, for many years now, had certainly been the truth. Ruth shot me a reproachful look and I realized with relief she had never told her father about my sister.

Mr. Simon was trim and tan, with a long, handsome face and thick, unnatural brown hair, acquired (I knew from Ruth) after the divorce. A nervous unease in his eyes belied the command of his telephone voice and the crunch of his handshake. I felt you could count Carol Simon's infidelities in the lines of his tanned forehead, but he led us through the house with the confident air of middle-aged prosperity.

The house had a kind of muffled hugeness, the floor flooded with thick pile carpet and crowded with velvet easy chairs. Mr. Simon's toupéed head participated in the over-upholstered aesthetic of the house. The high walls were covered with wallpaper that seemed to have more than two dimensions, and with an astonishing amount of ugly art, sentimental in subject matter and lurid in execution, as if Van Gogh had been commissioned by Hallmark.

"Oh, Daddy!" cried Ruth. "It's all furnished."

"Wait, Dot'll give you a whole tour. She's out by the pool nursing Dashiell. But I'll just show you one thing. This was my contribution."

He led us into a gargantuan, marble-floored dining room. He was a lot shorter than the depth of his voice or the height of his ceilings would have suggested. In the dining room stood three round tables with burgundy tablecloths, set with white china as if a reception for fifty had been planned. It looked like the dining room of a luxury liner. In the center of the room hung a huge chandelier, too large and too low for the room, an upside-down wedding cake, intended for a ceiling twice as high.

He was pointing to the chandelier, which must have weighed a thousand pounds. He led us directly under it. I had to stoop to avoid being tickled by a fringe of beveled crystal.

"Recognize it?" he said to me.

"Uh, no."

He seemed surprised, hurt.

"I'll give you a hint. It's from Manhattan."

What art-deco brothel for giant New Yorkers could it possibly have come from?

"Radio City Music Hall?"

"B. Altman. It used to hang in the men's department. When they went out of business a couple of years ago, I bought it at auction and had it stored. Cost me more to store than to buy. But worth it, huh?"

I had often passed the sad shell of B. Altman on Fifth Avenue and Thirty-fourth. As I walked up from ETNA on sunny days, I often thought that this must be how a city declines, how the Parthenon and the Colosseum fell empty.

"It's too bad about that store," I said.

"Don't get sentimental about department stores," Mr. Simon snapped, suddenly gruff. "They're not for the twenty-first century. Weak businesses die."

"As long as they don't kill Bloomingdale's," said a sweet southern voice coming toward us. "Because you know I was born to shop there."

"It's the mother herself," said Mr. Simon, beaming as his plump, blond, cheerful second wife came into view.

"Happy Mother's Day," said Ruth, kissing Dot.

"Ruth, you always wind up with such handsome men."

The "always" canceled the "handsome," but I shook her hand warmly and she leaned forward and kissed me.

She was smiling broadly, the upper lip rising slightly above the gum line, revealing the tombstone twinkle of overexposed tooth tops. Her sweatshirt was the same pool-blue as Mr. Simon's.

"And you!" she said to Ruth. "You just get prettier every time I see you."

"Yeah?" said Ruth, in the pleased, incredulous way she took compliments.

"Where's Dashiell?" asked Mr. Simon suddenly.

"He fell in the pool and I figured he'd just swim for it."

Mr. Simon looked wild with terror.

Dot gave a rich coloratura laugh. "I'm joking, Billy."

I could see from Ruth's face that no one else had ever called Will Simon "Billy."

"Mabel's giving him his nap. He had a nice meal"—she patted her breasts—"and now he's asleep."

We had made our way to a breakfast room between the dining room and kitchen, a room with sliding glass doors on two sides overlooking a swimming pool and a great expanse of lawn. The table was spread with lox and smoked sable, two small whitefish still in their gold jackets, bagels, olives, fruit salad and cheese.

"I hope you kids brought bathing suits," said Mr. Simon.

"Well, we didn't," said Ruth. "No one told us to. I didn't think you'd filled the pool."

"You can borrow one of mine, Sugar," said Dot. "I'm a twelve and I'd guess you're about a four, but you can knot it or something. Fact you can go in naked, for all we care."

"That's a joke," said Mr. Simon. "Joseph, I have plenty of spare trunks upstairs."

"Did you know your daddy's a big prude?" said Dot. "He'd wear trunks in the bathtub if I let him."

She laughed uproariously. Ruth, to my amazement, was laughing too. Mr. Simon looked uncomfortable, glancing at a fat Sunday paper and lapsing into silence.

There were whisker-fine lines of care radiating from Dot's laughing blue eyes, though she was probably no more than thirty-five. The band of corrugated pink gum above her teeth gave her pretty face a look of slippage. Despite her abundant good nature, something behind her smile and in the pale pouches under her made-up eyes hinted at sorrow.

Dot and Ruth talked for most of brunch. I kept checking Ruth's face for signs of woe, but she seemed more relaxed than I'd seen her in a long time, even when the conversation turned to her baby half brother. I heard Dot say, "Good gracious, that boy has doubled in size like a loaf of bread since you saw him last, I swear to God."

"Gracious," said Ruth, echoing Dot. "I just can't wait to see him." I thought I detected a faint southern drawl creeping into Ruth's speech as she leaned forward under Dot's spell.

I was pleased to note that she ate half a bagel with whitefish (no cream cheese) and a whole helping of fruit salad, though she ate it in her special order: kiwi, cantaloupe balls, orange sections, grapes.

I was opposite Mr. Simon, who looked up only occasionally from the business section of the Sunday *Times*. This left me looking dreamily past him at the blue immensity of the swimming pool.

Was it the newness of the house or my unfamiliarity with Mr. Simon, who was ignoring me, that made me feel such emptiness? A sense that nothing in the house had a history, like the clothing of a spy who has torn out all the labels so that he is untraceable. Except for the department-store chandelier, which hung huge and out of place, everything seemed nameless and inert, as if it had been dipped in the Lethe blue of the pool. Did Dot's southern Christian energies neutralize the northern neurotic Jewish vibes? I found myself associating the air-conditioning with a canceled quality to the house, an American blankness that passed for peace. Ruth herself, leaning conspiratorially toward Dot, lacked the identifying intensity I always looked for in her as a kind of landmark. Though we hadn't been there an hour, I felt almost homesick.

"So, Joe," said Mr. Simon, "the lease on my car is up."

He was the kind of man who did not make conversation so much as share information. I was particularly bad at this sort of exchange and I resented that he shortened my name, an impatient man's abbreviating impulse.

"Really?"

"I've been driving the Mercedes 420 SEL but I feel like I owe myself something sportier. Though of course with room for a baby seat in back," he added, glancing toward Dot. "You know, Mercedes is the safest car on the road. Biggest crash box."

I nodded, watching a cardinal that had settled on the diving board and caught my eye like a blood spot in an egg.

"What do you think of the 380 SEC? I know you can't really compare them."

That was certainly true. I had never heard of either.

"I've got the 380 on loan if you want to go for a spin later."

"After their swim," said Dot, looking up from her conversation with Ruth.

"Of course," Mr. Simon agreed hastily.

"Is there coffee?" Ruth asked quietly.

"Regular or unleaded?" Mr. Simon asked, rising to man the coffeemaker.

Dot was stacking our lunch plates in the dishwasher, humming to herself.

"Happy Mother's Day," said Ruth, when Dot had returned to the table. "These are for you."

"Baby, you shouldn't have." She opened the little box and dug a pink-nailed finger through the cotton balls Ruth had layered her gift with.

"Honey! They're little hearts, aren't they?"

"Onions," said Ruth, blushing.

"Gracious!" screamed Dot. "Vidalia! Oh, Billy, look!" She howled with laughter. "Come here. Come here and give old Dot a kiss." Like many southerners, she mocked her own manner of speech, as if she'd acquired it by watching *Gone With the Wind* too often.

Ruth walked around the table and was warmly embraced.

"They're just tremendous. We should carry your things in the Peach Tree—that's our gallery," Dot said to me. Mr. Simon had bought her a part interest in a gallery in White Plains, whence, I imagined, the ugly wall art. But Ruth was flushed with pleasure.

"You really like them?" she asked again, like a little girl.

"I *love* them," Dot said. "Will, aren't they wonderful? Shouldn't we carry her stuff?"

"Sure," her father said. "How many do you suppose you'd have to sell to pay for an hour with Dr. Hallo?"

"Will, you apologize," said Dot, as if to a little boy, but Mr. Simon glared at her and said, "This is between me and my daughter," with such grim purpose that she colored and busied herself with the dishes on the sideboard.

I was astonished by Will Simon's sudden rudeness, though it was in keeping with a certain sense of his personality I'd gleaned from the taped samples of his family conduct.

Ruth had frozen. She opened her mouth but no words came out. She was mute with rage.

"You and I have a few things to discuss," her father continued, levelly. "Things can't continue indefinitely. I have a family now."

Ruth's eyes glistened and I had a fleeting desire to speak up, but it was the baby who let out a cry from somewhere in the house, usurping even Ruth's tears. Mr. Simon pointed triumphantly at the ceiling, in the general direction of the sound.

Ruth had warned me that she would be forced, at some point in the visit, to beg for her allowance, especially now that her father had another mouth to feed—though he could well afford it. She had assured me that it was all just ritual. "He needs to feel in control," she'd said, "especially after the divorce." But Mr. Simon's jaw was set and his eyes had the fixed intensity I knew well from Ruth herself.

"You bill your clients four hundred and fifty dollars an hour," Ruth said bitterly. "But I guess my one little hour of help is too much."

Mr. Simon glanced uncomfortably in my direction.

"We'll go to my office," he said, between clenched teeth. Ruth followed obediently. She was trembling, white with anger, and as she followed her father out, she threw a tear-streaked glance back at me. Whether it was a look of reassurance or a plea for help I could not tell.

Dot and I were awkwardly alone for a moment. She looked at me apologetically and said softly, "He'll give her what she wants. He just needs to bark a little first."

She then excused herself to see to the crying child and I was left alone. I finished my coffee and tiptoed toward Will Simon's office, creeping close to the door in time to hear Ruth's muffled shout, "You can't stand having to spend money on me anymore, isn't that it? You can build this house, and buy a new car, and have a new baby. But old me is too expensive all of a sudden, isn't that it? How much did this house cost? How much?"

"None of your business," Mr. Simon snapped back, but he sounded stung. Their voices fell and I caught only a few more bitten-off fragments.

"No career for a smart young man with a Columbia degree," penetrated the thick door and sank into my heart with particular force. "Wasting my . . ."

I listened for what I hoped would be an impassioned defense of my character, but could make out nothing distinct, and at that point I slunk away, found the living room and took refuge in the arms of a velvet sofa.

A baby's cry still echoed through the huge house, as if Ruth had awakened the ghost of her own unhappy childhood.

As a consultant, Mr. Simon could hardly have approved of me. He paid Ruth's utilities and her Visa bill and gave her seven hundred dollars a month toward rent (more than my share). He must have concluded that the funds he passed on to Ruth were fungible and in some way subsidized my own slothful existence, though in fact Ruth had let me move in to avoid asking her father to pay her entire rent. But that would hardly have impressed him. His only comment, when I told him what I did for a living, was to say that my students would be better off learning Chinese. That's where the opportunities were now.

I undid my tie (I had left my jacket on a chair in the breakfast room) and felt suddenly chilly. Though it was a warm day, the house was as cold as a crisper and I lay on the couch in a kind of vegetable stupor.

Four hundred and fifty dollars an hour! That was more than I made in a week. I tried to calculate what I earned per hour and then broke it down per student. Twelve dollars an hour divided by how many students? I ran over the names of the students in my class, ticking them off like beads on an abacus, "Igor Kurasik, Boris Yevdosin, Galina Mendelsohn." Soon I forgot about the math, merely sounding the familiar names soothingly to myself, and so, counting Russians like sheep, I fell asleep.

Ruth woke me with a kiss after what felt like hours but had been in fact only twenty minutes or so. I sat up blinking. Ruth's eyes were red and she looked exhausted, but there was a triumphant cast to her features as she stood over me.

"Put this in your wallet," she said in an undertone, "before he changes his mind."

It was a check for seven thousand dollars.

I looked at her questioningly, but she did not want to discuss it.

"I earned it, believe me," was all she said.

She handed me a pair of salmon-pink swim trunks. "These are from my father. Let's go for a swim."

I changed upstairs in what must have been Dot's half of a his-and-hers bathroom. There were tiny bottles of bath oil and shampoo from the Helmsley Palace lined up along the sink, as if tiny people bathed and showered in its scalloped contours. Frilly perfumed night things hung on the back of the bathroom door. I undressed hastily and felt a strange clutch and shiver in my loins as I pulled Mr. Simon's bathing suit on.

Ruth was already in the water, wearing a borrowed red one-piece that made her look like a little girl playing dress-up. The straps kept slipping off her shoulders, and when she swam, water poured in the top and bulged it absurdly. She cursed and tried to hold it up, but I felt she was not unhappy in the enormous suit. I kept catching flashes of breast and belly through the looped and sagging openings.

"I wish we could take off our clothes," Ruth whispered.

Mr. Simon came out and activated the Jacuzzi next to the pool. "You've got to try this, it's amazing." He seemed to have forgotten the morning's unpleasantness. He smiled at us and strolled cheerfully back to the house.

Ruth and I stood together in the steaming Jacuzzi, two missionaries in a pot. The water was warm but the air on my face and shoulders was chilly.

"I have no childhood left," said Ruth. Her voice rose softly over the hum of an unseen motor and the quiet slurping of the pool. She had on a pair of Dot's sunglasses and it was hard to read her mood. "My father's thrown out everything from the old house. He wanted to wipe out all traces of my mother, but he wiped me out, too."

"You're still here, Ruth," I said.

The water was whipping her loose suit across her breasts. I reached out for her but she reminded me of the picture windows and pushed me away. Azaleas in bright colors surrounded the pool.

Ruth looked tough with her sunglasses on, her wet hair slicked back close and tight. I watched her large suit wobble in the water, one naked breast dodging into view.

"You're an Amazon," I said. "Your father can't hurt you."

She followed my gaze and studied her own breast without covering it.

"Amazons cut off one of their breasts so they could shoot their arrows better."

"Well, I didn't mean that."

Ruth slid lower into the heated water.

I looked down at our lower bodies, warped by the water. Ruth's legs tapered into a single taproot.

"And now he has his own baby," Ruth said, "it's like he doesn't even need me."

"Of course he does," I said, though I too had felt a disturbing, hermetic self-sufficiency about his life.

"I should have told him I'm pregnant and seen how he reacted."

I looked at her, but her head was tilted back and she was staring straight up at the sun. The water slurped and slapped around us.

"That's not funny," I said.

"I didn't mean it to be funny."

"Well, it's not. You don't do that to someone, even your father. And he did give you the money, just like you said he would."

Ruth lowered her gaze and stared at me hard behind her sunglasses.

"You think all I want from him is money?"

"No, of course not," I said hastily. "But whatever it is, you don't have to do or say something extreme to get him to care about you. You don't lie about life like that."

"You're really upset," she said, beginning to look upset herself, as if she had been insulted and were only just realizing it.

"Of course I am," I told her. "I don't find the thought of your needing an abortion amusing. I don't want to think of you subjecting yourself to that."

"Why an abortion?" Ruth demanded, offended. "You wouldn't want to have a baby with me?"

"Someday. Yes. Not now, of course. But this is hypothetical anyway, so what's the point?" I had moved closer to her, but she shrank from me.

"Ruth?"

"What?" she asked angrily.

"This is hypothetical," I repeated. "Isn't it?"

Ruth was silent. The line from her journal leaped into my mind. *Sex with Joseph. Disaster.* My heart was racing, an inner churning to match the roiling water.

"Are you telling me something?"

Ruth removed her sunglasses. She looked at me and said, in a low voice, "I'm pregnant, Joseph."

Though I was standing up in the hot tub I felt as if I were treading water, in danger of sinking down to bottomless depths.

"Ruth," was all I could say. "Ruth."

I took her hand, but she withdrew it.

"I wish I'd never told you," she said, harshly. "I wasn't going to. Forget it. I'll take care of it."

"I'll go with you," I said, but that only made things worse.

How could I not have known? And yet Ruth had written nothing beyond the word "disaster" and hadn't hinted anything to me at all. So much for our unspoken closeness. My head was spinning. And then, with terrible timing, Mr. Simon called us in to see his baby, now awake.

We showered and changed in different bathrooms. I came downstairs first and found Mabel, the black nanny, holding Dashiell. He was a pale-haired, peach-colored, wide-eyed baby, swathed like a blintz in a white blanket.

Dot began to coo and hold out her arms and say "Ooooooh, come to Mama, my baby precious," but Mr. Simon intercepted Mabel and lifted Dashiell out of her arms so that the white flannel fell off to reveal a little blue jumpsuit and tiny white socks.

"Look at that. Look at my son," he said. He tilted the boy toward me the way a waiter might tilt a bottle of Chablis at a customer.

"There's nothing more important, Joseph," he said, "nothing in the world."

The child was beautiful, and reached out his hands as if to embrace my head.

I felt that I was being shown my own child, Ruth's child, and I swelled with emotion. Ruth's wish to make room in her body for another living creature seemed suddenly a great omen of health. I would tell her I had been wrong. We would build our lives around her news.

But Ruth came into the room without looking at me. She had unwrapped our gift for Dashiell and shook it mechanically before the child's face. It made a warning sound, I thought, like a rattlesnake ready to strike.

"Look what your big sister gave you," said Dot, who was now holding her child. Mabel had left the room.

Dot took the rattle from Ruth and fit it into the baby's small grasp. Dashiell shook it once and threw it, with surprising force, to the ground.

Ruth picked up the rattle and shook it absently in her own delicate fist. I had taken all her joy away. I had ceded the field to Will Simon's own baby.

"Here," said Dot, "you hold him."

"Oh, I don't know," said Ruth.

"Sure, just keep his head up. Easiest thing in the world."

Ruth dropped the rattle on a chair and took Dashiell with careful hands, settling him on her lap. He was a cheerful baby, smiling and gurgling, full of bright awareness, but also, it seemed, distracted by some inner absorption. He sat facing Ruth, reaching out a small hand, first to her face, then to the more comfortable level of her breasts. He pressed the tender swelling with open fingers.

"Oh," said Ruth, startled.

"He thinks you're going to feed him," said Dot. "Ruth doesn't serve lunch," she told her son, "only Mommy does that. Mommy's just a big vending machine, isn't she?"

Tears were running down Ruth's cheeks, which Dot seemed to take for sisterly affection and which her father did not notice at all. But I knew their meaning and felt sick with guilt and confusion.

Dashiell was still trying to work the hidden springs of Ruth's breasts and Ruth defended herself by drawing him close so that he lay compressed against her heartbeat, where he went blissfully slack.

A look of quiet pleasure suffused Ruth's face. She stopped crying.

"He's so soft," she said, huskily.

"He likes you," said Dot.

"My son likes everybody," said Mr. Simon proudly, standing and looking down on the whole scene. "He's a very gregarious boy."

I must have been staring intently, for Dot said suddenly, "Let Joseph hold him."

Ruth detached Dashiell reluctantly. He had dug in like a kitten. She seemed unwilling to part with him, but at last she held him out. I could see a burning look of accusation in her eyes. The child seemed to tread the air, moving his arms and legs ineffectually.

Dot helped settle the child in my arms, but he remained standing up on the stage of my lap. I felt his tiny feet push into my thighs. A soft smell of powder and something earthier and more pungent filtered through the chlorine still in my nostrils.

Too little is made of the maternal feelings of men. I held the child around the middle and I felt, as the small head brushed my cheek, what I imagine Ruth had felt, a thrill of sweet being, a tender bliss. A wave of devotion came over me, his warm, soft-haired head touching my cheek, and I felt deeply stirred, protective, adoring. I would tell Ruth that I was wrong. We should marry and have a child. Who knows, perhaps my first impulse—that nothing could be worse for a woman obsessed with her body weight than pregnancy—was wrong. If everything contained its opposite, then perhaps a broken condom could make things whole. Ruth feared physical expansion and yet she wished to be pregnant. Maybe this of all things would heal her.

I still held Dashiell and laughed with pleasure, but the noise seemed to reverberate painfully in his small ears. He began to dance away from me, pushing out with his arms, making tiny noises that contained the seeds of fast-growing sobs. I held him firm and became mindful of a dampness under my hand, a cooling patch of drool on my shoulder.

Dashiell had begun to cry and I felt the brutal judgment of the child upon me as his choking sobs (so big for so small a child!) rang like a police siren and seemed to declare "This man here, he's the one."

Dot swooped down and took him away and walked little circles in the room, making *shush*ing noises, patting his back and whispering. Finally, she raised the blue sweatshirt, under which she wore no bra, and allowed Dashiell to nurse under the bunched canopy of blue. He sank against her, tranquil once more.

Mr. Simon insisted on driving us to the station so we could experience the Mercedes 300 SEC he had on loan. On our way outside I whispered to Ruth, "I was wrong. I'm sorry."

But Ruth took my arm and drew me closer.

"No," she whispered back darkly. "You were right."

The car was in the driveway and when we got there Mr. Simon let out an anguished cry. Small dusky footprints, which I recognized easily as the paw prints of a cat, were imprinted on the hood of the low-slung silver roadster.

"I'm going to kill that cat," said Mr. Simon. He took out a handkerchief to wipe away all traces of the offending animal. "At least there are no claw marks," he muttered, "or I'd set out poison."

The leather seats of Mr. Simon's car were the color of butterscotch and the sunroof was open, letting in the cool evening air as we drove. A pale scoop of moon was visible in the still-light sky.

"She corners pretty good, huh?" he called back to me, over the roar of the wind, and I agreed, though I was feeling ill in the back, which was big enough for a baby seat, perhaps, but too small for a man.

Fortunately, Mr. Simon quickly abandoned conversation, dialing Dot on the car phone to see if she needed anything from the store. Ruth, who sat beside him in the front, reclined her bucket seat all the way so that she was virtually in the back with me. Her head was just beyond my knees. Her eyes were shut, she appeared to have fallen instantly asleep. I watched Ruth and wondered about the tiny life inside her, a spark of myself rooted in her body.

Will Simon was working the wheel with one hand and holding the phone to his ear with the other. He chatted on idly and inaudibly, oblivious to his daughter beside him. But I looked down on her shut eyes and felt that even asleep it was Ruth who was driving. She was leading me past big houses and neat lawns, steering me toward the dark, unseen edge of the world.

Ruth wouldn't let me take her to the abortion clinic. She would not even let me plan the visit with her. One morning in the middle of the following week she said simply, "Today's the day."

"When?" I asked, knowing at once what she meant.

"Two o'clock."

"Can't I take you? Please. I'll call in sick."

"No."

"Will you at least tell me where?"

"Stop asking. I'll be fine."

I had already learned that Nadia, the companion of all Ruth's worst impulses, was going with her. My exclusion wounded me as much as the terrible thing itself. Ruth was removing her body from my care, at least for this one day, and I felt a bleak sense of failure and separation, of banishment, that was almost unbearable.

Ruth, however, moved around the apartment with a brisk energy that amazed me. There had already been tears and anger in the aftermath of our visit to Scarsdale, but that morning Ruth exhibited little emotion beyond a kind of anticipatory relief. She kissed me good-bye in a crisp, almost businesslike fashion. I was still in bed and felt more like the patient than the healer I hoped to be. I felt powerless and grim, a person to whom something bad had happened.

Ruth left quickly. I suspected she wanted to avoid more pleas from me to join her, but I felt she was also eager to have the thing over and done. She never referred to it as an abortion but as a "termination," at once more euphemistic and more terrible.

It took me all morning to wake up, and when I finally arrived at work I felt heavy, blanketed, distracted. I behaved like a buffoon in class, spilling my coffee and wiping it up with my eraser. When I erased the blackboard a moment later, I left a long wet streak and my class roared with laughter. And all the while I was wondering, "Is it time yet? Has it happened?" Like an expectant father, expecting—what?

The loneliness of the only child I had become, but not been born to be, overwhelmed me. It seemed to me suddenly that I had lost everything—not merely the unknown bundle of cells that would be taken away, but Ruth herself. Had I known where she was going I certainly would have met her there, whether she wanted me or not.

But what would I have done then? Would I have tried to talk her into keeping the child? Could I have? Should I have? Could I see myself as a father, when I earned almost no money and couldn't even find a way to care properly for Ruth? Could I see Ruth as a mother, able to nourish an infant, when she could scarcely nourish herself? How could a woman terrified of getting fat bear to carry a child?

And yet, as much as I feared that Ruth would see her worst fears enlarged in pregnancy, I felt, too, that having a child might truly heal her. Half of me hoped that she would change her mind. That I would come home from class and find her awkwardly apologetic, or even angrily defiant. "I'm keeping it." Imagining that scene filled me with joy and I knew suddenly what I would say to her if I knew where she had gone.

All hope of that vanished as soon as I got home. I found Ruth in the bedroom. The shades were drawn. I could barely see her shadowy form against the pillow, but I felt her lying there forlornly and knew that it had really happened. I tiptoed to the bed. The roses I had bought crinkled in their wrapper alarmingly, but Ruth didn't stir. The white sheet was pulled to her throat. She was in one of my white undershirts and her pale, thin arms rested at her sides on top of the sheet. My heart broke looking down at her.

She lay very still. I thought she was sleeping but her eyelids fluttered slowly.

"Who is that?" she asked softly.

"It's me," I said, sitting on the bed beside her.

"Oh, Joseph. I dreamed I was in the hospital and that Dr. Hallo came to see me. He brought me flowers. I must have smelled yours."

"It's me," I said again. "I'm right here."

I kissed her on the forehead and then the lips. Her hair was fanned out on the pillow. There was a circular Band-Aid on the inside of her arm. Had they put her to sleep?

"Are those roses for me?" she asked faintly.

"Yes, of course." I placed them beside her on the pillow so that she looked, though I hated to think it, like a body laid out for burial.

"Thank you," she said, smiling wanly.

"Did everything go all right?" The poverty of my words shamed me, but I did not know how else to ask.

"It all went fine," Ruth said, looking away.

"And you're okay?"

"Yes," she whispered. "I wouldn't mind a cup of tea."

I ran to the kitchen and brewed her special herbal mixture, glad to have something to do.

Max was gnawing a few fragments of dried food. I shook in more around his ears to keep him in the kitchen.

I brought Ruth her tea, and while she sipped it unwrapped the roses, snapping off thorns idly, waiting for her to speak. She did not. I went to the kitchen again for a vase and water.

Ruth seemed strangely serene when I returned, one hand resting on her stomach in a pregnant gesture that unnerved me. Her eyes seemed dreamily unfocused. I stuck the flowers in a corner on the floor. They made me ashamed, for I did not wish to feel like a visitor, like Dr. Hallo or anybody else, coming to see her in the hospital. I wished terribly that I had gone with her. More painfully, I wished that I hadn't let her go at all.

"Did they give you a general anesthetic?" I asked finally.

"No. It's all local. I fainted."

"Oh, Ruth!"

I took her hand, so small and helpless, and kissed it again and again.

"It's okay, Joseph. It's okay. It's better this way. You were right."

"No, I was wrong. I shouldn't have let you go."

"Don't tell me that now!" she said, her voice suddenly strong and accusing.

"I'm sorry, Ruth. I don't know what I'm saying. You did the right thing. I'm sorry."

"No, *I'm* sorry," she said, beginning to cry. "You're right. It was a mistake. I'll never have children. I just know it."

"Of course you will," I said, gripping her hands. "You'll have children."

"I want children with you."

"Absolutely," I said. "We'll have lots of children. Hundreds of children."

"Joseph, do you love me?"

"I love you, Ruth. I love you."

"Will you forgive me?"

"You haven't done anything."

"Please just forgive me."

"I forgive you," I said, ashamed that she sought some kind of absolution from me.

"Promise me we'll never talk about this."

"I promise." I was cupping her smooth tearful face in my hands.

"Never. Not another word. Never again."

"Never," I said.

"I'm going to try to sleep," said Ruth, kissing my hand.

It was only seven o'clock. I hadn't eaten dinner yet, but I switched off the reading light and lay down next to her, still in my clothes.

She curled up in the gloom beside me—the fetal position. Time passed thickly. Ruth was lying so still beneath the sheet I wondered, in a sudden panic, if she was breathing. I wanted to shake her, but held my breath to hear her breathe.

I had fantasized, briefly, that Ruth's pregnancy might offer a sort of remedy. She might come to see her body as more than an unwanted instrument of eating—she might come to see it as an instrument of life. Now I tried to tell myself that the opposite was true. That Ruth would wake up and feel not the empty, sterile gloom I felt filling me but a promise of new freedom and life. A termination of her sorrows.

Her body twitched suddenly, that strange sweep of electric life that passes through people as they fall asleep, as if, falling too fast, a hand has yanked them back to safety.

Perhaps, I told myself, an abortion is a kind of birth.

Summer

The days expanded. The sun expanded. Streets widened with heat, taxicabs grew a riper yellow. On the sidewalk lay dark piles of swollen, wrinkled garbage bags, bunches of enormous grapes turning into enormous raisins. It was only June, but already it felt like late summer.

I had begun teaching full-time. The breakup of the Soviet Union meant more work; new students came fast and furious that summer, often to drop out after only a day or two, as if all they required was a vaccination of English to set them right. Still, I felt useful in their presence. I had not resisted when a morning teacher quit and I was asked to take on a double load. I woke up early and no longer had time to scrutinize Ruth's diary after breakfast, or read until lunchtime in the library.

It was Ruth who now stayed home when I left in the morning for work. Her art classes had ended and her appointments with Dr. Hallo had now been moved to the middle of the day. She did not do well without structure, and I urged her to enroll in summer classes or to spend more time with friends. It was not good for her to be alone.

Something had broken in her after the abortion. Unlike the other calamities we'd endured, which had a binding effect on our relationship, this seemed to throw her back into a primitive and very private sorrow. There was a hermetic quality to her now—a vague suspiciousness I had not experienced since the early days of our relationship, a guilty defensiveness that put us both on edge.

So when Will Simon offered, in a fit of generosity, to send Ruth to Paris for six weeks I could not help thinking that a little time away from the roasting city might not be bad for her. Ever since she had been unable to join her high school French class on a three-week exchange program because she had lost too much weight, Paris had loomed as a magical city in Ruth's idealizing mind. She seemed cheered and motivated by the prospect of travel, though I couldn't help thinking that Mr. Simon, who did not approve of me and knew that I could not afford to go with her, enjoyed the idea of separating us for a while.

Ruth denied this and even offered to lend me the money to go with her, but the truth was that Blitstein had warned that anyone who left ETNA in its hour of need could not come back. He had also taken me aside and hinted that he was considering hiring an assistant and that if I made it through the summer I stood a chance of receiving this honor and a pay hike. This was hardly an incentive to stay and yet I did not wish to lose my job. I felt, even in the transient faces of my immigrants, an anchoring presence—a reassuring counterpoint to Ruth's etherealizing effect on me. Mainly, though, I needed the money.

Nadia planned to join Ruth for five of the six weeks. I would like to have talked Ruth out of this part of the plan but I held my tongue, for though I distrusted Nadia, I did not wish Ruth to be alone. And I had to admit that the gloom that had settled over Ruth since our visit to Scarsdale seemed to lift when she discussed her trip with Nadia.

They talked about setting up easels on the banks of the Seine, peddling jewelry for pocket money and haunting the museums and cafés. On the phone, planning their trip, they were giggly as high school girls going abroad for the first time. Ruth's laughter occasionally verged on the manic, and underneath she seemed full of secret dread, but the plans went forward. She had timed the trip for the last two weeks of July and all of August so that it would overlap with the four-week vacation of her psychiatrist.

Her separation from Hallo seemed to weigh more heavily on her than her separation from me. She confided this to her journal, which she was once more writing (and I, with greater stealth and irregularity, was still reading), and it wounded my pride more than her decision to go away. But Hallo wounded hers, unexpectedly, by telling her firmly that if her weight dropped below one hundred and seven pounds he would telephone her father and urge him to withhold the money for the trip. Shades of high school unhappiness! Ruth had come home fuming from a session, and, after prodding and cajoling, shared this ultimatum with me.

I was amazed. One hundred and seven was already five pounds less than I thought she weighed. Even more astonishing was that Hallo, the Freudian who scarcely ventured more than a raised eyebrow, would take so strong a stand. Did he think Ruth might again lapse into the outright abstention of her teenage years?

Ruth's body, once so familiar to me, was growing distant. She did not undress before me anymore and seldom held me close. I took this as private grief over the abortion, and decided that time would be the best remedy. When I saw her stalking swiftly out of the shower, more wood nymph than woman, I said nothing. Noticing how thin her legs were, how deep the hollows in her buttocks had become, like dents in a man's hat, I bit my tongue. Soon, I felt, when the invisible scars—about which she was silent in her diary—healed, she would again be mine.

My zeal for research, for explanations, had diminished. I told myself that this was my application of the Flekian principle of negative capability, but I wasn't feeling particularly capable, negatively or otherwise. It was more a temporary loss of faith in my ability to influence Ruth directly. Her withdrawal since the abortion had made me realize how powerless I was.

It may also be that I had looked into the fun-house mirror too long, had begun to see her body through her own distorting eyes. I half believed her when she told me she was eating more and would wind up above the required weight. When she told me about Hallo's ultimatum I ought to have realized that letting her go to Paris under any conditions at all was a terrible mistake. But I didn't try to stop her. Perhaps I knew I couldn't.

The date of Ruth's departure was fast approaching. She was endlessly preparing, making long lists of what she needed, and revising them ceaselessly. Clothing was a major problem and Ruth ransacked her closet in disgust, claiming that nothing fit her anymore. Many tears were shed over the purchase of a bathing suit, though why she would need one in Paris was beyond me.

In the evenings, when I was back from teaching, we would share a batch of herbed popcorn and watch *Children of Paradise* or Cocteau's *Beauty and the Beast* or another of the many French videos Ruth rented. Or she would sit curled up with her old college copy of *A la Recherche du temps perdu*, crying over the fate of poor Swann, doomed by foolish love, while she frantically looked up words in her *Petit Robert*.

I felt, in the excitement preceding Ruth's departure, a chance for a new beginning with her, and I put aside my feelings of jealousy and fear in the hope that she would return renewed. She went about her meals now with an added determination, like an athlete resolved to make weight, though I believe she took in not an ounce more than necessary. Certainly she still ruled her plate with an iron fork in an iron fist.

———

The night before she left for France we went out for dinner at Kayo's, Ruth's favorite Japanese restaurant on Columbus Avenue. I had suggested this place several days in advance so there would be no unnecessary anxiety attached to our last supper.

Once inside, however, I regretted the lean look of the place, and wished I had chosen a cozier restaurant. Ruth unsheathed her wooden chopsticks immediately and began nervously folding the paper sleeve into a little stand for them.

Ruth loved sushi for the care and beauty of its arrangement, each piece handcrafted by nimble fingers, the rice all combed in one direction as if each grain were magnetized. Japanese thinness inspired her, too: barring sumo wrestlers, it is a svelte culture. I also think the precut pieces relieved her of a certain anxiety—you *had* to eat each piece in one bite or it would fall apart. And the heady wasabi makes eating more a matter of inhalation than ingestion.

Wordlessly, she held up her chopsticks, still joined at the top. This was part of our ritual. Holding on to one stick, she let me take hold of the other and we snapped them apart like a wishbone. I had taken a lower grip than Ruth and she had come away with the top of my chopstick still fused to hers.

"You won," I said, handing her back her second chopstick. She whittled the two sticks together for a moment to smooth out the splinters. Her eyes were very green.

"You let me win," she said, matter-of-factly. "You always do."

I did not ask her what she had wished for.

The waiter came and Ruth ordered straightaway—in Japanese restaurants, Ruth had power of attorney over my dinner, since it was a shared meal. I was consulted, but this was merely a formality. She ordered three kinds of sushi: spicy tuna, yellowtail with scallions and salmon with avocado, and then raised the inevitable question—the waiter still bowed over us in his abbreviated black kimono—whether three rolls would be enough or if we should get a California roll just to be safe. I said a California roll would be fine with me.

Ruth decided to stick with three rolls of sushi but to add a bowl of miso soup. The soup arrived first, a ladleful of hot ocean. We passed the flower-painted tureen back and forth, sipping out of it as if it were a cup in a marriage ceremony. We hardly spoke but I knew from long practice not to take Ruth's silence personally.

When the waiter came again I ordered sake.

Ruth looked at me.

"It's a special occasion," I said. "We need to toast your trip."

Ordering without Ruth's approval seemed daring, reckless almost.

"I suppose so," she conceded. "I've never had sake."

"It's hot rice wine."

"I know what it is. Is it good?"

"Delicious," I told her.

I could see that she wanted to say something to me and I waited but she remained silent. Her face was blank and mysterious. I could not guess her thoughts.

The restaurant was crowded with couples. Some leaned whisperingly close together and some lounged comfortably back in their seats, some were young and some were old, some fed each other with chopsticks, some bickered. All of them were talking.

Outside the tatami room in the back of the restaurant shoes were lined up outside the sliding paper door and a woman in a bright red kimono, the only waitress in the place, was wobbling in and out on high wooden ceremonial shoes, carrying a tray. She looked like the wife in "The Rice Demon," small, obedient, with a flat, storybook face. What did she wear under her kimono?

Ruth sat scrunched up at the table as if she were trying to condense herself. This density, as always, drew me toward her as if she had more gravity than her size allowed. The other couples—the talkers, the eaters—were ordinary, dead, dull. They held no interest for me. Only the waitress in the red kimono, shuffling in those impossible shoes, and Ruth, compressed across the table, were present. The others might have been cardboard silhouettes.

Our sake arrived in a stone decanter with two ceramic cups. Ceremoniously, the brisk waiter filled each tiny cup with the warm wine. Ruth surprised me by raising hers in a toast.

"Joseph," she said, "I know it hasn't been easy. I owe you so much. You are my rock, you really are. And I'm trying."

"I know you are," I said.

"I'm going to come back a new woman. We'll begin again."

We clinked cups and Ruth brought the clear, sour liquid to her lips. She sipped, coughed and scowled.

"Are you all right?"

"I didn't expect it to taste like that."

"It takes getting used to."

"No, it's good."

Our sushi arrived, and Ruth placed a pink, transparent slice of ginger on her tongue to cleanse her palate, chewing cautiously.

"Can I ask you something?" she said at last. I was surprised to hear her speak.

"Of course."

"You promise you won't get mad?"

"I promise."

She waited another moment, staring at the food without touching it.

"Why don't you ever visit your parents?" she said at last.

It was not the question I was expecting.

"Joseph? Are you mad?"

"No," I told her. "I just don't know what to say. I've been busy. They've been busy."

"They invite you all the time."

That was true. My parents called often, urging me to come.

"I used to see them a lot. It's a phase."

"It's a phase that started," Ruth said quietly, looking away, "when you started living with me. Do you know that?"

"Coincidence."

"Is it?"

"Of course."

"You think I remind them of Evelyn, don't you? Or do I remind *you* of Evelyn? Are you afraid I'll get ideas?"

"Ruth! That's nonsense."

"Now you *are* mad."

"Yes, I am."

"You promised you wouldn't be."

"Well, that's such an outlandish accusation."

"Then forget I said it," Ruth said quickly. "It's just that . . . I don't want to remind you of Evelyn. There was a time I was almost jealous of her. But I don't want you to think I'm . . . like her. I want you to have faith in me."

My anger had melted away.

"I do have faith in you, Ruth."

"I'm glad," she said, and she did seem glad. "But promise me you'll visit them."

I said nothing.

"It's important, Joseph. For your own sake. Isn't it the anniversary of your sister's death soon?"

It was like Ruth to remember the date.

"End of August," I said. "Yes."

"It's a good time to go home," she said. "Visit them while I'm gone."

I reached across the table and touched Ruth's hand. I believe she took this as a pledge, and as an end to the discussion, for she began blending some soy sauce in a little porcelain saucer with a bit of wasabi, stirring it with the tip of her chopstick. She dipped her pinkie in and tasted the mixture furtively. She was back inside herself, which only made her departure more touching. She looked down at her meal as if it were a math problem on a final exam. Her mind seemed to whirl with private calculations. She took up her chopsticks and carefully pinched a piece of sushi off its low wooden altar.

What was it about Ruth that so moved me? She paid not the slightest attention to me and yet even her disregard had a transforming effect on me. How could I let her go? How could I let her out of my sight?

Ruth was concentrating intently on the remaining piece of sushi, seeing the world in a grain of rice. I had polished my share off ten minutes before, despite my resolve to wait for her. I studied the beautiful triangle of her face. Somewhere underneath lurked the real Ruth. It was this sense of concealment that made every encounter with her a kind of first date and kept me waiting, endlessly, for revelations. She caught me staring and lifted her lashes. The sake had gone to my head and Ruth's eyes, too, looked blurred with drink.

"Please don't study me like that," she said softly, blushing. "You're making me self-conscious." There was none of the defensive harshness in her that eating sometimes aroused.

I turned my attention away from her. The red kimono of the waitress caught my eye and then the long line of empty shoes outside the tatami room. At the sight of those empty shoes despair welled up in me.

"Don't go," I said, suddenly.

Ruth stared at me, her eyes wide.

"Don't go to Paris. Stay here with me."

A flushed, flattered look of confusion, almost mirth, suffused her face. She laid her chopsticks down and reached out her hand to me.

"Oh, Joseph," she said. "Do you really want me to stay?"

"Yes," I said.

"You mean that? Yes, I can see it in your face, you do." She was beaming with pleasure.

"I really do mean it," I told her, amazed at the emotion in my voice.

She looked at me with wonder, as if it were remarkable that anyone should truly want her to stay.

"It's too late now. The ticket's bought and everything."

She sounded unconvinced. I saw that she did not really want to go. That I could make her stay if I wanted to, if I begged her.

Perhaps if I proposed. For the second time the words were on my lips.

"Ruth—" I began.

She looked at me with fear and expectation.

"Marry me, Ruth. Stay here and marry me."

"Joseph!" There were tears in her eyes. "You don't want to marry me."

"But I do, Ruth. I do."

"No," she said. "But thank you. Ask me again someday. Not now. Don't ask me now."

I often wonder what would have happened if she had taken me up on my offer. At that moment I desperately wanted to cement her to me, to keep her always in my sight.

"Ruth, I'll miss you terribly."

We held hands across the table, my shirtsleeve in a little drip of soy sauce that spread like ink across my cuff.

"I'll miss you too," she said. She seemed relieved that I had not pressed my proposal. Had not begged. Had not disturbed things. Would she have stayed if I had persisted?

"I'll call and you'll call, too," she said. "Six weeks isn't so long."

"Don't take rides from Frenchmen on motorcycles."

Ruth smiled.

"Don't worry," she said. "I'll go everywhere on foot."

"And don't do everything Nadia does. She's . . . unreliable."

"Don't scare me," she said. "I'm scared enough."

"I'm sorry. There's nothing to be scared of. You're going to have a great time."

"I hope so."

"I know you will. *Magnifique.*"

The waiter arrived with my change and I let go of her hand to take it.

"I have to run to the bathroom," said Ruth, rising. "I'll meet you in front."

She threaded her way carefully through the diners, toward the back of the restaurant, past the row of empty shoes.

I looked out on Columbus Avenue. Well-dressed couples made the evening look cool. It was high summer, but the dummies in the clothing shop across the street were already dressed for fall.

Six weeks wasn't so long.

The morning after Ruth's departure I woke up with a headache—a piercing, lonely pain, though of shorter duration than usual, only fifteen minutes.

Afterward I drifted back to sleep and woke as if on the shore of some faraway place. I rose slowly, thinking of Ruth. I felt a faint echo of pain that had become so soft it was like a tiny hand touching my head. Sunlight filtered into the room and I opened the blinds and let in more, recoiling for a split second from the light but then welcoming it, feeling safe, for the god of pain had been appeased and would not come back that day.

I dressed slowly and made the bed. There was no damage, though there were days when I had to right overturned plants, sweep up the remains of a hurled and broken mug, recover books that, if encountered on the bed in the throes of a headache, I had flung away.

Once I had flung Max, though out of animal instinct or mere indifference he generally avoided me when I was sick. He had leaped on the bed, dangerous as a porcupine, each blade of fur a needle to my eye. I had seen, in the sick vision prompted by my migraine, that after an artery finally popped or the pain simply did me in, Ruth or the police would discover him nibbling my fingers or gnawing an eye. He had nuzzled my face and, in a mad burst of fury that drove a second knife into my temple, I tossed him and heard a sickening thud against the wall and a scramble under the bed, where I afterward found him sullen and suspicious, refusing to budge.

But nothing like that happened this time. I moved trance-like into the kitchen, where I put the kettle up and turned on the radio. A Haydn string quartet was playing, and though on plenty of days it might have meant nothing to me, in my slow and softened state it seemed perfect, beautiful, as if pain had opened me, made me more aware, more sensitive and grateful, and I saw why my father filled his office with music.

I raised the window, opened the refrigerator, and sat down with a container of strawberry yogurt. I sprinkled Grape-Nuts over it, but the crunch was too much for my face and head, delicate and warm as a new-laid egg, and I waited for the water to boil and the music to finish. I felt like Lazarus, newly risen, each note and breeze filled me with sleepy joy. The way sunlight fell on my hand seemed more beautiful than anything I had ever imagined.

I had an overwhelming desire to speak to Ruth, half expecting, in my trancelike state, that I could conjure her through the phone and she would appear in the kitchen. Ruth had left a slew of numbers where she and Nadia would be—a pension for the first few nights, with friends of friends for the following week, a professor's apartment for the last month, arranged by Mrs. Simon, who occasionally swapped her own apartment for a place in Paris and knew several academics there.

I tried to imagine where Ruth was at that moment. What she was thinking. Saying. Eating. Already I felt a gnawing insecurity, a disconcerting lack of knowledge. Though Ruth had only been gone a day I dialed, on impulse, the first number on the list taped to the refrigerator. It rang about ten times and then a woman's voice flashed by so fast I caught only its taunting cadence. Somehow I had imagined Ruth herself answering, and having prepared myself to hear her voice I was confused by the swift, confident, musical outburst. Frenchless myself, I could do no more than blurt out Ruth's name, which I repeated hopelessly several times to no effect. But there was no one there named Ruth, the woman, switching to broken English, insisted. It seemed a bad omen and I hung up distressed.

That evening, when I returned from teaching, there was a phone message from Ruth, who told me not only that she was staying at a different pension, but that the airline had lost her suitcase. The connection was poor, but she sounded upset. It was already 1:00 A.M. in France—too late to call—and the next morning, when I tried again, she was already gone. I spent the next day, on breaks from ETNA, frantically trying to track down her suitcase which, I learned, had been sent to Brussels but now seemed to be on another flight, though nobody was certain to where.

Uniting Ruth with her suitcase became an obsession, and I spent hours hollering at officials on both sides of the Atlantic. What would she wear? How would she cope? Ruth was a very neat and careful packer and had spent several days filling the large suitcase. I had been curious to examine its contents, but whenever she saw me hovering near she had shooed me away. Still, I had managed at the last minute to slip into the case a photograph Ruth had taken of me standing on the steps of Butler Library. Ruth had always liked the photo, and I hoped it would surprise and comfort her—though I suppose, too, it was a selfish act, for I did not want her to forget me.

Just how much I needed Ruth became painfully apparent in that first week. I hardly slept at all, I was in constant fear of another headache and had begun to feel, in my exhaustion and loneliness, a sort of madness creeping in. I had actually worn two different-colored shoes to ETNA one day, a source of delight for my students though disturbing to me. After my sister's death I had overheard whispered snippets of speculation from other family members—never my parents—that my sister had suffered from some undiagnosed mental malady, which explained her unexpected act of despair.

I had my own reasons for disbelieving this theory, knowing she had been sad for a long time. But I knew, too, that when my mother was a girl, a first cousin of hers had thrown herself under a train at the Atlantic Avenue subway station in Brooklyn. I had sometimes wondered whether there wasn't something in my family that was, if not mental illness, at least a kind of curse that made wanting to live a greater challenge. I had not thought about these things for a long time but now, in Ruth's absence, dark concerns began to resurface.

We spoke by telephone several times at last but the calls were awkward and full of intercontinental silence. It chilled me to hear Ruth's disembodied voice—I wanted to see her in the flesh, I wanted to touch her and make sure she wasn't slipping out of the material world. The distance magnified and distorted our emotions. When I suggested she come home she became offended and said I did not trust her. When I shared my fantasy of finding her in France, my arms full of her clothing, she actually laughed. The silences I found bearable across the dinner table were excruciating when stretched over six thousand miles. The emotional declarations we made before hanging up sounded desperate and final, shouted into a sucking void.

More comforting was Ruth's first letter. The familiar blue ink, the rounded letters I had seen illicitly in action in her diary on so many occasions, set my heart racing.

But the contents were brief and unsatisfying. The letter gave a quick account of her flight, her meeting up with Nadia two days later. The complaints were gentle—snooty waiters, pushy pedestrians, muggy weather. She took refuge in the museums: the Musée d'Orsay, the Pompidou, the Louvre. "I'm gorging myself on art," she wrote.

The letter ended with a reassuring word about her lost luggage. "Don't worry about the suitcase," she said. "You sounded more upset than even I was at first, but it doesn't bother me now. I feel freer without it. I really don't need much. It's hotter here than it was in New York. Maybe I don't need clothes. I feel like one of your Natashas, alone in a new place. I wish you were here. . . ."

I was stirred by the mildly flirtatious tone, though I did not enjoy the thought of Ruth strolling Godiva-like through the streets of Paris. More disconcerting was the idea that she didn't mind the loss of her things. Was this a sign of health, a newfound adaptability, or evidence of her renewed impulse to shuck the material shell of the world? That sixty-pound suitcase, heavy with home, was an anchor I wanted her to have. If only I were there to anchor her down myself.

But I was teaching in New York, where it was also hot enough to dream of life without clothes. It was so hot that summer that even Max lost his appetite and lay big and gray on the couch like a fallen cloud. I looked forward to the subway ride downtown—the new cars were cold as meat lockers. I hung from the metal loop as I rattled down to Union Square, planning my lesson for students who were stunned to discover that New York and Naples are on the same parallel. ETNA at least was air-conditioned—so powerfully that the women often wore shawls in class, though outside it was ninety-five degrees.

Blitstein had begun sharing the administrative details of ETNA with me, discussing the creation of new classes, the budget increase this would require, the possible expansion onto the twenty-ninth floor if we could get the lease. His services were in sudden demand, he was trembling with excitement, but it was with fading conviction that I faced my crowded classroom each morning. I performed the rudiments of speech like an actor stuck in a long-running play—I had read aloud the story about the Lower East Side a hundred times, I could recite from memory the paragraph about pets.

What was I doing there? I felt like my father, looking into endless open mouths, bottomless, infinite, one long tunnel of mortality. But my father understood the importance of distraction, and on those hot summer days I began to understand it too. I flung myself into teaching and even found that I had a knack for administrative details. And undoubtedly I continued to hope for something from my students—if only a piece of their invincible optimism, as if, standing before them, I might absorb their dogged faith in the future, their belief in the possibility of a new life.

But images of Ruth would not leave me. She haunted my imagination and I found myself invoking her in class in small private ways. I asked my students to picture Paris and describe it, to tell me what they would pack to take on a trip, what they would do if they were there. Blitstein would not have appreciated my impractical lessons, but it made me feel better to make my students scouts and spies, sending them after her on an invisible search.

After class, reluctant to go home, I often took long meandering walks that carried me past the Forty-second Street Library, closed at that hour. All those days of reading seemed strange and faraway, part of a dream, though one I wished to recapture. Ruth's illness had given more purpose to my life than anything had before, and now, without her, I felt bereft not merely of her presence, but of the reason for each day, of reason itself.

The speckled facade of the library was the color of dirty city snow, cooling to look at in the summer heat. I mounted the granite steps and stood before the nude marble statue of Beauty, pale in the failing light, and spoke, with an inner voice, to Ruth. I asked her if she was happy and if she was eating. I told her how sorry I was about the abortion and hoped it had not caused her too much pain. I apologized for failing to find her suitcase. I told her that I loved her. And sometimes, as if the giant marble statue were indeed the image of a goddess, I prayed for her return.

I always hurried past the burly figure of Truth, in which I saw the reproachful face of Flek, urging me to call. I did not wish to speak to him without Ruth in town. He would not, I felt, have approved of my behavior.

On one long, aimless walk home through the heat-warped city, I passed a little Italian restaurant, not far from the New School, where Ruth and I sometimes ate. I went inside and when the hostess asked if I was alone I told her, on impulse, that someone was joining me. She seated me at a booth in the back, where Ruth and I had once sat together. The waiter brought two waters and two menus.

I ordered for both of us, assuring the waiter that my wife would be arriving at any moment. I had never ordered for Ruth before. I decided she would want a salad, of course, but that there would be nothing wrong with a little pasta, and ordered her penne with pesto. I ordered a salad for myself, and a bowl of fettuccine.

The waiter asked if we would want the salads first and I told him no, bring everything together. Reluctantly, for he saw I was still alone, he did as I asked. I sat at the food-laden table, a prisoner of my own fantasy.

Meals, after my sister died, had been excruciating at home. The empty place where Evelyn had sat, the silence. The pain of eating when Evelyn could not. The very food seemed somehow an obscene indictment, proof of the guilt of the living. When I finally left home, the communal clamor of college dining had been a liberation. But here I was again, dining with ghosts.

I looked at the place set across the table, the steaming bowl of pasta, the cold salad, the bottle of wine I had ordered but had not touched, and began to cry. Alone in my booth I lost my appetite entirely. I paid amid the pitying looks of the entire restaurant.

When I got home that evening I found a letter from Ruth and two messages on the answering machine. The first was from my father, urging me to come home for the Jewish holidays, still over two months away. My mother had called the day before and I had not called back. I thought of Ruth, urging me to see them. In her absence I felt far more susceptible to their voices, to their pleas. "Come home, Joseph. Come home." I left a message on their office machine and told them I would try, though I knew I would not go.

The second message was from Felicia Thompson, an ETNA teacher who had always been particularly friendly to me and who had, the previous week, acted as an interpreter for me on one of my futile phone calls to France about what I now took to be Ruth's permanently lost suitcase. It was a short, friendly message inviting me to dinner later in the week. "I know you're all alone," she said, "and thought you might want some company."

While I considered Felicia's offer—it was safest, I decided, not to respond at all—I opened Ruth's letter, written on two sheets of fine onionskin paper. From the date I realized it was already two weeks old and would tell me nothing about her present state. Still, I read eagerly.

Dear Joseph,

Yesterday Nadia and I visited Rheims cathedral in a rented car. It's beautiful and huge and full of purple light. I felt tiny inside, just a little speck. Stones from the cathedral were sent to New York and are in the base of the statue of

Joan of Arc on Riverside Drive. She crowned Charles king at Rheims after leading his forces victoriously in battle and uniting France, and she was only twenty. I wanted to go to the tower of Rouen, where Joan was imprisoned and killed, but Nadia refused. When they burned Joan at the stake, her heart wouldn't burn. She wasn't afraid to die. I can't help feeling there's something very beautiful about the life of a saint like Joan. It makes me feel less alone here thinking about her, maybe because of the statue on Riverside Drive near where you are reading this letter.

Nadia's being impossible. She met some people she knows who live here and they go out every night and hang out in bars. I stay home most of the time because that's not me, but then suddenly I don't know who me is and I get scared. I don't really have a portable personality. I feel like the things that should keep me together are just tiny inside me, the way I was tiny in the cathedral. As soon as I write this I wonder what you'll think of me. You've probably had enough of my Sylvia Plathetudes. I don't mean to frighten you—you're one of the things that keeps me together.

I'm trying to draw every day. I was in the Luxembourg Gardens and I sketched a little child holding on to a big hand reaching down from the top of the page and I looked at it and said to myself, Where did that big hand come from? And suddenly I knew that it was your hand.

I love you,
Ruth

That night I dreamed I was walking around the reservoir in Central Park. A woman was walking ahead of me and I wanted to catch up to her, I felt I knew her. But the closer I got, the faster she walked. I called after her and she began to run. At last, when I was right behind her, she whirled to face me. I recognized, with terror, the statue of Joan of Arc, her sword raised high overhead. I woke with my heart pounding.

I could not fall asleep after that, and left the apartment early. I told myself I'd get some work done in the ETNA lounge before class, but I stayed on the train past my stop. As if still dreaming, I found myself at last at the graffitied outer door of Ernest Flek's loft.

I was buzzed into his apartment building and as I rose in the great, grinding elevator I thought about being there in winter with Ruth, and how much, and how little, had changed since then. I expected to see Flek, as I had that day, seated before me with a blanket on his lap. But when the elevator door opened, there, to my surprise, stood Carol Simon.

J oseph!" she said. "How wonderful to see you again."
She was wearing a big straw sun hat and a pale-blue dress—
a color Ruth often wore herself—which gave her a girlish
look. She kissed me warmly and took me briefly in her scented
arms.

She did not seem to find it strange that I had come for a
visit. She asked if I'd heard anything from Ruth.

"I got a letter yesterday," I said, unwilling to admit more.

"How nice," said Mrs. Simon. "I've hardly heard a word.
She must be having a *wonderful* time—though I'm sure she
misses you. It's a shame you couldn't go too."

"Yes."

"Well, you must be here for Ernest," she said, in her brisk,
cheerful way. "I'm so glad you've gotten to know him. You're
lucky you caught us. We're going to the country today for a
month."

I noticed, for the first time, several suitcases waiting to the
left of the elevator, and thought, with a pang, of Ruth's lost
luggage.

"A vacation wouldn't do you harm either," said the voice
of Ernest Flek. He was, in fact, in the very spot I had expected
to see him in, blocked by Ruth's mother, who now stepped
aside.

"I'm going to wait in the car," she announced. "Take your
time."

She kissed me again and got into the elevator.

"Well, Joseph," said Flek when I had approached. "Sit
down. Can I get you a cold drink? Coffee?"

I declined.

He was wearing a white polo shirt that exposed his dark, powerful arms.

"Where's Miranda?" I asked, scanning the vast room in case she might be crouching, undetected, beneath a table or chair.

"Camp," said Flek, with paternal pride.

"And you and Carol are going to the country?"

"You seem surprised."

I was surprised, but I was even more surprised by what seemed to happen to me in Flek's presence. I had not seen him for a long time—I did not, in fact, know him well, and yet I felt virtually obliged to say whatever popped into my head.

"I don't think you should be going away," I said, "with a woman like that."

"Like what, Joseph?"

"She's the problem," I blurted out, feeling Ruth speaking through me. "How can you be with her?"

"It doesn't surprise me that you believe that," Flek said calmly, "but you're wrong. You don't know Carol at all. Sit down," he said again, more firmly, motioning to a chair beside him. I sat.

Far from seeming perturbed by my abrupt outbursts, Flek seemed almost to encourage them—our visits contained a volatile mix of elements, part therapy session, part police investigation and part religious confession.

"How about your own parents? Have you visited them lately?"

"Everyone asks me that," I said, annoyed. "Ruth told me to see them before she went away, too."

"Ruth is right. By the way, how is she doing in Paris?"

"I don't know," I told him gloomily. "I got a letter yesterday dated two weeks ago. I have a strong feeling she isn't doing very well."

"And how are you doing?"

"Me? I'm fine."

"Headaches?"

"A few. That's not why I'm here, though. It's Ruth I want to talk about.

"Of course," he said. "But maybe it's time you talked a little more about yourself."

"But it's Ruth who's sick," I said. "It's Ruth who's alone."

"In the first place, she's not alone, as I understand it. In the second place, she's stronger than you imagine. And in the third place, you're not going to help her by inhabiting her illness. She's away now. Use this time."

I did not tell him about my sleepless nights, my pilgrimages to the library steps or my bizarre dinner for two the night before, but somehow I felt he knew.

"I'm worried about what might happen to her. What she might do. People do desperate things when they feel alone."

"Like your sister?"

"My sister has nothing to do with this."

"I think she does," Flek said gently. "You told me in the Harvard Club that you felt responsible for your sister's suicide. What did you mean by that?"

"Please don't ask me about my family," I said. His gentle coaxing threatened to distract me from the purpose of my visit and I felt mounting anxiety. "Don't you understand, it's Ruth. She needs me."

"You need her, Joseph. And I'm not sure it's for the noblest reasons. Ruth's illness is all about control—keeping chaos at bay, in her case through food. We all have different strategies for doing that, of course. I think yours is your obsession with her illness, but you can't use Ruth to replay your childhood with your sister. Or to hide from it."

The suggestion enraged me. I again felt like Ruth, whose moods changed with the speed of weather in the tropics. I was suddenly shouting, overcome by unexpected, bottomless rage.

"How dare you tell me that!" I shouted, my voice bouncing off the high ceiling as if I were yelling at myself. "You're the one using people. Teaching me about the body when you're only half a man yourself. Listening to my stories about Ruth because you don't have patients anymore. I worry about Ruth because I love her, which I guess is something you can't understand."

I had leaped to my feet—too quickly, for I was feelingly alarmingly light-headed. The medicine I took for my headaches always destabilized me, and I had, besides, forgotten to eat breakfast. I wobbled, grabbing hold of the back of Flek's chair, which, unanchored, rolled slightly beneath my grasp. I was hunched over Flek, who was looking at me more in concern than anger. He had reached out and taken my arm in his strong grasp.

"Sit down, Joseph," he said, levelly.

I did, already feeling ashamed of my outburst and baffled by it.

He pulled a clean, ironed handkerchief from his pants pocket and handed it to me. It was only then that I found I'd been weeping.

"I'm not saying you don't love Ruth," said Flek, in a conciliatory voice. "Certainly you do. I just think Ruth will be fine without you for a few weeks. What about you? You look like hell."

"I'm worried," I said softly, still feeling somewhat faint, as well as ashamed. "What if something happens to her? I'm responsible. I let her go. I knew about my sister and now it's too late. But Ruth . . ."

"Joseph!" Flek said sternly, as if calling me out of a trance. He had maneuvered his chair so that he sat directly before me, staring into my eyes. "Tell me about your sister. Why do you feel so responsible?"

His manner, despite my insulting outburst, was inviting, his expression stern but kind.

"She wrote a letter," I said at last.

"A suicide note?"

"I didn't know that's what it was. It was written several months before. A kind of pre-suicide note."

"And she sent it to you?"

"No," I told him. "I just found it."

"Where did you find it?"

"In her top drawer."

Flek smiled, not unkindly.

"Who was it addressed to?"

"Nobody. Or everybody, actually. It was addressed 'To the World.' "

"Like Emily Dickinson?" he asked. " 'This is my letter to the World/That never wrote to Me'?"

"Maybe," I told him. "She liked Emily Dickinson. I don't know. But she wrote a letter to the world and I'm the one who received it."

"You took it?"

"Yes. I took it out of her top drawer and kept it."

"And she never asked you about it?"

"No."

"Did you show it to your parents?"

"I didn't show it to anyone. I just kept it."

"Do you remember what it said?"

"Of course," I told him, taking out my wallet. "It's right here."

Even the unflappable Flek looked surprised at this.

"You carry it around?"

It was something I had not even told Ruth, eager though she was to learn about Evelyn, and I was surprised at how easily I volunteered the information now.

"It doesn't take up much room," I said, though as I explained this to Flek I realized, as if for the first time, just how strange it was that I had it at all.

I had taken the letter to college—as much to ensure that my mother wouldn't find it when she cleaned my room as to have it with me. I could not bear to throw it out. Eventually, carrying it simply became second nature. I moved it into each new wallet, where it lived uneasily among bus transfers and dollar bills and the occasional telephone numbers, a painful, but over the years oddly reassuring, presence.

"May I see it?" he asked, leaning forward slightly in his chair.

Still feeling light-headed, compliant, I opened my wallet and unfolded a small piece of ruled notebook paper, yellow with age, that had already been taped and retaped several times.

He took it in his large hands and as he read it to himself I recited it in my mind.

Dear world.

How are you? I don't care, it doesn't matter to me. What matters to me is how I am, and I am horrible. This is not a stage I am going through, this is for real. I don't see me changing for a really long time. Let me tell you something. I'm very unhappy right now. Boy, that seems typical. But, you see, you don't understand me anymore. It is not the usual, somehow, it is different this time. I feel like I'm at the end, like something has to happen now that I'm here, only nothing is happening. I'm still the same, and so is the rest of everybody. Why don't I change—why can't I understand myself? I'm full of emptiness inside. I feel very alone. I guess I don't like myself very much right now, even though theoretically I do. I have no hope left. Help me!

The letter was signed "Evie."

Flek sighed and handed the letter back to me.

"It's sad, Joseph. It's very sad. But this letter wasn't meant for you. And it is something any number of girls her age might have written without meaning anything at all."

"But I received it. I could have intervened."

"You're not responsible," Flek said. "And you need to stop believing you are. You need to stop going through top drawers in the hope of finding a letter like this again."

The buzzer rang, but Flek ignored it. He put his heavy hand on my arm.

"It's time to get down off the magic mountain, Joseph. It's time to enter life."

"Do people who are sane kill themselves?" I asked.

"Unfortunately," said Flek. "And people who are truly ill sometimes prove tougher than everyone around them. What makes you ask?"

"Some of my relatives," I told him, "thought Evie might have been sick, mentally—because there was so little warning. And because my mother had a cousin who . . . did the same thing. But I always knew it wasn't sudden, because of the letter. I knew how sad she was."

"The two have nothing to do with each other," Flek said. "God knows, sadness and mental illness are not incompatible. I have no idea about your sister's mental health and I doubt that's a question you'll ever answer. But knowing she was sad doesn't mean you knew what she would do."

"I could have helped her."

"Possibly," said Flek. "I'm sure your parents have suffered a great deal from that thought—and from the thought that they drove you away as well. I'm not saying your parents had nothing to do with your sister's isolation, but I certainly wouldn't say that they, or you, were responsible for what she did."

"They wanted us to have everything," I said. "They worked all the time."

"We are a precarious species, Joseph. Even in a loving family, a prosperous culture, there is plenty of sadness. Over a hundred years ago, Alexis de Tocqueville spoke of 'the strange melancholy which often haunts the inhabitants of democratic countries in the midst of their abundance, and the disgust at life which sometimes seizes upon them in the midst of calm and easy circumstances.' But you don't need more books to read. . . ."

The buzzer rang again, a long persistant trill, and Mrs. Simon's voice bounded into the apartment through the intercom.

"Ernest? I'm roasting down here."

I stood up.

"I should go myself," I said. "I'll be late for class."

"I'll be back in a month," said Flek. "You can always leave a message for me here."

I took his outstretched hand and shook it.

"Do you want me to take any of these downstairs?" I asked penitently, pointing to the suitcases against the wall.

"No, we have a driver. He'll do it. Tell Carol to send Charlie up and that I'll be down in five minutes," he said.

"Please forgive me," I began, but Flek cut me off.

"Forget it," he said. "I've heard much worse."

When I was already inside the elevator, before the door had shut, he called my name.

"Everyone makes his own choice to live or die," he said. "Make yours."

I arrived at ETNA eager to lose myself in a crowd of Russians. There were already several students in the lobby, two women were passing a package of plastic fingernails back and forth, someone was reading a Russian newspaper, a chess game was in progress, with a small crowd of kibbitzers smoking and pointing. The older Russians were most comfortable talking in the hallway, leaning conspiratorially together, a habit left over from the days when their offices were bugged.

There were few familiar faces in this crowd, so heavy had the influx of new immigrants been. I went unnoticed. The light in Blitstein's office was on and I crept quietly past.

Felicia was already in the teachers' lounge, reading the *Post* and eating a doughnut. She looked up when I came in. *"Ciao, bello,"* she said, in her breezy, flirtatious manner.

Felicia had spent a year in Rome, where ETNA had a branch, processing the Russians on their first stopover en route to America. When the flights became direct and the Rome office was closed, Felicia had come to New York to seek her fortune as an actress. She'd waited tables while auditioning for shows, but in the end she had gone back to ETNA, figuring that any audience was better than none, even if it knew no English.

I thanked her for her invitation and apologized for not responding. "I've been distracted," I told her vaguely.

"Some other time," she shrugged, wiping a flake of sugar glaze off her lip with her pinkie and smiling. "But is everything all right? You look awful."

"I'm okay," I told her, prying off the lid of my coffee. "I just didn't sleep much."

Felicia looked at me, wrinkling her nose with interest.

"Do you lead some kind of secret life we don't know about?" She giggled. "I thought you were so respectable."

Felicia was tall, large-boned, with straight black henna-reddened hair. Not quite pretty, she made you feel she was. She wore short skirts and heavy hiking boots and too much eye makeup, and when she taught she sat on the desk. Blitstein did not like her and she'd had more than one run-in with him, but he was desperate for teachers that summer so he kept her.

"I'm really getting sick of this place," said Felicia, lighting a cigarette. "I hear at Manhattan Community College they give you twenty dollars an hour. But you have to have a master's in English as a Second Language and learn about glottals and plosives and phonemes and shit like that. Sally's been taking classes. She told me."

I was only half listening to Felicia, but I found her chatter soothing. My conversation with Flek had unsettled me. I felt on the brink of a revelation and yet greatly in need of distraction.

"Of course," Felicia was saying, "the money's in Japanese businessmen, not Russians. I'm sick of Russians. They're worse than Italian men and they're not even cute. There's one guy in my class, Sergei, a real goon, who follows me home every day. It's beginning to get on my nerves."

She paused, took a long drag on her cigarette and looked at me.

"Kenneth tells me you live with your girlfriend," she said.

"Yes, usually—she's in Paris."

"Of course, the suitcase!" said Felicia. "Did you ever find it?"

"No," I said.

"Well, I'm sure it'll turn up. Maybe in ten years—it'll be like a time capsule. All kinds of things you've forgotten about."

I did not find Felicia's remark comforting, though she said it cheerfully. I wondered where Ruth would be, where I would be, in ten years. The office was filling up with other teachers and other conversations. I concentrated on my coffee and Felicia went back to her newspaper.

Felicia's remark had renewed my keen sense of loss. It was the fourth week of Ruth's absence. Today, I thought, I will buy a ticket to France. Flek had urged me to choose life, but why shouldn't that mean finding Ruth?

The bell rang its long note of childhood misery, putting an end to office discussion. We all filed out the door.

The day passed slowly and I was hoarse before it was half over. Instead of eating lunch I spent my break in a nearby travel agency pricing tickets to Paris. Eight hundred dollars was more than I had, but no cash was required for a reservation and I made one for Monday. I doubted I would use it, but it consoled me to know that I might. Teaching the second half of the day I already felt closer to Ruth and enjoyed teaching more than I had for a long time. At day's end, though, I was followed out of class by a newcomer in a Stalin mustache and a "Shit Happens" T-shirt, who badgered me all the way down the hall.

"Why you joke at Minsk? Minsk is big city. Minsk have one million peoples, Minsk is not joke. Brooklyn is joke."

Someone tapped me on the shoulder. I looked up and saw Felicia smiling at me.

"Teachers' meeting," she said, leading me away by the arm. The man from Minsk drifted off.

"I owe you one."

"Well, you can pay me off right now. Sergei's waiting for me." She nodded and I saw, standing by the elevator, an abject, bearded figure with a hangdog expression, eyeing us both.

"Walk out with me," she whispered in my ear.

Blitstein expected me, but his office was empty and I walked into the elevator with Felicia. Sergei joined us but was too shy to speak and on the sidewalk headed off in the opposite direction.

Felicia and I stood for a moment in silence. The heat surprised me after four hours of ETNA air-conditioning.

"I can't talk you into dinner?" Felicia asked. "You look like you could use a good meal."

She was right. I was still taking pills for my headaches, though I had not had one in many days, and the medicine disrupted my metabolism. In my hurry to see Flek that morning and to reserve a flight that afternoon, I had skipped both breakfast and lunch. Dinner would not have been a bad idea. But I declined Felicia's invitation.

"I've got some things to do," I said.

She shrugged, smiled, touched my arm lightly and walked off. I wanted to start walking too. I felt in need of my customary ramble home, but for some reason my feet would not move. The ETNA building was pitching weirdly to the right. I looked down in time to see my feet rushing up to meet me.

Memory for a moment was erased. Where was I? The voices were foreign. My head was on a soft pillow. My eyes, still shut, saw dancing darkness, and when I opened them, Ruth! It was Ruth! But her face resolved into other faces. I wasn't in bed, but on the sidewalk.

The man from Minsk, who had followed me out of class, had been standing near me on the street and caught me as I fell. He was kneeling patiently beside me, his hands cradling my head. Several other students were bending over me as well, along with Felicia, who had seen the commotion and doubled back. It was Felicia I had mistaken for Ruth.

"Is this one of the things you had to do?"

"I forgot to eat lunch," I said, wide awake now. "That's all."

"In that case," she said, "you really must eat dinner."

This time I didn't argue. The Russians were still hovering, poking me and murmuring, so that I felt like Gulliver stretched out on the Lilliputian shore. A woman who had been a doctor in Russia was trying to take my pulse, my wrist enclosed in her fingers as she consulted the huge face of her Russian wristwatch. I disengaged my arm from her grasp. Felicia helped me slowly to my feet.

I allowed her to lead me away, a little crowd of murmuring Russians still trailing us so that I wasn't sorry when she hailed a cab and bundled me into it.

She took me to a small Italian restaurant in the East Village, not far from ETNA but far enough away to avoid further encounters with my students. She was concerned about me, but not panicked. I felt suddenly that she was someone who had functioned in crises before, that this was nothing for her.

After eating an entire basket of bread with butter and swallowing several quick glasses of water, I began to feel sound again. Felicia sat patiently, talking little and watching me stuff bread into my mouth. The lingering effects of my blackout were, if anything, pleasant. A serenity had settled over me that made me feel impervious to further disruptions, as if illness were protective. I thought of Ruth forcing herself to throw up as a way to soothe her system, and I felt that I had come to understand yet another of her methods.

I was feeling sufficiently recovered that when Felicia said, "A little red wine will revive you—that's what they'd give you in Italy," I didn't contradict her. As it happened, red wine was terrible for my head, a red flag to the bull in my brain waiting to stick in his horns. But I hadn't had a headache in days and there is a certain dark recklessness that comes after lying on a city sidewalk.

We ordered dinner and Felicia ordered the wine.

"Something better than the house red," she told the waiter. "Something good."

"Celebrating?" he asked, and Felicia, to my astonishment, said, "We've just gotten engaged."

"Really!" said the waiter. "Hey!" he announced to the restaurant at large, "They just got engaged."

Somehow, after passing out in front of ETNA, I was not bothered by Felicia's joke. I saw the appeal these actors felt in acting, in wishing to be, however briefly, a new person. There were a few hoots and scattered applause. Felicia winked at me. The owner gave us a bottle of red on the house, and we raised our glasses in a toast.

"To marriage," I said.

Felicia and I clinked glasses.

The waiter was very attentive.

"How did you propose?" he asked me.

"Out on the street," I said.

"Did you get down on one knee?"

"No," I said.

"He got down on both knees," said Felicia. "In fact, he was basically lying down."

We both laughed, though my laughter rang hollow in my ears.

"You're a terrible actor," she said, after the waiter had left. "You have no conviction in your lies. We're supposed to be newly engaged. Where's your passion?"

She took my hands in hers.

"My God," she said, "your hands are ice!" She rubbed them vigorously. "We'll have to warm you up." She put my fingers to her lips and blew hot breath on them. Smoke from her cigarette clung to her lips like mist from uncorked champagne.

"You're not going to faint again?"

I said I wouldn't, though some part of me, deep inside, felt knocked out cold.

I remembered proposing to Ruth on her last night in New York and wondered how, if she had accepted, this scene might have happened with her—though the tiny Italian restaurant was cheering us on more than the Japanese place would have. Part of me felt that it *really was* happening with Ruth, though I was alive, too, to the artificial nature of the evening, and Felicia's presence. Nevertheless I embraced her lie as a welcome distraction, just as I saw blacking out as a kind of perverse gift my body had given me. Again I applied Ruth's contrarian formula, which viewed illness as the road to health, control as the path to freedom, denial as the way to fulfillment. In the restaurant, light-headed, this seemed to me a religious insight, the strange wisdom of her methods. If only she were there to share it.

From habit, I was keenly aware of Felicia's plate and noticed that she had ordered linguine with clam sauce, and ate without shame or restraint.

"You like to eat," I said, realizing, as soon as the words were out of my mouth, how insulting they might be to someone unfamiliar with my history. But Felicia did not seem offended.

"Of course I do," she said, with an odd knowingness. "I'm no angel. I like food. I like sex. I like wine."

She raised her glass again.

"To life," she said. It would have been a corny toast had Flek's exhortation not been ringing in my ears.

"To life," I repeated, though as I drank I felt an electric alarm run through my body, warning me of headaches, and the risks of medicine and alcohol. My sister, after all, had recklessly downed her pills with vodka and the memory made me feel close to her. Perhaps it was only this she was craving, a moment of forgetting, a new birth into someone else. A desire to be careless and free.

I downed my wine in one long swallow. If I blacked out again, so be it. But I did not black out and instead saw everything with perfect clarity and in that clarity wondered if I was making a fatal mistake.

"Choose life," Flek had said, but was I? It felt like the dark opposite of what he must have meant.

Since its early eruption in my life, I have hated disorder and feared its return. Ruth, heavy with her own grief, had somehow been my anchor. Now the chain had snapped and I was adrift in chaos. Felicia offered a weird distraction, a temporary mooring. I took one of her cigarettes in an effort to inoculate myself against strangeness. In the same spirit, I kissed her.

The evening was headed for its obvious conclusion, though it took time and more alcohol to fulfill. It followed dessert and coffee as well as the bottom three inches of several bottles we found in Felicia's apartment in various stages of fermentation. She lived in a studio carved out of the third floor of a tenement off First Avenue. A summer storm had begun as we left the restaurant and we'd arrived soaked. It was still pouring outside, and booming thunder. The windows in her place were closed against the rain. Elvis, her parakeet, was out of his little cage and flying around the room.

"You have a pet," I said.

"A pet?" screamed Felicia. "Did you say a pet?" And she recited, with minor variations, from the ETNA workbook: "A pet can be a dog or a cat, a parakeet or even a rabbit. Many Americans have pets. Sometimes they treat them like members of the family. They knit sweaters for their dogs. They take their rabbits to movies. They abuse their hamsters."

She burst into unbalanced laughter, knocking over a chair and laughing even harder.

"I found him in Tompkins Square Park," she said at last. "I took him home in my knapsack. I help the homeless."

She was drunk and so was I, though I'd had far less than she. My head was growing tender, though I had downed another pill with my last sip of wine. Elvis, pale blue as if he had been dipped in sky, flew in circles around the dark, untidy room-and-a-half.

"Is he tame?" I asked.

"If you were the size of a birdseed he'd peck you up in a second, but he's tame enough."

Elvis perched suddenly on the windowsill and shuffled himself like a pack of cards.

"A toast," cried Felicia, jumping up and filling two shot glasses with Cointreau. I had drunk as much as I could stand and after clinking glasses I set mine on the night table.

"You're cheating," she said.

"I took some medicine earlier," I said. "It really doesn't mix with alcohol."

"I used to take lithium," Felicia said, "but it made me pee all the time so I gave it up. Does your medicine make you pee all the time?"

We were sitting side by side on her unmade bed. Felicia drained her glass and, pressing her lips against mine, passed me the liqueur in a kiss of fire. I swallowed it down, gasping, aroused.

We kissed now without restraint. The emptiness within, the effect of my medicine, the fear of pain, the thoughts of Ruth and of my sister vanished.

"You're becoming a much better actor," she said, delighted.

The play wasn't over but the lights went out.

———

That night I dreamed I was back in my parents' house. I stood outside my sister's bedroom. The door was open although it was nighttime. Someone was sleeping in the bed, hidden under covers.

There was a light on and I walked inside. Beside the bed was a night table. I walked to the edge of the bed. The floor creaked, but the body in the bed did not wake up. I felt surrounded by sleep and darkness. I floated like the dream of the sleeping form. I felt like a dream inside a dream, but I did not wake up.

My sister's glasses were on the night table. Under them lay a book. The glasses lay there as if they continued to read into the night. They straddled the cleft between the two halves of the book and they were legs as well as glasses and somehow sexual. I leaned closer and tried to read the words on the page, but I could not. The handwriting was Ruth's, but the letters were foreign and meaningless. The sleeper stirred and then fell silent, a mute shape beneath the blankets. I wondered where my sister was.

I picked the glasses up, careful not to touch the lenses. The book looked naked without the glasses on top. I turned away from the indecent book.

I wondered again where my sister was. I put the glasses on.

My eyes burned and blurred. A great weight came down on them. I turned my head as if to clear things but the feeling followed me. The room changed its shape. It kept changing its shape, squeezing the furniture and the air and squeezing my eyes. I felt weak and dizzy. The room became a dark wave that broke over me.

I am going to be sick, I thought. I grabbed the glasses off my face and they fell to the floor with a clatter. One of the lenses popped out and lay at my feet. It looked like a watch without any time in it.

The figure on the bed woke and called my name. The voice was like a flash of lightning. The room had grown completely dark, but I saw a hand reach out to me. To turn on the lamp? To strike me? The arm reached out, and a great silent scream choked me awake.

———

I woke panting in a strange bed. Venetian blinds, half raised, threw ribs of light on the far wall. The windows were shut and the room was tropically hot. A pale blue parakeet perched serenely on a chair back, preening.

Felicia was not beside me. I found her in the bathroom, taking a shower. She stood under the spotlight of water, face upturned, eyes shut. She jumped when I touched her.

"Woa, I've seen *Psycho* too many times," she said. "Hey, you're dressed."

"I've really got to go," I said. Panic and guilt were at this point indistinguishable.

She squinted at me through the water. Cleansed of the eye makeup that had given her face a slightly tarnished look the night before, she had a pure, scoured appearance. I noticed, for the first time, that there were freckles on her nose and faint lines along the ridge of the cheekbone.

"Shampoo me," she said.

"I have to go."

She handed me a bottle of shampoo.

"It won't take long."

Despite my sense of urgency, I obeyed. The large shower curtain was parted, her back was to me and the cleft in her buttocks reminded me of the book in my dream. I leaned in enough to work the soap in, piling her hair onto her head, working my fingers deep into the sudsy lather, feeling the grit of hair against her scalp and the curved skull beneath. I was not fully awake and the warm water, the nearness of this woman's body, and the intoxicating fruity odor of shampoo misted my brain. Water drizzled onto me.

"Ooh, that feels great. You have wonderful hands."

My soapy hands had slid to her shoulders and in a horrified vision I saw myself choking her. Instead I reached around and held her breasts.

She tilted forward slightly, as if to push her breasts into my hands. Her spine tautened and I noticed an extra bone at the base, a tiny stub where fifty million years ago there'd been a tail.

"I thought you had to leave."

"I do," I said, letting go.

She turned and, naked, faced me with the full force of her body.

"You'd better make up your mind."

Looking at her now I realized that she was older than I was, perhaps ten years older. Her body had a different look and a subtly different shape from women I had known. Her breasts had an almost leisurely fall, there seemed an earthward tug on them, and on the swell of inner thigh, palely veined with blue.

I strained to remember what Ruth's body looked like, as if her body stirred inside this other woman's. My heart began to race.

"I have to go."

"Suit yourself," said Felicia, dragging the shower curtain shut as if modesty had suddenly overtaken her. "The door locks automatically."

She sounded matter-of-fact, resigned, but as I reached the door she added, in a scream that curdled my blood, "Don't let the bird out!"

It was still early. I walked aimlessly along the cracked side-walks and spurting fire hydrants of the hot neighborhood. It had stopped raining. Large milky puddles glinted in the sun, and the gutter ran with water. Traffic moved as in a dream, slow until I crossed its path and found it bearing down with unexpected speed that made me run. A police car nosed through a red light, releasing bubbles of sound.

An exhausted prostitute hobbled by on high heels, going home or still working the empty street. I had only glimpsed her face, yet it seemed familiar. Where had I seen that black hair and red lipstick, the sway of those hips? Could she be an ETNA student? There were plenty of rumors about prosti-tutes brought here by the Russian Mafia, abandoned mail-order brides, unlucky women who had fallen on hard times and turned to the streets.

Ilena! I took a few hurried steps toward her and called her name. Ilena! The woman turned and gave me a toothy grin.

"You can call me anything you want, honey."

"Oh, I'm sorry," I said, and hurried past.

"Asshole!" she yelled after me.

I felt I deserved the insult. Unshaven, in yesterday's clothes, my head battered by alcohol, I felt gross, physical. The city, too, seemed to bear a heavy material shell that morning. I was keenly aware of the broken crust of concrete underfoot, the brick facades and rusted scaffoldings. I felt a negating impulse to erase the weight of the world and, like my sister, escape the bonds of life.

Among the stores lining the waking street was a travel agency, and though they were still setting up I banged on the glass. A young Asian woman let me in reluctantly. I must have looked, in my rumpled state, like a fugitive, but she sat me down while she and the other agent booted their computers and prepared to begin the day. I stared at a poster of a frigid Alp and imagined myself already in the air, looking down.

I had made a reservation the day before, but I canceled it and made a new one, scheduled to leave Kennedy the following evening. I bought the nonrefundable ticket outright. Patty, my agent, scrutinized the face on my driver's license, squinting skeptically at me for several minutes, but at last took my check. As soon as I had the ticket in my hand I felt a surge of joy.

The purchase left me with less than a hundred dollars in my bank account, but I didn't care. There was something liberating about having cleaned myself out to visit Ruth. In two days I would be with her.

I walked the streets now with a lighter step. The ticket was in my breast pocket, folded in half as if I might board at any moment. Felicia and the night before were far behind me. I felt a new sense of purpose.

Perhaps we would stay in France for a while, abandon our lives here and begin again. Surely I could find some way to make money over there. Or we could drift east, to Prague, say. Several ETNA teachers had spent time there and assured me you could live cheaply and even eke out a living—waiting tables, tending bar.

The thought that I might work as a waiter filled me with perverse satisfaction. Perhaps Ruth and I could open a little place of our own. Ruth could sit in coffee shops for hours—where better to help her recover a normal appetite than in our own restaurant in romantic Prague, an old city waking to new life? Perhaps it would bring the final healing. Just the two of us in our own café from morning till night. We could live above the restaurant in one of those grand, neglected apartment-palaces.

I drifted along in my reverie, trying to think of a name for our little restaurant. Something in defiance of Ruth's illness, something to prove to us both that she had come full circle. Flek's tale of hunger denied, "The Rice Demon," had made a deep impression on Ruth, but people might mistake it for a Japanese restaurant. "The Golden Cage" had more of a middle European, fin-de-siècle sound. So did the title of Ruth's favorite Kafka story, "The Hunger Artist." Kafka himself (I discovered in the library) had been obsessed with food. He chewed every mouthful over a dozen times and dreamed of ending his days as a waiter in a Tel Aviv restaurant. Perhaps in his honor "The Hunger Artist" should be a bookstore café. Weren't the book and the body our two failed paths to mastery?

But the name I liked best was "Eve's Apple." Ruth had once joked that Adam's apple had stuck in his throat but Eve had avoided swallowing and should never have been expelled. The name would be a symbol of Ruth's defiance, her rebellion against the myth of Genesis, for all the apple of knowledge, of desire, of death still ruled us. It would be a private joke shared by two exiles, and Ruth did have a sense of humor about herself. She might even persuade her father to bankroll the venture. Surely Mr. Simon would endorse the enterprising spirit of his son-in-law to be.

The dream was so vivid that I actually saw our café, with Ruth's paintings on the wall (it would be a gallery, too) and great copper espresso machines behind the bar. The very streets around me began to seem like Prague, narrow and confusing. So much so that I soon realized I was lost.

A sign in scratched gold Hebrew lettering printed on glass caught my eye. It was not the first I had seen, but the others had merely contributed to my exotic fantasies. Now, however, I realized that I had wandered south and was roaming the Lower East Side.

I did not know the neighborhood well, and except for a brief trip with my ETNA students, it had been years since I'd spent any time there. The ETNA trip was intended to teach the Russians a little about the waves of immigrants that had preceded them, but they had been unmoved by the experience. Someday, when they were safely in the suburbs, they would no doubt tell their grandchildren about Brighton Beach and Midwood and the other areas of Brooklyn where they lived resentfully today, imbuing the very names with the luster and romance of legend.

But on that trip I had never seen them more bored. The very things that made them strong and appealing to me hardened them to any romanticized view of someone else's immigrant past. They were practical dreamers and I envied their vitality and purpose. I had been drawn to them out of my own wish for these things, and out of a wish, perhaps, to be at the beginning and not, as I felt, at the end. The end of *what* I could not quite have said.

My own great-grandparents had lived somewhere in this neighborhood, as I told my unimpressed students. My grandparents had moved to Brooklyn and my father, a dentist, had made it all the way to suburban New Jersey. It was a story meant to inspire them, but it didn't. "I make New Jersey myself," one of them told me. Another said, "New Jersey not so nice. I go to Scarsdale." A third, one of my more colloquial students, had said in his jeering manner, "How come you still stuck with immigrants?"—echoing the familiar Russian sentiment that anyone who taught Russians for a living must indeed be a loser.

I did not know where my great-grandparents had lived, but my father told stories of going to see them for the Jewish holidays. As a good student bound for a profession, he was treated with great respect. He had fond memories of crowded, hysterical, overfed religious gatherings. A live carp, kept in the bathtub, was waved over his head to atone for his sins and then clubbed to death for the pot.

My sister had been very taken with this and other stories. When she was in fifth grade and received an assignment to create a family tree, we all made the drive from New Jersey so that we could see where my father's grandparents had lived. My sister brought her Instamatic so she could snap pictures to tape onto her cardboard tree. Evelyn always took her schoolwork with the utmost seriousness. We *had* to find the tenement. We had to.

But we could not. My father couldn't remember where it was. He had been a small boy, the visits had stopped when he was still a child. He could, and already had, showed us the house in Borough Park he himself had grown up in. We had all been there to visit his parents—my grandparents—before they retired to Florida. But my sister wanted the old place, the mythic place. Like me, it seemed, she had a passion for immigrant origins, for large, vigorous families. You would have thought, walking down the street with her, that she expected to find a large happy family waiting to take her and the rest of us into its warm bosom.

But the Lower East Side was now Chinese, and though there hadn't been that much new construction, my father simply could not remember where the place was. There had been a great-aunt on Rivington Street, but were his grandparents on Orchard or Allen? In the end he wasn't even sure of that. They themselves had later moved into a kind of high-rise project of the undistinguished sort, visible here and there beyond the tenements.

"Why don't you just pretend it's this one?" my father had said, pointing to a building at random. "Go ahead, take a picture. No one will know. It certainly could have been this one."

This upset Evelyn enormously. She stamped her foot in fury on the cracked pavement. She wept. "I'll fail!" she wailed, "I'll fail!"

No one believed her, of course. Who would? She never failed. Her grades were always higher than my own but they did not come without effort. She poured hours of preparation into every assignment. Anything less than a perfect score seemed to diminish her whole being.

It was not simply about failing. She had a fantasy she'd shared with me that my parents, when they found the old place, would actually buy the tenement and we would all move there from New Jersey. Why not? We would live on one floor. Nana and Grandpa would come back from Florida to live on another floor. Beatrice, my mother's sister, who lived in Cleveland, would live on another floor with her whole family. And on the ground floor, my father could treat his patients.

Immediately I'd abused her confidence and announced her plan, declaring, at every crumbling, urine-stained, boarded-up building we came to, "Let's buy this one. It's perfect. Oooh, let's live here." My sister always laughed at my jokes until the moment came when she began to cry.

Now there were crack vials on the sidewalk. That my sister thought we could move back to such a place was absurd, though as I walked along I felt how beautiful, how mysterious, how heartbreaking her fantasy was. She wanted desperately and most of all for everyone to be happy and in one place.

It was why she helped out in my parents' office. I had hated this endless effort to insinuate herself into their work, but she joined them not because she cared about dentistry but because that was the only place to find them. My father had labored single-mindedly to build up his practice, and teeth were the only currency of value in my home. They jangled in every corner of our lives. Evelyn worked in the office because they did, and she pretended to be fascinated.

Why had no one seen how sad this was, and how much a bottomless need for love must have moved her to surrender her own childhood? My parents thought only what a good, if fragile, girl she was. And I was too busy resenting her devotion to notice what was happening. To wonder, as I wondered now, who she really was. There were so many moments when she obsessively labored to please those around her that she figured in certain remembered scenes more as a beloved, highstrung servant than a member of the family.

How fitting, though cruel for my parents, that it was Valium from their office that Evelyn had stolen and ultimately swallowed. She had brought the pills to trembling patients numerous times before she took them herself—a mortal taste of medicine, chased down with vodka from the seldom-used liquor cabinet, that cured her of sorrow for good.

I tried to remember where Katz's Delicatessen was, but could not. You had to look hard to find the Jewish stores at all amid the Chinese and Hispanic life stirring on the street. Most of the shops were shuttered. The synagogues were also closed, for sale, perhaps, though a few had scaffoldings that promised possible renovation.

The Jewish Lower East Side was hidden, an overgrown garden. It was the place my sister had wished us all to return to—boisterous, intimate, familial. The childhood of American Jews. I knew from my students how brutal immigrant life could be, but in Evelyn's mind it was the great antidote to the inert suburban world. She wanted to puncture the hermetic workaholic world my parents lived in. She wanted us all to begin anew in an old place. If only we could have.

What had happened—to my sister and then to Ruth? Was it what Flek had spoken of on that last visit, the "strange melancholy" that afflicts prosperous democracies? What was my sister's fantasy of turning back the clock and being again an immigrant family? Was it a healthy urge to live as my great-grandparents had at the energetic beginning of the century, instead of as my parents did at its exhausted end?

"I'm so sorry," she had written in the note she'd left behind, the one addressed to Mom and Dad, not the World. "I don't seem to know how to be happy." And, in the line directed terrifyingly to me, "Joseph, make them happy."

I wanted to find Katz's Deli, where my family had eaten together after the fruitless search to find the ancestral tenement. My sister was still panicking that her project had been ruined, her fantasy spoiled, her homework in doubt. When we all piled in I'd said, "Why don't we buy Katz's Deli? Nana and Grandpa could live over there, Aunt Beatrice could live in the kitchen, we could live in that booth . . ."

"Enough, Joseph," my mother had said, but I'd actually gotten my sister to smile. Still, the tears fell intermittently all during lunch. Why hadn't I realized that her desire for perfect outings and perfect grades and absolute harmony wasn't funny at all?

The only one who had taken her weeping seriously was the waiter, a rude, wrinkled man who carried a red cloth napkin draped over his forearm like a bullfighter's cape. In memory I pictured him stooped and humped like Mr. Blitstein. Certainly he'd had an accent. He was gruff, almost tyrannical in the way he moved among the tables, but he took pity on Evelyn and brought her a free cup of tea. When my father tried to send it back the waiter said "Don't worry, big spender, I'm not going to charge you. It's for the girl. Tea for tears."

That day in Katz's Delicatessen, Evelyn had left her food untouched. She wanted only the tea the waiter had brought her. But everyone ignored the untouched sandwich. We never took a family outing again once she was gone. . . .

An old Chinese woman hobbled up the street. A delivery boy pedaled past me. I wanted suddenly, with terrible longing, to be with Ruth. I should have married her. I should have made her stay. I needed her back.

Perhaps, I thought, looking around, Ruth and I could move down here. Find a two-bedroom apartment. Start a family. Why go to Prague? We could open Eve's Apple right here.

But as I wandered along the waking, graffitied streets, I felt a terrible haunting remorse that went beyond Ruth, beyond even Evelyn, and the more I walked, the more this nameless guilt assailed me. Ruth's body held a hollow secret. Inside the missing Ruth was a missing child.

The ghost had found its way back to me. Ruth had refused to speak of it. She had wished to forget the abortion completely. It was a photograph she had torn up and scattered to the wind. But I had found the negative. The lure of the shadow-world Flek had warned me against grew too great. I thought, for the first time, it seemed, that people really do have souls and that a soul had been summoned and dismissed. I felt it beating against me like a moth, as real as Ruth was real, though unseen. This was, weirdly, a kind of dark comfort.

But I had allowed this child to die. Evelyn—for surely that is what she would have been called. I felt certain it would have been a girl. Ruth, fascinated as she was with my sister, and with her name, which she uttered in a breathless whisper as if it were magic, would have agreed. My daughter, Evelyn. Evie! What else did we come into the world for but to create new life? To undo death. And I had failed. I had sacrificed my child.

Ruth, my sister and my shadow child merged, distracting me so that I was surprised to discover suddenly that it was raining. I walked along as large, slow drops fell heated from the sky. And I realized I was going to get a headache.

I tried to will it away, to ignore it, but already my left eye produced a tear, a sure sign of the pain to come. I lifted my face to let the rain carry it away, and indeed, strangely, the pain seemed to recede. It began to pour. The sidewalk boiled. I stood under the overhang of a small stone synagogue. The facade was melting away like an old tombstone and the double wooden doors looked closed for good. I heard a muffled din that might have been no more than wind and rain but it made me think of prayer.

Stirred by a strange impulse, I tried the door. It was locked. I banged futilely on the heavy door for a few moments but there was no response. The pain in my head was growing stronger. If I could only go inside, I thought, the pain would stop. I leaned against the door and tried to imagine the worshipers who had once prayed there. I saw them in hats, standing, feet pressed together as if they all stood on bathroom scales. I tried to imagine myself among them.

My parents wished me to come home for the anniversary of my sister's death, and for the Jewish holidays, when, for a day at least, they would share Ruth's belief that fasting would bring them favor. In my mind I heard them reciting Kaddish and felt myself join them. I recited aloud the prayer for the dead, and the mumbling rain responded. *Yisgadal V'yiskaddash sh'meh rabbah.* The ghost of the child beat in my breast pocket. Behind me my sister wandered, looking for a family that would take her in. *B'almah di vra chiruteh, v'yamlich malchuteh.* What were the dead? What were the living? Ruth, betrayed, sat alone and hungry somewhere in Paris. Where was my child?

The ghost rose like a balloon to my head, where I felt the shy pain quicken and grow bolder. It was madness to mourn for a child that had not been born but my unborn child kicked its feet into my brain. I had to go home. I resolved not to run or—my other great urge—to lie down on the soaked sidewalk. I resolved to walk my pain slowly home. I turned and left the shelter of the overhang, entering the rain with my head held high. I wore my headache like a crown.

The tiny red heart of the answering machine was beating when I got home, and Ruth's small, faraway voice informed me that she would be back in two days. She missed me. Nadia had left even earlier than expected. Ruth was calling from a pay phone because the phone in her apartment was not working. The connection was bad, clicking every few seconds like the scratch of an old record going round. There was a rush of foreign traffic and then static drowned her voice. I thought she might be crying.

I felt like crying myself. She was coming back! My headache had passed on the slow walk home, but the feeling of hopelessness and loss remained. Now I had the sense that a terrible dream had ended. Ruth and I could begin again. Never mind the nonrefundable ticket. My heart raced out to Ruth—I wanted to scoop her up, shelter her in the palm of my hand and carry her over the ocean myself. Magically, I felt that buying the ticket had made her return possible.

Max was dancing around the kitchen like a starved animal—which I suppose, after twenty-four hours, he was. I gave him food and changed his water. I left a message on Blitstein's machine telling him I would be out the rest of the week for personal reasons. Let him fire me—I didn't care. Ruth's return was all that mattered. I watered the plants, which were just alive enough to look dead. It seemed like months since I had been in the apartment and I planned, after a long nap, to do a thorough cleaning.

But first I sat down in the kitchen and made myself a cup of Ruth's witches' brew in honor of her return. I steeped it for five minutes, just as she did, watching the dark reddish color bleed into the water as if it did not want to mix. It gave off a fragrance of chamomile and dried roses, the flavor of Ruth's lips. Thirsty, chilled from the rain, I gulped it down.

Hearing Ruth's message had filled me with love and remorse. The note of feminine sadness in her voice seemed still to linger in the apartment, touching each object in the kitchen, waking the room from its bachelor's sleep. I saw it now as she would on entering: the stove top mottled with burned tomato sauce, the floor stained and unswept. Pots and pans piled on the counter, not hung on the wall racks I had mounted for Ruth when I moved in. The sloppy state of my soul, my own immoral excess of the night before, seemed discernible in the unkempt kitchen. I had defiled Ruth's temple. Lettuce was liquefying in the crisper. Everything needed a good scrubbing. I decided to skip my nap and to begin at once the rededication of the kitchen.

I was halfway through filling a bucket with hot water and Top Job when I felt an uncomfortable shifting in my bowels. Had I breathed in too much ammonia on an empty stomach? It seemed plausible as I sat, hunched on the toilet, my stomach cramping painfully, until I remembered the cup of tea I had drunk not five minutes before. I had eaten nothing all day, had a definite hangover, had suffered a headache and immeasurable amounts of guilt since my adventure with Felicia, but all at once I knew that those health-food flowers—senna and other emetic herbs—were a powerful laxative Ruth hid in a teacup the way alcoholics hide vodka in coffee mugs. My fears about Ruth returned. How would she look? How had she treated her body? I read her fortune in those tea leaves and felt afraid.

———

Two days later, Ruth came back. She wore clothes I had not seen before—baggy black pants, a white shirt buttoned to the throat and a dark-green oversized blazer with shoulder pads—altogether too much for the season. She had only her carry-on bag, filled to bursting, the strap pinching and raising one shoulder pad awkwardly. She set the bag down and we kissed and held each other. Her padded body felt light, unexpectedly small, as if, I thought guiltily, my arms had stretched for Felicia. But it was Ruth. Ruth was home!

The baggy pants gave her a vagabondish look. I regretted that I had not met her at the airport and swept her up in my arms as soon as she had touched down. She had cut her tawny hair short, and it framed the forlorn loveliness of her face in a way I found heartbreaking.

"You got your hair cut," I said, pressing my hands on either side of her face, covering her naked, delicate ears.

"It was so hot there I had to. Is it okay?"

In answer I kissed her forehead and then her lips. Her face and hands were cold, as if she had come in from a January day.

"Oh, Joseph, you're really here. It's you."

"It's me," I said, kissing her again.

"I had such a terrible time." And she burst into tears. "I hate Nadia. And I missed you so much. I even missed Max."

She sank down and held out her hand, but Max was not a cat who came when you called and she stood, wiping a tear from her nose.

"They found my suitcase, by the way—two days before I left. It's been halfway around the world. I told them to send it right home. Did it come yet?"

"No," I told her.

"Morons!" said Ruth, still emotional.

I held her again and felt, as I pressed her close, a desire to examine her, to make sure she was all right. I began removing her blazer but she detached herself.

"I'm going to wash up and change," she said. "I'm gross from the plane. Make me a cup of tea?" she added, with imploring eyes, before disappearing toward the bathroom.

Ruth was back, but I found myself still missing her. In the kitchen I felt the old longing, an odd mixture of erotic desire mingled with a burning need to know, directly, what had become of her body. I almost charged after her into the bathroom, where the shower hissed and fell, but instead I waited for the kettle to boil. I had no intention of brewing her poisonous tea. I had merely put the kettle on as a timer, to give Ruth a chance to change. When the whistle blew I would go in and see her.

Never had I felt so powerfully the mystery of Ruth's body. I tried to picture her in the shower, but Felicia's body kept intruding and soon I found it impossible to imagine a body accurately at all. I was reminded of my early adolescence, wondering just what a naked woman might look like, extrapolating from what I had seen in photographs and paintings and swimming pools, and what I had glimpsed of my sister's body at home.

Ten minutes later I found Ruth lying on our bed. She had changed into a baggy Columbia sweatshirt of mine and loose sweatpants of her own. Her short hair, wet from the shower, was pressed close to her head. I thought of the statue of Joan of Arc and shuddered inwardly, remembering my dream.

"I was just collecting myself for a minute," said Ruth. "The trip knocked me out. Why are you looking at me that way, Joseph? What's wrong?"

"Nothing's wrong," I said, coming over to her and taking her cool hand.

Ruth raised herself and sat up, facing me.

"Did you make me tea?" she asked.

"No," I said. "I tried that tea of yours while you were away and it made me sick."

Ruth colored. "You shouldn't have done that. It's very strong. It takes getting used to."

"Why would you want to get used to something like that?"

"Is that what's upsetting you? My tea?"

"No," I told her truthfully, "it's not the tea."

"Then what? What's wrong, Joseph? Is it my hair?"

"Your hair?"

"It'll grow back," Ruth said, putting a hand self-consciously to her bangs.

I couldn't help smiling at this ridiculous suggestion. I ran my own hand briefly over her damp head, marveling at the immediacy of the skull beneath my touch. My fingers tingled with the guilty memory of shampooing Felicia.

"It's not your hair," I said. Could I possibly tell her about Felicia? I held my tongue, which only made Ruth more alarmed. It was she who seemed guilty.

We sat in silence, Ruth avoiding my eyes, looking as if she expected a sentence of doom. She looked so small.

"You look different," I said at last.

"It *is* my hair!"

"No, Ruth, it's not. I just hope you didn't cut it to . . . diminish yourself." I was speaking with elliptical care so as not to set her off so soon after coming home. "I want you back the way you were."

I looked hard at her, trying to see the outline of her body under the bulky sweatshirt. She shifted uncomfortably under my gaze.

"It was so hot there, that's all," she said, defensively. "I didn't want to be burdened. It'll grow back. It's considered very stylish."

"I'm not worried about your hair."

As I spoke, I took hold of the lower edge of her sweatshirt and began to lift it, but she grabbed my wrist with surprising force.

"I'm so tired, Joseph," she said. "I'm just going to close my eyes for a few moments. Will you sit here with me?"

I sat beside her on the bed. We were silent for a long time and I thought Ruth really had fallen asleep until she said, her eyes still closed,

"Dot's pregnant again."

"Really! Why didn't you call me about it?"

"I don't know. The news upset me. You know how I feel."

"Why don't we just have a child of our own?"

Ruth opened her eyes with swift alarm.

"What?"

"Why worry about your father and Dot? We have it in ourselves to make life, too."

"Joseph, what's happened to you? You're speaking so strangely."

She propped herself up and put her hand to her head. I was afraid she was going to start talking about her hair again.

"It's the abortion, Ruth," I said. "I feel terrible about it. I know you asked me not to mention it but I can't help it."

Ruth hugged herself as if she were suddenly very cold. Her shoulders hunched. She hid inside herself and remained silent.

"Not now, Joseph. I can't have this conversation now."

"Why not?" I demanded suddenly. "Why not talk about it?"

"Because I don't want to." She looked at me imploringly, but I was feeling an unquenchable need to know. A new, angry thought came into my head.

"Is it because it wasn't mine?"

The look on Ruth's face was a cross between rage, disbelief and almost physical pain, as if my remark had truly cut into her.

"How dare you say that!" she said when she had found her voice.

"Well? Was I the father?"

Ruth looked away. She colored strongly and a new feeling of doubt and dizziness swept over me.

"It wasn't mine!" I shouted. "You cheated on me!"

"I didn't cheat on you," said Ruth, through tears. "I swear to God. I didn't."

"Then why not talk about it? How come you never mentioned it in all the time since it happened? Not in a letter. Not over the phone. Not in person. I can't get it out of my mind. Doesn't it bother you? Don't you have feelings?"

"You know I have feelings, Joseph," she said in a soft, wounded voice.

"For yourself!" I said, cruelly. "You're so busy mourning for yourself, you haven't thought once about the . . ."

"The what?" asked Ruth. "The child?" A faint smile crossed her lips but vanished quickly and she turned away from my stare.

"No!" I shouted. "Not the child! The abortion! That's what it is. Death!" I felt weak with rage I had not realized was in me.

"I didn't have an abortion," Ruth said quietly.

She wasn't looking at me but down at her lap. A feeling of new excitement began to fill me.

"Are you . . . ?"

"I'm not pregnant," she said, raising her eyes to mine with astonishment and, I almost thought, with pity. "I was never pregnant. I'm too thin, Joseph. I don't even menstruate anymore. When at first I didn't get my period—it's never been very regular—I did think, for one second, that maybe . . . It was a kind of dream, a fantasy, I was surprised to find I even had thoughts like that. To be full and fertile. I thought we'd share that for a little while, a week or so. I thought you'd be proud of me. But you were so horrified. I felt you'd killed that dream. I wanted you to think you'd really killed something. I was angry. I'm sorry. And then I thought, if you believed me, maybe I really did look, maybe I had grown . . ."

"Where did you go that day?" I demanded.

Ruth smiled grimly.

"I gave blood," she said. "I had to lie about my weight. I really did pass out."

Too thin to get pregnant. The obviousness of it, my own blindness suddenly overwhelmed me. What had happened to me?

"Take your sweatshirt off," I said.

Ruth sat there without moving.

"Take your sweatshirt off," I repeated, loudly.

I felt sick with anticipation as she sat there, hesitating. What would happen if Ruth refused? Would I undress her forcibly? Would it come to that?

It did not have to. Ruth carefully got up off the bed. She took a moment to steady herself, as if the blood in her was not flowing fast enough, but then she stood before me with trembling composure. It had been two months since I had seen her nude. Slowly and deliberately, she removed her sweatshirt—not shyly, as I would have thought, but matter-of-factly. She tossed it carelessly onto the floor. I could see as she stood there in her T-shirt—one of my T-shirts, too big in any case—that something horrible had happened. But I said, still not moving, "Take off the T-shirt."

She wore no bra and she did not need one. Her breasts now curved on either side into the pattern of her ribs. Her ribs looked like the folds of a curtain rising, drawn upward at the breastbone. She stood in self-starved marble pride as I watched her, her eyes wide as if only they were well fed.

Why is it that she did not look naked? There was no more to reveal, she had taken it all off. The dance of the seven veils was over, the last veil had been removed, but still something hid her from me. Her body itself was the last veil. What was behind it?

Something broke in me. I fell on her as if her bones belonged in my body and moved her back onto the bed. I kissed her head and face and freezing hands, her shoulders, even her poor breasts and ribs, her empty belly hollow at last. I enfolded her in my arms, wishing to dress her body in my own. There seemed no soft place on her where I could rest my head. Here was the book of the body, with no pages left to turn. I began to cry.

"I love you," I murmured. "I love you."

The bones of her embrace were painful. I closed my fingers easily around her wrist and slid them partly up her arm.

"It's like you're already dead," I said. "I can't hold you. It's like you've been in a concentration camp. You're slipping away. You're gone."

Ruth, who had not spoken, was busy detaching herself from my grasp.

"I'm right here," she said. "What are you talking about?"

She had broken away to gather up her clothes. She pulled her T-shirt on and as her head emerged I could see how angry she was. But I could not stop my own outpouring of love and remorse.

"Ruth, how could I have let this happen? I should never have let you go. You're so sick." I was weeping, kissing her, embracing her, literally watering her with tears. "I did this to you, Ruth. I did this. Forgive me."

But Ruth was pushing me away.

"You did not!" she said. I ignored her.

"Oh, Ruthie. Evie. Honey. I'm so sorry."

Ruth froze. Her eyes were bright with fury.

"How dare you!"

"What?"

"I'm Ruth. I'm not Evelyn."

"Of course you are."

"No, you think I'm somebody else. You don't know who I am. Talking about concentration camps. About Evelyn. About death! I'm just a girl from Westchester who has trouble with food. This isn't Germany, 1945. You can't liberate me. This is New York City. And you can't bring me back from the dead. I'M NOT DEAD. I'm not your sister, for God's sake. I'm Ruth Simon. Do you hear me? I'm Ruth Simon!"

"Ruth, what are you saying?"

"I'm not your science experiment."

"Of course not."

"Going to the library! You just want to solve me. You don't love me."

"I do, Ruth. I do."

"Get away from me with your sick dreams of death," Ruth said, stamping her foot in rage. "I thought you loved me. I thought you cared about me. Jesus, I thought you wanted me to get better, but that's not true, is it? You like me this way. This little striptease turns you on. Watching me take it all off till I'm just a handful of dust for you to cry over, so you can go say Kaddish with your father."

She had her thin arms through the sleeves of her shirt now and her sweatshirt was in her hand. Sobbing and furious, she was heading for the door.

I wished to stop her, but the truth of what she said paralyzed me. Did I want her to be sick? Was I in love not with Ruth but her illness? And was it possible that, in my desire to understand her relationship to food and to her body I had actually made her worse? Ruth had warned me repeatedly that she was, as she put it "bad news," but was it possible that it was I who was bad for her? The thought staggered me.

By the time I came to my senses Ruth was gone. I ran into the hall and down the stairs but she was not in the lobby. Ruíz, the super, was leaning idly against the door.

"She get into a cab," he said.

"So fast?"

"She was crying," he said, a note of accusation in his voice.

"Did she say where she was going?"

He shook his head.

"Such a nice girl," he said. "I hope she come back."

But Ruth did not come back. I waited by the phone and wondered what to do, whom to call. Would she do something desperate or had she merely gone to a friend's house? She might be in a coffee shop—one gloomy day she had spent five hours sitting in a café without eating anything, testing herself and, in some way, comforting herself despite the torment. Or perhaps she had simply taken the train to Scarsdale—though even in my panic my pride was too great to call her father and admit that the day she came home she had left me.

Around six that evening the buzzer rang and I ran to the door, only to find a messenger from the airline with Ruth's suitcase. I signed for it and dragged it hopefully into the bedroom, but hours passed and still no Ruth. I thought about calling the cops, but Ruth had not even been gone for eight hours. I tried Nadia—I'd called before—and again got no answer. Not even a machine. I let it ring and ring, for though it killed me to appeal to Nadia I was desperate.

I tried to reassure myself. Ruth, as she herself had pointed out, was not my sister. If self-starvation was slow-motion suicide it was also the expression of a wish to be rescued, to be noticed and cared for. This gave me hope. Besides, jumping into a cab did not seem like a prelude to desperate action. Still, how could I be sure? In the morning, I decided, I would call the police.

It was after midnight when, having heard nothing from Ruth, I at last went into the bedroom. The large leather-and-cloth suitcase, battered slightly from its travels, wasn't locked. I laid it flat and clicked up the tabs. Ruth's clothing lay neatly folded inside. Shirts, skirts, tights, underwear, dresses. I ran my hand along the border—was there a diary? I did not find one.

I passed my hand like a customs agent over all the different fabrics, feeling the sadness of empty clothes. I removed a leather sack full of makeup, and a moist plastic bag for mirror, comb, toothbrush, soap, shampoo, cream rinse, mousse, Noxzema, toothpaste. I don't know what I expected to find, but my hand trembled as it moved through her things, still looking for secrets.